# Into the Labyrinth

Bantam Spectra Books
by Margaret Weis and Tracy Hickman

THE DARKSWORD TRILOGY
Forging the Darksword
Doom of the Darksword
Triumph of the Darksword

DARKSWORD ADVENTURES

ROSE OF THE PROPHET
The Will of the Wanderer
The Paladin of the Night
The Prophet of Akhran

THE DEATH GATE CYCLE
Dragon Wing
Elven Star
Fire Sea
Serpent Mage
The Hand of Chaos
Into the Labyrinth

and by Margaret Weis

STAR OF THE GUARDIANS
The Lost King
King's Test
King's Sacrifice
Ghost Legion

A DEATH GATE NOVEL

# Into the Labyrinth

MARGARET WEIS

AND

TRACY HICKMAN

SPECTRA ™

BANTAM BOOKS
NEW YORK • TORONTO • LONDON • SYDNEY • AUCKLAND

INTO THE LABYRINTH
*A Bantam Book / December 1993*

Library of Congress Cataloging-in-Publication Data

Weis, Margaret.
  Into the labyrinth : a death gate novel / Margaret Weis and Tracy
Hickman.
    p.  cm.— (The death gate cycle ; v. 6)
  ISBN 0-553-09539-0 : $21.95
  I. Hickman, Tracy.   II. Title.   III. Series: Weis, Margaret.
Death gate cycle ;v. 6.
PS3573.E3978I58   1993
813'.54 — dc20                                              93-25414
                                                                CIP

*Published simultaneously in the United States and Canada*

*Bantam Books are published by Bantam Books, a division of Bantam Doubleday Dell Publishing Group, Inc. Its trademark, consisting of the words "Bantam Books" and the portrayal of a rooster, is Registered in U.S. Patent and Trademark Office and in other countries. Marca Registrada. Bantam Books, 1540 Broadway, New York, New York 10036.*

PRINTED IN THE UNITED STATES OF AMERICA

BVG          0 9 8 7 6 5 4 3 2 1

To Russ Lovaasen,
whose joy and love and courage
are the beacon fires,
shining brightly through the darkness,
guiding us home.

All our knowledge is,

ourselves to know.

◆

Alexander Pope,

*An Essay on Man*

# CHAPTER ♦ 1

# ABARRACH

♦

ABARRACH: WORLD OF STONE, WORLD OF DARKNESS LIT BY THE FIRES OF MOLTEN sea, world of stalagmites and stalactites, world of fire dragons, world of poisonous air and sulfurous fumes, world of magic.

Abarrach: world of the dead.

Xar, Lord of the Nexus, and now Lord of Abarrach, sat back in his chair, rubbed his eyes. The rune-constructs he was studying were starting to blur together. He'd almost made a mistake—and that was inexcusable. But he had caught himself in time, corrected it. Closing his aching eyes, he went over the construct again in his mind.

Begin with the heart-rune. Connect this sigil's stem to an adjoining rune's base. Inscribe the sigla on the breast, working upward to the head. Yes, that was where he'd gone wrong the first few times. The head was important—vital. Then draw the sigla on the trunk, finally the arms, the legs.

It was perfect. He could find no flaw. In his mind's eye, he imagined the dead body on which he'd been working rising up and living again. A corrupt form of life, admittedly, but a beneficial one. The corpse was far more useful now than it would have been moldering in the ground.

Xar smiled in triumph, but it was a triumph whose life span was shorter than that of his imaginary defunct. His thoughts went something like this:

I can raise the dead.

At least I am fairly certain I can raise the dead.

I can't be sure.

That was the pall over his elation. There were no dead for him to raise. Or rather, there were too many dead. Just not dead enough.

In bitter frustration, Xar slammed his hands down on the elaborately conceived rune-construct. The rune-bones[1] went flying, skittering and sliding off the table onto the floor.

Xar paid no attention to them. He could always put the construct together again. Again and again. He knew it as well as he knew the rune-magic to conjure up water. For all the good it would do him.

Xar needed a corpse. One not more than three days dead. One that hadn't been seized by these wretched lazars.[2] Irritably he swept the last few remaining rune-bones to the floor.

He left the room he used as his study, headed for his private chambers. On his way, he passed by the library. And there was Kleitus, the Dynast, former ruler (until his death) of Necropolis, the largest city on Abarrach. At his death, Kleitus had become a lazar— one of the living dead. Now the Dynast's gruesome form, which was neither dead nor alive, wandered the halls and corridors of the palace that had once been his. The lazar thought it was still his. Xar knew better, but he saw no reason to disabuse Kleitus of the notion.

The Lord of the Nexus steeled himself to speak to the Lord of the Living Dead. Xar had fought many terrible foes during his struggles to free his people from the Labyrinth. Dragons, wolfen, snogs, chaodyn—every monster the Labyrinth could create. Xar feared nothing. Nothing living. The lord couldn't help feeling a qualm deep in his bowels when he looked into the hideous, ever-shifting death-mask face of the lazar. Xar saw the hatred in the eyes —the hatred that the dead bore the living of Abarrach.

---

[1] A game played on Abarrach, similar to an ancient game known on Earth as mah-jongg. The playing pieces are inscribed with the sigla used by both Patryns and Sartan to work their magic. *Fire Sea*, vol. 3 of *The Death Gate Cycle*.

[2] The Sartan inhabiting Abarrach learned to practice the forbidden art of necromancy, began giving a dreadful type of life to the corpses of their dead. The dead became slaves, working for the living. If the dead are brought back too soon after death, the soul does not leave the body, but remains tied to it. These Sartan become *lazar*—fearful beings who inhabit simultaneously both the plane of the living and the realm of the dead. A lazar can find no peace, no rest. Its "life" is constant torment. *Fire Sea*, vol. 3 of *The Death Gate Cycle*.

An encounter with Kleitus was never pleasant. Xar generally avoided the lazar. The lord found it uncomfortable talking to a being who had one thought on his mind: death. Your death.

The sigla on Xar's body glowed blue, defending him from attack. The blue light was reflected in the Dynast's dead eyes, which glittered with disappointment. The lazar had tried once, on Xar's arrival, to kill the Patryn. The battle between the two had been brief, spectacular. Kleitus had never tried it again. But the lazar dreamed of it during the endless hours of his tormented existence. He never failed to mention it when they came together.

"Someday, Xar," said Kleitus, the corpse talking, "I will catch you unawares. And then you will join us."

". . . join us," came the unhappy echo of the lazar's soul. The two parts of the dead always spoke together, the soul being just a bit slower than the body.

"It must be nice for you to have a goal still," Xar said somewhat testily. He couldn't help it. The lazar made him nervous. But the lord needed help, information, and Kleitus was the only one—so far as Xar could determine—who might have it. "I have a goal myself. One I would like to discuss with you. If you have the time?" Nervousness made Xar sarcastic.

Try as he might, Xar could not look for long at the lazar's face. It was the face of a corpse—a murdered corpse, for Kleitus had himself been slain by another lazar, had then been brought back to hideous life. The face would sometimes be the face of one long dead, and then suddenly it would be the face of Kleitus as he had been when he was alive. The transformation occurred when the soul moved into the body, struggled to renew life, regain what it had once possessed. Thwarted, the soul flew out of the body, tried vainly to free itself from its prison. The soul's continual rage and frustration gave an unnatural warmth to the chill, dead flesh.

Xar looked at Kleitus, looked away hastily.

"Will you accompany me to the library?" Xar asked with a polite gesture, his gaze anywhere but on the corpse.

The lazar followed willingly. Kleitus had no particular desire to be of assistance to the Lord of the Nexus, as Xar well knew. The lazar came because there was always the possibility that Xar might weaken, inadvertently lower his defenses. Kleitus came because he hoped to murder Xar.

Alone in the room with the lazar, Xar considered briefly summoning another Patryn to stand guard. He immediately abandoned the idea, was aghast at himself for even thinking such a thing. Not only would such a summons make him appear weak in the eyes of his people—who worshipped him—but he wanted no one else to know the subject of his discussions.

Consequently, though he did so with misgivings, Xar shut the door made of braided kairn grass, marked it with Patryn runes of warding so that it could not be opened. He drew these runes over faded Sartan runes, Sartan magic that had long ago ceased to function.

Kleitus's lifeless eyes sprang suddenly to life, focused on Xar's throat. The dead fingers twitched in anticipation.

"No, no, my friend," Xar said pleasantly. "Another day, perhaps. Or would you like to come again with the circle of my power? Would you like to feel again my magic starting to unravel your existence?"

Kleitus stared at him with unblinking hatred. "What do you want, Lord of the Nexus?"

". . . Nexus," came the sad echo.

"I want to sit down," Xar said. "I've had a wearing time of it. Two days and nights on the rune-construct. But I have solved it. I now know the secret to the art of necromancy. I can now raise the dead."

"Congratulations," said Kleitus, and the dead lips curled in a sneer. "You can now destroy your people as we destroyed ours."

Xar let that pass. The lazar tended to have a dark outlook on things. He supposed he couldn't blame them.

The lord took his seat at a large stone table whose top was covered with dusty volumes: a treasure-trove of Sartan lore. Xar had spent as much time studying these works as possible, considering the myriad duties of a lord about to lead his people to war. But this time spent among the Sartan books was minute compared to the years Kleitus had spent. And Xar was at a disadvantage: he was forced to read the material in a foreign language—the Sartan language. Although he had mastered that language while in the Nexus, the task of breaking down the Sartan rune-structure, then rebuilding it into Patryn thought, was exhausting and time-consuming.

Xar could never, under any circumstances, think like a Sartan. Kleitus had the information Xar needed. Kleitus had delved deep into these books. Kleitus was—or had been—a Sartan himself. He knew. He understood. But how to worm it out of the corpse? That was the tricky part.

Xar wasn't fooled by the lazar's shambling walk and blood-thirsty demeanor. Kleitus was playing a far more subtle game. An army of living, warm-blooded beings had recently arrived on Abar-rach—Patryns, brought here by Xar, brought here to train for war. The lazar hungered after these living beings, longed to destroy the life that the dead coveted and at the same time found so abhorrent. The lazar could not fight the Patryns. The Patryns were too power-ful.

But it required an immense outlay of the Patryns' magic to sustain life in the darksome caverns of Abarrach. The Patryns were beginning to weaken—ever so slightly. So had the Sartan weakened before them; so had many of the Sartan died.

Time. The dead had time. Not soon, but inevitably, the Patryn magic would start to crumble. And then the lazar would strike. Xar didn't plan to be here that long. He had found what he'd come to Abarrach to find. Now he just needed to determine whether or not he'd really found it.

Kleitus did not sit down. The lazar can never rest in one place long, but are constantly moving, wandering, searching for some-thing they have lost all hope of discovering.

Xar did not look at the animated corpse, shuffling back and forth in front of him. He looked instead at the dusty volumes lying on the table.

"I want to be able to test my knowledge of necromancy," Xar said. "I want to know if I can actually raise the dead."

"What is stopping you?" Kleitus demanded.

". . . stopping you?"

Xar frowned. The annoying echo was like a buzzing in his ears, and it always came just when he was about to speak, interrupting him, breaking the chain of his thought.

"I need a corpse. And don't tell me to use my own people. That is out of the question. I personally saved the life of every Patryn I brought with me from the Nexus."

"You gave life," said Kleitus. "You have the right to take it."

". . . take it."

"Perhaps," Xar said loudly over the echo. "Perhaps that is true.

And if there were more of my people—far more—I might consider it. But our numbers are few and I dare not waste even one."

"What do you want of me, Lord of the Nexus?"

". . . Nexus?"

"I was talking to one of the other lazar, a woman named Jera. She mentioned that there were Sartan—living Sartan—still on Abarrach. A man named . . . um . . ." Xar hesitated, appeared at a loss.

"Balthazar!" Kleitus hissed.

"Balthazar . . ." mourned the echo.

"Yes, that was the name," Xar said hastily. "Balthazar. He leads them. An early report I received from a man called Haplo—a Patryn who once visited Abarrach—led me to believe that this Sartan Balthazar and his people all perished at your hands. But Jera tells me that this is not true."

"Haplo, yes, I recall him." Kleitus did not seem to find the memory a pleasant one. He brooded for a long moment, the soul flying in, struggling, flying out of the body. He came to a halt in front of Xar, stared at the lord with shifting eyes. "Did Jera tell you what happened?"

Xar found the corpse's gaze disconcerting. "No," he lied, forcing himself to remain seated when it was his instinct to get up and flee to a far corner. "No, Jera did not. I thought perhaps you—"

"The living ran before us." Kleitus resumed his restless walk. "We followed. They could not hope to escape us. We never tire. We need no rest. We need no food. We need no water. At last we had them trapped. They made a pitiable stand before us, planning to fight to save their miserable lives. We had among us their own prince. He was dead. I had brought him back to life myself. He knew what the living had done to the dead. He understood. Only when the living are all dead can the dead be free. He swore he would lead us against his own people.

"We readied for the kill. But then one of our number stepped forward—the husband of this very Jera. He is a lazar. His wife murdered him, raised him up, gave him the power we command. But he betrayed us. Somehow, somewhere, he had found a power of his own. He has the gift of death, as did one other Sartan who came to this world, came through Death's Gate—"

"Who was that?" Xar asked. His interest, which had been lagging through the lazar's long-winded discourse, was suddenly caught.

"I don't know. He was a Sartan, but he had a mensch name," said Kleitus, irritated at the interruption.

"Alfred?"

"Perhaps. What difference does it make?" Kleitus seemed obsessed with telling his tale. "Jera's husband broke the spell that held the prince's corpse captive. The prince's body died. The prison walls of his flesh crumbled. The soul floated free." Kleitus sounded angry, bitter.

". . . floated free." The echo was wistful, longing.

Xar was impatient. Gift of death. Sartan nonsense.

"What happened to Balthazar and his people?" he demanded.

"They escaped us," Kleitus hissed. His waxen hands clenched in fury. "We tried to go after them, but Jera's husband was too powerful. He stopped us."

"So there *are* Sartan still living on Abarrach," Xar said, fingers drumming the table. "Sartan who can provide the corpses I need for my experiments. Corpses who will be troops in my army. Do you have any idea where they are?"

"If we did, they would not still be living," Kleitus said, regarding Xar with hatred. "Would they, Lord of the Nexus?"

"I suppose not," Xar muttered. "This husband of Jera's. Where is *he*? Undoubtedly he knows how to find the Sartan?"

"I do not know where he has gone. He was in Necropolis until you and your people arrived. He kept us out of our city. Kept me out of my palace. But you appeared, and he left."

"Afraid of me, no doubt," Xar said offhandedly.

"He fears nothing, Lord of the Nexus!" Kleitus laughed unpleasantly. "*He* is the one of whom the prophecy speaks."

"I heard about a prophecy." Xar waved a negligent hand. "Haplo said something about it. He viewed prophecies much as I view them, however. Wishes, nothing more. I give them little credence."

"You should give this one credence, Patryn. So the prophecy is spoken: 'He will bring life to the dead, hope to the living, and for him the Gate will open.' That is the prophecy. And it has come to pass."

". . . come to pass."

"Yes, it has come to pass," Xar echoed the echo. "*I* am the one who has brought the prophecy to fulfillment. It speaks of *me*, not some perambulating corpse."

"I think not . . ."

". . . think not."

"Of course it has!" Xar said irritably. " 'The Gate will open . . .' The Gate *has* opened."

"*Death's* Gate has opened."

"What other gate is there?" Xar demanded, annoyed and only half-listening, hoping to steer the conversation back to where it had started.

"The Seventh Gate," Kleitus replied.

And this time the echo was silent. Xar glanced up, wondering what was the matter with it.

"Your talk of armies, of conquest, of traveling from world to world . . . What a waste of time and effort." Kleitus gave a rictus smile. "When all you need to do is step inside the Seventh Gate."

"Indeed?" Xar frowned. "I have been through many gates in my lifetime. What is so special about this one?"

"It was inside this chamber—the Seventh Gate—that the Council of Seven sundered the world."

". . . sundered the world."

Xar sat silent. He was stunned. The implications, the possibilities . . . *if* Kleitus was right. *If* he was telling the truth. *If* this place still existed . . .

"It exists," said Kleitus.

"Where is this . . . chamber?" Xar asked, testing, still not entirely believing the lazar.

Kleitus appeared to ignore the question. The lazar turned to face the bookcases that lined the library. His dead eyes—occasionally alight with the flitting soul—searched for something. At last his withered hand, still stained with the blood of those it had murdered, reached out and lifted a small, thin volume. He tossed the book on the desk in front of Xar.

"Read," Kleitus said.

". . . read," came the sad refrain.

"It looks like a children's primer," Xar said, examining it with some disdain. He had himself used books like these, found in the Nexus, to teach the Sartan runes to the mensch child Bane.

"It is," said Kleitus. "It comes from the days when our own children were alive and laughing. Read."

Xar studied the book suspiciously. It appeared to be genuine. It was old, extremely old—to judge by the musty smell and brittle, yellowed parchment. Carefully, fearful that the pages might crumble to dust at a touch, he opened the leather cover, read silently to himself.

*The Earth was destroyed.*

*Four worlds were created out of the ruin. Worlds for ourselves and the mensch: Air, Fire, Stone, Water.*

*Four Gates connect each world to the other: Arianus to Pryan to Abarrach to Chelestra.*

*A house of correction was built for our enemies: the Labyrinth.*

*The Labyrinth is connected to the other worlds through the Fifth Gate: the Nexus.*

*The Sixth Gate is the center, permitting entry: the Vortex.*

*And all was accomplished through the Seventh Gate.*

*The end was the beginning.*

That was the printed text. Beneath, in a crude scrawl, were the words *The beginning was our end.*

"You wrote this," Xar guessed.

"In my own blood," Kleitus said.

". . . blood."

Xar's hands shook with excitement. He forgot about the Sartan, about the prophecy, about the necromancy. This—this was worth it all!

"You know where the gate is? You will take me there?" Xar rose eagerly to his feet.

"I know. The dead know. And I would be only too happy to take you, Lord of the Nexus . . ." Kleitus's face writhed, the soul flitting restlessly in and out of the corpse. The hands flexed. "*If* you met that requirement. Your death could be arranged . . ."

Xar was in no mood for humor. "Don't be ridiculous. Take me there now. Or, if that is not possible"—the thought came to the lord that perhaps this Seventh Gate was on another world—"tell me where to find it."

Kleitus appeared to consider the matter, then shook his head. "I don't believe I will."

". . . I will."

"Why not?" Xar was angry.

"Call it . . . loyalty."

"This—from a man who slaughtered his own people!" Xar sneered. "Then why tell me about the Seventh Gate, if you refuse to take me to it?" He had a sudden thought. "You want something in exchange. What?"

"To kill. And keep on killing. To be rid of the smell of warm blood that torments me every moment that I live . . . and I will live forever! *Death* is what I want. As to the Seventh Gate, you don't need me to show you. Your minion has been there already. I should think *he* would have told you."

". . . death . . . you . . ."

"What minion? Who?" Xar was confounded a moment, then asked, "Haplo?"

"That could be the name." Kleitus was losing interest.

". . . name."

"Haplo knows the location of the Seventh Gate!" Xar scoffed. "Impossible. He never mentioned it . . ."

"*He* doesn't know," Kleitus responded. "No one *living* knows. But his corpse would know. It would want to return to that place. Raise up this Haplo's corpse, Lord of the Nexus, and he will lead you to the Seventh Gate."

"I wish I knew your game," Xar said to himself, pretending once more to peruse the child's book, covertly observing the lazar. "I wish I knew what *you* were after! What is the Seventh Gate to *you*? And why do *you* want Haplo? Yes, I see where you're leading me. But so long as it's the same direction I'm traveling . . ."

Xar shrugged and lifted the book, read aloud.

" 'And all was accomplished through the Seventh Gate.' How? What does that mean, Dynast? Or does it mean anything? It is hard to tell; you Sartan derive so much pleasure out of playing with words."

"I would guess it means a great deal, Lord of the Nexus." A flicker of dark amusement brought real life to the dead eyes. "What that meaning is, I neither know nor care."

Reaching out his hand, its flesh bluish white and dappled with blood, its nails black, Kleitus spoke a Sartan rune, struck the door.

The Patryn sigla protecting the door shattered. Kleitus walked through it and left.

Xar could have held the runes against the Dynast's magic, but the lord didn't want to waste his energy. Why bother? Let the lazar leave. He would obviously be of no further use.

The Seventh Gate. The chamber where the Sartan sundered the world. Who knows what powerful magic exists inside there still? thought Xar.

If, as he claims, Kleitus knows the location of the Seventh Gate, then he doesn't need Haplo to show him. He obviously wants Haplo for his own purposes. Why? True, Haplo eluded the Dynast's clutches, escaped the lazar's murderous rampage, but it seems unlikely that Kleitus would hold a grudge. The lazar loathes *all* living beings. He wouldn't single out just one unless he had a special reason.

Haplo has something or knows something Kleitus wants. I wonder what? I must keep Haplo to myself, at least until I find out . . .

Xar picked up the book again, stared at the Sartan runes until he had them memorized. A commotion in the hallway, voices calling his name, disturbed him.

Leaving the desk, Xar crossed the room, opened the door. Several Patryns were roaming up and down the corridor.

"What do you want?"

"My Lord! We've been searching all over!" The woman who had answered paused to catch her breath.

"Yes?" Xar caught her excitement. Patryns were disciplined; they did not ordinarily let their feelings show. "What is it, Daughter?"

"We have captured two prisoners, My Lord. We caught them coming through Death's Gate."

"Indeed! This is welcome news. What—"

"My Lord, hear me!" Under normal circumstances, no Patryn would have dared interrupt Xar. But the young woman was too excited to contain herself. "They are both Sartan. And one of them is—"

"Alfred!" Xar guessed.

"The man is Samah, My Lord."

Samah! Head of the Sartan Council of Seven.

Samah. Who had been held in suspended animation long centuries on Chelestra.

Samah. The very Samah who had brought about the destruction of the worlds.

Samah. Who had cast the Patryns into the Labyrinth.

At that moment, Xar could almost have believed in this higher power Haplo kept yammering about. And Xar could almost have thanked it for giving Samah into his hands.

# CHAPTER 2

ABARRACH

♦

SAMAH. OF ALL THE WONDERFUL PRIZES. SAMAH. THE SARTAN WHO HAD THOUGHT up the plot to sunder the world. The Sartan who had sold the idea to his people. The Sartan who had taken their blood and the blood of countless thousands of innocents in payment. The Sartan who had locked the Patryns in the prison hell of the Labyrinth.

"And," Xar said to himself suddenly, his gaze going back to the book, "the Sartan who undoubtedly knows the location of the Seventh Gate! Not only that, but he will probably refuse to tell me where it is or anything about it." Xar rubbed his hands. "I will have the inordinate pleasure of forcing Samah to talk!"

There are dungeons in the palace of stone on Abarrach. Haplo had reported their existence to Xar. Haplo had very nearly died in the dungeons of Abarrach.

Xar hastened through the rat's warren of corridors that led downward to the dungeons—the "catacombs," as they had been euphemistically known during the reign of the Sartan.

What had those early Sartan used the catacombs for? Prisons for the malcontents among the mensch? Or perhaps the Sartan had even tried housing the mensch down here, away from the corrupt atmosphere of the caverns above, the atmosphere that was slowly poisoning every living thing the Sartan had brought with them. According to Haplo's report, there were rooms down here, other rooms besides prison cells. Large rooms, big enough to hold a fair number of people. Sartan runes, traced along the floor, led the way, for those who knew the secrets of their magic.

Torches burned in sconces on the wall. By their light, Xar caught an occasional glimpse of these Sartan runes. Xar spoke a word—a Sartan word—and watched the sigla flicker feebly to life, glow a moment, then die, their magic broken and spent.

Xar chuckled. This was a game he played around the palace, a game of which he never tired. The sigla were symbolic. Like their magic, the power of the Sartan had shone briefly, then died. Broken, spent.

As Samah would die. Xar rubbed his hands together again in anticipation.

The catacombs were empty now. In the days before the accidental creation of the dread lazar, the catacombs had been used to house the dead, both types of dead: those who had been reanimated and those awaiting reanimation. Here they stored the corpses for the three days requisite to being brought back to life. Here, too, were the occasional dead who had already been brought back to life but who had proved a nuisance to the living. Kleitus's own mother had been one of these.

But now the cells were empty. The dead had all been freed. Some had been turned into lazar. Others, dead too long to be of use to the lazar—like the queen mother—were left to wander vaguely around the halls. When the Patryns arrived, such dead had been rounded up, formed into armies. Now they awaited the call to battle.

The catacombs were a depressing place in a world of depressing places. Xar had never liked coming down here, and had not done so after his first brief tour of inspection. The atmosphere was heavy, dank and chill. The smell of decay was rank, lingering on the air. It was even palpable to the taste. The torches sputtered and smoked dismally.

But Xar didn't notice the taste of death today. Or if he did, it left a sweet flavor in his mouth. Emerging from the tunnels into the cellblock, he saw two figures in the shadows, both keeping watch for him. One was the young woman who had summoned him. Marit was her name. He'd sent her on ahead to prepare for his arrival. Although he could not see her clearly in the murky dimness, he recognized her by the sigla glowing faintly blue in the darkness; her magic acting to keep her alive in this world of the living dead. The other figure Xar recognized by the fact that the sigla on this man's skin did *not* glow. That and the fact that one of his red eyes did.

"My Lord." Marit bowed with deep reverence.

"My Lord." The dragon-snake in man's form bowed, too, but never once did the one red eye (the other eye was missing) lose sight of Xar.

Xar didn't like that. He didn't like the way the red eye was always staring at him, as if waiting for the moment the lord would lower his guard, when the red eye could slide swordlike inside. And Xar did not like the lurking laughter he was positive he could see in that one red eye. Oh, its gaze was always deferential, subservient. The laughter was never there when Xar looked into the eye directly. But he always had the feeling that the eye gleamed mockingly the moment he glanced away.

Xar would never let the red eye know it bothered him, made him uneasy. The lord had even gone so far as to make Sang-drax (the dragon-snake's mensch name) his personal assistant. Thus Xar kept *his* eye on Sang-drax.

"All is in readiness for your visit, Lord Xar." Sang-drax spoke with the utmost respect. "The prisoners are in separate cells, as you commanded."

Xar peered down the row of cells. It was difficult to see by the feeble light from the torches—they too seemed to be coughing in the ruinous air. Patryn magic could have lit this foul place as bright as day on the sunny world of Pryan, but the Patryns had learned from bitter experience that one didn't waste one's magic on such luxuries. Besides, having come from the dangerous realm of the Labyrinth, most Patryns felt more at ease under the protection of darkness.

Xar was displeased. "Where are the guards I ordered?" He looked at Marit. "These Sartan are tricky. They might well be able to break free of our spells."

She glanced at Sang-drax. Her glance wasn't friendly; she obviously disliked and distrusted the dragon-snake. "I was going to post them, My Lord. But this one prevented me."

Xar turned a baleful gaze on Sang-drax. The dragon-snake in Patryn form gave a deprecating smile, spread his hands. Patryn runes adorned the backs of those hands, similar in appearance to the runes tattooed on Xar's hands and on Marit's. But the sigla on Sang-drax's hands didn't glow. If another Patryn attempted to read them, the runes wouldn't make any sense. They were strictly for show; they had no meaning. Sang-drax was not a Patryn.

Just what he was Xar wasn't certain. Sang-drax called himself a "dragon," claimed he came from the world of Chelestra, claimed he and others of his kind were loyal to Xar, living only to serve Xar and further his cause. Haplo referred to these creatures as dragon-snakes, insisting that they were treacherous, not to be trusted.

Xar saw no reason to doubt the dragon or dragon-snake or whatever it was. In serving Xar, Sang-drax was only showing good sense. Still, the lord didn't like that unblinking red eye, or the laughter that wasn't in it now but almost certainly would be when Xar's back was turned.

"Why did you countermand my orders?" Xar demanded.

"How many Patryns would you require to guard the great Samah, Lord Xar?" Sang-drax asked. "Four? Eight? Would even that number be sufficient? This is the Sartan who sundered a world!"

"And so we have *no* guards to guard him. That makes sense!" Xar snorted.

Sang-drax smiled in appreciation of the humor, was immediately serious again. "He is under constraint now. A mensch child could guard him, in his state."

Xar was worried. "He is injured?"

"No, My Lord. He is wet."

"Wet!"

"The sea water of Chelestra, My Lord. It nullifies the magic of *your kind.*" The voice lingered over the last two words.

"How did Samah come to soak himself in sea water before entering Death's Gate?"

"I cannot imagine, Lord of the Nexus. But it proved most fortuitous."

"Humpf! Well, he will dry out. And then he will need guards—"

"A waste of manpower, My Lord Xar. Your people are few in number and have so many matters of urgent importance to deal with. Preparing for your journey to Pryan—"

"Ah, so I am going to Pryan, am I?"

Sang-drax appeared somewhat confused. "I thought that was my lord's intent. When we discussed the matter, you said—"

"I said I would *consider* going to Pryan." Xar eyed the dragon-snake narrowly. "You seem to be unusually interested in getting me to that particular world. Is there any special reason, I wonder?"

"My lord has said himself that the tytans of Pryan would make formidable additions to his army. And, in addition, I think it quite likely that you might find the Seventh Gate on—"

"The Seventh Gate? How did you come to find out about the Seventh Gate?"

Sang-drax was now definitely confused.

"Why . . . Kleitus told me you were searching for it, Lord."

"He did, did he?"

"Yes, Lord. Just now."

"And what do *you* know of the Seventh Gate?"

"Nothing, Lord, I assure you—"

"Then why are you discussing it?"

"The lazar brought it up. I was only—"

"Enough!" Xar had rarely been so angry. Was he the only person around here who *didn't* know about the Seventh Gate? Well, that would soon end.

"Enough," Xar repeated, casting a sidelong glance at Marit. "We will speak of this matter later, Sang-drax. *After* we have dealt with Samah. I trust I will receive many of the answers to my questions from him. Now, as to guards—"

"Allow me to serve you, Lord. I will use my own magic to guard the prisoners. That will be all you need."

"Are you saying that your magic is more powerful than ours? Than Patryn magic?" Xar asked the question in a mild tone. A dangerous tone, to those who knew him.

Marit knew him. She drew a step or two away from Sang-drax.

"It is not a question of whose magic is more powerful, My Lord," Sang-drax replied humbly. "But let us face facts. The Sartan have learned to defend against Patryn magic, just as you, My Lord, can defend against theirs. The Sartan have *not* learned to fight our magic. We defeated them on Chelestra, as you will remember, Lord—"

"Just barely."

"But that was before Death's Gate had been opened, My Lord. Our magic is much more powerful now." Again the threatening softness. "I was the one who captured these two."

Xar looked at Marit, who confirmed this fact with a nod. "Yes," she conceded. "He brought them to us, where we stood guard, at the gates of Necropolis."

The Lord of the Nexus pondered. Despite Sang-drax's protestations, Xar didn't like the implied conceit of the dragon-snake's statement. The lord also didn't like admitting that the creature had a point. Samah. The great Samah. Who among the Patryns could guard him effectively? Only Xar himself.

Sang-drax appeared ready to argue further, but Xar cut the dragon-snake's words short with an impatient wave of his hand. "There is only one sure way to prevent Samah's escape, and that is to kill him."

Sang-drax demurred. "But surely you require information from him, My Lord . . ."

"Indeed," Xar said with smooth satisfaction. "And I will have it —from his corpse!"

"Ah!" Sang-drax bowed. "You have acquired the art of necromancy. My admiration is boundless, Lord of the Nexus."

The dragon-snake sidled closer; the red eye gleamed in the torchlight. "Samah will die, as you command, My Lord. But—there is no need for haste. Surely he should suffer as your people have suffered. Surely he should be made to endure at least a portion of the torment your people have been made to endure."

"Yes!" Xar drew in a shivering breath. "Yes, he will suffer. I will personally—"

"Permit me, My Lord," Sang-drax begged. "I have a rather special talent for such things. You will watch. You will be pleased. If not, you have only to take my place."

"Very well." Xar was amused. The dragon-snake was almost panting with eagerness. "I want to speak to him first, though. Alone," he added, when Sang-drax started to accompany him. "You will wait for me here. Marit will take me to him."

"As you wish, My Lord." Sang-drax bowed again. Straightening, he added in solicitous tones, "Be careful, My Lord, not to get any of the sea water on yourself."

Xar glowered. He looked away, looked back quickly, and it seemed to him that the red eye glinted with laughter.

The Lord of the Nexus made no reply. Turning on his heel, he stalked down the row of empty cells. Marit walked beside him. The sigla on the arms and hands of both Patryns glowed with a blue-red light that was not entirely acting in response to the poisonous atmosphere of Abarrach.

"You don't trust him, do you, Daughter?"[1] Xar asked his companion.

"It is not for me to trust or distrust anyone whom my lord chooses to favor," Marit answered gravely. "If my lord trusts this creature, I trust my lord's judgment."

Xar nodded in approval of the answer. "You were a Runner,[2] I believe?"

"Yes, My Lord."

Slowing his steps, Xar laid his gnarled hand on the young woman's smooth, tattooed skin. "So was I. We didn't either of us survive the Labyrinth by trusting in anything or anyone other than ourselves, did we, Daughter?"

"No, My Lord." She seemed relieved.

"You will keep your eye on this one-eyed snake, then."

"Certainly, My Lord."

Noticing Xar glancing around impatiently, Marit added, "Samah's cell is down here, My Lord. The other prisoner is being held at the opposite end of the cellblock. I deemed it wise not to put them too close together, although the other prisoner appears harmless."

"Yes, I forgot there were two. What about this other prisoner? Is he a bodyguard? Samah's son?"

"Hardly that, My Lord." Marit smiled, shook her head. "I'm not even certain he's a Sartan. If he is, he's deranged. Odd," she added, thoughtfully, "but if he were a Patryn, I would say he suffers from Labyrinth sickness."

---

[1] Marit is not his daughter in the literal sense of the word. Xar considers all Patryns his children, since he was the one who brought them forth out of the darkness of the Labyrinth. It is not known whether Xar fathered any natural children of his own. If so, the youngest would be old by Patryn standards, at least past their Seventieth Gate. Since few Patryns trapped in the Labyrinth live even half that long, we must assume that Xar's true children, if he had any, are long since dead.

[2] Those who live in the Labyrinth are divided into two categories: Runners and Squatters. Runners live and travel alone, their only object to escape the Labyrinth. Squatters live in large groups. Their object is also escape, but they place greater value on the survival and perpetuation of their race.

"Probably an act. If the man was mad, which I doubt, the Sartan would never permit him to be seen in public. It might harm their status as demigods. What does he call himself?"

"A bizarre name. Zifnab."

"Zifnab!" Xar pondered. "I've heard that before . . . Bane spoke . . . Yes, in regard to—" Casting a sharp look at Marit, Xar shut his mouth.

"My Lord?"

"Nothing important, Daughter. I was thinking out loud. Ah, I see we are nearing our destination."

"Here is the cell of Samah, My Lord." Marit gave the man inside a cool, dispassionate glance. "I will return to guard our other prisoner."

"I think the other will get along well enough on his own," Xar suggested mildly. "Why not keep our snaky friend company?" He motioned with his head back toward the opening of the cellblock tunnels, where Sang-drax stood watching them. "I do not want to be disturbed in my conversation with the Sartan."

"I understand, My Lord." Marit bowed and left, walking back down the long, dark corridor flanked by rows of empty cells.

Xar waited until she had reached the end and was speaking to the dragon-snake. When the red eye turned upon Marit and away from Xar, the Lord of the Nexus approached the prison cell and looked inside.

Samah, head of the Sartan governing body known as the Council of Seven, was—in terms of years—far older than Xar. Yet because of his magical sleep—one which had been supposed to last only a decade but had inadvertently lasted centuries—Samah was a man in the prime of middle age.

Strong, tall, he had once had hard, chiseled features and a commanding air. Now the sallow skin sagged from his bones; the muscles hung loose and flaccid. The face, which should have been lined with wisdom and experience, was creviced, haggard, and drawn. Samah sat listlessly on the cold stone bed, his head and shoulders bowed in dejection, despair. His robes, his skin were sopping wet.

Xar clasped his hands around the bars, drew close for a better look. The Lord of the Nexus smiled.

"Yes," he said softly, "you know what fate awaits you, don't you, Samah? There is nothing quite as bad as the fear, the anticipation. Even when the pain comes—and your death will be very pain-ful, Sartan, I assure you—it won't be as bad as the fear."

Xar gripped the bars harder. The blue sigla tattooed on the backs of his gnarled hands were stretched taut; the enlarged knuckles were as white as exposed bone. He could scarcely draw breath; for long moments he couldn't speak. He had not thought to feel such passion in the presence of his enemy, but suddenly all the years—years of battle and suffering, years of fear—returned to him.

"I wish"—Xar almost choked on his words—"I wish I could let you live a long, long time, Samah! I wish I could let you live with that fear, as my people have lived with it. I wish I could let you live centuries!"

The iron bars dissolved beneath Xar's squeezing hands. He never noticed. Samah had not raised his head, did not look up at his tormentor. He sat in the same attitude, but now his hands clenched.

Xar entered the cell, stood over him.

"You can't escape the fear, never for a moment. Not even in sleep. It's there in your dreams. You run and run and run until you think your heart must burst and then you wake and you hear the terrifying sound that woke you and you get up and you run and run and run . . . all the time knowing it is hopeless. The claw, the tooth, the arrow, the fire, the bog, the pit will claim you in the end.

"Our babies suck fear in their mother's milk. Our babies don't cry. From the moment of birth, they're taught to keep quiet—out of fear. Our children do not laugh either. Who knows who might be listening?

"You have a son, I am told. A son who laughs and cries. A son who calls you 'Father,' a son who smiles like his mother."

A shiver crawled over Samah's body. The lord didn't know what nerve he had hit, but he reveled in the discovery and kept probing.

"Our children rarely know their own parents. A kindness—one of the few we can do for them. That way they don't become attached to their parents. It doesn't hurt so much when they find them dead. Or watch them die."

Xar's hatred and fury were slowly suffocating him. There wasn't enough air in Abarrach to sustain him. Blood beat in his head, and the lord feared for an instant that his heart might rupture. He raised his head and howled, a savage scream of anguish and rage that was like the heart's blood bursting from his mouth.

The howl was horrifying to hear. It reverberated through the catacombs, growing louder by some trick of the acoustics, and stronger, as if the dead in Abarrach had picked it up and were adding their own fearful cries to those of the Lord of the Nexus.

Marit blanched and gasped and shrank in terror against the chill wall of the prison. Sang-drax himself appeared taken aback. The red eye shifted uneasily, darting swift glances into the shadows, as if seeking some foe.

Samah shuddered. The scream might have been a spear driven through his body. He closed his eyes.

"I wish I didn't need you!" Xar gasped. Foam frothed his mouth; spittle hung from his lips. "I wish I didn't need the information you have locked in that black heart. I would take you to the Labyrinth. I would let you hold the dying children, as I have held them. I would let you whisper to them, as I have whispered: 'All will be well. Soon the fear will end.' And I would let you feel the envy, Samah! The envy when you gaze down upon that cold, peaceful face and know that, for this little child, the fear is over. While for you, it has just begun . . ."

Xar was calm now. His fury was spent. He felt a great weariness, as if he had spent hours fighting a powerful foe. The lord actually staggered as he took a step, was forced to lean against the stone wall of the prison cell.

"But unfortunately, I do need you, Samah. I need you to answer a . . . question." Xar wiped his mouth with the sleeve of his robe, wiped the chill sweat from his face. He smiled, a mirthless, bloodless smile. "I hope, I sincerely hope, Samah, Head of the Council of Seven, that you choose *not* to answer!"

Samah lifted his head. The eyes were sunken, the skin livid. He looked truly as if he were impaled on his enemy's spear. "I do not blame you for your hatred. We never meant . . ." He was forced to pause, lick dry lips. "We never meant any of the suffering. We never meant for the prison to turn deadly. It was to be a test . . . Don't you understand?"

Samah gazed at Xar in earnest appeal. "A test. That was all. A difficult test. One meant to teach you humility, patience. One meant to diminish your aggression . . ."

"Weaken us," Xar said softly.

"Yes," said Samah, slowly lowering his head. "Weaken you."

"You feared us."

"We feared you."

"You hoped we would die . . ."

"No." Samah shook his head.

"The Labyrinth became the embodiment of that hope. A secret hope. A hope you dared not admit, even to yourselves. But it was whispered into the words of magic that created the Labyrinth. And it was that secret, terrible hope that gave the Labyrinth its evil power."

Samah did not answer. He sat again with his head bowed.

Xar shoved himself away from the wall. Coming to stand in front of Samah, the lord put his hand beneath the Sartan's jaw, wrenched his head up and back, forced Samah to look up.

Samah flinched. He wrapped his hands around the old man's wrists, tried to free himself from the lord's grasp. But Xar was powerful. His magic was intact. The blue runes flared. Samah gasped in agony, snatched his hands away as if he had touched burning cinders.

Xar's thin fingers bit deeply and painfully into the Sartan's jaw.

"Where is the Seventh Gate?"

Samah stared, shocked, and Xar was pleased to see—at last—fear in the Sartan's eyes.

"Where is the Seventh Gate?" He squeezed Samah's face.

"I don't know . . . what you're talking about," Samah was forced to mumble.

"I'm so glad," Xar said pleasantly. "For now I will have the pleasure of teaching you. And you *will* tell me."

Samah managed to shake his head. "I'll die first!" he gasped.

"Yes, you probably will," Xar agreed. "And *then* you'll tell me. Your corpse will tell me. I've learned the art, you see. The art you came here to learn. I'll teach you that, too. Though it will be rather late to do you much good."

Xar released his hold, wiped his hands on his robes. He didn't like the feel of the sea water, could already notice it starting to weaken the rune-magic. Turning tiredly, he walked out of the cell. The iron bars sprang back into place as he passed by.

"My only regret is that I lack the strength to instruct you myself. But one waits who, like me, also wants revenge. You know him, I believe. He was instrumental in your capture."

Samah was on his feet. His hands clasped the bars of the cells. "I was wrong! My people were wrong! I admit it. I can offer no excuse, except that maybe we *do* know what it is like to live in fear. I see it now. Alfred, Orla . . . Orla." Samah closed his eyes in pain, drew a deep breath. "Orla was right."

Opening his eyes, gazing intently at Xar, Samah shook the bars of his cell. "But we have a common enemy. An enemy who will destroy us all. Destroy both our peoples, destroy the mensch!"

"And that enemy would be?" Xar was toying with his victim.

"The dragon-snakes! Or whatever form they take. And they can take any form they choose, Xar. That is what makes them so dangerous, so powerful. That Sang-drax. The one who captured me. He is one of them."

"Yes, I know," said Xar. "He has been very useful."

"*You* are the one being used!" Samah cried in frustration. He paused, trying desperately to think of some way to prove his point. "Surely one of your own would have warned you. That Patryn, the young man. The one who came to Chelestra. He discovered the truth about the dragon-snakes. He tried to warn me. I didn't listen. I didn't believe. I opened Death's Gate. He and Alfred . . . Haplo! That's the name he called himself. Haplo."

"What do you know of Haplo?" Xar asked in a low voice.

"He learned the truth," Samah said grimly. "He tried to make me see it. Surely, he must have told it to you, his lord."

So this is the thanks I get, is it, Haplo? Xar asked the dark shadows. This is gratitude for saving your life, my son. Betrayal.

"Your plot failed, Samah," Xar said coolly. "Your attempt to subvert my faithful servant failed. Haplo told me everything. He admitted everything. If you're going to speak, Sartan, speak to some purpose. Where is the Seventh Gate?"

"Haplo obviously didn't tell you everything," Samah said, lip curling. "Otherwise you would know the answer to your question. *He* was there. He and Alfred, at least so I gathered from something Alfred said. Apparently your Haplo trusts you no more than my Alfred trusts me. I wonder where we went wrong . . ."

Xar was stung, though he took care not to show it. Haplo again! Haplo knows. And I don't! It was maddening.

"The Seventh Gate," Xar repeated as if he hadn't heard.

"You're a fool," Samah said tiredly. Letting loose of the bars, he lapsed back on the stone bench. "You're a fool. As I was a fool. You doom your people." He sighed. His head sank into his hands. "As I have doomed mine."

Xar made a sharp, beckoning gesture. Sang-drax hastened down the dank and gloomy corridor.

The lord was having a difficult time. He wanted Samah to suffer, of course, but he also wanted Samah dead. Xar's fingers twitched. He was already drawing, in his own mind, the runes of necromancy that would begin the terrible resurrection.

Sang-drax entered the Sartan's cell. Samah did not look up, though Xar saw the Sartan's body stiffen involuntarily, bracing to endure what was coming.

What *was* coming? Xar wondered. What would the dragon-snake do? Curiosity made the lord forget momentarily his eagerness to see it all end.

"Commence," he said to Sang-drax.

The dragon-snake made no move. He did not raise his hand against Samah, did not summon fire or conjure steel. Yet suddenly Samah's head jerked up. He stared at something only he could see, his eyes widening in horror. He raised his hands, tried to use the Sartan runes to defend himself, but since he was wet with the magic-nullifying sea water of Chelestra, the magic would not work.

And perhaps it would not have worked anyway, for Samah was fighting a foe of his own mind, an enemy from somewhere in the depths of his own consciousness, brought to life by the insidious talents of the dragon-snake.

Samah screamed and leapt to his feet and flung himself against the stone wall in an effort to escape.

There was no escape. He staggered as beneath a tremendous blow, screamed again—this time in pain. Perhaps sharp talons were rending his skin. Perhaps fangs had torn his flesh or an arrow had thudded into his breast. He sank to the floor, writhing in agony. And then he shuddered and lay still.

Xar watched a moment, frowned. "Is he dead?" The lord was disappointed. Though he could commence his rune-magic now, death had come too quickly, been too easy.

"Wait!" the dragon-snake cautioned. He spoke a word in Sartan.

Samah sat up, clutching a wound that was not there. He stared around in terror, remembering. He gave a low, hollow cry, ran to the other side of his cell. Whatever was attacking him struck again. And again.

Xar listened to the Sartan's fearful screams, nodded in satisfaction.

"How long will this go on?" he asked Sang-drax, who was lounging back against a wall, watching, smiling.

"Until he dies—truly dies. Fear, exhaustion, terror will eventually kill him. But he'll die without a mark on his body. How long? That depends on your pleasure, Lord Xar."

Xar ruminated. "Let it continue," he decided finally. "I will go and question the other Sartan. He may be far more willing to talk with the yells of his compatriot ringing in his ears. When I return, I will ask Samah one more time about the Seventh Gate. Then you may finish it."

The dragon-snake nodded. After taking another moment to watch Samah's body twitch and jerk in agony, Xar left the Sartan's cell, proceeding down the corridor to where Marit waited in front of the cell of the other Sartan.

The one called Zifnab.

# CHAPTER ✦ 3

## ABARRACH

✦

THE OLD MAN HUDDLED IN HIS CELL. HE LOOKED PATHETIC AND RATHER PALE. Once, when a bubbling cry of excruciating torment was wrenched from Samah, the old man shuddered and put the tip of his yellowed white beard to his eyes. Xar watched from the shadows, deciding that this wretched relic would probably collapse into a trembling heap if the lord stamped his foot at him.

Xar approached the cell, signed Marit to use her rune-magic to remove the bars.

The old man's wet robes clung to his pitifully thin body. His hair trailed in a sodden mass down his back. Water dripped from the straggly beard. On the stone bed beside him was a battered pointed hat. The old man had from all appearances been attempting to wring the water from the hat, which had a twisted and maltreated look about it. Xar stared hard and suspiciously at the hat, thinking it might be a hidden source of power. He received the odd impression that it was sulking.

"That is your friend you hear screaming," said Xar conversationally, sitting down beside the old man, taking care to keep himself from getting wet.

"Poor Samah," the old man said, trembling. "There are those who would say he deserves this, but"—his voice softened—"he was only doing what he believed to be right. Much as you have done, Lord of the Nexus."

The old man lifted his head, looked intently at Xar with a disconcertingly shrewd expression. "Much as you have done," he repeated. "If only you'd left it there. If only *he'd* left it there." He inclined his head in the direction of the screams and gave a gentle sigh.

Xar frowned. This wasn't precisely what he'd had in mind. "The same thing will be happening to you shortly, Zifnab—"

"Where?" The old man peered around curiously.

"Where what?" Xar was growing irritated.

"Zifnab? I thought"—the old man looked deeply offended—"I thought this was a private cell."

"Don't try any of your tricks on me, old fool. I won't fall for them . . . as did Haplo," Xar said.

Samah's cries ceased for a moment, then began again.

The old man was regarding Xar with a blank expression, waiting for the lord to proceed. "Who?" he asked politely.

Xar was strongly tempted to commence torturing him right then and there. He contained himself by a great effort of will. "Haplo. You met him in the Nexus, beside the Final Gate, the gate that leads to the Labyrinth. You were seen and overheard, so don't play stupid."

"I never *play* stupid!" The old man drew himself up haughtily. "Who saw me?"

"A child. His name is Bane. What do you know about Haplo?" Xar asked patiently.

"Haplo. Yes, I do seem to remember." The old man was growing anxious. He stretched out a wet and shaking hand. "Youngish chap. Blue tattoos. Keeps a dog?"

"Yes," Xar growled, "that is Haplo."

The old man grabbed Xar's hand, shook it heartily. "You *will* give him my regards—"

Xar yanked his hand away. The lord stared at his skin, displeased to note the weakening of the sigla wherever the water touched them.

"So I am to give Haplo—a Patryn—the regards of a Sartan." Xar wiped his hand on his robes. "Then he *is* a traitor, as I have long suspected."

"No, Lord of the Nexus, you are mistaken," said the old man earnestly and rather sadly. "Of all the Patryns, Haplo is the *most* loyal. He will save you. He will save your people, if you will let him."

"Save *me?*" Xar was lost in astonishment. Then the lord smiled grimly. "He had better look to saving himself. As you should do, Sartan. What do you know about the Seventh Gate?"

"The citadel," the old man said.

"What?" Xar asked with feigned carelessness. "What did you say about the citadel?"

The old man opened his mouth, was about to reply, when he suddenly let out a shriek, as though he'd been kicked. "What did you do that for?" he demanded, whirling around and confronting empty air. "I didn't say anything. Well, of course, but I thought that you . . . Oh, very well."

Looking sullen, he turned back around, jumped when he saw Xar. "Oh, hullo. Have we met?"

"What about the citadel?" Xar recalled hearing something about a citadel, but he couldn't remember what.

"Citadel?" The old man looked vague. "What citadel?"

Xar heaved a sigh. "I asked about the Seventh Gate and you mentioned the citadel."

"It's not there. Definitely *not* there," the old man said, nodding emphatically. Twiddling his thumbs, he looked nervously around his cell, then said loudly, "Pity about Bane."

"What about Bane?" Xar questioned, eyes narrowing.

"Dead, you know. Poor child."

Xar couldn't speak, he was so amazed. The old man kept rambling on.

"Some would say it wasn't his fault. Considering the way he was raised and all that. Loveless childhood. Father an evil wizard. Boy didn't stand a chance. I don't buy that!" The old man looked extremely fierce. "That's the problem with the world. No one wants to take responsibility for his actions anymore. Adam blames the apple-eating incident on Eve. Eve says the serpent made her do it. The serpent claims that it's God's fault for putting the tree there in the first place. See there? No one wants to take responsibility."

Somehow Xar had lost control of the situation. He was no longer even enjoying Samah's tormented screams. "What about Bane?" he demanded.

"And you!" the old man shouted. "You've smoked forty packs of cigarettes a day since you were twelve and now you're blaming a billboard for giving you lung cancer!"

"You are a raving lunatic!" Xar started to turn away. "Kill

him," he ordered Marit. "We'll learn nothing from this fool while
he's alive . . ."

"What were we talking about? Ah, Bane." The old man sighed,
shook his head. He looked at Marit. "Would *you* care to hear about
him, my dear?"

Marit silently asked Xar, who nodded.

"Yes," she said, seating herself gingerly beside the old man.

"Poor Bane." He sighed. "But it was all for the best. Now there
will be peace on Arianus. And soon the dwarves will be starting up
the Kicksey-winsey . . ."

Xar had heard enough. He stormed out of the cell. He was very
nearly irrational with fury—a drunken sensation he didn't like. He
forced himself to think logically. The flame of his anger was
quenched, as if someone had shut off one of the gas jets that gave
light to this palace of tomb-like darkness. He beckoned to Marit.

She left the old man, who in her absence continued talking to
his hat.

"I don't like what I am hearing about Arianus," Xar said in a
low voice. "I don't believe the doddering old fool, but I have long
sensed that something was wrong. I should have heard from Bane
before now. Travel to Arianus, Daughter. Find out what is going on.
But be careful to take no action! Do not reveal yourself—to anyone!"

Marit gave a brief nod.

"Prepare for the journey," Xar continued, "then come to my
chambers for your final instructions. You will use my ship. You
know how to navigate Death's Gate?"

"Yes, Lord," Marit answered. "Shall I send someone down here
to take my place?"

Xar considered. "Send one of the lazar. Not Kleitus," he added
hastily. "One of the others. I may have some questions for them
when it comes time to raise Samah's body."

"Yes, Lord." Marit bowed respectfully and left.

Xar remained, glaring into Zifnab's cell. The old man had apparently forgotten the Patryn's existence. Rocking from side to side,
Zifnab was snapping his fingers and singing to himself. " 'I'm a soul
man. Ba-dop, da-ba-dop, da-ba-dop, da-ba-dop. Yes, I'm a soul
man . . .' "

Xar hurled the cell bars back into place with grim delight.

"I'll find out from your corpse who you really are, old fool. And
you'll tell me the truth about Haplo."

Xar strode back down the corridor toward Samah's cell. The screams had ceased for the moment. The dragon-snake was peering in through the bars. Xar came up behind him.

Samah lay on the floor. He appeared near death; his skin was clay-colored and glistened with sweat. He was breathing spasmodically. His body twitched and jerked.

"You're killing him," Xar observed.

"He proved weaker than I thought, Lord," Sang-drax said apologetically. "However, I could dry him off, permit him to heal himself. He would still be weak, probably too weak to attempt to escape. However, there would be a danger—"

"No." Xar was growing bored. "I need information. Rouse him enough that I may speak to him."

The bars of the cell dissolved. Sang-drax walked inside, prodded Samah with the toe of his boot. The Sartan groaned and flinched. Xar stepped in. Kneeling beside Samah's body, the Lord of the Nexus put his hands on either side of the Sartan's head and raised it from the ground. The lord's touch was not gentle; long nails dug into Samah's gray flesh, leaving glistening trails of blood.

Samah's eyes wrenched open. He stared at the lord and shivered in terror, but there was no recognition in the Sartan's eyes. Xar shook the man's head, dug his fingers to the bone.

"Know me! Know who I am!"

Samah's only reaction was to gasp for breath. There was a rattling in his throat. Xar knew the signs.

"The Seventh Gate! Where is the Seventh Gate?"

Samah's eyes widened. "Never meant . . . Death . . . Chaos! What . . . went wrong . . ."

"The Seventh Gate!" Xar persisted.

"Gone." Samah shut his eyes, spoke feverishly. "Gone. Sent it . . . away. No one knows . . . Rebels . . . Might try . . . undo . . . Sent it . . ."

A bubble of blood broke on Samah's lips. His eyes fixed in his head, staring in horror at something only he could see.

Xar dropped the head. It fell limp and unresisting, struck the stone floor with a crack. The lord laid his hand on Samah's inert chest, put his fingers on the Sartan's wrist. Nothing.

"He is dead," Xar said, cool with controlled excitement. "And his last thoughts are of the Seventh Gate. Sent the Gate away, he claims! What nonsense. He proved stronger than you thought, Sang-drax. He had the strength to continue this deceit to the end. Now, quickly!"

Xar ripped apart Samah's wet robes, laying bare the still chest. Producing a dagger—its blade was marked with runes—the lord set the sharp tip over Samah's heart and pierced the skin. Blood, warm and crimson, flowed from beneath the knife's sharp edge. Working swiftly and surely, repeating the sigla beneath his breath as he drew them on the skin, Xar used the knife to carve the runes of necromancy into Samah's dead flesh.

The skin grew cool beneath the lord's hand; the blood flowed more sluggishly. The dragon-snake stood nearby, watching, a smile lighting the one good eye. Xar did not look up from his work. At the sound of footsteps approaching, the Lord of the Nexus said merely, "Lazar? Are you here?"

"I am here," intoned a voice.

". . . am here," came the sighing echo.

"Excellent."

Xar sat back. His hands were covered with blood; the dagger was dark with it. Lifting his hand above Samah's heart, Xar spoke a word. The heart-rune flashed blue. Fast as lightning, the magic spread from the heart-sigil to the sigil touching it, from that sigil to the one touching it, and soon blue light was flickering and dancing all over the body.

An eerie, glowing form wavered into being near the body, as if the dead man's shadow were made of light instead of darkness. Xar drew in a shivering breath of awe. This pallid image was the phantasm—the ethereal, immortal part of every living being, what the mensch called the "soul."

The phantasm tried to pull away from the body, tried to free itself, but it was caught in the husk of chill and bloody flesh and could only writhe in an agony comparable to that experienced by the body when it had lived in torment.

Suddenly the phantasm disappeared. Xar frowned, but then saw the dead eyes pathetically lit from within: a mockery of life, the spirit joining momentarily with the body.

"I have done it!" Xar cried in exaltation. "I have done it! I have brought life back to the dead!"

But now what to do with it? The lord had never seen one of the dead raised; he had only heard descriptions from Haplo. Appalled and sickened by what he had seen, Haplo had kept his descriptions brief.

Samah's dead body sat bolt upright. He had become a lazar.

Startled, Xar fell back a step. He caused the runes on his skin to glow bright red and blue. The lazar are powerful beings who come back to life with a terrible hatred of all things living. A lazar has the strength of one who is past feeling pain and fatigue.

Naked, his body covered with bloody tracings of Patryn sigla, Samah stared around in confusion, the dead eyes occasionally flickering with pitiable life when the phantasm flitted inside.

Shaken by his triumph, overawed, the lord needed time to think, to calm himself. "Lazar, say something to it." Xar motioned, his hands trembling with excitement. "Speak to it." He drew back against a far wall to watch and to exult in his achievement.

The lazar, a man, obediently stepped forward. Before death—which had obviously come by violence, to judge by the cruel marks still visible on the corpse's throat—the man had been young and comely. Xar paid scant attention to the lazar beyond a brief glance to assure himself that it wasn't Kleitus.

"You are one of my people," said the lazar to Samah. "You are Sartan."

"I am . . . I was," said the voice of the corpse.

"I am . . . I was," came the dismal echo from the trapped phantasm.

"Why did you come to Abarrach?"

"To learn necromancy."

"You traveled here to Abarrach," repeated the lazar, its voice a lifeless monotone, "to learn the art of necromancy. To use the dead as slaves to the living."

"I did . . . I did."

"And you know now the hatred the dead bear for the living, who keep them in bondage. For you see, do you not? You see . . . freedom . . ."

The phantasm coiled and wrenched in a futile attempt to escape. The hatred on the face of the corpse as it turned its sightless—yet all too clear-seeing—eyes to Xar caused even the Patryn to blanch.

"You, lazar," the Lord of the Nexus interrupted harshly, "what are you called?"

"Jonathon."

"Jonathon, then." The name meant something to Xar, but he couldn't think what. "Enough talk of hatred. You lazar are free now, free from the weaknesses of the flesh that you knew when you were alive. And you are immortal. It is a great gift we living have given you . . ."

"One we would be happy to share," said the lazar of Samah in a low, dire voice.

". . . to share," came the fearful echo.

Xar was displeased; the rune-glow that came from his body flared. "You waste my time. There are many questions I will ask you, Samah. Many questions you will answer for me. But the first, the most important, is the one I asked you before you died. Where is the Seventh Gate?"

The countenance of the corpse twisted; the body shook. The phantasm peered out through the lifeless eyes with a sort of terror. "I will not . . ." The blue lips of the corpse moved, but no sound came out. "I will not . . ."

"You will!" Xar said sternly, though he was somewhat at a loss. How do you threaten one who feels no pain, one who knows no fear? Frustrated, the lord turned to Jonathon. "What is the meaning of this defiance? You Sartan forced the dead to reveal all their secrets. I know, because Kleitus himself told me this, as did my minion, who was here previously."

"This man's will was strong in his life," the lazar answered. "You raised him too quickly, perhaps. If the body had been allowed to remain quiet for the requisite three days, the phantasm would have left the body and then the soul—the will—could no longer have any effect on what the body did. But now the defiance that died with him lives still."

"But will he answer my questions?" Xar persisted, frustration growing.

"He will. In time," Jonathon answered, and there was sorrow in the echoing voice. "In time he will forget all that meant anything to him in life. He will know only the bitter hatred of those who still live."

"Time!" Xar ground his teeth. "How much time? A day? A fortnight?"

"I cannot say."

"Bah!" Xar strode forward, came to stand directly before Samah. "Answer my question! Where is the Seventh Gate? What do you care now?" he added in wheedling tones. "It means nothing to you. You defy me only because that's all you remember how to do."

The light in the dead eyes flickered. "We sent it . . . away . . ."

"You did not!" Xar was losing patience. This wasn't turning out as he had foreseen. He'd been too eager. He should have waited. He *would* wait the next time. When he killed the old man. "Sending the gate away makes no sense. You would keep it where you could use it again if need be. Perhaps you *did* use it—to open Death's Gate! Tell me the truth. Does it have something to do with a citadel—"

"Master!"

The urgent cry came bounding down the corridor. Xar jerked his head toward the sound.

"Master!" It was Sang-drax, calling and gesturing wildly from the end of the corridor. "Come swiftly! The old man is gone!"

"Dead, then?" Xar grunted. "All for the best. Now let me be—"

"Not dead! Gone! He is gone!"

"What trick is this?" Xar demanded. "He couldn't be gone! How could he escape?"

"I do not know, Lord of the Nexus." Sang-drax's sibilant whisper shook with a fury that startled even Xar. "But he is gone! Come and see for yourself."

There was no help for it. Xar cast a final baleful look at Samah, who appeared completely oblivious to what was going on. Then the lord hastened down the corridor.

When the Lord of the Nexus had left, when his voice could be heard rising strident and angry from the far end of the cellblock, Jonathon spoke, quietly, softly.

"You see now. You understand."

"Yes!" The phantasm peered out of the lifeless eyes in despair, as the living man had once peered out of his prison cell. "I see now. I understand."

"You always knew the truth, didn't you?"

"How could I admit it? We had to seem to be gods. What would the truth have made us?"

"Mortal. As you were."

"Too late. All is lost. All is lost."

"No, the Wave corrects itself. Rest upon it. Relax. Float with it, let it carry you."

The phantasm of Samah appeared irresolute. It darted into the body, fled out of it, but could not yet escape. "I cannot. I must stay. I have to hang on . . ."

"Hang on to what? To hatred? To fear? To revenge? Lie back. Rest upon the Wave. Feel it lift you up."

The corpse of Samah remained seated on the hard stone. The eyes stared up at Jonathon. "Can they forgive me . . . ?"

"Can you forgive yourself?" the lazar asked gently.

Samah's body—an ashen and blood-covered shell—laid slowly down on the stone bed. It shuddered, then was still. The eyes grew dark and now truly lifeless.

Jonathon reached out his hand, closed them.

Xar, suspecting some trick, stared hard into Zifnab's cell. Nothing. No sight of the wet and bedraggled old Sartan.

"Hand me that torch!" Xar commanded, peering about in baffled outrage.

The Lord of the Nexus banished the cell bars with an impatient wave of his hand and strode into the cell, flashing the light into every part of it.

"What do you think you will find, Lord?" Sang-drax snarled. "That he is playing at peekaboo in a corner? I tell you, he is gone!"

Xar didn't like the dragon-snake's tone. The lord turned, held the light so that it would flare into the dragon's one good eye. "If he has escaped, it is your fault! You were supposed to be guarding him! Sea water of Chelestra!" Xar sneered. "Takes away their power! Obviously it didn't!"

"It did, I tell you," Sang-drax muttered.

"But he can't get far," Xar reflected. "We have guards posted at the entrance to Death's Gate. He—"

The dragon-snake hissed suddenly—a hiss of fury that seemed to wrap its coils around Xar and squeeze the breath from his body. Sang-drax pointed a rune-covered hand at the stone bed. "There! There!" He could say no more; the breath gurgled in his throat.

Xar held the torchlight to shine on the spot. The lord's eyes caught a glint, a sparkle that came from something on the stone. He reached down, picked it up, held it to the light.

"It's nothing but a scale—"

"A dragon's scale!" Sang-drax glared at it with enmity, made no move to touch it.

"Perhaps." Xar was noncommittal. "A lot of reptiles have scales, not all of them dragons. And what of it? It has nothing to do with the old man's disappearance. It must have been here for ages—"

"Undoubtedly you are right, Lord of the Nexus." Sang-drax was suddenly nonchalant, though his one good eye remained fixed on the scale. "What could a dragon—one of my cousins, for instance —possibly have to do with that daft old man? I will go and alert the guard."

"I give the orders—" Xar began, but his words were wasted. Sang-drax had vanished.

The lord stared around at the empty cell, fuming, a disturbing and unfamiliar unease jabbing deep beneath his skin.

"What is going on?" he was forced to ask himself, and the simple fact that he had to ask that question indicated to the Lord of the Nexus that he had lost control.

Xar had known fear many times in his life. He knew fear every time he walked into the Labyrinth. But still he was able to walk in; he was able to grapple with his fear and put it to use, channel its energy into self-preservation, because he knew that he was in control. He might not know which enemy the Labyrinth was going to hurl at him, but he knew every enemy that existed, knew their strengths and their weaknesses.

But now. What was going on? How had that feeble-minded old man escaped? Most important, what did Sang-drax fear? What did the dragon-snake know that he wasn't telling?

"Haplo didn't trust them," the lord said to himself, glaring at the scale he held in his hand. "He warned me not to trust them. So did that fool who lies dead over there. Not"—Xar scowled—"that I believe any claim of either Haplo's or Samah's. But I am beginning to believe that these dragon-snakes have their own goals, which may or may not coincide with mine.

"Yes, Haplo warned me against them. But what if he did so only to blind me to the fact that he is in league with them? They called him 'Master' once.[1] He admitted as much to me. And Kleitus talks to them. Perhaps they are all in league against me."

Xar stared around the cell. The torchlight was failing; the shad-

---

[1] *Serpent Mage*, vol. 4 of *The Death Gate Cycle*.

ows grew darker, began to close in around him. It was nothing to him whether or not he had light. The sigla on his body compensated, would make the darkness bright if he chose. He did choose. He tossed away the useless torch and drove away the shadows with his own magic. He didn't like this world, this Abarrach. He felt constantly stifled, smothered. The air was foul, and though his magic nullified the poison, it could not sweeten the stench of the sulfurous fumes, remove the rank odor of death.

"I must make my move, and quickly," he said.

He would start by determining the location of the Seventh Gate.

Xar left Zifnab's cell, strode rapidly back down the corridor. The lazar that called itself Jonathon (where had Xar heard that name? Haplo, undoubtedly, but in what connection?) stood in the corridor. Jonathon's body itself was unmoving; the phantasm roved restlessly about it in a manner that Xar found extremely disconcerting.

"You have served your purpose," Xar told it. "You may go."

The lazar made no response. It did not argue. It simply walked away.

Xar waited until it had shambled back down the corridor. Then, putting the disquieting lazar out of his mind, along with the dragon scale and Sang-drax, Xar turned his attention to what was important. To Samah.

The corpse lay on the stone bed. It looked as if it slumbered peacefully. Xar found this more irritating than ever.

"Get up!" he snapped. "I want to speak with you."

The corpse did not move.

A feeling of panic invaded the lord's body. He saw then that the eyes were closed. No lazar that he had ever seen went about with its eyes closed, any more than a living person. Xar bent over the corpse, lifted one of the flaccid eyelids.

Nothing looked back at him. No unholy light of life glimmered and winked. The eyes were empty. The phantasm was gone, fled.

Samah was free.

# CHAPTER ♦ 4

# NECROPOLIS

# ABARRACH

♦

I_T DID NOT TAKE MARIT LONG TO PREPARE FOR HER JOURNEY. SHE SELECTED_ clothes to wear on Arianus, choosing among the wardrobes left behind by the Sartan, murdered by their own dead. She selected a garment that would conceal the runes on her body, one that would make her look human. Packing this, along with several of her favorite sigla-inscribed weapons, Marit transported the bundle to a Patryn ship floating on Abarrach's lava sea. Then she returned to the castle of Necropolis.

She walked through halls still stained with blood from the dreadful Night of the Risen Dead—the term the lazar used when they spoke of their triumph. The blood was Sartan blood, blood of her enemies, and so the Patryns had made no attempt to remove it, left it splattered on the walls and floors. The dried blood of the Sartan, mingled with the broken runes of their magic, became a symbol to the Patryns of the ultimate defeat of their ancient foe.

Other Patryns passed Marit on her way to her lord's study. They exchanged no greetings, wasted no time in idle conversation. The Patryns Xar had brought with him to Abarrach were the strongest and toughest of a strong, tough breed. Almost all had been Runners. Each had made it either to the Final Gate or near enough. Most had ultimately been rescued by Xar; there were few Patryns alive today who did not owe their lives to their lord.

Marit took pride in the fact that she had fought with her lord, side by side, in the grueling struggle to win her own freedom from the Labyrinth. . . .

She was near the Final Gate when she was attacked by gigantic birds with leather wings and flesh-tearing teeth, who would first disable a victim by pecking out his eyes, then gorge on the warm, still-living flesh.

Marit fought the birds by altering her own form to that of a bird —a gigantic eagle. Her talons ripped jagged holes in the leather wings; her plummeting dives knocked many from the sky.

But, as is the way of the Labyrinth, its heinous magic grew powerful in the face of defeat. The numbers of shrieking leather-winged birds increased. She was hit countless times, wounded by tooth and claw. Her strength gave out. She fell to land. Her magic could no longer support her altered state. She changed back to her own shape and fought what she knew would be a losing battle, as the horrid flapping things swirled about her face, trying to get at her eyes.

Her skin was torn and bleeding. She was knocked to her knees by striking blows from behind. She was nearly ready to give up and die when a voice thundered over her.

"Rise, Daughter! Rise and battle on. You are not alone!"

She opened her eyes, already dimming with approaching death, and saw her lord, the Lord of the Nexus.

He came like a god, wielding balls of flame. He stood protectively over her until she regained her feet. He gave her his hand, gnarled and wrinkled but beautiful to her, for it brought her not only life but hope and renewed courage. Together they fought until the Labyrinth was forced to retreat. The birds—those that survived —flapped away with shrill squawks of disappointment.

Marit fell then. The Lord of the Nexus lifted her in his strong arms and bore her through the Final Gate, carried her to freedom.

"I pledge you my life, Lord," she whispered to him, her last words before she lost consciousness. "Always . . . forever . . ."

He had smiled. The lord had heard many such pledges, knew that they would all be redeemed. Marit had been chosen to travel to Abarrach by her lord. She was just one of many Patryns he'd brought with him, all of whom would be willing to give their lives for the man who had given life to them.

Approaching the study now, Marit was disturbed to see a lazar wandering the halls outside. At first, she thought it was Kleitus and was about to order him off. Admittedly the castle had once been his.

But the lazar had no business here. Closer examination, which Marit made with extreme repugnance, revealed this lazar to be the one she had sent to serve her lord in the dungeons. What was it doing here? If she could have supposed such a thing possible, she would have said the lazar was lingering in the halls, listening to the voices that came through the closed door.

Marit was about to order it to be gone, when another voice—the eerie echoing voice of another lazar—forestalled her words.

"Jonathon!" Kleitus came shambling along the corridor. "I heard the Patryn lord raging over his failure to raise the dead. It occurred to me that you might have had something to do with that. I was right, it seems."

"It seems . . ." The echo was mournful.

They were both speaking Sartan, a language Marit found uncomfortable and disturbing to hear, but one she understood. She backed into the shadows, hoping to learn something to her lord's advantage.

The lazar called Jonathon slowly turned. "I could give you the same peace I gave Samah, Kleitus."

The Dynast laughed, a terrible sound, made awful by the echo. It wailed in despair. "Yes, I'm certain you would gladly reduce me to dust!" The corpse's bluish-white hands flexed, long-nailed fingers twitched. "Consign me to oblivion!"

"*Not* oblivion," Jonathon corrected. "Freedom." His gentle voice and its soft echo coincided with the despairing echo of Kleitus, producing a sad, yet harmonic note.

"Freedom!" Kleitus gnashed his rotting teeth. "I'll give you freedom!"

". . . freedom!" The echo howled.

Kleitus rushed forward, skeletal hands clutching at Jonathon's throat. The two corpses grappled together, Jonathon's wasted hands closing over Kleitus's wrists, trying to drag the other off him. The lazar struggled, nails digging into flesh, drawing no blood. Marit watched in horror, disgusted by the sight. She made no move to intervene. This was not her fight.

A cracking sound. One of Kleitus's arms bent at a sickening angle. Jonathon flung his opponent off him, sent the Dynast reeling back against the wall. Kleitus nursed his broken limb, glared at the other lazar in rage and bitter enmity.

"You told Lord Xar about the Seventh Gate!" Jonathon said,

standing over Kleitus. "Why? Why hasten to what you must see as your own destruction?"

Kleitus was massaging his broken arm, muttering Sartan runes. The bone was starting to re-form; thus the lazars kept their rotting bodies functional. Looking up at Jonathon, the corpse grinned hideously. "I didn't tell him its location."

"He will find out."

"Yes, he will find out!" Kleitus laughed. "Haplo will show him. Haplo will guide him to that room. They will all be inside the chamber together . . ."

". . . together . . ." The echo sighed dismally.

"And you—waiting for them," said Jonathon.

"I found my 'freedom' in that chamber," Kleitus said, blue-gray lips curled in a sneer. "I'll help them find theirs! As you will find yours—"

The Dynast paused, turned his head to stare directly at Marit with his strange eyes, which were sometimes the eyes of the dead and sometimes the eyes of the living.

Marit's skin prickled; the runes on her arms and hands glowed blue. Silently, she cursed herself. She had made a sound, nothing more than a sharp intake of breath, but it had been enough to give her away.

No help for it now. She strode boldly forward.

"What are you lazars doing here? Spying on my lord? Begone," Marit commanded, "or must I summon Lord Xar to make you leave?"

The lazar known as Jonathon departed immediately, gliding down the blood-spattered corridor. Kleitus remained, eyeing her balefully. He seemed about to attack.

Marit began to weave a rune-spell in her mind. The sigla on her body glowed brightly.

Kleitus withdrew into the shadows, walking with his shuffling gait down the long hall.

Shivering, thinking that any living enemy, no matter how fearsome, was far preferable to these walking dead, Marit was about to knock on the door when she heard from within her lord's voice, raised in anger.

"And you did not report this to me! I must find out what goes on in my universe from a doddering old Sartan!"

"I see now that I was mistaken in not telling you, Lord Xar. I offer as my excuse only the fact that you were deeply involved in the study of necromancy and I did not want to disturb you with grievous news." It was Sang-drax. The dragon-snake was whining again.

Marit wondered what she should do. She did not want to get involved in an argument between her lord and the dragon-snake, whom she heartily disliked. Yet her lord had ordered her to report to him at once. And she could not very well remain standing out here in the hallway. She would look as much an eavesdropper as the lazar. Taking advantage of a lull in the conversation, a lull that perhaps arose from Xar's being speechless with rage, Marit knocked timidly on the kairn-grass door.

"Lord Xar, it is I, Marit."

The door swung open by Xar's magical command. Sang-drax bowed to her with slimy officiousness. Ignoring him, Marit looked at Xar.

"You are engaged, Lord," she said. "I can return—"

"No, my dear. Come in. This concerns you and your journey." Xar had regained his calm demeanor, though his eyes still flashed when they turned to the dragon-snake.

Marit stepped inside and shut the door behind her, first glancing outside to make certain the hall was empty.

"I found Kleitus and another lazar outside your door, my lord," she reported. "I think they were attempting to overhear your words."

"Let them!" Xar said, without interest. He then spoke to Sang-drax.

"You fought Haplo on Arianus. Why?"

"I was attempting to prevent the mensch from seizing control of the Kicksey-winsey, Lord," the dragon-snake replied, cringing. "The machine's power is immense, as you yourself have surmised. Once it is in operation, it will not only change Arianus, but will affect all the other worlds as well. In the hands of the mensch—" Sang-drax shrugged, leaving that terrible possibility to the imagination.

"And Haplo was assisting the mensch?" Xar pursued.

"Not only assisting them, Lord," said the dragon-snake. "He actually provided them with information—undoubtedly obtained from that Sartan friend of his—on how to operate the great machine."

Xar's eyes narrowed. "I don't believe you."

"He has a book, written in four languages: Sartan, elven, human, and dwarven. Where else could he have obtained it, Lord, but from the one who calls himself Alfred?"

"*If* what you say is true, he must have had it with him, then, when he last saw me in the Nexus," Xar muttered. "Why would Haplo do such a thing? What reason?"

"He wants to rule Arianus, Lord. And perhaps the rest of the four worlds as well. Isn't that obvious?"

"And so the mensch, under Haplo's guidance, are about to start up the Kicksey-winsey." Xar's fist clenched. "Why didn't you tell me this before?"

"Would you have believed me?" Sang-drax asked softly. "Though I have lost an eye, I am not the one who is blind. You are, Lord of the Nexus. Look! Look at the evidence you have amassed—evidence indicating one thing. Time and again Haplo has lied to you, betrayed you. And you permit it! You love him, Lord. Your love has blinded you as surely as his sword almost blinded me."

Marit trembled, astounded at the dragon-snake's temerity. She waited for Xar's fury to thunder around them.

But Xar's clenched fist slowly relaxed. His hand shook. Leaning on his desk, he turned away from Sang-drax, away from Marit.

"Did you slay him?" the lord asked heavily.

"No, Lord. He is one of your people, and so I took care not to kill him. I left him critically wounded, however, for which I apologize. Sometimes I do not know my own strength. I tore his heart-rune open. Seeing him near death, I realized what I had done and, fearing your displeasure, withdrew from the battle."

"And that is how you came to lose your eye?" Xar asked wryly, glancing around. "*Withdrawing* from the battle?"

Sang-drax glowered; the single red eye glowed, and Marit's defensive runes suddenly glimmered to life. Xar continued to regard the dragon-snake with apparent calm, and Sang-drax lowered his eyelid, extinguishing the red glow.

"Your people are skilled warriors, Lord." The single eye slid to Marit and flared briefly; then its gleam was doused again.

"And what is Haplo's condition now?" Xar asked. "Not good, I should think. It takes time to heal the heart-rune."

"True, Lord. He is exceedingly weak and will not soon recover."

"How did Bane come to die?" Xar asked mildly enough, though his own eyes flickered dangerously. "And why did Haplo attack you?"

"Bane knew too much, Lord. He was loyal to you. Haplo hired a mensch called Hugh the Hand, an assassin friend of Alfred's, to murder Bane. This done, Haplo seized control of the great Kicksey-winsey for himself. When I attempted to stop him—in your name, My Lord Xar—Haplo drove the mensch to attack me and my people."[1]

"And they *defeated* you? *Mensch* defeated you?" Xar was regarding Sang-drax with disgust.

"They did not defeat us, Lord," Sang-drax answered with dignity. "As I said, we withdrew. We feared the Kicksey-winsey might suffer harm if we pursued the battle. We knew that you did not want the great machine damaged, and so, in deference to your wishes, we left Arianus."

Sang-drax looked up; the single eye gleamed. "There was no urgency. What my lord wants, my lord will take. As to the mensch, they may have found peace for the time being, but they will soon misplace it. Such is their way."

Xar glared at the dragon-snake, who stood chastened and abashed before him. "What is happening on Arianus now?"

"Alas, Lord, as I said, our people all left. I can send them back, if you truly believe it necessary. However, might I suggest that my lord's true interest lies in Pryan—"

"Pryan again! What is so important about Pryan?"

"The dragon's scale that was discovered in the old man's cell—"

"Yes, what about it?" Xar demanded impatiently.

"Such creatures come from Pryan, Lord." Sang-drax paused, then added in a low voice, "In the ancient days, Lord, these dragons were servants of the Sartan. It has occurred to me that perhaps the Sartan left something behind on Pryan that they wished to keep secret, well guarded, undisturbed . . . such as the Seventh Gate."

Xar's anger cooled. He was suddenly thoughtful. He had just

---

[1] Those who have read about the dragon-snakes before will note the difference between Sang-drax's account of the Battle of the Kicksey-winsey and the truth, as recorded in *The Hand of Chaos*, vol. 5 of *The Death Gate Cycle*.

recalled where he'd heard about the citadels of Pryan. "I see. And you say these dragons exist only on this world?"

"Haplo himself reported so, Lord. And it was there he ran into the crazed old Sartan. Undoubtedly the dragon and the old Sartan have returned to Pryan. And if they were able to travel here, to Chelestra, who knows but that next time they will return with an army of tytans?"

Xar was not about to let the dragon-snake see his excitement. "Perhaps I will go to Pryan," he said noncommittally. "We will discuss this later, Sang-drax. Know that I am displeased with you. You are dismissed."

Flinching beneath the lash of Xar's anger, the dragon-snake slunk out of the lord's presence.

Xar was silent long moments after Sang-drax's departure. Marit wondered if he had changed his mind about sending her to Arianus, since he'd heard what was happening from the dragon-snake. He was apparently thinking along the same lines, for he said to himself, "No, I do not trust him!"

But was he, Marit wondered suddenly, speaking of Sang-drax . . . or of Haplo?

He turned to her, decision made.

"You will travel to Arianus, Daughter. You will learn the truth of the matter. Sang-drax kept this concealed from me for a reason, and I do not believe it was to save me from grief! Although," he added in a softer tone, "the betrayal of one of my own people, particularly Haplo . . ."

He paused a moment, thoughtful. "I have read that in the ancient world, before the Sundering, we Patryns were a stern and cold people who did not love, who prided ourselves on never feeling affection, not even for each other. Lust was permissible, encouraged, for lust perpetuates our species. The Labyrinth taught us many hard lessons. I wonder if it didn't teach us to love." Xar sighed. "Haplo's betrayal has inflicted a pain on me worse than any I have endured from the creatures of the Labyrinth."

"I do not believe he would betray you, Lord," said Marit.

"No?" Xar asked, gazing at her intently. "And why not? Is it possible that you love him, too?"

Marit flushed. "That is not the reason. I do not believe any Patryn could be so disloyal."

He stared at her as if probing for some deeper meaning. She returned his gaze steadfastly, and he was satisfied.

"That is because your heart is true, Daughter. And therefore you cannot conceive of one that is false." He paused, then said, "If Haplo *is* proven a traitor—not only to me, but to our people—what punishment would he merit?"

"Death, Lord," said Marit calmly.

Xar smiled, nodded. "Well spoken, Daughter. Tell me," he added with that same piercing stare, "have you ever rune-joined with any man or woman, Marit?"

"No, Lord." She was at first startled by his question, then understood what he was truly asking. "You are mistaken, Lord, if you think that Haplo and I—"

"No, no, Daughter," Xar interrupted smoothly. "I do not ask because of that—although I am glad to hear it. I ask for another, more selfish reason."

Walking to his desk, Xar lifted a long bodkin that lay on it. Also on his desk was a jar of ink, so blue as to be almost black. He muttered over the ink several words of the rune-language used by the Patryns. Then he drew his hood back from his face and lifted the long hair that fell over his forehead to reveal a single blue sigil tattooed there.

"Will you rune-join with me, Daughter?" he asked gently.

Marit stared at him in astonishment; then she fell to her knees. Her fists clenched, she bowed her head. "Lord, I am not worthy of this honor."

"Yes, Daughter. Most worthy."

She remained kneeling before him, lifted her face to his. "Then, yes, Lord, I will rune-join with you, and count it the greatest joy of my life." Reaching to the open-necked blouse she wore, she ripped it open, laying bare her rune-marked breasts.

Over the left breast was tattooed her own heart-rune.

Xar brushed back Marit's brown hair from her forehead. Then his hand sought her breasts, which were firm and small and rode high upon the strong muscles of her chest. His hand moved down over her smooth, slender neck to cup and fondle her left breast.

She closed her eyes and shivered, more in awe than in pleasure, at his touch.

Xar noticed. His gnarled hand ceased its caress. She heard him sigh. "Few times I regret my lost youth. This is one."

Marit's eyes flared open. She burned with shame that he should so mistake her. "Lord, I will gladly warm your bed—"

"Ah, that is what you would be doing, Daughter—*warming* my bed," Xar said dryly. "I am afraid I could not return the favor. The fire died in these loins of mine long ago. But our minds will join, if our bodies cannot."

He placed the point of the bodkin on the smooth skin of her forehead and pricked her flesh.

Marit shuddered, though not at the pain. From the moment of birth, Patryn children are tattooed at various times throughout their lives. They not only become accustomed to the pain but are taught to endure it without flinching. Marit shuddered at the rush of magic into her body, magic which flowed from the lord's body to her own, magic which would grow stronger as he formed the sigla which would bind them together—his heart-rune, entwined with hers.

Over and over he repeated the process, inserting the bodkin into Marit's smooth skin more than a hundred times until the complicated pattern was completely drawn. He shared her ecstasy, which was of the mind rather than the body. After the ecstasy of rune-joining, sexual coupling is generally a letdown.

When he had finished his work and set down the blood- and ink-stained bodkin, he knelt before her and took her in his arms. The two pressed their foreheads together, sigil touching sigil, the circles of their beings closing in one. Marit cried out in gasping pleasure and went limp and trembling in his grasp.

He was pleased with her and held her in his arms until she grew calm again. Then he put his hand on her chin and looked into her eyes.

"We are one. No matter that we are apart, our thoughts will fly each to the other as we desire."

He held her with his eyes, his hands. She was transfixed, adoring. Her flesh was soft and pliable beneath his fingers.

It seemed to her as if all her bones had dissolved at his touch, his look.

"You did once love Haplo." He spoke gently.

Marit hesitated, then lowered her head in shameful, silent acquiescence.

"So did I, Daughter," Xar said softly. "So did I. That will be a bond between us. And if I deem that Haplo must die, you will be the one to slay him."

Marit lifted her head. "Yes, Lord."

Xar regarded her doubtfully. "You speak quickly, Marit. I must know for certain. You lay with him. Yet you will kill him?"

"I lay with him. I bore his child. But if my lord commands, I will kill him."

Marit's voice was calm and even. He would sense no hesitation, feel no tension in her body. But then a thought came to her. Perhaps this was some sort of test . . .

"Lord," she said, clasping her hands over his, "I have not incurred your displeasure. You do not doubt *my* loyalty—"

"No, Daughter—or, I should say, Wife." He smiled at her.

She kissed the hands she held in hers.

"No, Wife. You are the logical choice. I have seen inside Haplo's heart. He loves you. You and you alone, among our people, can penetrate the circle of his being. He would trust you where he would trust no one else. And he will be loath to harm you—the mother of his child."

"Does he know about the child?" Marit asked, astonished.

"He knows," said Xar.

"How could he? I left him without telling him. I never told anyone."

"Someone found out." Xar asked the next question, frowning. "Where is the child, by the way?"

Again Marit had the sense that she was being tested. But she could make only one answer, and that was the truth. She shrugged. "I have no idea. I gave the baby to a tribe of Squatters."[2]

Xar's frown eased. "Most wise, Wife." He disengaged himself from her grasp, rose to his feet. "It is time for you to depart for Arianus. We will communicate through the rune-joining. You will report to me what you find. Most particularly, you will keep your arrival on Arianus secret. You will not let Haplo know he is under

---

[2] This sounds callous, but it was a common practice among the Runners to give their children to the tribes of the more settled Squatters, with whom a baby would have a far greater chance for survival.

observation. If I deem he must die, you must take him by surprise."

"Yes, Lord."

" 'Husband,' Marit," he said, chiding her gently. "You must call me 'Husband.' "

"That is far too great an honor for me, Lor—Hus—Husband," she stammered, alarmed that the word should come to her lips with such difficulty.

He brushed his hand across her forehead.

"Cover the sigil of rune-joining. If he saw it, he would recognize my mark and know at once that you and I have become one. He would suspect you."

"Yes, Lor—Husband."

"Farewell, then, Wife. Report to me from Arianus at your earliest opportunity."

Xar turned from her, went to his desk. Sitting down without another look, he began to flip through the pages of a book, his brow furrowed in concentration.

Marit was not surprised at this cold and abrupt dismissal by her new husband. She was shrewd enough to know that the rune-joining had been one of convenience, made in order to facilitate her reporting to him from a far distant world. Still, she was pleased. It was a mark of his faith in her. They were bound for life and, through the exchange of magic, could now communicate with each other through the combined circle of their beings. Such closeness had its advantages, but its disadvantages as well—particularly to the Patryns, who tended to be loners, keep to themselves, refuse to permit even those closest to them to intrude on their inner thoughts and feelings.

Few Patryns ever formally rune-joined. Most settled for simply joining the circle of their beings.[3] Xar had conferred on Marit a great honor. He had set his mark[4] on her, and anyone who saw it would

---

[3] Haplo describes such a ceremony in *Dragon Wing*, vol. 1 of *The Death Gate Cycle*.

[4] Either the elder inscribes the rune on the younger, or the one who is first joined inscribes the rune on the one who is not. If both have been previously joined, they inscribe the runes on each other. Once rune-joined, Patryns are forbidden to join with any other, so long as their rune-mate remains alive.

know they had joined. His taking her to wife would increase her standing among the Patryns. On his death, she might well assume leadership of her people.

To Marit's credit, she was not thinking of that. She was touched, honored, dazzled, and overwhelmed, unable to feel anything but her boundless love for her lord. She wished that he would live forever so that she could serve him forever. Her one thought was to please him.

The skin on her forehead burned and stung. She could feel the touch of his hand on her naked breast. The memory of that blessed pain and the memory of his touch would remain with her forever.

She left Abarrach, sailing her ship into Death's Gate. It never occurred to her to report to Xar the conversation she'd overheard between the two lazar. She had, in her excitement, forgotten all about it.

Back in Necropolis, in his study, Xar settled down at his desk, took up again one of the Sartan texts on necromancy. He was in a good humor. It is a pleasant thing to be worshipped, adored, and he'd seen worship and adoration in Marit's eyes.

She had been his to command before, but she was doubly his now, bound to him body and mind. She would open herself to him completely, as had so many others before her. Unwritten law prohibits a Patryn from joining with more than one person, so long as the rune-mate is still alive. But Xar *was* the law, as far as he was concerned. He had discovered that rune-joining opened up many hearts' secrets to him. As for revealing his secrets to others, Xar was far too disciplined mentally to permit such a thing to happen. He revealed as much of himself as he deemed it useful to reveal, no more.

He was pleased with Marit, as he would have been pleased with any new weapon that came into his hand. She would do readily whatever needed to be done—even if it meant slaying the man she had once loved.

And Haplo would die knowing he'd been betrayed.

"Thus," said Xar, "I will be avenged."

# CHAPTER ♦ 5

## THE FORTRESS

## OF THE BROTHERHOOD

## SKURVASH, ARIANUS

♦

"He's arrived," came the report. "Standing out front."

The Ancient looked at Ciang, pleading in his eyes. The formidable elf woman had only to say . . . No, she had merely to nod . . . and Hugh the Hand would be dead. An archer sat in a window above the entrance. If the elf woman, sitting stiff and upright in her chair, barely inclined her smooth, skull-like head, the Ancient would leave her presence and carry a wooden knife, with Hugh's name carved in it, to the archer. The archer would without hesitation send a shaft into Hugh's breast.

Hugh knew this. He was taking an enormous risk, returning to the Brotherhood. The knife had not been sent around on him[1] (if it had been, he would not have been alive at the moment), but the word had been whispered among the membership that Ciang was displeased with Hugh the Hand, and he had been shunned. No one would kill him, but no one would help him either. A shunning was one step away from the wooden knife. A member finding himself shunned had better get to the Brotherhood and argue his case fast. Thus no one was surprised at Hugh's arrival at the fortress, though a few were disappointed.

To have been able to claim that you killed Hugh the Hand, one

---

[1] An expression used among the Brotherhood to indicate a member marked for death. See Appendix I, "The Brotherhood," *The Hand of Chaos*, vol. 5 of *The Death Gate Cycle*.

of the greatest assassins the Guild had fostered—such a boast would have been worth a fortune.

No one dared do it without sanction, however. Hugh was—or had been—one of Ciang's favorites. And though her protective arm was gnarled and wrinkled and spotted with age, it was spotted with blood as well. No one would touch Hugh unless Ciang commanded it.

Ciang's small, yellow teeth sank into her lower lip. Seeing this gesture and knowing it for indecision, the Ancient's hopes rose. Perhaps one emotion could still touch the woman's insensate heart. Not love. Curiosity. Ciang was wondering why Hugh had come back, when he knew his life was nothing but a word on her lips. And she couldn't very well find out from his corpse.

The yellow teeth gnawed flesh. "Let him come in to me."

Ciang spoke the words grudgingly and with a scowl, but she'd said them and that was all the Ancient needed to hear. Fearful she might change her mind, he hastened out of the room, his crooked old legs moving with more speed than they'd used in the past twenty years.

Grabbing hold of the huge iron ring attached to the door, the Ancient himself swung it open.

"Come in, Hugh, come in," the Ancient said. "She has agreed to see you."

The assassin stepped inside, stood unmoving in the dim entryway until his eyes adjusted to the light. The Ancient eyed Hugh quizzically. Other people the Ancient had seen in this position had been limp with relief—some so limp he'd been forced to carry them in. Every member of the Brotherhood knew about the archer. Hugh knew that he'd been a curt nod away from certain death. Still, there was no sign of it on his face, which was harder than the fortress's granite walls.

Yet perhaps the penetrating eyes of the Ancient did catch a flicker of feeling, though not what the Ancient had expected. When the door offering life instead of death had opened to Hugh the Hand, he had appeared, for an instant, disappointed.

"Will Ciang see me this moment?" Hugh asked, voice gruff and low. He raised his hand, palm outward, to show the scars that crossed it. Part of the ritual.

The Ancient peered at the scars intently, though he had known this man for more years than the elder could recall. This, too, was part of the ritual.

"She will, sir. Please go on up. May I say, sir," the Ancient added, his voice trembling, "that I am truly glad to see you well."

Hugh's grim and dark expression relaxed. He laid his scarred hand on the old man's bird-bone–fragile arm in acknowledgment. Then, setting his jaw, the Hand left the old man, began the long climb up the innumerable stairs to Ciang's private quarters.

The Ancient peered after him. The Hand had always been a strange one. And perhaps the rumors about him were true. That would explain a lot. Shaking his head, knowing that he would likely never find out, the Ancient resumed his post at the door.

Hugh walked slowly up the stairs, looking neither to the left nor to the right. He wouldn't see anyone anyway, and no one would see him—one of the rules of the fortress. Now that he was here, he was in no hurry. So certain had he been of his death at the hands of the archer that he hadn't given much thought to what he would do if he didn't die. As he walked, tugging nervously on one of the braided strands of the beard which straggled from his jutting chin, he pondered what he would say. He rehearsed several variations. At length he gave up.

With Ciang, there was only one thing to say—the truth. She probably already knew it anyway.

He traversed the silent, empty hallway paneled in dark, highly polished, and extremely rare wood. At the end, Ciang's door stood open.

Hugh paused outside, looked in.

He had expected to see her seated at her desk, the desk marked with the blood of countless initiates into the Guild. But she was standing in front of one of the diamond-paned windows, looking out at the wilds of the isle of Skurvash.

Ciang could see everything worth seeing from that window: the prosperous town—a smuggler's haven—rambling along the shoreline; the craggy forest of the brittle hargast trees that separated town from fortress; the single narrow path that led from town to fortress (a dog walking along that path could be seen by every lookout in the Brotherhood); and beyond and above and below, the sky, in which the isle of Skurvash floated.

Hugh's hand clenched; his mouth was so dry he could not for a moment announce himself; his heart beat rapidly.

The elf woman was old; many considered her the oldest living person in Arianus. She was small and fragile. Hugh could have crushed her with one of his strong hands. She was dressed in the bright-colored silken robes the elves fancy, and even at her age there was a delicacy, a grace, a hint of what reputedly had once been remarkable beauty. Her head was bald, the skull exquisitely shaped, the skin smooth and without blemish, an interesting contrast to the wrinkled face.

The absence of hair made her slanted eyes appear large and liquid, and when she turned—not at the sound but at the absence of sound—the penetrating look from those dark eyes was the arrow shaft that had not, until now, lodged in his breast.

"You risk much coming back, Hugh the Hand," Ciang said.

"Not as much as you might think, Ciang," he replied.

His answer was neither flippant nor sarcastic. He spoke in a voice pitched low, its tone dull and lifeless. That arrow shaft, it seemed, would have robbed him of very little.

"Did you come here hoping to die?" Ciang's lip curled. She despised cowards.

She had not moved from her place by the window, nor had she invited Hugh into her room, asked him to be seated. A bad sign. In the ritual of the Brotherhood, this meant that she, too, was shunning him. But he was endowed with the rank of "hand," next to her own —"arm"—the highest ranking in the Brotherhood. She would grant him the favor of listening to his explanation before she passed sentence.

"I wouldn't have been disappointed if the arrow had found its mark." Hugh's expression was grim. "But no. I didn't come here looking for death. I have a contract." He grimaced as he spoke. "I've come for help, advice."

"The contract from the Kenkari." Ciang's eyes narrowed.

Despite all he knew of Ciang, Hugh was surprised at her knowledge of this. His meeting with the Kenkari—the sect of elves who held in their care the souls of elven dead—had been shrouded in secrecy. So Ciang had her spies even among that pious sect.

"No, it is not *from* them," Hugh explained, frowning. "Though they are the ones who are forcing me to fulfill it."

*"Forcing* you? To fulfill a contract—a sacred commitment? Do you mean to tell me, Hugh the Hand, that you would not have done so if the Kenkari had not *forced* you?"

Ciang was truly angry now. Two spots of crimson stained her wrinkled cheeks, mounted up from the wizened neck. Her hand stretched forth like a claw, pointing a skeletal, accusatory finger at him.

"The rumors we have heard about you are true, then. You have lost your nerve." Ciang started to turn around, started to turn her back on him. Once she did, he was a dead man. Worse than dead, for without her help he would not be able to fulfill his contract, and that meant he would die dishonored.

Hugh broke the rules. He walked into the room uninvited, strode across the carpeted floor to Ciang's desk. On the desk was a wooden box, encrusted with sparkling gems. Hugh lifted the lid.

Ciang paused, looked back over her shoulder. Her face hardened. He had broken her unwritten law, and if she decided against him his punishment would now be far more severe. But she appreciated bold and daring moves, and this was certainly one of the boldest anyone had ever made in her presence. She waited to see the outcome.

Hugh reached into the box, pulled out a sharp dagger whose golden hilt was fashioned in the shape of a hand—palm flat, fingers pressed together, the extended thumb forming the crosspiece. Taking the ceremonial dagger, Hugh advanced to stand before Ciang.

She regarded him coolly, with detached curiosity, not in the least frightened. "What is this?"

Hugh fell on his knees. Raising the dagger, he offered it—hilt first, blade pointed at his breast—to Ciang.

She accepted it, her hand wrapping around the hilt with loving skill.

Hugh drew back the collar of his shirt, laid bare his neck. "Stab me here, Ciang," he said, voice harsh and chill. "In the throat."

He did not look at her. His eyes stared out the window, into the dusk. The Lords of Night were spreading their cloaks across Solarus; evening's shadows were crawling over Skurvash.

Ciang held the dagger in her right hand. Stretching forth her left, she grabbed hold of the twisted strands of beard, jerked his head upward and around to face her—also giving her better leverage if she did decide to slit his throat.

"You have done nothing to deserve such an honor, Hugh the Hand," she said coldly. "Why do you demand your death at my hand?"

"I want to go back," he said in a lifeless monotone.

Ciang was rarely startled, but this statement, made so calmly and flatly, took her by surprise. She released him, fell back a step, and peered intently into the man's dark eyes. She saw no gleam of madness. Only an emptiness, as if she looked into a dry well.

Hugh grasped the leather jerkin he wore, wrenched it apart. He ripped the shirt seam wide.

"Look at my chest. Look well. The mark is hard to see."

He was a dark-complexioned man; his breast was matted with thick, curly black hair, beginning to gray.

"Here," he said and guided Ciang's unresisting hand to the part of his breast over the heart.

She looked closely, running her fingers through his chest hair, their touch like bird claws scraping over his flesh. He shivered; the flesh rose in small bumps.

Ciang drew in a deep breath, snatched her hand away. She stared at him in awe slowly crystallizing into understanding.

"The rune-magic!" she breathed.

His head bowed as if in defeat, Hugh sank back on his heels. One hand went to his breast, convulsively grasping the shirt and drawing the two torn halves together again. The other hand clenched into a fist. His shoulders slumped; he stared unseeing at the floor.

Ciang stood over him, the dagger still balanced in her hand but now forgotten. She had not known fear in a long, long time. How long she couldn't even remember. And then it hadn't been fear like this—a crawling worm in the bowels.

The world was changing, changing in drastic ways. Ciang knew it. She wasn't afraid of change. She had looked into the future and was ready to meet it. As the world changed, so would the Brotherhood. There would be peace among the races now—humans, elves, and dwarves would live together in harmony. The cessation of war and rebellion would be a blow to the organization at first; peace might even mean that the humans and the elves would imagine themselves strong enough to attack the Brotherhood. Ciang doubted that, however. Too many human barons, too many elven lords owed the Brotherhood too many favors.

Ciang wasn't afraid of peace. True peace would be obtained only if every elf and human and dwarf had his or her head cut off and heart cut out. So long as there was life, there would be jealousy, greed, hatred, lust, and so long as there were heads to think and hearts to feel, the Brotherhood would be there to act.

Ciang didn't fear the future in a world where all things were equal. But this—this upset the balance. Knocked over the scale. She must deal with it swiftly, if she could. For the first time in her life, Ciang doubted herself. That was the root of the fear.

She looked at the dagger, dropped it to the floor.

Ciang placed her hands on Hugh's gaunt and hollow cheeks, lifted his head gently. "My poor boy," she said to him softly. "My poor boy."

His eyes dimmed with tears. His body shuddered. He hadn't slept, hadn't eaten for so long he had lost the need for either. He fell into her hands like rotten fruit.

"You must tell me everything," she whispered. Ciang pressed the man's unresisting head against her bony breast, crooned over him. "Tell me everything, Hugh. Only then can I help you."

He squeezed his eyes shut, trying to keep back the tears, but he was too weak. He gave a wrenching sob, covered his face with his hands.

Ciang held him, rocked with him back and forth. "Tell me everything . . ."

# CHAPTER ✦ 6

## THE FORTRESS

## OF THE BROTHERHOOD

## SKURVASH, ARIANUS

✦

"I AM NOT IN TO ANYONE THIS NIGHT," CIANG TOLD THE ANCIENT WHEN HE tottered up to her chambers, carrying a message from another member begging an audience.

The Ancient nodded and closed her door behind him as he left, leaving the two alone.

Hugh was now composed again. Several glasses of wine and a hot meal, which he wolfed from the tray placed on the bloodstained desk, restored his physical and, to some extent, his mental strength. He was so far improved as to recall his outburst with chagrin, flushing darkly when he thought about it. Ciang shook her head at his stammered apology.

"It is no small matter," she said, "to brush up against a god."

Hugh smiled bitterly. "God. Alfred—a god."

Night had fallen; the candles were lighted.

"Tell me," Ciang repeated.

Hugh began at the beginning. He told her about the changeling Bane, about the evil wizard Sinistrad, about being hired to kill Bane and falling under the little boy's spell. He told Ciang about falling also under the spell of the boy's mother, Iridal—not a magic spell but one of plain and ordinary love. He told Ciang, unashamed, how he had forsaken the contract to kill the child for love of Iridal and how he had planned to sacrifice his life for her son.

And the sacrifice had been made.

"I died," Hugh said, shuddering at the remembered pain and horror. "I knew torment—terrible torment, far worse than any mortal agony a man can suffer. I was made to see inside myself, see the evil, heartless creature I had become. And I was sorry. Truly sorry. And then . . . I understood. And when I understood, I was able to forgive myself. And I was forgiven. I knew peace . . . And then it was all snatched away."

"He . . . Alfred . . . brought you back."

Perplexed, Hugh looked up. "You believe me, Ciang. I never thought . . . That was why I didn't come . . ."

"I believe you." Ciang sighed. Her hands, resting on the desk, trembled slightly. "I believe you. Now." She stared at his chest. Though it was covered, the rune-mark seemed to shine through the fabric. "I might not if you had come back then. However, what is done is done."

"I tried to go back to my old life, but no one would hire me. Iridal said that I'd become mankind's conscience. Any who plotted evil deeds saw their own evil in my face." The Hand shrugged. "I don't know if that's true or not. At any rate, I hid myself away in the monastery of the Kir monks. But she found me."

"The woman you brought here—Iridal, the boy's mother. She knew you were alive?"

"She was with Alfred when he . . . did this." Hugh placed his hand on his breast. "Alfred denied it afterward, but Iridal knew what she had seen. She left me to myself, though. She was afraid . . ."

"The touch of the god," Ciang murmured, nodding.

"And then her son, Bane, turned up again, with the elves. The boy was well named. He was planning to destroy the peace being arranged between Prince Rees'ahn and King Stephen. With the help of the Kenkari, Iridal and I set out to free Bane from the elves, but the boy betrayed us to them. The elves held Iridal hostage, forced me to agree to kill Stephen. As the supposed heir, Bane would take over the human rulership and he would betray them to the elves."

"And Stephen's assassination was the job you bungled," Ciang put in.

Hugh flushed again, glanced up at her, gave a rueful smile. "So you heard about that, too? I planned to get myself killed. It was the only way I could think of to save Iridal. Stephen's guards would take care of me. The king would know Bane was behind it. He'd deal with the boy. But again, I didn't die. The dog jumped the guard who was about to—"

"Dog?" Ciang interrupted. "What dog?"

Hugh began to reply; then an odd look crossed his face. "Haplo's dog," he said softly. "That's strange. I hadn't thought of it until now."

Ciang grunted. "More about that in its proper place. Continue your story. This Bane died. His mother killed him, just as he was about to kill King Stephen. Yes." She smiled at Hugh's look of amazement. "I heard all about it. The mysteriarch, Iridal, returned to the High Realms. You did not go with her. You went back to the Kenkari. Why?"

"I owed them a debt," Hugh said slowly, turning his wine glass around and around in his hand. "I had sold them my soul."

Ciang's eyes widened. She sat back in her chair. "They do not deal in human souls. Nor would the Kenkari buy the soul of any man—human or elven."

"They wanted mine. Or at least I thought they did. You can understand why, of course." Hugh drank down the wine at one gulp.

"Of course." Ciang shrugged. "You had died and had returned. Your soul would have been one of great value. But I can also understand why they did not take it."

"You can?" Hugh paused in the act of pouring himself another glass to focus on her. He was drunk, but not drunk enough. He could never get drunk enough.

"The souls of the elves are held in constraint to serve the living. They are prevented from going beyond. Perhaps they do not even know that such peace as you describe exists." Ciang pointed a bony finger. "You are a danger to the Kenkari, Hugh the Hand. You are more of a threat to them dead than you are alive."

Hugh gave a low whistle. His face darkened. "I never thought of that. The bastards. And I thought . . ." He shook his head. "They acted so compassionate . . . And all the time looking out for their own."

"Have you ever known anyone who did not, Hugh the Hand?" Ciang rebuked him. "Once you would not have fallen for such wiles. You would have seen clearly. But you are changed. At least now I know why."

"I will see clearly again," Hugh said softly.

"I wonder." Ciang stared at the bloodstains on the desk. Absently her fingers traced them. "I wonder." She fell silent, absorbed in thought.

Hugh, troubled, did not disturb her.

At length she raised her eyes, regarded him shrewdly. "You mentioned a contract. Who has hired you and for what?"

Hugh moistened his lips, this part coming reluctantly. "Before he died, Bane made me agree to kill a man for him. The man named Haplo."

"The one who traveled with you and Alfred?" Ciang looked surprised at first; then she smiled grimly. It was all starting to make sense. "The one with the bandaged hands."

Hugh nodded.

"Why must this Haplo die?"

"Bane said something about some lord of his wanting Haplo out of the way. The kid was persistent, kept after me. We were coming up on Seven Fields, where Stephen was camped. I had too much to do to fool with a child's whim. I agreed, to shut him up. I wasn't intending to live that long anyway."

"But you did live. And Bane died. And now you have a contract with the dead."

"Yes, Ciang."

"And you were not going to keep it?" Ciang was disapproving.

"I'd forgotten about the damn thing!" Hugh said impatiently. "Ancestors take me, I was supposed to die! The Kenkari were supposed to buy my soul."

"And they did—only not quite the way you expected."

Hugh grimaced. "They reminded me of the contract. Said my soul is bound to Bane. I'm not free to give it to them."

"Elegant." Ciang was admiring. "Elegant and very neat. And so, elegantly and neatly, they escape this great danger that you present to them."

"Danger?" Hugh slammed his hand on the desk. His own blood was there, taken from him years ago when he had been an initiate into the Brotherhood. "What danger? How do they know about this? They were the ones who showed me this mark!" He clutched at his breast as if he would rip out his flesh.

"As for how they know, the Kenkari have access to the ancient books. And then, you see, the Sartan favored them. Told them their secrets . . ."

"Sartan." Hugh looked up. "Iridal mentioned that word. She said Alfred—"

"—is a Sartan. That much is obvious. Only the Sartan could use the rune-magic, or so they claimed. But there were rumors, dark rumors, of another race of gods—"

"Gods with marks like this, covering their entire bodies? Known as Patryns? Iridal told me about them, too. She guessed that this Haplo was a Patryn."

"Patryn." Ciang lingered over the word, tasting it. Then she shrugged. "Perhaps. Many years have passed since I read the ancient texts, and then I wasn't interested. What had these gods—Patryn or Sartan—to do with us? Nothing. Not anymore."

She smiled, the thin and puckered lips, outlined in red that seeped into the wrinkles, made her look as though she had drunk the blood on her desk. "For which we are grateful."

Hugh grunted. "And now you see my problem. This Haplo has runes like mine tattooed all over his body. They glow with a strange light. Once I tried to jump him. It was like wrapping my hands around a lightning bolt." He made an impatient gesture. "How do I kill this man, Ciang? How do I kill a god?"

"This is why you came to me?" she asked, lips pursed. "To seek my help?"

"Help . . . death, I'm not sure." Hugh rubbed his temples, which were starting to throb from the wine. "I had nowhere else to go."

"The Kenkari gave you no assistance?"

Hugh snorted. "They almost fainted even talking about it. I forced them to give me a knife—more to have a laugh at them than anything else. Lots of people have hired me to kill for lots of reasons, but I never saw one of them start blubbering over his intended victim."

"The Kenkari wept, you say?"

"The one who handed me the knife did. The Keeper of the Door. He damn near couldn't turn loose of the weapon. I almost felt sorry for him."

"And what did he say?"

"Say?" Hugh frowned, thinking, trying to weave his way among the wine fumes. "I didn't pay much attention to what he said —until he came to the part about this." Hugh thumped himself on the chest. "The rune-magic. About how I wasn't to disrupt the workings of the great machine. And I was to tell Haplo that Xar wanted him dead. That's it. That's the name of this lord of his. Xar. Xar wants him dead."

"The gods fight among themselves. A hopeful sign for us poor mortals." Ciang was smiling. "If they kill each other off, we will be free to go on with our lives without interference."

Hugh the Hand shook his head, not understanding, not caring.

"God or no, Haplo is my mark," he muttered. "How am I supposed to kill him?"

"Give me until tomorrow," Ciang said. "I will study on it this night. As I said, it has been a long time since I read the ancient texts. And you must sleep, Hugh the Hand."

He didn't hear her. Wine and exhaustion had combined to rob him—mercifully—of his senses. He lay sprawled on her desk, his arms stretched out over his head, his cheek resting on the blood-stained wood. The wine glass was still clutched in his hand.

Ciang rose to her feet. Leaning on her desk for support, she walked slowly around to stand over him. In her younger days, long, long ago, she would have taken him for her lover. She had always preferred human lovers to elven. Humans are hot-blooded, aggressive—the flame that burns shorter burns brighter. Then, too, humans die off in good time, leave you free to pursue another. They don't live long enough to make nuisances of themselves.

Most humans. Most who were not god-touched. God-cursed.

"Poor fly," Ciang murmured, her hand on the man's shoulder. "What dreadful sort of web do you struggle in? And who, I wonder, is the spider who has spun it? Not the Kenkari. I begin to think I was mistaken. Their own butterfly wings may be caught in this tangle as well.

"Should I help you? Should I act in this? I can, you know, Hugh." Ciang ran her hand absently through the mass of matted black and gray hair that straggled, uncombed, down his back. "I can help. But why should I? What is in it for me?"

Ciang's hand began to tremble. She rested it on the back of his chair, leaned on the chair heavily. The weakness was back. It came over her more frequently now. A dizziness, a shortness of breath. She clung to the chair grimly, stoically, waited for it to pass. It always passed. But a time was coming when it would grow worse. The time when it would claim her.

"You say that dying is hard, Hugh the Hand," Ciang said when she could breathe again. "That does not surprise me. I've seen death enough to know. But I must admit I am disappointed. Peace. Forgiveness. Yet first we are called to account.

"And I thought there would be nothing. The Kenkari, with their foolish soul-boxes. Souls living in the gardens of their glass dome. What nonsense. Nothing. All is nothing. I gambled on that." Her hand curled over the back of the chair. "I've lost, seemingly. Unless you are lying?"

Bending over Hugh, she looked at him closely, hopefully. Then she sighed, straightened. "No, the wine doesn't lie. And neither have you, Hand, in all the years I've known you. Called to account. Wickedness. What wickedness have I *not* done? But what can I do to make amends? I've thrown my dice upon the table. Too late to snatch them back. But maybe another throw, eh? Winner take all?"

Cunning, shrewd, the old woman peered into the dark shadows. "Is it a bet?"

A soft knock fell on the door. Ciang chuckled to herself, half-mocking, half-serious. "Enter."

The Ancient thrust the door open, hobbled inside.

"Ah, me," he said sadly when he saw Hugh the Hand. He looked questioningly at Ciang. "Do we leave him here?"

"We are neither of us strong enough to move him, my old friend. He will do well enough where he is until morning."

She extended her arm. The Ancient took it. Together—his failing strength supporting her faltering steps—they walked slowly the few paces across the dark hall to Ciang's sleeping chambers.

"Light the lamp, Ancient. I will be reading late this night."

He did as she instructed, lighting the glow lamp and placing it on the stand beside her bed.

"Go into the library.[1] Bring me any books you find written on

---

[1] The library of the Brotherhood is quite extensive, according to Haplo's notes on the subject. As one might expect, there are the volumes devoted to the making and use of almost any weapon imaginable—human and elven and dwarven, mundane and magical. Innumerable volumes concern botany and herb lore, particularly as they relate to poisons and antidotes. There are books on venomous snakes and the deadlier types of spiders, books on snares and traps, books on the care and handling of dragons.

There are also books of an unexpected nature: books on the inner workings the Sartan. And bring me the key to the Black Coffer. Then you may retire."

"Very good, madam. And I'll just get a blanket to cover Hugh the Hand."

The Ancient was bobbing his way out when Ciang stopped him.

"My friend, do you ever think about death? Your own, I mean."

The Ancient didn't even blink. "Only when I have nothing better to do, madam. Will that be all?"

---

of the hearts and minds of humans, elves, dwarves, and even those earlier beings—the Sartan. Philosophical treatises in an assassins' guild? Odd. Or perhaps not. As the saying goes, "When tracking a victim, you should try to fit your feet into his footprints."

# CHAPTER ♦ 7

## THE FORTRESS

## OF THE BROTHERHOOD

## SKURVASH, ARIANUS

♦

Hᴜɢʜ sʟᴇᴘᴛ ʟᴀᴛᴇ ᴛʜᴇ ɴᴇxᴛ ᴍᴏʀɴɪɴɢ, ᴛʜᴇ ᴡɪɴᴇ ᴅᴜʟʟɪɴɢ ʜɪs ᴍɪɴᴅ, ᴘᴇʀᴍɪᴛᴛɪɴɢ exhaustion to lay claim to the body. But it was the heavy, unrefreshing sleep of the grape, which causes one to wake with the brain sodden and aching, the stomach queasy. Knowing that he would be groggy and disoriented, the Ancient was there to guide Hugh's stumbling steps to a large water barrel placed outside the fortress for the refreshment of the lookouts.[1] The Ancient dipped in a bucket, handed it to Hugh. The Hand dumped the contents over his head and shoulders, clothes and all. Wiping his dripping face, he felt somewhat better.

"Ciang will see you this morning," said the Ancient when he deemed Hugh capable of understanding his words.

Hugh nodded, not quite capable yet of replying.

"You will have audience in her chambers," the Ancient added.

Hugh's eyebrows rose. This was an honor accorded to few. He glanced down ruefully at his wet and slept-in clothes. The Ancient, understanding, offered to provide a clean shirt. The old man hinted at breakfast, but Hugh shook his head emphatically.

Washed and dressed, the throbbing in his temples receding to an ache behind his eyeballs, Hugh presented himself once again to Ciang, the Brotherhood's "arm."

---

[1] A measure of the Brotherhood's wealth. Nowhere else in the Mid Realms would one find a water barrel sitting out in the open, unguarded, its precious contents free to all takers.

Ciang's chambers were enormous, sumptuously and fancifully decorated in the style elves admire and humans find ostentatious. All the furniture was of carved wood, extremely rare in the Mid Realms. The elven emperor Agah'ran would have opened his painted eyelids wide with envy at the sight of so many valuable and beautiful pieces. The massive bed was a work of art. Four posts, carved in the shapes of mythological beasts, each perched on the head of another, supported a canopy of wood decorated with the same beasts lying outstretched, paws extended. From each paw dangled a golden ring. Suspended from the rings was a silken curtain of fabulous weave, color, and design. It was whispered that the curtain had magical properties, that it accounted for the elven woman's longer than normal life span.

Whether or not that was true, the curtain was marvelously lovely to look on and seemed to invite admiration. Hugh had never before been inside Ciang's personal quarters. He stared at the shimmering multicolored curtain in awe, lifted his hand and reached out to it before it occurred to him what he was doing. Flushing, he started to snatch his hand back, but Ciang, seated in a high-backed monstrosity of a chair, gestured.

"You may touch it, my friend. It will do you some good."

Hugh, recalling the rumors, wasn't certain that he wanted to touch the curtain, but to do otherwise would offend Ciang. He ran his fingers over it gingerly and was startled to feel a pleasurable exhilaration tingle through his body. At this he did snatch his fingers back, but the feeling lasted and he found his head clear, the pain gone.

Ciang was seated on the opposite side of the large room. Diamond-paned windows, which stretched from ceiling to floor, admitted a flood of sunlight. Hugh walked across the bright bands of light spanning the ornate rugs to stand before the high-backed wooden chair.

The chair was said to have been carved by an admirer of Ciang's, given to her as a present. It was certainly grotesque. A skull leered at the top. The blood-red cushions that supported Ciang's frail form were surrounded by various ghostly spirits twining their way upward. Her feet rested on a footstool formed of crouching, cringing naked bodies. She waved a hand in a gracious gesture to a chair opposite hers, a chair which Hugh was relieved to see was perfectly ordinary in appearance.

Ciang dispensed with meaningless pleasantries and struck, arrow-like, at the heart of their business.

"I have spent the night in study." She rested her hand, gnarled and almost fleshless but elegant in its movement and grace, on the dusty leather cover of a book in her lap.

"I am sorry to have disturbed your sleep," Hugh began to apologize.

Ciang cut him off. "To be honest, I could not have slept otherwise. You are a disturbing influence, Hugh the Hand," she added, looking at him with narrowed eyes. "I will not be sorry to see you go. I have done what I could to speed you on your way." The eyelids—lashless, as the head was hairless—blinked once. "When you are gone, do not come back."

Hugh understood. The next time there would be no hesitation. The archer would have his orders. Hugh's face set hard and grim. "I would not have come back in any case," he said softly, staring at the cringing bodies, bent to hold Ciang's small and delicate-boned feet. "If Haplo doesn't kill me then I must find—"

"What did you say?" Ciang demanded sharply.

Hugh, startled, glanced up at her. He frowned. "I said that if I don't kill Haplo—"

"No!" Ciang's fist clenched. "You said 'If Haplo doesn't kill *me* . . . !' Do you go to this man seeking his death or your own?"

Hugh put his hand to his head. "I . . . was confused. That's all." His voice was gruff. "The wine . . ."

". . . speaks the truth, as the saying goes." Ciang shook her head. "No, Hugh the Hand. You will not come back to us."

"Will you send the knife around on me?" he asked harshly.

Ciang considered. "Not until after you have fulfilled the contract. Our honor is at stake. And therefore, the Brotherhood will help you, if we can." She glanced at him and there was an odd glint in her eye. "If you want . . ."

Carefully she closed the book and placed it on a table beside the chair. From the table she lifted an iron key, which hung from a black ribbon. Extending her hand to Hugh, she allowed him the privilege of helping her to stand. She refused his assistance in walking, making her way slowly and with dignity to a door on a far wall.

"You will find what you seek in the Black Coffer," she told him.

The Black Coffer was not a coffer at all but a vault, a repository for weapons—magical or otherwise. Magical weapons are, of course, highly prized, and the Brotherhood's laws governing them are strict and rigorously enforced. A member who acquires or makes such a weapon may consider it his or her own personal possession, but must apprise the Brotherhood of its existence and how it works. The information is kept in a file in the Brotherhood's library, a file which may be consulted by any member at any time.

A member needing such a weapon as he finds described may apply to the owner and request the weapon's loan. The owner is free to refuse, but this almost never happens, since it is quite likely that the owner himself will need to borrow a weapon someday. If the weapon is not returned—something else that almost never happens —the thief is marked, the knife sent around.

On the owner's death, the weapon becomes the property of the Brotherhood. In the case of elderly members, such as the Ancient, who come back to the fortress to spend their remaining years in comfort, the deliverance of any magical weapons is easily facilitated. For those members who meet the sudden and violent end considered an occupational hazard, collecting the weapons of the deceased can present a problem.

These have sometimes been irrevocably lost, as in cases where the body and everything on it have been burned in a funeral pyre or tossed in rage off the floating isles into the Maelstrom. But so prized are the weapons that once the word goes around that the owner has died (which it does with remarkable swiftness) the Brotherhood is quick to act. All is done quietly, circumspectly. Very often grieving family members are surprised by the sudden appearance of strangers at their door. The strangers enter the house (sometimes before the body is cold) and leave almost immediately. Usually an object leaves with them—the black coffer.

To facilitate the passing on of valuable weapons, members of the Brotherhood are urged to keep such weapons in a plain black box. This has become known as the black coffer. It is thus natural that the repository for such weapons in the Brotherhood's fortress should have become known—in capital letters—as the Black Coffer.

If a member requests the use of a weapon kept in the Black Coffer, he or she must explain in detail the need and pay a fee proportionate to the weapon's power. Ciang has the final say on who gets what weapons, as well as the price to be paid.

Standing before the door of the Black Coffer, Ciang inserted the iron key into the lock and turned it.

The lock clicked.

Grasping the handle of the heavy iron door, she pulled. Hugh was ready to assist her if she asked, but the door, revolving on silent hinges, swung easily at her light touch. All was dark inside.

"Bring a lamp," Ciang ordered.

Hugh did so, catching up a glow lamp that stood on a table near the door, probably for this very purpose. Hugh lit the lamp, and the two entered the vault.

It was the first time Hugh the Hand had ever been inside the Black Coffer. (He had always taken pride in the fact that he had never needed enhanced weaponry.) He wondered why he was being accorded this honor now. Few members were ever permitted inside. When a weapon was needed, Ciang either fetched it herself or sent the Ancient to do so.

Hugh entered the enormous stone-lined vault with quiet step and subdued heart. The lamp drove the shadows back but could not banish them. A hundred lamps with the brightness of Solarus could not banish the shadow that hung over this room. The tools of death created their own darkness.

Their numbers were inconceivable. They rested on tables, reclined against the walls, were sheltered beneath glass cases. It was too much to take in all at one glance.

The light flashed off the blades of knives and daggers of every conceivable shape and type, arranged in a vast, ever expanding circle—a sort of metal sunburst. Pikes and poleaxes and spears stood guard around the walls. Longbows and short were properly displayed, each with a quiver of arrows, undoubtedly the famous elven exploding arrows so feared by human soldiers. Rows of shelving contained bottles and vials, small and large, of magical potions and poisons—all neatly labeled.

Hugh walked past one case filled with nothing but rings: poison rings, snake-tooth rings (containing a tiny needle tipped with snake venom), and magical rings of all sorts, from rings of charming (which grant the user power over the victim) to rings of warding (which protect the user against rings of charming).

Every item in the Black Coffer was documented, labeled in both the human and elven (and, in certain rare cases, dwarven) languages. Words to magical spells—should any be needed—were recorded. The value of it all was incalculable. Hugh's mind boggled.

Here was stored the true wealth of the Brotherhood, worth far more than all the barls and jewels of the elven and human royal treasuries combined. Here was death and the means to deal it. Here was fear. Here was power.

Ciang led the way through the veritable maze of shelves, cabinetry, and cases, to an unimportant-looking table shunted off to a distant corner of the room. Only one object rested on that table, an object hidden under a cloth that might once have been black but, covered with dust, looked gray. The table appeared to be chained to the wall by thick cobwebs.

No one had ventured near this table in a long, long time.

"Set the lamp down," Ciang told him.

Hugh obeyed, placing the lamp on a case containing a vast assortment of blow-darts. He looked curiously at the cloth-covered object, thinking there was something strange about it, but not certain what.

"Look at it closely," Ciang ordered, echoing his thought.

Hugh did so, bending cautiously near it. He knew enough about magical weapons to respect this one. He would never touch it or anything pertaining to it until its proper use had been carefully explained—one reason Hugh the Hand had always preferred not to rely on such weapons. A good steel blade—hard and sharp—is a tool you can trust.

Hugh straightened, frowning, tugging on the braided strands of beard dangling from his chin.

"You see?" Ciang asked, almost as if she were testing him.

"Dust and cobwebs over everything else, but no dust or cobwebs anywhere on the object itself," Hugh replied.

Ciang breathed a soft sigh, regarded him almost sadly. "Ah, there are not many like you, Hugh the Hand. Quick eye, quick hand. A pity," she ended coolly.

Hugh said nothing. He could offer no defense, knew that none was invited. He stared hard at the object beneath the cloth, could make out the shape by the fact that dust lay all around it but not over it—a dagger with a remarkably long blade.

"Put your hand on it," Ciang said. "You may do so safely," she added, seeing the flash in Hugh's eye.

Hugh held his fingers gingerly above the object. He wasn't afraid, but he was loath to touch it, as one is loath to touch a snake or a hairy spider. Telling himself it was just a knife (yet wondering why it was covered with a black cloth), he rested his fingertips on it. Startled, he jerked his hand back. He stared at Ciang.

"It moved!"

She nodded, unperturbed. "A quivering. Like a live thing. Barely felt, yet strong enough to shake off the dust of centuries, strong enough to disturb the web-weavers. Yet it is not alive, as you will see. Not alive as *we* know life," she amended.

She plucked away the black cloth. The dust that caked the edges flew up, formed a nose-tickling cloud that caused them both to back off, wiping the grime and the horrible clinging wispy sensation of cobweb from face and hands.

Beneath the cloth—an ordinary metal dagger. The Hand had seen far better-crafted weapons. In shape and design, it was exceedingly crude, might have been made by some smith's child, attempting to learn his parent's craft. The hilt and crosspiece were forged of iron that appeared to have been beaten into shape while it was cooling. The marks of each hammer blow were plain on both hilt and crosspiece.

The blade was smooth, perhaps because it was made of steel, for it was bright and shiny in contrast to the hilt's dull finish. The blade had been affixed to the hilt with molten metal, the traces of soldering plain to see. The only things that made this knife at all remarkable were the strange symbols etched on the blade. The symbols were not the same as—yet they were reminders of—the one traced on Hugh's chest.

"The rune-magic," said Ciang, her bony finger hovering above, carefully not touching the blade.

"What does the thing do?" Hugh asked, regarding the weapon with disdain mingled with disgust.

"We do not know," Ciang answered.

Hugh raised an eyebrow, regarded her questioningly. She shrugged. "The last brother to use it died."

"I can understand why." Hugh grunted. "Trying to go up against a mark using a kid's toy."

Ciang shook her head. "You do not understand." She raised her slanted eyes to his, and again there was that strange glint. "He died of shock." She paused, looked down at the weapon, and added, almost casually, "He had grown four arms."

Hugh's jaw sagged. Then he snapped his mouth shut, cleared his throat.

"You don't believe me. I don't blame you. I didn't believe it myself. Not until I saw it with my own eyes." Ciang stared at the cobwebs as if they wove time. "It was many cycles ago. When I became 'arm.' The dagger had come to us from an elven lord, long ago, when the Brotherhood first began. It was kept in this vault, with a warning. A curse was on it, so the warning went. A human, a young man, scoffed at the notion. He did not believe in the curse. He took the knife—for it is written that 'he who masters the knife will be invincible against all foes. *Not even the gods* will dare oppose him.' "

She eyed Hugh as she said this. "Of course," she added, "this was in the days when there were no gods. Not anymore."

"What happened?" Hugh asked, trying not to sound skeptical. He was, after all, talking to Ciang.

"I am not certain. The partner, who survived, could not give us a coherent account. Apparently the young man attacked his mark, using the knife, and suddenly it was not a knife. It changed to a sword—enormous, whirling, many-bladed. Two ordinary arms could not hold it. Then it was that two more arms sprouted from the young man's body. He stared at his four arms and dropped dead— of terror and shock. His partner eventually went mad, threw himself off the isle. I don't blame him. I saw the body. The man had four arms. I dream of it still sometimes."

She was silent, lips pursed. Hugh, looking at that hard, pitiless face, saw it blanch. The compression of the lips was to hold them firm. He looked at the knife and felt his stomach crawl.

"That incident could have been the end of the Brotherhood." Ciang glanced at him sideways. "You can imagine what rumor would have made of this. Perhaps we—the Brotherhood—had cast the dreadful curse upon the young man. I acted swiftly. I ordered the body brought here under cover of darkness. The partner also. I questioned him before witnesses. I read the tract to them—the tract that came with the knife.

"We agreed that it was the knife itself that was cursed. I forbade its use. We buried the grotesque body in secret. All brothers and sisters were ordered, on pain of death, not to speak of the incident.

"That was long ago. Now," she added softly, "I am the only one left alive who remembers. No one, not even the Ancient, whose grandfather had not yet been born when this occurred, knows about

the cursed knife. I have written the injunction against its use in my
will. But I have never told the story to anyone. Not until now."

"Cover it up," Hugh said grimly. "I don't want it." His frown
darkened. "I've never used magic before—"

"You have never been asked to kill a god before," Ciang said,
displeased.

"The dwarf, Limbeck, claims they're not gods. He said Haplo
was almost dead when the dwarf first saw him, just like any ordinary man. No, I will not use it!"

Two red spots of anger appeared in the woman's skull-like face.
She seemed about to make a bitter rejoinder, then paused. The red
spots faded; the slanted eyes were suddenly cool. "It is your choice,
of course, my friend. If you insist on dying in dishonor, that is your
own affair. I will not argue further except to remind you that another's life is at stake here. Perhaps you have not considered this?"

"What other life?" Hugh demanded, suspicious. "The boy,
Bane, is dead."

"But his mother lives. A woman for whom you hold strong
feelings. Who knows but that if you fail and fall, this Haplo would
not go after her next? She knows who he is, what he is."

Hugh thought back. Iridal had said something to him about
Haplo, but the assassin couldn't remember what. They'd had little
time to talk. His mind had been on other things—the dead child he
had carried in his arms, Iridal's grief, his own confusion at being
alive when he was supposed to be dead. No, whatever she'd said to
him about the Patryn, Hugh had lost in the horror-tinged mists of
that terrible night. What had it to do with him anyway? He was
going to give the Kenkari his soul. He was going to return to that
beautiful, peaceful realm . . .

Would Haplo try to find Iridal? He had taken her son captive.
Why not her? Could Hugh afford to take the chance? He owed her
something, after all. Owed her for having failed her.

"A tract, you said?" he asked Ciang.

Her hand slid into the large pockets of her voluminous robes,
withdrew several sheets of vellum held together by a black ribbon
tied around them. The vellum was old and discolored, the ribbon
tattered and faded. She smoothed it with her hand.

"I read it again last night. The first time I have read it since that
dreadful night. Then I read the tract aloud, to the witnesses. Now I
will read it to you."

Hugh flushed. He wanted to read it, study it in private, but he didn't dare insult her. "I have put you to so much trouble already, Ciang—"

"I must translate it for you," she said with a smile that indicated she understood. "It is written in High Elven, a language spoken after the Sundering, a language that is all but forgotten now. You would not be able to understand it."

Hugh had no further objections.

"Bring me a chair. The text is long and I am weary of standing. And put the lamp close."

Hugh brought a chair, set it in a corner beside the table on which rested the "cursed" knife. He remained standing outside the circle of lamplight, not sorry to keep his face hidden in the shadows, his doubts concealed. He didn't believe it. Didn't believe any of it.

Yet he wouldn't have believed a man could die and come back to life again either.

And so he listened to the tale.

# CHAPTER 8

# THE ACCURSÉD

# BLADE

✦

SINCE YOU ARE READING THIS, MY SON, I AM DEAD AND MY SOUL HAS GONE TO Krenka-Anris, to help in the liberation of our people.[1] Since it has come to open war, I trust that you will acquit yourself honorably in battle, as have all those who bear this name who have gone before you.

I am the first of our family to set down this account on paper. Before now, the story of the Accurséd Blade was whispered to the eldest son from his father's deathbed. Thus my father told me and thus his father before him and so on back to before the Sundering. But since it seems likely that my deathbed may be the hard ground of a battlefield and that you, my beloved son, will be far away, I leave this account to be read after my death. And so you will take an oath, my son, by Krenka-Anris and by my soul, that you will pass this account to your son—may the Goddess bless your lady-wife and deliver her safely.

In the armory is a box with a pearl-inlaid lid that holds the ceremonial dueling daggers. You know the one, I am certain, for as a child you expressed your admiration for the daggers, an admiration much misplaced, as you know by now, being a seasoned warrior

---

[1] By this we assume that the writer was a member of the Tribus elven clan, who were battling their Paxar cousins in the war that became known as the Brother-blood. See *The Hand of Chaos*, vol. 5 of *The Death Gate Cycle*, for details. Additional note: this manuscript can now be found in Haplo's collection.

yourself.[2] You have undoubtedly wondered why I kept the fool things, much less accorded them room in the armory. Little did you know, my son, what those daggers concealed.

Select a time when your lady-wife and her retinue have left the castle. Dismiss the servants. Make absolutely certain that you are alone. Go to the armory. Take up the box. On the lid, you will note that in each corner there is a butterfly. Press down *simultaneously* on the butterflies in the upper right corner and the lower left. A false bottom at the left-hand side will slide open. *Please, my son, for the sake of my soul and your own, do not place your hand in this box!*

Inside you will see a knife much less prepossessing than those that nestle above it. The knife is made of iron and appears to have been forged by a human. It is exceedingly ugly and misshapen, and, I trust, you will have as little desire to touch it, once you see it, as I had when I first looked at it. Yet, alas, you will be curious, as I was curious. I beg you, *beg you*, my dear, dear son, to fight against your curiosity. Look at the blade and see its hideous aspect and heed the warning of your own inner senses, which will recoil in horror before it.

I did not heed that warning. And it brought me a grief that has forever cast a shadow over my life. With this dagger, this Accurséd Blade, I murdered my beloved brother.

I imagine you growing pale with shock as you read this. It was always claimed that your uncle died of wounds suffered at the hands of human attackers, who waylaid him on a lonely stretch of road near our castle. That story was not true. He died by my hand, in the armory, probably not far from the spot where you now stand. But I swear, I swear by Krenka-Anris, I swear by the sweet eyes of your mother, I swear by the soul of my dear brother, that it was the blade that killed him—not I!

---

[2] The ancient elven custom of dagger-dueling had gone out of favor by this time, probably because so many elves were fighting for their lives on the battle-field. Dueling came to the fore under the peaceful reign of the Paxar, providing a way for youths to test their courage without placing anyone in real danger. As this elf implies, the daggers were meant more for show than actual use, often having jeweled handles and fancifully shaped blades.

The rules of the duel were complicated. The intent was to slash an ear. An elf walking around with a cropped "human" ear was an object of ridicule. To avoid scarring the face or damaging eyes, elaborate headgear was worn that left only the ears exposed.

This is what happened. Forgive the handwriting. Even now, as I relate this, I find I am shaking from the horror of that incident, which happened well over a hundred years ago.

My father died. On his deathbed, he told my brother and me the story of the Accursèd Blade. It was a rare and valuable artifact, he said, which had come from a time when two races of dread gods ruled the world. These two races of gods hated and feared each other and each sought to rule over those they called *mensch:* humans, elves, and the dwarves. Then came the God Wars—terrible battles of magic that raged over an entire world until at last, fearing defeat, one race of gods sundered the world.

Mostly the gods fought these wars among themselves, but sometimes, if they were outnumbered, they recruited mortals to assist them. Of course, we would be no match for the magical attacks of the gods, and so the Sartan (we know the gods by that name) armed their mensch supporters with fantastic magical weapons.

Most of these weapons were lost during the Sundering, as many of our people were lost, or so the tales relate. Yet a few remained with those who survived and were kept in their possession. This knife is, according to family legend, one of those weapons. My father told us he had called in the Kenkari, to verify the fact.

The Kenkari could not say for certain that the weapon was pre-Sundering, but they did agree that it was magical. And they warned him that its magic was potent and advised him never to use it. My father was a timid man and the Kenkari frightened him. He had this box built specially to hold the weapon, which the Kenkari deemed Accursèd. He placed the blade in the box and never looked at it again.

I asked him why he did not destroy it, and he said that the Kenkari had warned him not to try. Such a weapon could never be destroyed, they said. It would fight to survive and return to its owner, and as long as it was in his possession, he could guarantee that it would not have the power to do harm. If he attempted to rid himself of it—perhaps throw it into the Maelstrom—the weapon would simply fall into the hands of another and might do great damage. He vowed to the Kenkari that he would keep it safe and he made each of us take the same solemn oath.

After his death, as my brother and I were settling our father's affairs, we recalled the story of the knife. We went to the armory, opened the box, and found the knife in the false bottom. Knowing my father's timidity and also his love of romantic stories, I am afraid that we discounted much of what he had said. This plain and ugly knife was forged by a god? We shook our heads, smiling.

And, as brothers will, we fell to play. (We were young at the time of my father's death. That is the only excuse I can offer for our heedlessness.) My brother grabbed one of the dueling daggers and I took what we were jokingly calling the Accurséd Blade. (Goddess forgive my unbelief!) My brother took a playful slash at me with his dagger.

You will not believe what happened next. I am not certain I believe it myself, to this day. Yet I saw it with my own eyes.

The knife felt strange in my hand. It quivered, as if it were a live thing. And suddenly, when I started to thrust it playfully at my brother, the knife squirmed like a snake and I held—not a knife, but a sword. And before I knew what was happening, the sword's blade had passed clean through my brother's body. It pierced his heart. I will never, never—perhaps not even after my death—forget the look of shocked and awful surprise on his face.

I dropped the blade and caught him in my arms, but there was nothing I could do. He died in my embrace, his blood flowing over my hands.

I think I cried out in terror. I am not certain. I looked up to find our old retainer standing in the door.

"Ah," An'lee said, "now you are the sole heir."

He assumed, you see, that I had slain my brother in order to gain our father's inheritance.

I protested that he was wrong. I told him what had happened, but naturally he did not believe me. How could I blame him? I did not believe myself.

The knife had altered its form again. It was as you see it now. I knew that if An'lee did not believe me, no one else would. The scandal would ruin our family. Fratricide is punishable by death. I would be hanged. The castle and lands would be confiscated by the king. My mother would be thrown out into the streets, my sisters left disgraced and dowerless. Whatever my private grief (and I would have gladly confessed and paid the penalty), I could not inflict such harm upon the family.

An'lee was loyal, offered to help me conceal my crime. What could I do but go along with him? Between us, we smuggled my unfortunate brother's body out of the castle, carried it to a place far distant—known to be frequented by human raiders—and dumped it in a ditch. Then we returned home.

I told my mother that my brother had heard reports of human raiding parties and had gone to investigate. When the body was found, days later, it was assumed that he'd run afoul of those he sought. No one suspected a thing. An'lee, faithful servant, took the secret to his grave.

As for me, you cannot imagine, my son, the torture I have endured. At times I thought my guilt and grief would drive me mad. Night after night I lay awake and dreamed longingly of hurling myself off the parapet and ending this agony forever. Yet I had to go on living, for the sake of others, not my own.

I meant to destroy the knife, but the warning that the Kenkari had given my father burned in my mind. What if it should fall into other hands? What if it should kill again? Why should another suffer as I had? No, as part of my penance, I would keep the Accurséd Blade in my possession. And I am forced to hand it on to you. It is the burden our family bears and must bear until time's end.

Pity me, my son, and pray for me. Krenkra-Anris, who sees all, knows the truth and will, I trust, forgive me. As will, I hope, my beloved brother.

And I adjure you, my son, by all that you hold dear—by the Goddess, by my memory, by your mother's heart, by your lady-wife's eyes, by your unborn child—that you keep the Accurséd Blade safe and that you never, never touch it or again look upon it.

May Krenka-Anris be with you.

Your loving father.

# CHAPTER ✦ 9

# THE FORTRESS

# OF THE BROTHERHOOD

# SKURVASH, ARIANUS

✦

Ciang finished reading, looked up at Hugh.

He had stood silently as she read the missive, his hands thrust into the pockets of his leather pants, his back leaning against the wall. Now he shifted his weight from one foot to the other, crossed his arms, stared down at the floor.

"You do not believe," Ciang said.

Hugh shook his head. "A murderer trying to wriggle out from under his deed. He claims no one suspected, but someone obviously did, and he's trying to square himself with his kid before going off to war."

Ciang was angry. Her lips disappeared into a thin, bitter line. "If you were an elf, you would believe. Such oaths he swears are not made lightly, even in this day and age."

Hugh flushed. "I'm sorry, Ciang. I meant no disrespect. It's just . . . I've seen magical weapons in my time and I've never seen one do anything like that. Or even close."

"And how many men have you met who were dead and came back to life, Hugh the Hand?" Ciang demanded, voice soft. "And how many men have you seen with four arms? Or do you now refuse to believe me as well?"

Hugh lowered his gaze, stared again at the floor. His face darkening, his visage grim, he glanced at the knife. "Then how does it work?"

"I do not know," Ciang answered, her gaze, too, on the crude-looking weapon. "I cannot say. I have my own surmises, but that is all they are—surmises. You now know all the facts that I know."

Hugh stirred restlessly. "How did the knife come into the Brotherhood's possession? Can you tell me that?"

"It was here when I came. But the answer is not so difficult to imagine. The elven war was long and costly. It ruined many elven families. Perhaps this noble family fell on hard times. Perhaps a younger son was forced to seek his fortune and sought it in the Brotherhood. Perhaps he brought the Accurséd Blade with him. Krenka-Anris is the only one who knows the truth now. The man who was my predecessor turned it over to me with this missive. He was human. He had not read this, could not understand it. Which was, undoubtedly, why he permitted the knife to be loaned out."

"And you never have allowed anyone to use it?" Hugh asked, studying her intently.

"Never. You forget, my friend," Ciang added, "I helped them bury the man with four arms. Then, too, no one of us before has ever been forced to kill a god."

"And you think this weapon will do that?"

"If you believe this account, it was designed for just such a purpose. I have spent the night studying the Sartan magic, for though this man you must kill is not one of them, the basis for both their magicks is basically the same."

Ciang rose to her feet, moved slowly from her chair to stand near the table on which lay the knife. As she spoke, she ran a long-nailed finger delicately over the hilt, along its battered metal. She was careful, however, not to touch the blade itself, the blade marked with the runes.

"A Paxar wizard, who lived in the days when the Sartan were still living in the Mid Realms, made an attempt to learn the secrets of Sartan magic. Not unusual. The wizard Sinistrad did the same, or so I am told." Ciang's gaze slid in Hugh's direction.

He frowned, nodded, but said nothing.

"According to this wizard, Sartan magic is far different from elven magic—or human magic—in that the magic does not rely on manipulating natural occurrences, as in the case of humans, or using it to enhance mechanics, as do we elves. Such magicks work either with what is past or what is here and now. Sartan magic controls the future. And that is what makes it so powerful. They do this through controlling the possibilities."

Hugh looked baffled.

Ciang paused, considered. "How shall I explain? Let us suppose, my friend, that we are standing in this room when suddenly thirteen men rush through that door to attack you. What would you do?"

Hugh gave a rueful grin. "Jump out the window."

Ciang smiled, rested her hand on his arm. "Ever prudent, my friend. That is why you have lived long. That would be one possibility, of course. There are many weapons here. They provide you with numerous other possibilities. You might use a pike to keep your enemies at bay. You could shoot the elven exploding arrows into their midst. You might even fling one of the human fire-storm potions at them. All possibilities you could choose.

"And there are others, my friend. Some more bizarre, but all possibilities. For example, the ceiling could unexpectedly give way and crush your enemies. Their combined weight could cause them to drop through the floor. A dragon could fly through the window and devour them."

"Not likely!" Hugh laughed grimly.

"But you admit it is possible."

"Anything's *possible*."

"Almost. Though the more improbable the probability, the more power is required to produce it. A Sartan has the ability to look into the future, scan the possibilities, and choose the one that suits him best. He summons it forth, causes it to happen. That, my friend, is how you came back to life."

Hugh was no longer laughing. "So Alfred looked into the future and discovered the possibility—"

"—that you survived the wizard's attack. He chose that one and you returned to life."

"But wouldn't that mean I had never died?"

"Ah, here we delve into the forbidden art of necromancy. The Sartan were not permitted to practice it, according to the wizard—"

"Yes, Iridal said something about that. One reason Alfred denied having used his magic on me. 'For every one who is brought back to life untimely, another dies untimely,' she said. Bane, perhaps. Her own son."

Ciang shrugged. "Who knows? It is probable that if Alfred had been present when the wizard attacked you, the Sartan could have saved your life. In that case, you would not have died. But you were already dead. A fact that could not be altered. Sartan magic cannot change the past, it can only affect the future. I spent long hours considering this last night, my friend, using the wizard's text for reference, although he did not bother to consider necromancy, since the Sartan were not then practicing it.

"We know that you died. You experienced an afterlife." Ciang grimaced slightly as she said this. "And now you are alive. Think of this as a child playing at leapfrog. The child starts at this point. He leaps over the back of the child in front of him, arrives at his next point. Alfred cannot change the fact that you died. But he can leap over it, so to speak. He moves from back to front—"

"And leaves me trapped in the middle!"

"Yes. That is what I believe has happened. You are not dead. Yet you are not truly alive."

Hugh stared at her. "I mean no offense, Ciang, but I can't accept this. It just doesn't make sense!"

Ciang shook her head. "Perhaps I cannot either. It is an interesting theory. And it helped me to pass the long hours of the night. But now, back to this weapon. Knowing more about how the Sartan magic works, we can start to understand how this weapon works—"

"Assuming Patryn magic works like Sartan."

"There may be some differences—just as elven magic is different from human. But I believe—as I said—that the basics are the same. First let us consider this account of the elf lord who killed his brother. Let us assume that he is telling the truth. What, then, do we know?

"He and his brother are engaged in a friendly contest, using knives. But the weapon that he has chosen does not know the contest is a friendly one. It only knows that it is fighting an opponent wielding a knife . . ."

"And so it counters. And it does so by turning itself into a superior weapon," Hugh said, regarding the blade with more interest. "That much makes sense. A man comes at you with a knife. If you have the ability to choose your weapon, you'll take a sword. He never has a chance to get within your guard."

He looked up at Ciang, awed. "And you think the weapon itself *chose* to become a sword?"

"Either that," said Ciang slowly, "or it reacted to the elf lord's wish. What if he was thinking, academically, of course, that a sword would be a perfect weapon to use against his knife-wielding opponent. Suddenly he holds the sword in his hand."

"But surely the man who had four arms didn't wish for two more arms?" Hugh protested.

"Perhaps he wished for a larger weapon and he ended up with one so large and heavy that four arms were required to wield it." Ciang tapped the knife's hilt with her fingernail. "It is like the faery story we heard as children—the beautiful young maiden wished for immortal life, and her wish was granted. But she forgot to ask for eternal youth and so she grew older and older, her body withered to a husk. And thus she was doomed to live on and on."

Hugh had a sudden vision of himself, doomed to such an existence. He looked at Ciang, who had lived far longer than the longest-lived elf . . .

"No," she answered his unspoken question. "I never encountered a faery. I never went looking for one. I will die. But you, my friend—I am not so certain. This Sartan Alfred is the one who is in control of your future. You must find him to regain your soul's freedom."

"I will," said Hugh. "Just as soon as I rid the world of this Haplo. I will take the knife. I may not use it. But it could come in handy. 'Possibly,' " he added with a twisted smile.

Ciang inclined her head, granting him permission.

He hesitated a moment, hands flexing nervously, then—conscious of the elf woman's slanted eyes on him—he swiftly wrapped the knife in its black velvet cloth and picked it up. He held it in his hand, keeping it away from his body, eyeing it suspiciously.

The blade did nothing, though it seemed he could feel it quiver, pulse with whatever magic life it possessed. He started to thrust it into his belt, thought better of it, continued to hold it. He would need a sheath for it, one that he could sling over his shoulder, to keep from coming into contact with the weapon. The touch of the metal knife, squirming like an eel in his hand, was unnerving.

Ciang turned to walk back toward the entrance. Hugh gave her his arm. She accepted it, though she took pains not to lean on him. They walked at a slow pace.

A thought occurred to Hugh. His face reddened. He came to a halt.

"What is it, my friend?" Ciang said, feeling the arm she held grow tense.

"I . . . cannot pay for this, Ciang," he said, embarrassed. "What wealth I had I gave to the Kir monks. In return for letting me live with them."

"You will pay," said Ciang, and her smile was dark and mirthless. "Take the Accursèd Blade away, Hugh the Hand. Take your accursèd self away as well. That will be your payment to the Brotherhood. And if you ever return, the next payment will be taken in blood."

# CHAPTER ♦ 10

## TERREL FEN, DREVLIN

## ARIANUS

♦

MARIT HAD NO DIFFICULTY NAVIGATING DEATH'S GATE. THE JOURNEY WAS FAR easier, now that the gate was open, than the first terrifying journeys her compatriot, Haplo, had made. The choice of destination flashed before her eyes: the fiery lava cauldrons of the world she had just left, the sapphire and emerald jewel that was the water world of Chelestra, the lush jungles of the sunlit world of Pryan, the floating isles and grand machine of Arianus. And inserted into these, a world of wondrous beauty and peace that was unrecognizable, yet tugged at her heart strangely.

Marit ignored such weak and sentimental yearnings. They made little sense to her, for she had no idea what world this was and she refused to indulge in idle speculation. Her lord—her husband—had told her about the other worlds, and he had not mentioned this one. If Xar had thought it was important, he would have informed her.

Marit selected her destination—Arianus.

In the blinking of an eyelid, her rune-covered ship slid through the opening in Death's Gate, and she was almost instantly plunged into the violent storms of the Maelstrom.

Lightning cracked around her, thunder boomed, wind buffeted and rain lashed her ship. Marit rode out the storm calmly, watched it with mild curiosity. She knew from having read Haplo's reports on Arianus what to expect. Soon the storm's fury would abate, and then she could safely land her ship.

Until the storm passed by, she watched and waited.

Gradually the lightning strikes grew less violent; the thunder sounded from a distance. The rain still pattered on the ship's hull, but softly. Marit could begin to see, through the skudding clouds, several floating isles of coralite, arranged like stair-steps.

She knew where she was. Haplo's description of Arianus, given to her by Xar, was precise in detail. She recognized the islands as the Steppes of Terrel Fen. She guided her ship among them and came to the vast floating continent of Drevlin. She landed her ship at the first site available on the shoreline. For though the ship was guarded by rune-magic and would not therefore be visible to any mensch not specifically looking for it, Haplo would see it and know it at once.

According to Sang-drax's information, Haplo was last known to be in the city that the dwarves on this world called Wombe, on the western side of Drevlin. Marit had no very clear idea where she was, but she assumed by the proximity of the Terrel Fen that she had landed near the continent's edge, possibly near where Haplo himself had been brought to recover from the injuries sustained on that first visit, when his ship had crashed into the Terrel Fen.[1]

Looking out the ship's porthole, Marit could see what she presumed was part of the wondrous machine known as the Kicksey-winsey. She found it amazing. Haplo's description and her lord's further explanation had not prepared her for anything like this.

Built by the Sartan to provide water to Arianus and energy to the other three worlds, the Kicksey-winsey was an unwieldy monstrosity that sprawled across a continent. Of fantastic shape and design, the immense machine was made of silver and gold, brass and steel. Its various parts were formed in the shape of either human or animal body parts. These metal arms and legs, talons and claws, ears and eyeballs might once, long ago, have formed recognizable wholes. But the machine—having run on its own for centuries—had completely distorted them in nightmarish fashion.

Steam escaped from screaming human mouths. Gigantic bird talons dug up the coralite; tigerish fangs chewed up hunks of ground and spit it out. At least that's what would have been happening if the machine had been operating. As it was, the Kicksey-

---

[1] Marit does not know it, but her ship lands not far from the site on which Hugh the Hand and Alfred and Bane landed the *Dragon Wing*. The part of the machine she sees is in the city of Het.

winsey had come to a complete and mysterious halt. The reason for the halt—the opening of Death's Gate—had been discovered;[2] the dwarves now possessed the means to turn the great machine back on.

At any rate, that's what Sang-drax had reported. It was up to Marit to find out the truth.

She scanned the horizon, which seemed littered with body parts. She was no longer interested in the machine, but watched to see if anyone had noticed her ship landing. The runes would invoke the possibility that anyone not specifically searching for a ship would not see it, thus rendering the ship practically invisible. But there was always the chance, minute though it might be, that some mensch staring at this one particular patch of ground could see her ship. They couldn't damage it; the runes would see to that. But an army of mensch crawling around her ship would be a distinct nuisance, to say nothing of the fact that word might get back to Haplo.

But no army of dwarves came surging out over the rain-swept landscape. Another storm was darkening the horizon. Already much of the machine was lost in sullen, lightning-charged clouds. Marit knew from Haplo's early experience that the dwarves would not venture out into the storm. Satisfied that she was safe, she changed her clothes, putting on the Sartan clothing she had brought with her from Abarrach.

"How do those women stand this?" Marit muttered.

It was the first time she'd worn a dress,[3] and she found the long skirts and tight bodice confining, clumsy, and bulky. She frowned down at it. The Sartan fabric was scratchy against her skin. Though she told herself it was all in her mind, she felt extremely uncomfortable, suddenly, wearing the clothes of an enemy. A dead enemy at that. She decided to take the dress off.

Marit stopped herself. She was being foolish, behaving illogically. Her lord—her husband—would not be pleased. Studying her

---

[2] *The Hand of Chaos,* vol. 5 of *The Death Gate Cycle.*

[3] Women in the Labyrinth, particularly Runners, dress in leather trousers and vests, all rune-enhanced, as do the men. Squatter women, who are foragers and gatherers, will occasionally wear skirts that assist them in these tasks. Such skirts are worn over the trousers and can thus be easily removed if the women need to flee or fight a pursuing foe.

reflection in the porthole glass, Marit was forced to admit that the dress was perfect camouflage. She looked exactly like one of the mensch, whose pictures she'd seen in her lord's—her husband's—books. Not even Haplo, should he chance to see her, would know her.

"Not that he'd likely know me anyway," she said to herself, walking around the ship's cabin, trying to get used to the long skirts, which kept tripping her until she learned to take small steps. "We've each passed through too many gates since that time."

She sighed as she said it, and the sigh alarmed her. Pausing, she stopped to consider her feelings, examine them for any weakness, much as she would examine her weapons before going into battle. That time. The time they'd been together . . .

The day had been long and arduous. Marit had spent it battling—not a monster of the Labyrinth, but a piece of the Labyrinth itself. It had seemed as if the very ground were possessed by the same evil magic that ruled the prison-world on which the Patryns had been cast. Her destination—the next gate—lay on the other side of a razorback ridge. She had seen the gate from the top of the tree where she'd spent the night, but she couldn't reach it.

The ridge was smooth rock on the side she needed to climb, ice-smooth rock that was nearly impossible to scale. Nearly impossible, but not absolutely. Nothing in the Labyrinth was ever absolutely impossible. Everything in the Labyrinth offered hope—teasing hope, mocking hope. One more day and you will reach your goal. One more battle and you can rest in safety. Fight on. Climb on. Walk on. Keep running.

And this ridge was like that. Smooth rock, yet broken by tiny fissures that provided a way up, if raw and bleeding fingers could be forced inside. And just when she was about to pull herself over the top, her foot would slip—or had the crack in which she'd dug her toe deliberately closed? When did the hard surface beneath her foot change suddenly to gravel? Was it sweat that caused her hand to slip or did that strange wetness bleed from the rock itself?

Down she slithered, cursing and grasping at plants to try to stop her fall, plants that jabbed hidden thorns into her palms or that came uprooted easily in her grasp and fell down with her.

She spent a full day in attempting to negotiate the ridge, ranging up and down it in an effort to find a pass. Her search proved

futile. Night was nearing and she was no closer to her goal than she
had been that morning. Her body ached; the skin of her palms and
feet (she had removed her boots to try to scale the rock) was cut and
bleeding. She was hungry and had no food, for she had spent the
day climbing, not hunting.

A stream ran at the base of the ridge. Marit bathed her feet and
hands in the cool water, watched for fish to catch for dinner. She
saw several, but suddenly the effort needed to catch them eluded
her. She was tired, far more tired than she should have been, and
she knew it was the weariness of despair—a weariness that could be
deadly in the Labyrinth.

It meant you didn't care anymore. It meant you found a quiet
place and lay down and died.

Dabbling her hand in the water, unable to feel the pain anymore, unable to feel anything now, she wondered why she should
bother. What use? If I cross this ridge, there will only be another.
Higher, more difficult.

She watched the blood trail out of the cuts on her hands,
watched it flow into the clear water, swirl down the stream. In her
dazed mind, she saw her blood sparkle on the water's surface, form
a trail that led to a jog in the stream bank. Lifting her gaze, she saw
the cave.

It was small, set into the embankment. She could crawl in there
and nothing could find her. She could crawl into its darkness and
sleep. Sleep as long as she wanted. Forever, maybe.

Marit plunged into the water, waded the stream. Reaching the
other side, she crept into the shallows near the bank, advanced
slowly, keeping to the cover of trees that lined the stream. Caves in
the Labyrinth were rarely unoccupied. But a glance at her rune-
tattooed skin showed her that if there was anything inside, it wasn't
particularly large or threatening. Likely she could make short work
of it, especially if she surprised it. Or maybe, just once in her life, she
would be lucky. Maybe the cave would be empty.

Nearing it, not seeing or hearing anything, her sigla giving no
indication of danger, Marit sprang out of the water and hurriedly
covered the short distance to the entrance. She did draw her knife—
her one concession to danger—but that was more out of instinct
than because she feared attack. She had convinced herself that this
cave was empty, that it was hers.

And so she was extremely startled to find a man sitting comfortably inside.

At first Marit didn't see him. Her eyes were dazzled by the setting sun slanting off the water. The cave's interior was dark and the man sat very quietly. But she knew he was there by his scent and, in the next moment, his voice.

"Just hold right there, in the light," he said, and his voice was quiet and calm.

Of course he was calm. He'd watched her coming. He'd had time to prepare. She cursed herself, but she cursed him more.

"The hell with the light!" She bounded inside, heading for the sound of his voice, blinking rapidly to try to see him. "Get out! Get out of my cave!"

She was inviting death at his hands and she knew it. Perhaps she wanted it. He had warned her to stay in the light for a reason. The Labyrinth occasionally sent its own deadly copies of Patryns against them—boggleboes, as they were known. They were exactly like Patryns in all respects, except that the sigla on their skin were all backward, as if one were looking at one's reflection in a lake.

He was on his feet in an instant. She could see him now and was impressed, in spite of herself, with the ease and quickness of his movement. He could have killed her—she was armed and had sprung right at him—but he didn't.

"Get out!" She stamped her foot and gestured with her knife.

"No," he said and sat back down.

She had apparently interrupted him in a project of some sort, for he took hold of something in his hands—she couldn't see what because of the shadows and the sudden tears stinging her eyes—and began working at it.

"But I want to die," she told him, "and you're in the way."

He glanced up, coolly nodded. "What you need is food. You probably haven't eaten all day, have you? Take what you want. There's fresh fish, berries."

She shook her head. She was still standing, the knife in her hand.

"Suit yourself." He shrugged. "You've been trying to scale the ridge?" He must have seen the cuts on her hand. "Me, too," he continued on his own. She gave him no encouragement. "For a week. I was just sitting here thinking, when I heard you coming, that two people might be able to do it together. If they had a rope."

He held up the thing in his hands. That was what he was doing, braiding a rope.

Marit flung herself down on the floor. Reaching for the fish, she grabbed a hunk and began to eat hungrily.

"How many gates?" he asked, deftly twisting the vines together.

"Eighteen," she said, watching his hands.

He glanced up, frowning.

"Why are you looking at me like that? It's true," she said defensively.

"I'm just surprised you've lived that long," he said. "Considering how careless you are. I heard you coming all the way up the stream."

"I was tired," she said crossly. "And I didn't really care. You can't be much older. So don't talk like a headman."[4]

"That's dangerous," he said quietly. Everything he did was quiet. His voice was quiet; his movements were quiet.

"What is?"

"Not caring."

He looked up at her. Her blood tingled.

"Caring's more dangerous," she said. "It makes you do stupid things. Like not killing me. You couldn't have known I wasn't a boggleboe, not with just that single quick glimpse."

"You ever fought a boggleboe?" he asked.

"No," she admitted.

He smiled, a quiet smile. "A boggleboe doesn't usually commence an attack by bounding in and demanding that I get out of its cave."

She couldn't help herself. She laughed. She was beginning to feel better. It must have been the food.

"You're a Runner," he said.

"Yes. I left my camp when I was twelve. So I really do have more sense than I showed just now," she said, flushing. "I wasn't thinking right." Her voice softened. "You know how it gets sometimes."

[4] Leader of a tribe of Squatters, known for wisdom.

He nodded, kept working. His hands were strong and deft. She edged nearer. "Two people could make it across that ridge. I am called Marit." She drew back her leather vest, revealed the heart-rune tattooed on her breast—a sign of trust.

He set down the rope. Drawing back his own leather vest, he showed his heart-rune. "I'm Haplo."

"Let me help," she offered.

Lifting a huge tangle of vines, she began sorting them out so that he could twine them into rope. As they worked, they talked. Their hands touched often. And soon, of course, it was necessary that she sit very close beside him so that he could teach her how to braid the rope correctly. And soon after that, they shoved the rope to the back end of the cave, to get it out of their way . . .

Marit forced herself to relive the night, was pleased to feel no unwelcome emotions, no warmed-over, leftover attraction. The only touch that could send fire through her now was her lord's touch. She wasn't surprised that this should be so. After all, there had been other caves, other nights, other men. None quite like Haplo, perhaps, but then even Xar had acknowledged that Haplo was different from other men.

It would be interesting to see Haplo again. Interesting to see how he had changed.

Marit deemed herself ready to proceed. She had learned how to maneuver in the long skirts, though she didn't like them and wondered how a woman, even a mensch, could permit herself to be permanently encumbered in such a manner.

Another storm broke over Drevlin. Marit paid little attention to the slashing rain, the tumbling thunder. She would not have to venture out in it. Magic would take her to her destination. Magic would take her to Haplo. She had only to be careful that the magic didn't take her too near.[5]

Marit pulled on a long cloak, covered her head with the hood. She cast one final glance at herself. She was satisfied. Haplo cer-

---

[5] A Patryn who knows another Patryn may act on the possibility that he or she is with this Patryn and the magic will bring them together. But just as a Patryn must be able to visualize a location before being taken there, so Marit must be able to visualize Haplo before she can use the magic to join him.

tainly wouldn't recognize her. As for the mensch . . . Marit shrugged.

Having never before met a human—or any other mensch—she had, as do most Patryns, little respect for them. She looked like one of them, she planned on blending in with them, and figured that they would never notice the difference.

It did not occur to her to think that dwarves might question the sudden appearance of a human female in their midst. To her the mensch were all alike. What was one more rat in the pack?

Marit began to trace the sigla in the air, spoke them, watched them catch fire and burn. When the circle was complete, she walked through it and disappeared.

# CHAPTER ◆ 11

## WOMBE, DREVLIN

## ARIANUS

◆

AT ANY OTHER TIME IN THE LONG AND, SOME MIGHT SAY, INGLORIOUS HISTORY OF Drevlin, the sight of a human female walking the glimmerglamp-lit halls of the Factree would have occasioned considerable astonishment, not to mention wonder. No human female since the beginning of the world had set foot on the Factree floor. Those few human males who had done so had done so only recently, being part of a ship's crew who had assisted the dwarves in the historic Battle of the Kicksey-winsey.

If discovered, Marit wouldn't have been in any danger, except perhaps being "why'd" and "how'd" and "what'd" to death—the dwarves' deaths, not her own, for Marit was not a Patryn who had learned the lesson of patience in the Labyrinth. What she wanted she took. If anything got in her way, she removed it. Permanently.

Fortunately, Marit happened to arrive in the Factree at one of those moments in history that are both precisely the right moment and precisely the wrong moment. She arrived at precisely the right moment for herself, precisely the wrong moment for Haplo.

At this very moment, when Marit was materializing inside the Factree, stepping out of the circle of her magic, which had altered the possibility that she was here and not somewhere else, a contingent of elves and humans were gathering with the dwarves to form a historic alliance. As usual on such occasions, the high and the mighty could not conduct this business without being observed by the lower and humbler. Thus, a vast number of representatives of all the mensch races were wandering around the Factree floor for the first time ever in the history of Arianus. These included a group of human females from the Mid Realms, ladies-in-waiting to Queen Anne.

Marit kept to the shadows, observed and listened. At first, noting the number of mensch about, she feared she might have stumbled on a mensch battle, for Xar had told her that mensch invariably fought among themselves. But she soon realized that this was not a meeting to fight but what appeared to be a party—of sorts. The three groups were obviously uncomfortable together, but under the watchful eyes of their rulers, they were making every effort to get along.

Humans were talking with elves; dwarves were stroking their beards and endeavoring to make conversation with the humans. Whenever several members of any race broke off and began to group together, someone would come by and disperse them. In the confusion and strained atmosphere, no one was likely to notice Marit.

She added to this possibility a spell that would further protect her—enhancing the likelihood that anyone not looking for her would not see her. Thus she was able to walk from group to group, keeping apart but listening to their conversations. Through her magic, she understood all mensch languages, so she was soon able to figure out what was going on.

Her attention was drawn to a gigantic statue of a robed and hooded man—she recognized it with distaste as a Sartan—not far from her. Three men stood near the statue; a fourth sat on its base. From what she overheard, the three men were the mensch rulers. The fourth was the universally acclaimed hero who had made peace in Arianus possible.

The fourth man was Haplo.

Keeping to the shadows, Marit drew near the statue. She had to be careful, for if Haplo saw her, he might recognize her. As it was, he lifted his head and glanced swiftly and keenly around the Factree, as if he had heard a faint voice speak his name.

Marit swiftly ended the spell she had cast over herself to protect herself from the mensch's view, and shrank back even farther into the darkness. She felt what Haplo must be feeling: a tingle in the blood, a brushing of invisible fingers across the back of the neck. It was an eerie but not unpleasant sensation—like calling to like. Marit had not realized such a thing would happen, could not believe that the feelings they shared were this strong. She wondered if this phenomenon would occur between any two Patryns who happened to be alone together on a world . . . or if this was something between Haplo and her.

Analyzing the situation, Marit soon came to the conclusion that two Patryns meeting anywhere in a world of mensch would be attracted to each other, as iron to the lodestone. As for her being attracted to Haplo, that was not likely. She barely recognized him.

He looked older, much older than she remembered. Not unusual, for the Labyrinth aged its victims rapidly. But his was not the grim, hard look of one who has fought daily for his life. Haplo's look was haggard and hollow-cheeked, sunken-eyed—the look of one who has fought for his soul. Marit didn't understand, didn't recognize the marks of internal struggle, but she vaguely sensed it and strongly disapproved of it. He looked sick to her, sick and defeated.

And at the moment, he looked puzzled as well, trying to place the unheard voice that had spoken to him, trying to find the unseen hand that had touched him. At length he shrugged, put the matter out of his mind. He returned to what he'd been doing, petting his dog, listening to the mensch.

The dog.

Xar had told Marit about the dog. She had found it difficult to believe that any Patryn could indulge in such a weakness. She had not doubted her lord's word, of course, but she considered that he might have been mistaken. Marit knew now he had not been. She watched Haplo stroke the animal's smooth head, and her lip curled in a sneer.

Her attention shifted from Haplo and his dog to the mensch and their conversation. A dwarf, a human, and an elf stood together beneath the statue of the Sartan. Marit dared not cast any magic that would bring their words to her, and so she had to go nearer them.

She did so, moving noiselessly, keeping to the opposite side of the statue. Her main fear was being discovered by the dog, but it appeared to be totally absorbed in and concerned for its master. Its liquid eyes were fixed on him anxiously, and it would occasionally put a paw on his knee, offering a touch of comfort.

"And you are feeling quite well now, Your Majesty?" The elf was speaking to the human.

"Yes, thank you, Prince Rees'ahn." The human, a king of some sort, grimaced, put his hand to his back. "The wound was deep, but fortunately hit nothing vital. I have some stiffness that will be with me the rest of my life, according to Trian, but at least I'm alive, for which I thank the ancestors—and the Lady Iridal." The king looked grim, shook his head.

The dwarf was staring up at each tall mensch in turn, peering at them through squinted eyes, as if he were extremely nearsighted. "A child attacked you, you say? That boy we had down here— Bane? Pardon me, King Stephen." The dwarf blinked rapidly. "But is this normal behavior among human children?"

The human king looked somewhat put out at this question.

"He doesn't mean any offense, Sire," Haplo explained, with his quiet smile. "Limbeck—the High Froman—is only curious."

"Why, yes," said Limbeck, his eyes round. "I didn't mean to imply— Not that it would matter, mind you. It's just that I was wondering if maybe all human—"

"No," said Haplo shortly. "They don't."

"Ah." Limbeck stroked his beard. "I'm sorry," he added somewhat nervously. "That is, I don't mean I'm sorry that all human children aren't murderers. I mean I'm sorry I—"

"That's quite all right," said King Stephen stiffly, but with a smile lurking about the corners of his lips. "I understand completely, High Froman. And, I must admit that Bane was not a very good representative of our race. Neither was his father, Sinistrad."

"No." Limbeck appeared subdued. "I remember him."

"A tragic situation all around," said Prince Rees'ahn, "but at least good has come out of evil. Thanks to our friend Haplo"—the elf placed a slender hand on Haplo's shoulder—"and that human assassin."

Marit was shocked, disgusted. A mensch behaving in such a familiar manner, treating a Patryn as if they were equals. And Haplo permitting it!

"What was that assassin's name, Stephen?" Rees'ahn was continuing. "Something odd, even for humans—"

"Hugh the Hand." Stephen spoke with distaste.

Rees'ahn kept touching Haplo's shoulder; elves were fond of touching, hugging. Haplo appeared uncomfortable at the mensch's caress; Marit gave him credit for that. He managed to evade it politely by rising to his feet, sliding out from under.

"I was hoping to talk to Hugh the Hand," Haplo said. "You don't happen to know where he is, Your Majesty?"

Stephen's face darkened. "I do not. And frankly I don't want to know. And neither should you, sir. The assassin told the wizard he had another 'contract' to fulfill. It is Trian's belief," Stephen added, turning to Rees'ahn, "that this Hugh the Hand is a member of the Brotherhood."

Rees'ahn frowned. "A nefarious organization. We should make it one of our top priorities, when peace is established, to wipe out that nest of vipers. You, sir." He turned to Haplo. "Perhaps you could assist us in this undertaking. I understand from our friend, the High Froman here, that your magic is quite powerful."

So Haplo had revealed his magical powers to the mensch. And from the way it looked, the mensch were all quite taken with him. Revered him. As they should, of course, Marit was quick to allow— but they should be revering him as the *servant* of the master, not the master. And now was the perfect opportunity for Haplo to inform them of Xar's coming. The Lord of the Nexus would rid the world of this Brotherhood, whatever it might be.

But Haplo was only shaking his head. "I'm sorry. I can't help you. In any case, I think my powers might have been overrated." He smiled down at Limbeck. "Our friend here is a little nearsighted."

"I saw it all," Limbeck insisted stubbornly. "I saw you battle that evil dragon-snake. You and Jarre. She whumped it with her ax." The dwarf swung vigorously through the motions. "Then you jabbed it with your sword. Wham! Stabbed it in the eye. Blood all over the place. I saw it, King Stephen," reiterated Limbeck.

Unfortunately, he addressed Queen Anne, who had come up to stand beside her husband.

A female dwarf jabbed the male dwarf in the ribs.

"*That's* the king, Limbeck, you druz," she said, grabbing hold of Limbeck's beard and tugging on him until he faced the right direction.

Limbeck was not in the least upset over the mistake. "Thank you, Jarre, my dear," he said, smiling, and blinked benignly at the dog.

The mensch's talk turned to other matters, to the war on Arianus. A combined force of humans and elves was attacking the island of Aristagon, battling an emperor and his followers who had taken refuge in a palace there. Marit wasn't interested in the doings of the mensch. She was far more interested in Haplo.

He had gone suddenly gray; his own smile had slipped. His hand went to his heart, as if his wound still pained him. He leaned back against the statue to mask his weakness. The dog, whining, crept to his side and pressed against Haplo's leg.

Marit knew then that Sang-drax had been telling the truth—Haplo had been critically wounded. Privately she had doubted it. She knew and respected Haplo's ability; she had little use for the dragon-snake, who, as far as she could tell, possessed minimal magical powers, perhaps in the same category as mensch. Certainly none as strong as Patryn magic. She could not see how such a creature could have inflicted a dire wound on Haplo. But she had no doubts now. She recognized the symptoms of a heart-rune injury, a blow that would strike to the core of a Patryn's being. Difficult to heal—alone.

The mensch continued to talk, about how they would start up the Kicksey-winsey, what would happen when they did. Haplo stood silent through their conversation, stroking the dog's smooth head. Marit, not understanding the discussion, only half-listened. This wasn't what she wanted to hear. Suddenly Haplo stirred and spoke, interrupting an involved explanation of whirley-gears and whump-rotors from the dwarf.

"Have you warned your people to take precautions?" Haplo was asking. "According to what the Sartan wrote, the continents will begin to move once the Kicksey-winsey is activated. They'll move slowly, but they will move. Buildings could fall down. People might die of fright if they don't know what is going on."

"We've informed them," Stephen said. "I've sent the King's Own to every part of our lands, carrying the news. Though whether the people will listen is another matter. Half of them don't believe us, and the half who do have been told by the barons that it's some sort of elven plot. There've been rioting and threats to depose me. And what will happen if this doesn't work . . ." The king's face darkened. "Well, I don't like to think about that."

Haplo shook his head, looked grave. "I can't promise anything, Your Majesty. The Sartan intended to align the continents within a few years of their settling here. They planned to do so before the continents were even inhabited. But when their plans went wrong and they disappeared, the Kicksey-winsey kept on working and building and repairing itself—but without any guidance. Who knows but that during this time it may have done some irreparable damage to itself?

"The only thing in our favor is this: down through the generations, the dwarves have continued to do exactly what the Sartan taught them to do. The dwarves have never deviated from their original instructions, but passed them on religiously from father to son, mother to daughter. And so the dwarves have not only kept the Kicksey-winsey alive, but they've kept it from running amuck, so to speak."

"It's all . . . so strange," said Stephen with a distrustful glance at the glimmerglamps and the catwalks and the hooded silent figure of the Sartan, holding a dark eyeball in its hand. "Strange and terrifying. I don't understand any of it."

"In fact," Queen Anne added quietly, "my husband and I are beginning to wonder if we haven't made a mistake. Perhaps we should just let the world go along as it is. We've gotten on well enough before now."

"But we haven't," Limbeck argued. "Your two races have fought wars over water for as long as any of you can remember. Elf fought elf. Human fought human. Then we all fought each other and came close to destroying everything we have. I may not be able to see anything else clearly, but I can see this. If we've no need to fight over water, we've got a chance to find true peace."

Limbeck fished about in his coat, came out with a small object, and held it up. "I have this—the book of the Sartan. Haplo gave it to me. He and I have gone over it. We believe the machine will work, but we can't guarantee it. The best I can say is that if anything *does* start to go wrong, we can always shut the Kicksey-winsey down and then see if we can fix it."

"What about you, Prince?" Stephen turned to Rees'ahn. "What about your people? What do they think?"

"The Kenkari have informed them that drawing the continents together is the will of Krenka-Anris. No one would dare oppose the Kenkari—openly at least," the prince said with a rueful smile. "Our people are prepared. We have already started to evacuate the cities. The only ones we have not been able to warn are the emperor and those holed up in the Imperanon with him. They refuse to allow the

Kenkari inside; they have even fired arrows at them, which has never happened in all the history of our people. My father is undoubtedly mad."

Rees'ahn's face hardened. "I have little sympathy for him. He murdered his own people to obtain their souls. But there are those inside the Imperanon who are innocent of wrongdoing, who support him out of misguided loyalty. I wish there was some way of warning them. But they refuse to talk to us even under a flag of truce. They'll have to take their chances."

"You're all agreed to do this, then?" Haplo asked, looking at each in turn.

Rees'ahn said he was. Limbeck's beard wagged in hearty enthusiasm. Stephen looked at his queen, who hesitated, then nodded once, briefly. "Yes, we're agreed," he said at last. "The High Froman is right. It seems to be the one chance we have for peace."

Haplo pushed himself away from the statue, against which he'd been leaning. "Then it's settled. Two days from this day we start up the machine. You, Prince Rees'ahn, and you, Your Majesties, should go back to your kingdoms, try to keep the people from panicking. Your representatives can remain here."

"I will go back to the Mid Realms. Trian will be present in my stead," Stephen said.

"And I will leave behind Captain Bothar'el, a friend of yours, I believe, High Froman," said Prince Rees'ahn.

"Wonderful, wonderful!" Limbeck clapped his hands. "Then we're all set."

"If that is all you need me for," Haplo said, "I will go back to my ship."

"Are you all right, Haplo?" the female dwarf asked, regarding him anxiously.

He smiled down at her, his quiet smile. "Yes, I'm all right. Just tired, that's all. Come on, dog."

The mensch bade him farewell, speaking to him with obvious deference, concern evident on their faces. He held himself straight and tall; his step was firm, but it was apparent to all observers—including the one unseen observer—that he was exerting all his strength to keep moving. The dog padded behind, its own worried eyes on its master.

The others shook their heads, spoke of him in anxious tones.

Marit's lip curled in scorn. She watched him leave, not using his magic but heading for the open Factree door like any mensch.

Marit considered following him, immediately abandoned the idea. Away from the mensch, he would certainly sense her presence. She'd heard all she needed to hear anyway. She lingered only a moment, to listen to the mensch, for they were talking about Haplo.

"He is a wise man," Prince Rees'ahn was saying. "The Kenkari are greatly impressed with him. They urged me to ask him if he would act as intermediary ruler over us all during this period of transition."

"Not a bad idea," Stephen admitted thoughtfully. "The rebellious barons might agree to a third party settling the disputes that must inevitably arise between our people. Especially since he looks human, if you don't count those odd pictures on his skin. What do you think, High Froman?"

Marit didn't wait to hear what the dwarf thought. Who cared? So Haplo was going to rule over Arianus. Not only had he betrayed his lord, but he had supplanted him!

Moving far away from the mensch, into the very darkest regions of the Factree, Marit stepped back through the circle of her magic.

If she had waited a moment, this is what she would have heard:

"He will not do it," said Limbeck softly, looking after Haplo. "I've already asked him to stay here and help our people. We have much to learn if we are to take our place among you. But he refused. He says he must go back to his world, to wherever it is he came from. He must rescue a child of his who is trapped there."

"A child," said Stephen, his expression softening. He took hold of his wife's hand. "Ah, then, we will say no more to him of his staying. Perhaps in saving one child he will make up in some small measure for the child who was lost."

But Marit heard none of this. It might have made no difference if she had. Once on board her ship, as violent storm winds buffeted the vessel, she placed her hand over the mark on her forehead and closed her eyes.

A vision of Xar came to her mind.

"Husband"—she spoke aloud—"what the dragon-snake says is true. Haplo is a traitor. He gave the Sartan book to the mensch. He plans to help the mensch start this machine. Not only that, but the mensch have offered him the rulership of Arianus."

"Then Haplo must die," came back Xar's thought, his response immediate.

"Yes, Lord."

"When the deed is done, Wife, send me word. I will be on the world of Pryan."

"Sang-drax has convinced you to travel to that world," said Marit, not altogether pleased.

"No one convinces me to do what I do not choose to do, Wife."

"Forgive me, Lord." Marit's skin burned. "You know best, of course."

"I am going to Pryan in company with Sang-drax and a contingent of our people. While there, I hope to be able to enslave the tytans, use them to aid our cause. And I have other matters to pursue on Pryan. Matters in which Haplo may be helpful."

"But Haplo will be dead—" Marit began, and then stopped, overwhelmed with horror.

"Indeed, he will be dead. You will bring me Haplo's corpse, Wife."

Marit's blood chilled. She should have expected this, should have known Xar would make such a demand. Of course, her lord must interrogate Haplo, find out what he knew, what he'd done. Far easier to interrogate his corpse than his living person. The memory of the lazar came to her; she saw its eyes, which were dead, yet dreadfully alive . . .

"Wife?" Xar's prodding was gentle. "You will not fail me?"

"No, Husband," said Marit, "I will not fail you."

"That is well," said Xar, and withdrew.

Marit was left alone in the lightning-blue darkness to listen to the rain thrumming on the ship's hull.

# CHAPTER ♦ 12

## GREVINOR

## VOLKARAN ISLES

## ARIANUS

♦

"WHAT POSITION DO YOU SEEK?" THE ELF LIEUTENANT BARELY GLANCED UP AT Hugh the Hand as he shuffled forward.

"Wingman, Master," Hugh answered.

The lieutenant kept his eyes on his crew lists. "Experience?"

"Aye, Master," Hugh replied.

"Any references?"

"Want to see me lash marks, Master?"

Now the lieutenant lifted his head. The delicate elven features were marred by a frown. "I don't need a troublemaker."

"Only bein' honest, Master." Hugh chuckled, grinned. " 'Sides, what better references could ye want?"

The elf took in Hugh's strong shoulders, broad chest, and callused hands—all marks of those who "lived in harness," as the saying went—humans who had been captured and forced to serve as galley slaves aboard the elven dragon ships. The elf was apparently impressed not only with Hugh's strength, but with his candor.

"You look old for this line of work," remarked the lieutenant, a faint smile on his lips.

"Another point in me favor, Master," Hugh returned coolly. "I'm still alive."

At this the lieutenant definitely seemed impressed. "True. A good indication. Very well, you're . . . um . . . hired." The elf's lips pursed, as if the word was difficult to say. Doubtless the lieutenant was thinking with regret of the old days when all that wingmen earned was their food and water and the whip. "A barl a day, plus your food and water. And the passenger's paying a bonus for a smooth trip there and back."

Hugh argued a bit, just to make it look good, but couldn't eke out another barl, though he did win an extra water ration. Shrugging, he agreed to the terms and put his X on the contract.

"We set sail tomorrow when the Lords of Night pull back their cloaks. Be here tonight, on board, with your gear. You'll sleep in harness."

Hugh nodded and left. On his way back to the squalid tavern where he'd spent the night, again keeping in character, he passed "the passenger," emerging from the crowd of people who were standing on the docks. Hugh the Hand recognized the passenger— Trian, King Stephen's wizard.

Crowds of people stood gawking at the unusual sight of an elven ship swinging at anchor in the human port city of Grevinor. Such a sight had not been seen since the days when the elves occupied the Volkaran Islands. Children, too young to remember, stared in excited awe and wonder, tugged their parents closer to marvel at the brightly colored garb of the elven officers, their flute-like voices.

The parents watched with grim faces. They remembered—all too well. They remembered the elven occupation of their lands and had no love for their former enslavers. But the King's Own stood guard around the ship; their war-dragons circled overhead. What comments were made were made beneath the breath, therefore; all took care that the Royal Wizard should not hear them.

Trian stood among a knot of courtiers and noblemen who were either accompanying him on his journey, seeing him off, or attempting to make last-minute deals with him. He was pleasant, smiling, polite, hearing everything, seeming to promise all in return, but actually promising nothing. The young wizard was adept at court intrigue. He was like the rune-bone player at the fair who can play at any number of games at the same time, remembering every move, beating handily every opponent.

Almost every opponent. Hugh the Hand walked right past him. Trian saw him—the wizard saw everyone—but did not give the ragged sailor a second glance.

Hugh smiled grimly, shoved his way through the crowd. Showing himself to Trian had not been an act of bravado. If Trian had recognized Hugh as the assassin the wizard had once hired to murder Bane, the wizard would have shouted for the guards. In that case, Hugh wanted a crowd around him, a city to hide in.

Once on board, it was not likely that Trian would descend into the ship's belly to hobnob with the galley slaves—or rather, the wingmen, the term now being officially used—but with the wizard, one never knew. Far better to test the disguise here in Grevinor than aboard the small dragon ship, where all the guards had to do was wrap Hugh's legs and arms in bowstrings and toss him overboard into the Maelstrom.

Having obtained a weapon to kill Haplo, the assassin's next problem had been reaching Haplo. The Kenkari had told him that the Patryn was in Drevlin, in the Low Realms—a place nearly impossible to reach under the best of circumstances. Ordinarily, flying to somewhere in Arianus would not be difficult for Hugh, who was expert at handling both dragons and the small, one-person dragon ships.

But small ships did not fare well in the Maelstrom, as Hugh the Hand knew from bitter past experience. And dragons, even the giant ones, would not venture into the treacherous storm. It had been Ciang who had discovered, through her numerous contacts, that the wizard Trian would be flying down the day before the ceremony that would mark the starting up of the Kicksey-winsey.

The wizard, one of the king's most valued counselors, had remained behind to keep an eye on the rebellious barons. When king and queen returned to renew their iron grip on power, Trian would sail to Drevlin to make certain that human interests were represented when the giant machine started up and did whatever it was supposed to do.

Hugh had once served as a galley slave aboard an elven dragon ship. He guessed that the elves would likely need replacement men when they stopped in Grevinor to pick up Trian. Operating the wings of the dragon ships was dangerous and difficult work. A voyage rarely passed without a wingman being injured or killed.

Hugh had not judged wrong. Once in port, the first thing the elven captain did was post a notice stating that he needed three wingmen—one to work and two for spares. It would not be easy to find replacements to fly into the Maelstrom. No matter that the pay was a barl a day—a fortune to some on the Volkaran isles.

The Hand returned to the tavern, made his way to the filthy

common room where he'd spent the night on the floor. He gathered up his blanket and knapsack, paid his bill, and sauntered out. He paused to study his reflection in the dirty, cracked windowpane. Small wonder that Trian hadn't known him. Hugh barely knew himself.

He had shaved every hair from his head—face, scalp, all completely bare. He'd even—at the cost of pain that had brought tears to his eyes—yanked out most of his thick black eyebrows, leaving only a scraggly line that slanted upward to his forehead, making his narrow eyes look abnormally large.

Having been protected from the sun by his hair and beard, his chin and scalp had stood out in pallid contrast to the rest of his face. He'd used the boiled-down bark of a hargast tree to stain brown the pale skin. Now he looked as if he'd been bald all his life. There hadn't really been a chance Trian would recognize him.

There wasn't a chance Haplo would recognize him.

Hugh the Hand returned to the ship. Sitting on a barrel on the docks, he observed closely all who came and went, watched Trian boarding, watched the other members of the wizard's party boarding.

Once assured that no one else he knew had gone onto the ship, Hugh the Hand boarded as well. He'd been faintly concerned (or was it faintly hopeful?) that Iridal might be among the party of mysteriarchs accompanying the king's wizard. Well, Hugh was just as glad she wasn't. *She* would have recognized him. Love's eyes were hard to fool.

Hugh put the woman firmly out of his mind. He had a job to do. He reported to the lieutenant, who turned him over to a mate, who led him into the ship's belly, showed him his harness, and left him to meet his fellow crewmen.

No longer slaves, the humans now took pride in their work. They wanted to win the offered bonus for a smooth trip and asked Hugh more questions about his experience than had the elf lieutenant who hired him.

The Hand kept his answers short and to the point. He promised he'd work as hard as any of them, and then made it plain that he wanted to be left alone.

The others went back to their boning and dicing; they'd lose the bonus to each other a hundred times before they had it in their pockets. Hugh felt to make certain the Cursed Blade, as he had dubbed it, was in his knapsack; then he lay down on the deck beneath his harness and pretended to sleep.

The wingmen didn't earn their bonus that trip. They didn't even come close. There were times when Hugh the Hand guessed that Trian must be sorry he hadn't offered more for simply setting him down on Drevlin alive. Hugh needn't have worried about Trian recognizing him, for the Hand saw nothing of the wizard during the voyage, until the ship finally came to a shuddering landing.

The Liftalofts[1] were located in the eye of the perpetual storm that swept over Drevlin. The Liftalofts were the one place on the continent where the storms would swirl away, let Solarus beam through the scudding clouds. Elven ships had learned to wait to land until such times—the only safe times. They set down in relative calm and during this brief period (another storm was already massing on the horizon) swiftly offloaded the passengers.

Trian appeared. His face was partly muffled, but the wizard looked decidedly green. Leaning weakly on the arm of a comely young woman who was aiding his faltering steps, Trian stumbled down the gangplank. Either the wizard had no magical cure for airsickness or he was playing on the young woman's sympathy. Whatever the case, he glanced neither right nor left, but departed from the vicinity as if he couldn't leave the ship fast enough. Once on the ground, he was met by a contingent of dwarves and fellow humans, who—seeing the coming storm—cut short the speeches and whisked the wizard away to a place of dryness and safety.[2]

Hugh knew how Trian felt. Every muscle in the assassin's body ached and burned. His hands were raw and bleeding; his jaw was

---

[1] "Nine gigantic arms made of brass and steel thrust up out of the coralite—some of them soaring several menka into the air. Atop each arm was an enormous hand whose thumb and fingers were made of gold with brass hinges at each of the joints and at the wrist. The hands were . . . large enough to have grasped one of the enormous waterships and held it in a golden palm. . . ." Thus Haplo describes the Liftalofts in *Dragon Wing*, vol. 1 of *The Death Gate Cycle*.

[2] It appears from this text that the ship has landed on the ground. Those who read Haplo's first account of an elven ship arriving at the Liftalofts will recall that the dragon ship remained in the air. These early waterships were accustomed to leaving before the next storm hit, and while Haplo provides no explanation for the difference, it is logical to assume that elven ships intending to

swollen and bruised—one of the straps controlling the wings had snapped loose in the storm and struck him across the face. For long moments after the ship had landed, Hugh lay on the deck and wondered that they weren't all dead.

But he didn't have time to dwell on his misery. And as for the swollen face, he couldn't have paid money for a better addition to his disguise. With luck, the ache in his head and the ringing in his ears would go away in a few hours. He gave himself that amount of time to rest, wait for a lull in the storm, and rehearse his next course of action.

The crew would not be allowed ashore. Nor, after having sailed through the horrific storm, would they be at all eager to venture out into it. Most had dropped from exhaustion; one—who'd been hit in the head by a broken beam—was unconscious.

In the old days, before the alliance, the elves would have chained up the galley slaves when the ship landed—despite the storm. Humans were known for being reckless, foolhardy, and lacking in common sense. Hugh wouldn't have been much surprised to see the guards descending into the belly anyway—old habits die hard. He waited tensely for them to show up; their presence would have been an extreme inconvenience to him. But they didn't.

Hugh thought it over, decided it made sense—from the captain's viewpoint at least. Why put a guard over men who are costing you a barl a day (payable at the end of the voyage)? If one wants to jump ship without collecting his pay, fine. Every captain carried spare wingmen, the mortality rate among them being high.

The captain might well cause a furor when he discovered one of his crew missing, but Hugh doubted it. The captain would have to report the matter to a superior officer on shore, who would have his hands full with the dignitaries and would be highly annoyed at being bothered over such a minor problem. Likely the ship's captain himself would be the one reamed out.

"Why in the name of the ancestors can't you hang on to your humans, sir? High Command'll have your ears for this when you get back to Paxaria!"

No, Hugh's disappearance would probably not even be

---

stay for long periods were forced to set down on the ground to ride out the storm.

reported. Or if it was, it would be conveniently forgotten soon after.

The storm winds were dropping; the thunder was rumbling in the distance. Hugh didn't have much time. He dragged himself to his feet, grabbed his knapsack, and staggered off to the head. The few elves he passed never gave him a second glance. Most were too exhausted by the rigors of the flight even to open their eyes.

In the head, he made most convincing retching sounds. Groaning occasionally, he pulled from the knapsack a lump that looked like nothing so much as the insides of the knapsack. Once Hugh brought the cloth out, however, it began immediately to change color and texture, perfectly matching the wooden hull of the ship. Anyone looking at him would think he was acting very strangely, seemingly dressing himself in nothing. And then he would, to the observer's eyes, disappear altogether.

Much against their will, the Kenkari had provided him with the magical chameleon-like clothing of the Unseen. They didn't have much choice except to accede to Hugh's demands. After all, they were the ones who wanted him to kill Haplo. The clothes had the magical power to blend in with their background, rendering those who wore them practically invisible. Hugh wondered if they were the same clothes he'd worn into the palace that ill-fated night when he and Iridal had stumbled into Bane's trap. He couldn't be sure, and the Kenkari wouldn't tell. Not that it mattered.

Hugh discarded his own clothes—crude homespun that befitted a sailor—and dressed himself in the long, flowing pants and tunic of the Unseen. The clothes, made for elves, were a tight fit. A hood covered his head, but his hands remained bare; he could not hope to fit human hands into elven gloves. But he had learned, the last time he wore the garments, to keep his hands hidden in the folds of the tunic until time to use them. By then, if anyone saw him, it would be too late.

Hugh retrieved his knapsack, which held one more disguise and his pipe, though he would not dare use the latter. Few people smoked stregno, and both Trian and Haplo were likely to notice someone who did, recall Hugh the Hand to mind. The Cursed Blade, safely tucked into its sheath, he wore slung over his shoulder, concealed beneath his clothing.

Moving slowly, allowing the magical fabric time to adjust itself to its surroundings, the assassin glided past the elven guards, who had come up on deck during the lull in the storm to take advantage of the brief moment of sunshine and fresh air. Talking among themselves about the marvels soon to be witnessed when the great machine came on, they once looked straight at Hugh and saw nothing. He glided from the elven ship with as much ease as the freshening wind glided over it.

Hugh the Hand had been on Drevlin before, with Alfred and Bane.[3] He knew his way around as he knew his way around any place he'd ever been and more than a few he hadn't. The nine gigantic brass and golden arms thrusting up from the ground were known as the Liftalofts. The elven ship had landed right in the center of a circle formed by the arms. Near the circle's perimeter stood another arm, this one shorter than the rest, known as the Short Arm. Inside this arm was a circular staircase that led up to the nine drooping and lifeless hands atop the nine arms. Darting inside the stairwell, Hugh cast a quick glance around, ascertained that the place was empty and he was alone. He shed the clothes of the Unseen, made what would be his final change of costume.

He had ample time; another storm had crashed down on Drevlin, and he dressed with care. Examining himself in the polished metal interior wall of the staircase, he decided he was too dry to be believable, and stepped outside. In an instant he was drenched to the rich fur lining of his embroidered cape. Satisfied, he returned to the safety of the Short Arm and waited with the patience that all successful assassins know is the true foundation of their craft.

The curtain of rain parted enough so that he could see the elven ship through it—the storm was blowing over. Hugh the Hand was just about to venture out when he saw a female dwarf heading in his direction. He decided it would be more in character to wait for her arrival, and stayed where he was. But when she drew near, Hugh began to curse softly.

Of all the luck! He knew her! And she knew him!

Jarre—Limbeck's girlfriend.

There was no help for it now. He would have to trust to his altered appearance and considerable acting ability.

Splashing heedlessly through puddles, Jarre was peering upward continually at the sky. Hugh deduced that another ship must

---

[3] *Dragon Wing*, vol. 1 of *The Death Gate Cycle*.

be expected, probably carrying the elven contingent of dignitaries. Good, she would be preoccupied and might not pay much attention to him. He braced himself. She opened the door, bustled inside.

"I say!" Hugh rose haughtily to his feet. "It's about time!"

Jarre skidded to a halt, stared at him in astonishment—Hugh was pleased to note that she showed no recognition. He kept his hood up, casting his face into shadow but not hiding it, which might have looked suspicious.

"Wha—what are you doing here?" the dwarf stammered in her own language.

"Don't gabble at me in that strange tongue," Hugh returned pettishly. "You speak human. I know you do. Everyone who is anyone does." He sneezed violently, took the opportunity to draw up the collar of his cape around the lower part of his face, began to shiver. "There, you see, I'm catching my death. I'm wet to my skin." He sneezed again.

"What are you doing here, sir?" Jarre repeated in passable human. "Did you get left behind?"

"Left behind? Yes, I was left behind! Do you think I sought shelter in this beastly place because I wanted to? Was it my fault I was too sick to walk when we landed? Does anyone wait for me? No, no, and no. They're off like arrows, leaving me to the tender mercies of the elves. By the time I staggered onto deck, my friends were nowhere in sight. I made it this far when the storm hit, and now look at me." Hugh sneezed again.

Jarre's mouth twitched. She was about to laugh, thought better of it, and changed it into a polite cough instead.

"We're meeting another ship, sir, but if you'll wait, I'll be happy to show you to the tunnels—"

Hugh glanced outside, saw a whole group of dwarves trudging through the puddles. His sharp eyes picked out the leader, Limbeck. Hugh scanned the rest of the crowd intently, thinking Haplo might be with them. He wasn't.

Hugh drew himself up in offended dignity. "No, I will not wait! I'm halfway to dying of poomonia. If you will simply have the goodness to point me in the correct direction . . ."

"Well . . ." Jarre hesitated, but it was obvious she had more important things to do than fool with a sopping wet human numbskull. "See that enormous big building way, way over there? That's the Factree. Everyone's inside." She cast an eye at the distant storm clouds. "If you hurry, you should just about make it before the next downpour hits."

"Not that it would matter." Hugh sniffed. "I can't get much wetter, can I? Thank you, m'dear." He offered her a hand that resembled a wet fish, lightly twiddled his fingers near hers, and retrieved the hand before she could actually touch it. "You've been most kind."

Wrapping his cloak around him, Hugh stalked out of the Liftalofts to meet the startled stares of the dwarves (discounting Limbeck, who was gazing around in blissful myopia and didn't see him at all). Giving them a look that consigned them all unfavorably to their ancestors, Hugh flung his cape over his shoulder and strode past them.

A second elven dragon ship was descending, carrying the representatives from Prince Rees'ahn. Those meeting it soon forgot Hugh, who splashed his way to the Factree, ducking inside just as another storm swooped down on Wombe.

Throngs of elves, humans, and dwarves were gathered in the enormous area that had been, so legend had it, the birthplace of the fabulous Kicksey-winsey. All present were eating and drinking and treating each other with the nervous politeness of longtime enemies now suddenly friends. Again Hugh searched the crowd for Haplo.

Not here.

Just as well. Now was not the time.

Hugh the Hand made his way to a fire that was burning inside an iron barrel. He dried his clothes, drank some wine, and greeted his fellow humans with outflung arms, leaving them to think confusedly that they must know him from somewhere.

When anyone tried to ask—in a roundabout way—who he was, Hugh looked faintly insulted, replied vaguely that he was "in the party of that gentleman over there, Baron [sneeze, cough], standing by that thingamabob [wave of the hand]."

A polite bow and wiggle of the fingers to the baron. Seeing this obviously wealthy, well-dressed gentleman bowing to him, the baron bowed politely back. The questioner was satisfied.

The Hand took care not to talk to one person too long, but he made certain that he said something to everyone.

By the end of several hours every human in the Factree, including a pale and ill-looking Trian, would have been prepared to swear that he or she had been friends with the richly dressed and politely spoken gentleman for eons.

If they could just think of his name . . .

# CHAPTER ♦ 13

## WOMBE, DREVLIN

## ARIANUS

♦

THE DAY DAWNED FOR THE TURNING ON OF THE GREAT MACHINE. THE DIGNITARIES gathered in the Factree, forming a circle around the statue of the Manger. The High Froman of the dwarves, Limbeck Bolttightner, would have the honor of opening the statue, being the first to descend into the tunnels, leading the way to the heart and brains of the Kicksey-winsey.

This was Limbeck's moment of triumph. He held the precious Sartan book[1] in his hand (not that the book was necessary; Limbeck had memorized it completely, besides which he couldn't really see it unless he held it up level with his nose), and with Jarre at his side (now Madam High Froman), accompanied by a host of dignitaries, Limbeck Bolttightner approached the Manger. The dwarf, who had

---

[1] Foreseeing their doom, realizing they would be forced to leave Arianus without completing their task, the Sartan left detailed instructions informing the mensch how to operate the Kicksey-winsey. The book was written in three languages, dwarven, elven, and human, as well as Sartan. Unfortunately, at this time the mensch races were already at war, divided by hatred and prejudice. The book fell into the hands of the Kenkari elves, a powerful religious order.

Giving in to their own fears, particularly of the humans, the Kenkari hid the book and suppressed all knowledge of it. The current Speaker of the Soul— a studious man who, like Limbeck, suffered from insatiable curiosity—came upon the book and knew instantly what wonderful miracles it could bring to his world. He, too, was afraid of the humans, however, until an incident occurred that caused him to see true evil. He then gave the book to Haplo, to be given to the dwarves. *The Hand of Chaos,* vol. 5 of *The Death Gate Cycle.*

started this wondrous upheaval by simply asking "Why?", gave the statue a gentle shove.

The figure of the robed and hooded Sartan turned on its base. Before descending Limbeck paused a moment, stared down into the darkness.

"Take it one step at a time," Jarre advised him in an undertone, conscious of the dignitaries gathered around, waiting for them to proceed. "Don't go too fast and hold on to my hand and you won't fall."

"What?" Limbeck blinked. "Oh, it's not that. I can see fine. All those blue lights,[2] you know, make it quite easy. I was just . . . remembering."

Limbeck sighed and his eyes misted over, and suddenly the blue lights were more blurred in his vision than before, if such a thing was possible. "So much has happened, and most of it right here in the Factree. They held my trial here, when I first realized that the Manger was trying to tell us how the machine worked, and then the fight with the coppers—"

"When Alfred fell down the stairs and I was trapped in there with him and we saw his beautiful people, all dead." Jarre took hold of Limbeck's hand and squeezed it tight. "Yes, I remember."

"And then we found the metal man and I found that room with the humans and elves and dwarves all getting along together.[3] And I realized that *we* could be like that." Limbeck smiled, then sighed again. "And after that came the horrible fight with the dragon-snakes. You were a hero, my dear," he said, looking at Jarre with pride. He saw her clearly, if he could see nothing else clearly in this world.

She shook her head. "All I did was fight a dragon-snake. You fought monsters that were far bigger and ten times more horrible. You fought ignorance and apathy. You fought fear. You forced people to think, to ask questions and demand answers. You are the true

---

[2] Sartan runes placed to guide the way down the stairs.

[3] Ironically, what Limbeck saw was a gathering of the evil dragon-snakes, who had taken on forms of the mensch in order to insinuate themselves into the world. Haplo knows the truth, but, seeing that Limbeck is quite taken with the idea that the races can live and work together in peace, Haplo has never told the dwarf what he really saw.

hero, Limbeck Bolttightner, and I love you, even if you are a druz sometimes." She said the last in a whisper and then leaned over to kiss him on the side-whiskers, in front of all the dignitaries and half the population of dwarves on Drevlin.

There was much cheering, and Limbeck blushed to the roots of his beard.

"What's the delay?" asked Haplo softly. Quiet, keeping to the shadows, away from the other mensch, he stood near the statue of the Manger. "It's safe. You can go down there now. The dragon-snakes are gone."

At least they're not down in the tunnels anymore, he added, but he added it to himself. Evil was in the world and would always be in the world, but now, with the prospect for peace among the mensch races, evil's influence was lessened.

Limbeck blinked in Haplo's general direction. "Haplo, too," he said to Jarre. "Haplo's a hero, too. He's the one really responsible."

"No, I'm not," Haplo said hastily, irritably. "Look, you'd better get on with this. The people on the other continents above will be waiting. They might start to get nervous if there's a delay."

"Haplo's right," said Jarre, ever practical. She tugged Limbeck toward the entrance to the stairway.

The dignitaries crowded around the statue, preparing to follow. Haplo stayed put. He was feeling uneasy and could find no reason for it.

He looked, for the hundredth time, at the sigla tattooed on his skin, the runes that would warn him of danger. They did not glow with their magical warning, as they would have if danger had threatened—if the dragon-snakes were lurking somewhere below, for instance. But he felt the warning still, a prickling of the skin, a tingle of nerve-endings. Something was wrong.

He retreated into the darkness, planning to take a close look at everyone in the crowd. The dragon-snakes might disguise themselves effectively as mensch, but their glinting red reptile eyes would give them away.

Haplo hoped to remain unnoticed, forgotten. But the dog, excited by the noise and activity, was not about to be left out of the celebrations. With a cheerful bark, it bounded away from Haplo's side and dashed for the stairs.

"Dog!" Haplo made a lunge for the animal and would have caught it, but at that moment he was conscious of movement behind him, movement felt rather than seen, of someone drawing near him, a whispered breath on the back of his neck.

Distracted, he glanced around and missed in his grab for the dog. The animal joyfully leapt for the stairs and promptly entangled itself among the august limbs of the High Froman.

There was a perilous moment when it seemed that the dog and Limbeck would mark this historic occasion by tumbling down the stairs in a confused tangle of fur and beard. But the quick-thinking Jarre grabbed hold of both her renowned leader and the dog, each by their respective napes, and managed to sort them out and save the day.

Keeping firm hold of the dog in one hand and Limbeck in the other, Jarre glanced around. She had never really been all that fond of dogs.

"Haplo!" she called in a stern and disapproving tone.

No one was near him. He was quite alone, not counting the various dignitaries all lined up at the head of the stairs, waiting for their chance to descend. Haplo stared at his hand. For one instant, he had thought the runes were about to activate, to prepare to defend him from imminent attack. But they remained dark.

It was a strange sensation, one he'd never before experienced. He was reminded of a candle flame, extinguished by a breath. Haplo had the disquieting feeling that someone had, with a breath, extinguished his magic. But that wasn't possible.

"Haplo!" Jarre called again. "Come get this dog of yours!"

No help for it. Everyone in the Factree was looking at him and smiling. Haplo had lost all opportunity of remaining comfortably anonymous. Scratching at the back of his hand, he made his way to the top of the stairs and, with a grim expression, ordered the animal to his side.

Aware from its master's tone that it had done something wrong, but not quite certain why all the fuss, the dog pattered meekly up to Haplo. Sitting in front of the statue, the animal lifted a contrite paw, asking to be forgiven. This proceeding highly amused the dignitaries, who gave the dog a round of applause.

Thinking the applause was for him, Limbeck bowed solemnly, then proceeded down the stairs. Haplo, the crowd pressing behind him, had no choice but to join the procession. He cast one quick glance backward, saw nothing. No one was lurking about the statue. No one was paying any particular attention to him.

Perhaps he'd imagined it. Perhaps he was weaker from his injury than he'd thought.

Puzzled, Haplo followed Limbeck and Jarre, the Sartan runes lighting their way into the tunnels.

Hugh the Hand stood against a wall, in the shadows, watching the rest of the mensch file down the stairs. When the last one was down, he would follow—silent, unseen.

He was pleased with himself, satisfied. He knew now what he needed to know. His experiment had been successful.

"A Patryn's magic is said to warn him of danger," Ciang had told Hugh, "much as what we call our sixth sense warns us of danger, except that theirs is far more accurate, far more refined. The runes they have tattooed on their skin flare with a bright light. This not only warns them of danger, but acts as a defensive shield."

Yes, Hugh remembered—painfully—the time in the Imperanon when he'd tried to attack Haplo. A blue light had flared and a jolt like a lightning bolt had shot through the assassin's body.

"It would seem to me logical that for this weapon to work, it must somehow break down or penetrate the Patryn's magic. I suggest you experiment," Ciang had advised him. "See what it does."

And so Hugh had experimented. That morning, when the group of dignitaries assembled in the Factree, Hugh the Hand was among them. The assassin spotted his prey immediately on entering.

Recalling what he knew of Haplo, the Hand guessed that the quiet, unassuming Patryn would keep to the background, out of the sunlight, as the saying went, staying hidden in the shadows—making Hugh's task relatively simple.

The Hand was not wrong. Haplo stood apart, near that huge statue the dwarves called the Manger. But the dog was with him. Hugh cursed himself softly. He had not forgotten about the dog, but he was simply amazed to find it with its master. The last Hugh had seen of the animal, it had been with him and Bane in the Mid Realms. Shortly after saving Hugh's life, the dog had disappeared. The assassin had not been particularly grateful to the dog for its action, and hadn't bothered to go looking for it.

He had no idea how it had managed to make its way from the Mid Realms to the Low Realms, and he didn't much care. The dog was going to prove a damn nuisance. If need be, he'd kill it first. Meanwhile, Hugh had to see how close he could get to the Patryn, see if the Cursed Blade reacted in any way.

Drawing the knife, keeping it hidden in the folds of his cloak, Hugh drifted into the shadows. The glimmerglamps, which would have turned the Factree's night into bright day, were dark, since the Kicksey-winsey that ran them was not working. The humans and elves had brought oil lamps and torches, but these did little to penetrate the darkness of the cavernous building. It was easy for Hugh the Hand, dressed in the clothes of the Unseen, to join that darkness, become one with it.

He crept silently up behind his quarry, came to a halt, waited patiently for the right time to make his move. Too many in Hugh's trade, driven by fear or nervousness or eagerness, rushed to the attack instead of waiting, observing, preparing mentally and physically for the correct moment, which always came. And when it came, you had to know it, you had to react—often in only a splinter of an instant. It was this ability to wait patiently for that moment, to recognize it and act upon it, that had made Hugh the Hand great.

He bided his time, thinking as he did so that the knife had adapted itself wonderfully to his hand. He couldn't have hired a smith to design a hilt that suited him as well. It was as if the blade had molded itself to his flesh. He watched, waited, keeping his attention more on the dog than on its master.

And the moment came.

Limbeck and Jarre were starting down the stairs when suddenly the High Froman stopped. Haplo leaned over to talk to him; Hugh couldn't catch what they were saying, nor did he care. Then the dwarves started down the stairs.

"I wish," Hugh muttered to himself, "the damn dog would go along."

At that moment, the dog sprang after them.

Hugh the Hand was startled by the coincidence but was quick to take advantage of the opportunity. He glided forward. His knife hand slid out from beneath the folds of his cape.

He was not surprised to notice that Haplo was suddenly aware of him. The Hand had a healthy respect for his opponent, had not expected this to be easy. The knife writhed in Hugh's grip—a repulsive sensation, as if he were holding a snake. He advanced on Haplo, waiting grimly for the telltale runes to flare to life, in which case he was prepared to freeze, letting the night-blending magic fabric of the Unseen protect him from sight.

But the runes didn't react. No blue light flared. This appeared to discomfit Haplo, who had sensed a threat and looked to his body for confirmation, only to see nothing.

Hugh the Hand knew in that instant that he could kill Haplo, that the Patryn's magic had failed him, that the knife must have affected it and would affect it again.

But now was not the time to strike. Too many people. And it would disrupt the ceremony. The Kenkari had been most precise in their instructions—on no account was Hugh the Hand to disrupt the turning on of the Kicksey-winsey. This had been a test of his weapon. He now knew it worked.

It was a pity that he'd alerted Haplo to possible danger. The Patryn would be on his guard, but that was not necessarily a bad situation. A man looking over his shoulder is a man who will trip and fall on his face—a common jest among the Brotherhood. Hugh the Hand wasn't planning to ambush his victim, take him by surprise. Part of the assassin's contract—again, a part on which the Kenkari had been most specific—was that he was to tell Haplo, in his final moments, the name of the man who had ordered his death.

The Hand observed the procession from the darkness. When the last elf lord had disappeared down the stairs, the assassin followed, unheard, unseen. His time would come, a time when Haplo was cut off from the crowd, isolated. And at that moment, the Patryn's magic would fail him. The Cursed Blade would see to that.

Hugh the Hand had only to follow, watch, and wait.

# CHAPTER ♦ 14

## WOMBE, DREVLIN

## ARIANUS

♦

"Look!" limbeck exclaimed, coming to a halt with a suddenness that caused several people traipsing along at his heels to stumble into him. "There's my sock!"

The Sartan tunnels were shadowed and eerie, lit only by the blue rune-lights that flickered along the base of the wall. These runes were leading the party to its destination—or so all of them devoutly hoped, although more than a few were beginning to have serious doubts. No one had brought torches or lamps, Limbeck having assured them all that the tunnels were well lighted. (So they were, to a dwarf.)

Since the departure of the dragon-snakes, the feeling of evil that had wafted through the tunnels like the foul smell of something dead and decaying was no longer prevalent. But there remained in the tunnels a sensation of lingering sadness, regret for mistakes made in the past, regret that there had been no future in which to correct them. It was as if the ghosts of the builders of the Kicksey-winsey walked among them, benevolent but sorrowful.

*We're sorry.* The words seemed to whisper from the shadows. *So very sorry . . .*

Hearts were subdued. The dignitaries bunched together in the darkness, glad to feel the touch of a warm hand—be it human, elven, or dwarven. Trian was visibly moved, and Jarre was just beginning to feel a choke in her throat when Limbeck made his discovery.

"My sock!"

Eagerly the dwarf hurried over to the wall, proudly pointed out a bit of string running along the floor.

"I beg your pardon, High Froman?" Trian was not certain he'd understood the words, which were spoken in dwarven. "Did you say something about a . . . er . . ."

"Sock," Limbeck said for the third time. He was about to launch into the exciting tale, which had come to be one of his favorites—all about how they had discovered the metal man, how then Haplo had been captured by the elves, and how he, Limbeck, had been left alone, lost in the tunnels with no way out and only his socks standing between him and disaster.

"My dear," said Jarre, giving his beard a tweak, "there isn't time."

"But I'm certain there will be after the machine is up and running," Trian hastened to add, seeing that the dwarf appeared extremely disappointed. "I would really enjoy hearing your tale."

"You would?" Limbeck brightened.

"Most assuredly," said Trian with such eagerness that Jarre regarded him with suspicion.

"At least," said Limbeck, starting out again, Trian at his side, "now I know we're going in the right direction."

This statement appeared to comfort the vast majority of the procession. They hurried after Limbeck. Jarre lagged behind.

She was sad and grumpy on the day that should have been the most joyous of her life, and she didn't understand why.

A cold, wet nose prodded her in the back of the leg.

"Hullo, dog," she said dispiritedly, timidly patting its head.

"What's wrong?" Haplo asked, coming up beside her.

She looked startled. She'd supposed he was in front, with Limbeck. But then Haplo was rarely where you thought he ought to be.

"Everything's changing," said Jarre with a sigh.

"That's good, isn't it?" Haplo asked. "It's what you wanted. What you and Limbeck worked for. What you risked your lives for."

"Yes," Jarre admitted. "I know. And change will be good. The elves have offered to let our people move up to our ancestral homes in the Mid Realms. Our children will play in the sunshine. And, of course, those who want to stay down here and work on the machine can stay."

"Now your work will have meaning, purpose," Haplo said. "Dignity. It won't be slave labor."

"I know all that. And I don't want to go back to the old days. Not really. It's just . . . well . . . there was a lot of good mixed in with the bad. I didn't see it then, but I miss it now. Do you understand?"

"Yes," said Haplo quietly. "I understand. Sometimes I'd like to go back to the way things used to be in my life. I never thought I'd say that. I didn't have much, but what I did have, I didn't value. Trying to get something else, I let what was important get away. And when I got what I wanted, it turned out to be worthless without the other. Now I might lose it all. Or maybe I've already lost it past finding."

Jarre understood without understanding. She slid her hand inside Haplo's. They walked slowly after Limbeck and the others. She wondered a little why Haplo should choose to stay in the back of the procession; it was almost as if he were keeping watch. She noticed he glanced continually this way and that, but he didn't seem to be afraid—which would have made *her* afraid. He just seemed puzzled.

"Haplo," Jarre said suddenly, reminded of another time when she'd walked hand in hand with another person down in these tunnels. "I'm going to tell you a secret. Not even Limbeck knows."

Haplo said nothing, but he smiled encouragingly down at her.

"I'm going to see to it that no one"—she stared hard at the wizard Trian as she spoke—"that no one ever bothers the beautiful dead people. That no one finds them. I don't know how I'm going to do it yet, but I will." She brushed her hand across her eyes. "I can't bear to think of the humans, with their loud voices and prying hands, barging into that hushed tomb. Or the elves with their twitterings and high-pitched laughs. Or even of my people clumping about with their big, heavy boots. I'll make certain that it all stays quiet. I think Alfred would want it that way, don't you?"

"Yes," said Haplo. "Alfred would want it that way. And I don't believe you have to worry," he added, squeezing her hand. "The Sartan magic will take care of its own. No one will find that room who isn't meant to."

"Do you think so? Then I don't need to worry?"

"No. Now, you'd better go on ahead. I think Limbeck's looking for you."

Indeed, the procession had straggled to a halt again. Limbeck could be seen in the front, in the reflected glow of the Sartan sigla, peering myopically into the shadows.

"Jarre?" he was calling.

"He's such a druz," said Jarre fondly, and started to hurry back up to the front of the line. "Won't you come, too?" she asked Haplo, hesitating. "Are you feeling all right?"

"Just a little weakness." Haplo lied easily. "Let go of the past, Jarre. Reach out to the future with both hands. It will be a good one for you and your people."

"I will," said Jarre decisively. "After all, you gave us that future." She had a sudden funny feeling that she would never see him again.

"Jarre!" Limbeck was getting worried.

"You'd better run along," Haplo told her.

"Good-bye," she faltered, a smothering ache in her chest. Leaning down, she gave the dog a hug that nearly choked the animal; then, blinking back sudden and inexplicable tears, she ran off to join Limbeck.

Change—even good change—was hard. Very hard indeed.

The procession halted outside a door marked by gleaming blue Sartan runes. Bathed in the soft blue light, Limbeck marched up to the door and, acting according to Jarre's instructions (she held the book, reading out directions), the dwarf drew with a stubby finger the Sartan rune that completed the circle of runes on the door.

The door swung open.

A strange clanking sound could be heard within, coming toward them. The elves and humans held back, curious but alarmed.

Limbeck, however, marched right in. Jarre hurried to stay at his side. The wizard Trian nearly tripped on the dwarves' heels, hastening in behind.

The room they entered was brightly lighted by globes hanging from the ceiling. The light was so bright after the darkness of the tunnels that they had to shade their eyes momentarily.

A man made all of metal—silver and gold and brass—walked over to meet them. The metal man's eyes were jewels; it moved stiffly. Sartan runes covered its body.

"It's an automaton," announced Limbeck, recalling Bane's

word. The dwarf waved his hand at the metal man with as much pride as if he'd made it himself.

Awed, Trian stared at the automaton, and at the huge glass eyeballs that lined the walls, each eye gazing out watchfully on a certain part of the great machine. The wizard looked around dubiously at the banks of gleaming metal adorned with glass boxes and small wheels, levers, and other fascinating and unfathomable objects.

None of the levers or gears or wheels was moving. All held perfectly still, as if the Kicksey-winsey had fallen asleep and was waiting for the sunlight to shine on closed eyelids, when it would awake.

"The gate is open. What are my instructions?" asked the metal man.

"It speaks!" Trian was agog.

"Of course it does," Limbeck said proudly. "It wouldn't be much use otherwise."

He gulped in excitement, reached out a shaking hand for Jarre. She caught hold of his hand in hers, held on to the book in the other. Trian was trembling in excitement.

One of the human mysteriarchs, peering in nervously through the door, had broken down and was weeping uncontrollably.

"All lost," he was blubbering incoherently, "all lost, for all these many centuries."

"Now found," Trian breathed. "And bequeathed to us. May the ancestors make us worthy."

"What do I say to the metal man, my dear?" Limbeck quavered. "I . . . want to make sure I get it right."

" 'Put your hand on the wheel of life and turn,' " Jarre read the directions in dwarven.

Trian translated the words into elven and human for those crowding around the door.

"Put your hand on the wheel of life and turn," Limbeck ordered the automaton. The dwarf's voice cracked at first, but, gathering his confidence, he boomed out the last words so that even Haplo, standing alone and forgotten in the hall, heard them.

A gigantic wheel made of gold was affixed to one of the metal walls. Runes were etched all around the wheel. The metal man obediently clanked its way over to the wheel. The automaton placed its hands on the wheel and then looked back with its jeweled eyes at Limbeck.

"How many times do I turn it?" the mechanical voice intoned.

" 'One for each of the worlds,' " said Jarre, sounding doubtful.

"That is correct," said the metal man. "Now, how many worlds are there?"

None of them who'd studied the book was sure about this part. The answer wasn't given. It was as if the Sartan assumed the number would be common knowledge.

They had consulted Haplo. He'd shut his eyes, as if he were seeing moving pictures—like those in the Sartan magic lantern—in his mind.

"Try the number seven," Haplo had advised them, but wouldn't say how he arrived at the answer. "I'm not sure myself."

"Seven," Jarre repeated with a helpless shrug.

"Seven," said Limbeck.

"Seven worlds," murmured Trian. "Can such a thing be?"

Apparently it could, for the automaton nodded and, reaching up its hands, took hold of the wheel and gave it a mighty turn.

The wheel shuddered; its gears squealed from long disuse, but it moved.

The metal man began to speak, saying a word every time it turned the wheel. No one could understand what it said except Haplo.

"The first world, the Vortex," said the automaton in Sartan.

The wheel revolved with a protesting, grinding sound.

"The Vortex," Haplo repeated. "I wonder . . ." His musings were cut short.

"The Labyrinth," the metal man intoned.

Again the wheel turned.

"The Nexus," said the automaton.

"The Labyrinth, then the Nexus." Haplo considered what he was hearing. He quieted the dog, which had begun to howl dismally—the squealing of the wheel hurt its sensitive ears. "Both of those in order. Perhaps that means the Vortex is in the—"

"Arianus," said the metal man.

"It said us!" Jarre cried in delight, recognizing the Sartan word for their world.

"Pryan. Abarrach. Chelestra." At each name in the roll call, the metal man gave the wheel another turn.

When it came to the last name, it stopped.

"Now what?" Trian asked.

" 'Heaven's fire will spark life,' " Jarre read.

"I'm afraid we were never very clear on that part," Limbeck said in apology.

"Look!" cried Trian, pointing to one of the crystal eyeballs that looked out upon the world.

Terrible thunderclouds, darker and more ferocious than any that had been seen before on Drevlin, were massing in the skies above the continent. The land grew pitch-black. The very room in which they stood, so brightly lit, seemed darker, though they were far, far beneath the ground.

"My—my goodness," stammered Limbeck, eyes round. Even without his spectacles, he could see the boiling clouds swirling over his homeland.

"What have we done?" Jarre gasped, crowding close to Limbeck.

"Our ships," cried the elves and the humans. "This will wreck our ships. We'll be stranded down here—"

A bolt of jagged lightning shot from the clouds, struck one of the metal hands of the Liftalofts. Arcs of fire swirled around the hand, flashed down the metal arm. The arm twitched. Simultaneously hundreds of other spears of lightning slanted down from the heavens, struck hundreds of metal hands and arms, all over Drevlin. The eyeballs focused on each. The mensch gazed from one to the other in terrified astonishment.

" 'Heaven's fire'!" announced Trian suddenly.

And at that moment all the machinery in the room came to life. The wheel on the wall began to turn of its own accord. The glass eyeballs started to blink and rove, shifting their gazes to different parts of the great machine. Arrows encased in glass boxes began to inch their way upward.

On all parts of Drevlin, the Kicksey-winsey came back to life.

Immediately the metal man left the large wheel and headed for the levers and the small wheels. The mensch scrambled to get out of its way, for the automaton let nothing stop it.

"Look, oh, look, Limbeck!" Jarre was sobbing and didn't know it.

The whirley-wheels were whirling, the 'lectric zingers zinging, the arrows arrowing, the flash-rafts flashing. The dig-claws began furiously digging; gears were gearing and pulleys pulling. The glimmerglamps burst into light. Bellows sucked in great breaths and whooshed them out, and warm air wafted once again through the tunnels.

The dwarves could be seen swarming out of their homes, hugging each other and whatever parts of the machine they could conveniently hug. The scrift-bosses appeared in their midst and immediately began bossing, which was what they were supposed to do, so no one minded. All the dwarves went back to work, just as they had before.

The metal man was working, too, the mensch taking care to keep out of its way. What it was doing, no one had any idea, when suddenly Limbeck pointed to one of the eyeballs.

"The Liftalofts!"

The storm clouds roiled and swirled around the circle of the nine huge arms, forming a hole through which the sun shone on a waterspout, which was no longer working.

In the old days, the spout had funneled the water collected from the Maelstrom into a water pipe lowered from Aristagon. Elves had seized control of the pipe, and of the life-giving water, thus bringing about the first of many wars. But when the Kickseywinsey had ceased to work, the waterspout had no longer functioned—for anybody.

Would it begin working now?

"According to this," said Jarre, reading from the book, "some of the water harvested from the storm will be heated until it turns to steam and hot water; then that steam and hot water will shoot up into the sky . . ."

Slowly the nine hands attached to the nine arms rose straight up in the air. Each hand opened, its metal palm lifted to the sun. Then each hand seemed to catch hold of something, like an invisible string attached to an invisible kite, and began the motion of pulling the string, pulling the kite.

Above, in the Mid Realms and the High, the continents shuddered, moved, began slowly to shift their positions.

And suddenly a sparkling geyser of water burst out of the waterspout. Higher it rose, higher and higher, clouds of steam billowing around it, obscuring it from view.

"It's starting," said Trian softly, reverently.

# CHAPTER ✦ 15

# VOLKARAN ISLES

# ARIANUS

✦

KING STEPHEN STOOD ON THE BATTLEGROUND OF SEVEN FIELDS, OUTSIDE HIS royal pavilion, watching and waiting for what many in his realm believed would be the end of the world. His wife, Queen Anne, stood beside him, their baby daughter safe in her arms.

"I felt something that time," Stephen said, peering down at the ground below his feet.

"You keep saying that," Anne told him with fond exasperation. "I didn't feel anything."

Stephen grunted but didn't argue. The two of them had decided to cease the constant bickering that had been all for show anyway. Now they publicly revealed their love for each other. It had been quite amusing, those first few weeks after the peace treaty with the elves had been signed, to watch the various factions, who had supposed they were playing the king and queen off each other, flop about in confusion.

A few barons were trying to stir up trouble and succeeding, in large part because most humans still distrusted the elves and had grave reservations about peace among the races. Stephen kept quiet, bided his time. He was wise enough to know that hatred was a weed that would not wilt just because the sun was shining on it. Patience would be needed to uproot it. With luck and care, his daughter might live to see the weed die. Stephen knew he probably would not.

Still, he had done what he could to help. He was pleased. And if this crazy machine of the dwarves worked, so much the better. If not, well, he and Rees'ahn and the dwarf—what was his name? Bolt-something—would find a way.

A sudden hubbub from the shoreline attracted Stephen's attention. The King's Own were posted on watch, and now most of them were peering cautiously over the edge of the floating island, exclaiming and pointing.

"What the devil—" Stephen started forward to see for himself what was going on, and ran into a messenger coming to report.

"Your Majesty!" The messenger was a young page, so excited he bit his tongue trying to speak his piece. "W-w-water!"

Stephen had no need to move another step, for now he could see . . . and feel. A drop of water on his cheek. He stared in wonder. Anne, next to him, gripped his arm.

A fountain of water shot up past the island, soaring high into the sky. Stephen craned his neck, nearly fell over backward trying to see. The geyser ascended to a height that the king guessed must be somewhere below the Firmament, then cascaded downward in a sparkling shower like a gentle spring rain.

Steaming hot when it burst up out of Drevlin, the water was cooled by the air through which it passed, still more by the cold air near the ice floes that formed the Firmament. It was tepid when it hit the upturned faces of the humans, who stared in awe at the miracle showering down around them.

"It's . . . beautiful!" Anne whispered.

Solarus's bright rays burst through the clouds and struck the cascading water, transforming the transparent curtain into shining bands of color. Rings of rainbow hue surrounded the geyser. Droplets of water glittered and glistened, began to gather in the sagging tops of the tents. The baby laughed until a drop hit her squarely in the nose; then she wailed in dismay.

"I'm positive I felt the ground move that time!" Stephen said, wringing water from his beard.

"Yes, dear," said Anne patiently. "I'm going to take the baby inside before she catches her death."

Stephen stayed outside, reveling in the deluge, until he was soaking wet to his skin and then some. He laughed to see the peasants rushing around with buckets, determined to catch every drop of the commodity that was so precious it had become the monetary standard in human lands (one barl equaled one barrel of water). Stephen could have told them they were wasting their time. The water would fall and keep on falling without end, so long as the Kicksey-winsey kept working. And knowing the energetic dwarves, that would be forever.

He wandered for hours around the battlefield, which had now become a symbol of peace, for it was here that he and Rees'ahn had signed the peace accord. A dragon flashed down through the water, its wet wings shining in the sunlight. Coming to rest on the ground, it shook itself all over, appearing to enjoy its shower.

Stephen squinted against the sunlight, trying to see the rider. A female, to judge by the clothing. The King's Own were giving her respectful escort.

And then he knew her. Lady Iridal.

Stephen frowned, resentful. Why the devil was she here? Did she have to ruin this wonderful day? At the best of times, she made him damned uncomfortable. Now, since she'd been forced to kill her own son to save the king's life, Stephen felt even worse. He glanced longingly toward his tent, hoping Anne would come to his rescue. The tent flap not only remained closed, but a hand could be seen popping out, tying it shut.

Queen Anne wanted even less to do with the Lady Iridal than the king.

Lady Iridal was a mysteriarch, one of the most powerful magi in the land. Stephen had to be polite. He splashed through the puddles to meet her.

"My Lady," he said gruffly, giving her his wet hand.

Iridal took it coolly. She was extremely pale, but composed. She kept the hood of her cape over her head, protecting herself from the water. Her eyes, which had once shone as brightly as the rainbows in the water, were now gray, clouded with a sorrow that would remain with her until she died. But she seemed at peace both with herself and with the tragic circumstances of her life. Stephen still felt uncomfortable around her, but now the feeling was one of sympathy, no longer guilt.

"I bring you news, Your Majesty," said Iridal when the polite formalities and exchange of wonderments over the water were finished. "I have been with the Kenkari on Aristagon. They sent me to tell you that the Imperanon has fallen."

"Is the emperor dead?" Stephen asked eagerly.

"No, Sire. No one is quite certain what happened, but from all indications, Agah'rahn disguised himself in the magical garments of the Unseen and, with their aid, managed to slip away in the night. When his people discovered that the emperor had fled, leaving them to die alone, they surrendered peacefully to Prince Rees'ahn."

"That is welcome news, My Lady. I know the prince was loath to have to kill his own father. Still, it is a shame Agah'rahn escaped. He could yet cause mischief."

"There is much in this world that will yet cause mischief," Iridal said, sighing. "And always will. Not even this miracle of water can wash it away."

"Yet perhaps now we are armored against it," Stephen told her, smiling. "There!" He stamped his foot. "Did you feel that?"

"Feel what, Sire?"

"The ground shake. This island is moving, I tell you! Just as the book promised."

"If so, Your Majesty, I doubt you could feel it. According to the book, the movement of the isles and continents would take place very, very slowly. Many cycles will go by before all are in their proper alignment."

Stephen said nothing; the last thing he wanted to do was argue with a mysteriarch. He was convinced he had felt the ground move. He was certain of it. Book or no book.

"What will you do now, Lady Iridal?" he asked, changing the subject. "Will you return to the High Realms?"

He was immediately uncomfortable asking this question, wished he hadn't thought of it. Her son was buried up there, as was her husband.

"No, Your Majesty." Iridal grew paler, but answered him quite calmly. "The High Realms are dead. The shell that protected them has cracked. The sun parches the land; the air is too hot to breathe."

"I'm sorry, Lady," was all Stephen could think of to say.

"Do not be sorry, Your Majesty. It is better this way. As for me, I am going to serve as a liaison between the mysteriarchs and the Kenkari. We are going to pool our magical talents and learn from each other, to the benefit of all."

"Excellent!" said Stephen heartily. Let the blasted wizards keep to themselves, leave decent people alone. He'd never really trusted any of them.

Iridal smiled slightly at his enthusiasm. Undoubtedly she guessed what he was thinking, but was polite enough to say nothing. Now it was she who changed the subject. "You have just returned from Drevlin, haven't you, Your Majesty?"

"Yes, Lady. Her Majesty and I were there with the prince, looking things over."

"Did you, by chance, see the assassin, Hugh the Hand?" A crimson stain spread over Iridal's cheeks when she spoke the name.

Stephen scowled. "No, thank the ancestors. Why would I? What would he be doing down there? Unless he has another contract—"

Iridal's flush deepened. "The Kenkari . . ." she began, then bit her lip, fell silent.

"Who's he supposed to kill?" Stephen asked grimly. "Me or Rees'ahn?"

"No . . . please . . . I . . . must have been mistaken." She looked alarmed. "Don't say anything . . ."

Making him a low curtsy, she drew her hood farther over her face, turned, and hurried back to her dragon. The creature was enjoying its bath and didn't want to fly. She rested her hand on its neck, said soothing words to it, keeping it under her magical control. The dragon shook its head, flapped its wings, a blissful expression on its face.

Stephen hastened for his tent, planning to reach it before Iridal thought of something else to tell him and came back. Once there, he would inform the guard that he wasn't to be disturbed. He should probably find out more about the assassin, but he wasn't going to get the information from her. He'd put Trian on the mystery, when the wizard returned.

As it was, though, Stephen was glad he had spoken to Iridal. The news she brought was good. Now that the elven emperor was gone, Prince Rees'ahn would be able to take over and work for peace. The mysteriarchs would, Stephen hoped, become so interested in Kenkari magic that they would stay out of his hair. As for this business with Hugh the Hand, perhaps the Kenkari had wanted the assassin out of the way, sent him to his doom in the Maelstrom.

"Trust a bunch of elves to dream up something sneaky like that!" Stephen muttered into his beard. Realizing what he'd said, he glanced around hurriedly to make certain no one had heard.

Yes, prejudice was going to take a long time to die.

On his way to his tent, he took out his purse and dumped all the barls into a puddle.

# CHAPTER ♦ 16

## WOMBE, DREVLIN

## ARIANUS

♦

THE DOG WAS BORED.

Not only bored, but hungry and bored.

The dog didn't blame its master for this state of affairs. Haplo wasn't well. The jagged wound across the heart-rune had healed, but it had left a scar, a white weal slashing across the sigil that was the center of Haplo's being. Haplo had attempted to tattoo over it, to close the sigil, but for some reason unknown to both the dog and its master, the pigment wouldn't take on the scar tissue; the magic wouldn't work.

"Probably some sort of venom, left by the dragon-snake," Haplo had reasoned when he'd calmed down enough to be reasonable.

The first few moments after he'd discovered that his wound wouldn't completely heal had, in the dog's estimation, rivaled the storm raging outside their ship. The dog had deemed it wise to retreat during the outburst to a place of safety under the bed.

The dog simply couldn't understand all the fuss. Haplo's magic was as strong as ever—or so it seemed to the dog, who, after all, should know, having been not only a witness to some of Haplo's more spectacular feats, but a willing participant in them as well.

The knowledge that his magic was in good working order hadn't pleased Haplo as the dog had hoped it would. Haplo grew silent, withdrawn, preoccupied. And if he forgot to feed his faithful dog, well, the dog couldn't complain much because Haplo often forgot to feed himself.

But there came a time when the dog could no longer hear the glad cries of the mensch, celebrating the wondrous workings of the Kicksey-winsey, because the rumblings of its own empty stomach drowned out the noise. The animal decided enough was enough.

They were down in the tunnels. The metal thing that looked like a man and walked like a man but smelled like one of Limbeck's tool boxes was clanking about, doing nothing interesting that the dog could see, yet receiving all sorts of lavish praise. Only Haplo wasn't interested. He leaned against one of the walls of the tunnel, in the shadows, staring at nothing.

The dog cocked an eye in Haplo's direction and gave a bark that expressed the following thoughts: "Very well, Master. The man-thing without a smell has turned on the machine that hurts our ears. Our little and our big friends are happy. Let's go and eat."

"Hush, dog," said Haplo and patted the animal absentmind-edly on the head.

The dog sighed. Back on board the ship hung rows and rows of sausages—fragrant, stomach-filling sausages. The dog could see them in its mind, could smell them, could taste them. The animal was torn. Loyalty prompted it to stay with its master, who might get into serious trouble on his own.

"However," reasoned the dog, "a dog who is faint with hunger is not a dog who would be much good in a fight."

The animal whined, wriggled against Haplo's leg, and cast a longing look back down the tunnel, the way they'd come.

"You have to go out?" Haplo demanded, eyeing the dog with irritation.

The dog considered the matter. This hadn't been what it in-tended. And, well, no, it didn't have to go out. Not in the way Haplo meant. Not at the moment. But at least they both would be out—anywhere else besides this rune-lit tunnel.

The dog indicated, by pricking its ears straight up, that yes, indeed, it did have to go out. Once out, there was just a short jaunt to the ship and the sausages.

"Go on, then," said Haplo impatiently. "You don't need me. Don't get lost in the storm."

Lost in the storm! Look who's talking about being lost! Still, the dog had received permission to go and that was the main thing, although permission had been received based on a fraudulent prem-ise. The dog's conscience jabbed it on this point, but hunger pangs hurt worse than conscience pangs and the dog trotted off without giving the matter further consideration.

It was only when the dog was halfway up the stairs leading out of the tunnels, near another man that had no smell but looked like Alfred, that the dog realized it had a problem.

The animal could not get back onto the ship without assistance.

The dog drooped. Its steps faltered. Its tail, which had been waving jauntily in the air, sagged. It would have flopped down on its belly in despair if it hadn't been at that moment ascending a staircase, which made flopping uncomfortable. The dog dragged itself up the stairs. Near the man that had no smell but looked like Alfred, the dog sat down to scratch an itch and consider its current problem.

Haplo's ship was completely guarded by Patryn rune-magic. Not a problem for the dog, who could slide inside the sigla as easily as if it were greased. But paws are not meant to open doors. And while doors and walls had not stopped the dog when it was going to rescue its master, such obstacles might well stop it from sneaking inside to steal sausages. Even the dog could admit that there was a distinct difference.

There was also the unfortunate fact that Haplo kept the sausages hanging up near the ceiling, well out of the reach of hungry dogs. Another point the animal had not considered.

"This simply is not my day," the dog said, or words to that effect.

It had just heaved another sigh and was considering biting something to ease its frustration when it caught a scent.

The dog sniffed. The scent was familiar, belonged to a person the dog knew well. The man's scent was an odd variety, composed of a mixture of elf and human, combined with the flavor of stregno and held together by a sharp smell of danger, of nervous anticipation.

The dog bounded to its feet, searched the room for the source of the scent, and came upon it almost immediately.

His friend, his master's friend—Hugh the Hand. The man had shaved off all his hair for some reason, which the dog didn't bother to try to figure out. Not many of the things people did ever made sense.

The dog grinned, wagged its tail in friendly recognition.

Hugh didn't respond. He seemed disconcerted by the dog's

presence. He growled at it, kicked at it with his foot. The dog understood that it was not welcome.

This wouldn't do. Sitting down, the dog lifted a paw to be shaken. For some reason which the animal could never fathom, people found this inane gesture charming.

It appeared to work. The dog couldn't see the man's face, which was hidden beneath a hood (people were so very strange), but the animal knew Hugh was now regarding it with interest. The man squatted down on his haunches, beckoned the dog to come closer.

The dog heard the man's hand move inside the cloak, although the man was trying very hard to move it silently. Hugh the Hand drew something forth with a scraping sound. The dog smelled iron tinged with old blood, a scent the dog didn't like much, but this was no time to be choosy.

Hugh accepted the dog's paw, shook it gravely. "Where's your master? Where's Haplo?"

Well, the dog couldn't see launching into a lengthy explanation at this point. The animal jumped to its feet, eager to go. Here was someone who could open doors, someone who could snag sausages off their hooks. And so the dog told a lie.

It barked once and looked out the Factree door, in the direction of Haplo's ship.

One must note that the dog didn't consider this a lie. This was a mere matter of taking the truth, gnawing at it a bit, and then burying it for later. His master wasn't on the ship at this precise moment —as the dog was leading Hugh to believe—but he soon would be.

In the meanwhile, the dog and Hugh would have a nice visit and share a sausage or two. Time for explanations later.

But, of course, the man couldn't react simply and logically. Hugh the Hand stared around distrustfully, as if expecting Haplo to leap out at him any moment. Not seeing Haplo, Hugh the Hand glared at the dog.

"How did he get past me?"

The dog felt a howl of frustration rising in its throat. Damn the man. There were all sorts of ways Haplo could have slipped past him. Magic, for one . . .

"I guess he must have used his magic," Hugh the Hand muttered, standing up. There was the scraping sound again, and the smell of iron and old blood was considerably diminished, to the dog's relief.

"So why did he sneak off?" Hugh the Hand was asking. "Maybe he suspects something's up. That must be it. He's not the type to take chances. But then what are *you* doing running around loose?" The man was staring at the dog again. "He didn't send you out looking for me, did he?"

Oh, for the love of all that was greasy! The dog could have cheerfully bitten the man. Why did everything have to be so complicated? Hadn't this fellow ever been hungry before?

The dog assumed an innocent air, cocked its head to one side, gave the man a melting look with its dark eyes, and whined a bit to protest being falsely accused.

"I guess not," Hugh the Hand said, studying the animal intently. "He couldn't know it's me who's after him, for one thing. And you—you might be my ticket on board his ship. He'd let you in. And when he sees I'm with you, he'll let me in as well. Come on, then, mutt. Lead the way."

Once this man made up his mind, he moved quickly. The dog had to give him credit for that, and so it chose to overlook (for the moment) the use of the highly insulting "mutt."

The dog danced off, dashed out the Factree door. The man followed along closely behind. He appeared slightly daunted at the sight of the tremendous storm raging over Drevlin, but after a moment's hesitation in the entrance, he drew his hood up over his head and advanced grimly into the wind and rain.

Barking back at the thunder, the dog splashed gleefully through puddles, heading for the ship—a hulking mass of rune-glimmering darkness, barely visible through the slanting rain.

Of course, there would come the moment when, once on the ship, Hugh the Hand would discover that Haplo wasn't on board. Which moment might be rather ticklish to handle. The dog hoped, however, that the moment would come only *after* the man had been persuaded to hand over a few sausages.

Once its stomach was full, the dog felt capable of anything.

# CHAPTER ✦ 17

## WOMBE, DREVLIN

## ARIANUS

✦

ALONE IN THE HALLWAY, HAPLO TOOK A LOOK INSIDE THE AUTOMATON'S ROOM. The mensch were talking excitedly among themselves, moving from one glass eye to the next, gazing out at the marvels of the new world. Limbeck was standing squarely in the center of the room, giving a speech. Jarre was the only one listening to him, but he never noticed that he had such a small audience, nor did he much care. Jarre regarded him with loving eyes—her eyes would see quite well enough for the two of them.

"Good-bye, my friends," Haplo told them both from the hallway, where they couldn't possibly hear him. He turned around and left.

Arianus would be at peace now. An uneasy peace, riven with cracks and splits. It would break and crumble and threaten more than once to fall down and crush everyone beneath. But the mensch, guided by their wise leaders, would shore the peace up here, patch it up there, and it would stand, strong in its imperfection.

Which was not what he'd been ordered to do.

"It had to be this way, Lord Xar. Otherwise the dragon-snakes . . ."

Haplo's hand went, unknowing, to his breast. The wound bothered him sometimes. The scar tissue was inflamed, painful to the touch. He scratched at it absently, winced, and snatched his hand away, cursing. Looking down, he saw his shirt spotted with blood. He'd broken the wound open again.

Emerging from the tunnels, he climbed the stairs, halted at the top, stood before the statue of the Manger. It reminded him more than ever of Alfred.

"Xar won't listen to me, will he?" Haplo asked the statue. "Any more than Samah listened to you."

The statue didn't respond.

"But I've got to try," Haplo insisted. "I've got to make my lord understand. Otherwise we're all in danger. And then, when he knows the danger of the dragon-snakes, he can fight them. And I can return to the Labyrinth, find my child."

Oddly, the thought of going back into the Labyrinth no longer terrified him. Now, at last, he could walk back through the Final Gate. His child. And her child. Perhaps he'd find her as well. The mistake he'd made—letting her go—would be rectified.

"You were right, Marit," he said to her silently. " 'The evil inside us,' you said. Now I understand."

Haplo stood staring up at the statue. Once, when he had first seen it, the statue of the Sartan had seemed to him awful, majestic. Now it looked tired, wistful, and faintly relieved.

"It was tough being a god, wasn't it? All that responsibility . . . and no one listening. But your people are going to be all right now." Haplo rested his hand on the metal arm. "You don't have to worry about them any longer.

"And neither do I."

Once outside the Factree, Haplo headed for his ship. The storm was letting up; the clouds were starting to roll away. And so far as Haplo could see, there wasn't another storm in sight. The sun might actually shine on Drevlin—all of Drevlin, not just the area around the Liftalofts. Haplo wondered how the dwarves would cope.

Knowing dwarves, they'd probably be opposed to it, he decided, smiling at the thought.

Haplo slogged through the puddles, taking care to keep clear of any part of the rumbling Kicksey-winsey that looked as if it might swing, trundle, roll, or smash into him. The air was filled with the various sounds of the machine's intense activity: whistles and hoots, beeps and grindings, the zap of electricity. A few dwarves had actually ventured outside and were peering up at the sky with doubt.

Haplo looked swiftly to his ship, was pleased to see that no one and nothing was near it—this included the Kicksey-winsey. He was not so pleased to note that the dog wasn't around either. But then, Haplo was forced to admit, *I haven't been very good company of late. Probably the dog was off chasing rats.*

The storm clouds broke up. Solarus burst through, streaming down between the breaks in the clouds. In the distance, a cascade of rainbow colors shimmered around the spouting geyser. The sunlight made the great machine suddenly beautiful—it gleamed on the bright silver arms, glinted off fanciful golden fingers. The dwarves stopped to stare at the amazing sight, then hurriedly shaded their eyes and began to grumble about the brightness of the light.

Haplo stopped, took a long look around.

"I won't be back here," he said to himself suddenly. "Ever again."

The knowledge didn't cause him sorrow, only a kind of wistful sadness, much as he'd seen on the face of the Sartan statue. It wasn't a feeling of ill omen. But it was a feeling of certainty.

He wished, after all, that he'd said good-bye to Limbeck. And thanked him for saving his life. Haplo couldn't remember that he ever had. He almost turned around, then kept going straight ahead, toward his ship. It was better this way.

Haplo removed the runes from the entrance, was about to open the hatch when he stopped again, looked around again.

"Dog!" Haplo called.

An answering "whuff" came from inside. From *far* inside the ship. Say, around the hold area, where the sausages were hung . . .

"So that's what you've been up to," Haplo called out grimly. He opened the door and stepped in.

Pain burst at the base of his skull, exploded behind his eyes, and propelled him, struggling, into darkness.

Chill water, splashing on his face, brought Haplo instantly to consciousness. He was wide awake and alert, despite the ache in his head. He found himself lying on his back, his wrists and ankles bound securely with a length of his own rope. Someone had ambushed him. But who? Why? And how had whoever it was gotten on board his ship?

*Sang-drax. The dragon-snake. But my magic should have warned me . . .*

Haplo's eyes flicked opened involuntarily when the water hit him, but he closed them almost immediately. Groaning, he let his head loll sideways. Then he lay still, pretending to black out again, hoping to hear something to tell him what was happening.

"Come off it. Quit shamming."

Something—probably the toe of a boot—prodded Haplo in the side. The voice was familiar.

"I know that old trick," the voice continued. "You're awake, all right. I can prove it if you want me to. A kick in the side of the knee. Feels like someone's driving a red-hot poker into your flesh. No one can play dead through the pain."

The shock of recognizing the voice, more than the threat—which to Haplo, with his protective runes, was no threat at all—caused him to open his eyes. He stared up dazedly at the man who had spoken.

"Hugh the Hand?" he said groggily.

The Hand grunted in acknowledgment. He was seated on a low wooden bench that ran along the bulkheads. He had a pipe in his mouth, and the noxious odor of stregno wafted through the ship. Although he looked relaxed, he was watchful and undoubtedly had a weapon ready.

Not that any mensch weapon could hurt Haplo. But then, no mensch could possibly break through his magic, sneak on board his ship. Nor could any mensch ambush him.

He'd figure this out later, once he was free of these ropes. Haplo called on the magic that would remove his bonds, dissolve the ropes, burn them away . . .

Nothing happened.

Astounded, Haplo tugged at the ropes, to no avail.

Hugh the Hand watched, puffed on his pipe, said nothing. Haplo had the odd impression that the Hand was as curious as the Patryn about what was going forward.

Haplo ignored the assassin. He took time to analyze the magic, something he hadn't bothered to do, since a routine spell of this sort was second nature. He scanned the possibilities, only to discover that there was only one possibility—he was bound securely with strong rope. All other possibilities had disappeared.

No, not disappeared. They were still there; he could see them, but they were unavailable to him. Accustomed to having innumerable doors open to him, Haplo was shocked to find that now all but one were shut and locked.

Frustrated, he pulled hard at the bonds, tried to free himself. The rope cut painfully into his wrists. Blood trickled over the sigla on his forearms. Sigla that should have been burning bright red and blue, sigla that should have been acting to free him.

"What have you done?" Haplo demanded, not afraid, just amazed. "How did you do this?"

Hugh the Hand shook his head, removed the pipe from his mouth. "If I told you, you might find a way to fight it. Seems a pity to let you die without knowing, but"—the assassin shrugged—"I can't take the chance."

"Die . . ."

Haplo's head hurt like hell. None of this was making sense. He closed his eyes again. He wasn't trying to fool his captor anymore. He was simply trying to ease the pain in his skull long enough to figure out what was going on.

"I've sworn to tell you one thing before I kill you," Hugh the Hand said, rising to his feet. "That's the name of the person who wants you dead. Xar. That name mean anything to you? Xar wants you dead."

"Xar!" Haplo's eyes flared open. "How do you know Xar? He wouldn't hire you—a mensch. No, damn it, this doesn't make any sense!"

"He didn't hire me. Bane did. Before he died. He said I was to tell you that Xar wants you dead."

Haplo went numb. *Xar wants you dead.* He couldn't believe it. Xar might be disappointed with him, angry with him. But want him dead?

No, Haplo said to himself, that would mean Xar is afraid of me. And Xar isn't afraid of anything.

Bane. This was *his* doing. It had to be.

But now that Haplo had figured that out, what did he plan to do about it?

Hugh the Hand stood over him. The assassin was reaching into his cloak, probably for the weapon he was going to use to finish the job.

"Listen to me, Hugh." Haplo hoped to distract the assassin with talk while he tried surreptitiously to loosen his bonds. "You've been tricked. Bane lied to you. *He* was the one who wanted me dead."

"Doesn't matter." Hugh the Hand drew a knife out of a sheath strapped behind his back. "A contract's a contract, no matter who made it. I took it. I'm honor-bound to carry it out."

Haplo didn't hear. He was staring at the knife. Sartan runes! But how? . . . Where? . . . No, damn it, that didn't matter! What mattered was that now he knew—sort of—what was blocking his magic. If he only understood how the runes worked . . .

"Hugh, you're a good man, a good fighter." Haplo stared hard at the knife. "I don't want to have to kill you—"

"Good thing," Hugh the Hand remarked with a grim smile. "Because you're not going to have the chance."

Concealed in Haplo's boot was a rune-covered dagger of his own. He acted on the probability that the dagger wasn't in his boot but in his hands.

The magic worked. The knife was in Haplo's hands. But at the same instant the knife in the assassin's hand was suddenly a double-bladed ax.

Hugh fumbled, nearly dropped the heavy weapon, but quickly recovered, held on to it.

So that's how the magic works, Haplo realized. Ingenious. The knife can't stop my magic, but it can limit my choices. It will let me fight, because it can counteract whatever weapon I choose to use. And the weapon works on its own, obviously, judging by the look on Hugh's face. He was more shocked than I was.

Not that this helps much, since the Sartan knife will always give him the upper hand. But does it react to all magic? Or just to a threat . . .

"I'll make your death quick," Hugh the Hand was saying. He gripped the ax in both hands, raised it over Haplo's neck. "If you people have any prayers to say, you'd best say them."

Haplo gave a low whistle.

The dog—sausage grease on its nose—trotted out from the hold. It paused to regard its master and Hugh with amazed curiosity. Obviously this was a game . . .

*Take him!* Haplo ordered silently.

The dog looked puzzled. *Take him, Master? He's our friend! I saved his life. He was kind enough to feed me a sausage or two. Surely you're mistaken, Master.*

*Take him!* Haplo ordered.

The dog might have, for the first and only time in its life, disobeyed. But at that moment Hugh raised the ax.

The dog was baffled. The game had suddenly turned ugly. This couldn't be allowed. The man must be making a mistake. Silently, not growling or barking, the dog jumped for Hugh.

The Hand never knew what hit him. The animal struck him solidly from behind. The assassin lost his balance; the ax flew from his hands, thudded harmlessly into the wall. Hugh stumbled, fell. The human's heavy weight crashed down on top of Haplo.

Hugh the Hand gave a great groan. His body stiffened. Haplo felt a rush of warm blood cover his hands and arms.

"Damn!" Haplo pushed on the assassin's shoulder, rolled him over onto his back.

Haplo's knife protruded from the man's gut.

"Damn it! I didn't mean— Why the hell did you—" Cursing, Haplo crouched over the man. A major artery had been severed. Blood was pulsing out of the wound. Hugh was still alive, but he wouldn't be for long.

"Hugh," Haplo said quietly. "Can you hear me? I didn't mean to do this."

The man's eyes flickered open. The Hand seemed almost to smile. He tried to speak, but the blood rattled in his throat. His jaw fell slack. The eyes fixed. His head rolled to one side.

The dog trotted over, pawed at the dead man. *Game's over. That was fun. Now it's time to get up and play again.*

"Leave him alone, boy," Haplo said, shoving the dog back.

The dog, not understanding but having the idea that this was all somehow its fault, flopped down on its belly. Nose between its paws, it gazed from its master to the man, who was now lying quite still. The dog hoped someone would tell it what was going on.

"You of all people," Haplo said to the corpse. "Damn it!" He beat gently on his leg with a clenched fist. "Damn it all. Bane! Why Bane—and why this? What cursed fate put this weapon into your hands?"

The Sartan weapon lay on the blood-spattered deck beside the body. The weapon, which had been an ax, was now again a crude knife. Haplo didn't touch it. He didn't want to touch it. The Sartan runes etched into its metal were hideous, repulsive, reminded him of the corrupt Sartan runes he'd seen on Abarrach. He left it where it was.

Angry at Hugh, himself, fate—or whatever one might call it— Haplo stood up, stared grimly out the ship's porthole.

The sun was pouring down on Drevlin with blinding intensity. The rainbow geyser sparkled and danced. More and more dwarves were coming up to the surface, staring around them in dazzled bewilderment.

"What the devil am I going to do with the body?" Haplo demanded. "I can't leave it here, on Drevlin. How would I explain what happened? And if I just dump it out, the humans will suspect the dwarves of murder. All hell will break loose. They'll all be back right where they started.

"I'll take him back to the Kenkari," he decided. "They'll know what to do. Poor bastard—"

A great and terrible cry of rage and anguish, coming from directly behind him, froze Haplo's heart to awed stillness. He was unable to move for an instant, his brain and nerves fused by fear and disbelief.

The cry was repeated. Haplo's icy blood surged through his body in chilling waves. Slowly he turned around.

Hugh the Hand was sitting up, looking down at the knife hilt protruding from his stomach. Grimacing as if in memory of the pain, the assassin took hold of the hilt and pulled the blade out. With a bitter curse, he hurled the weapon—stained with his own blood—away from him. Then he let his head sink into his hands.

It took only a moment for the initial shock to wear off, for Haplo to understand what had happened. He said one word.

"Alfred."

Hugh the Hand looked up. His face was ravaged, haggard; the dark eyes burned. "I was dead, wasn't I?"

Wordlessly Haplo nodded.

Hugh's hands clenched; fingernails dug into flesh. "I . . . couldn't leave. I'm trapped. Not here. Not there. Will it be like this always? Tell me! Will it?"

He sprang to his feet. He was nearly raving. "Must I know death's pain and never its release? Help me! You have to help me!"

"I will," Haplo said softly. "I can."

Hugh halted, regarded Haplo with suspicion. His hand went to his breast, tore open the bloodstained shirt. "You can do something about *this*? Can you get rid of it?"

Haplo saw the sigil, shook his head. "A Sartan rune. No, I can't. But I can help you find the one who can. Alfred put it there. He's the only one who can free you. I can take you to him, if you have the courage. He's imprisoned in—"

"Courage!" Hugh gave a roaring laugh. "Courage! Why do I need courage? I can't die!" His eyes rolled in his head. "I don't fear death! It's life I'm scared of! It's all backward, isn't it? All backward."

He laughed and kept laughing. Haplo heard a high, thin note, of hysteria, of madness. Not surprising, after what the human had endured, but he couldn't be permitted to indulge in it.

Haplo caught hold of Hugh's wrists. The assassin, scarcely knowing what he was doing, struggled violently to free himself.

Haplo held him fast. Blue light shone from the runes on Haplo's hands and arms, spread its soothing glow to Hugh the Hand. The light wrapped itself around him, twined up his body.

The Hand sucked in his breath, stared at the light in awe. Then his eyes closed. Two tears squeezed out from beneath his lids, trailed down his cheeks. He relaxed in Haplo's hold.

Haplo held him, drew him into the circle of his being. He gave his strength to Hugh, took Hugh's torment into himself.

Mind flowed into mind; memories became tangled, shared. Haplo flinched and cried out in agony. It was Hugh the Hand, his potential killer, who supported him. The two men stood, locked in an embrace that was of spirit, mind, and body.

Gradually the blue light faded. Each man's being returned to its own sanctuary. Hugh the Hand grew calm. Haplo's pain eased.

The Hand lifted his head. His face was pale, glistening with sweat. But the dark eyes were calm. "You know," he said.

Haplo drew a shivering breath and nodded, unable to speak.

The assassin stumbled backward, sat down on a low bench. The dog's tail stuck out from underneath. Hugh's resurrection had apparently been too much for it.

Haplo called to the animal. "Come on, boy. It's all right. You can come out now."

The tail brushed once across the deck, disappeared.

Haplo grinned and shook his head. "All right, stay there. Let this be a lesson about purloining sausages."

Glancing out the porthole, Haplo saw several of the dwarves, blinking in the sunlight, looking curiously in the ship's direction. A few were even pointing and beginning to wander toward the ship. The sooner they left Arianus, the better.

Haplo put his hands on the steering mechanism, began speaking the runes, to make certain that all were unbroken, that the magic was ready to take them back through Death's Gate.

The first sigil on the steering stone caught fire. The flames spread to the second, and so on. Soon the ship would be airborne.

"What's happening?" Hugh the Hand asked, staring suspiciously at the glowing runes.

"We're getting ready to leave. We're going to Abarrach," said Haplo. "I have to report to my lord . . ." He paused.

*Xar wants you dead.*

No! Impossible. It was Bane who wanted him dead.

"Then we'll go find Alf—" Haplo began, but never finished.

Everything that was three-dimensional suddenly went flat, as if all juice and pulp and bone and fiber were sucked out of every object aboard the ship. Without dimension, brittle as a dying leaf, Haplo felt himself pressed back against time, unable to move, unable to so much as draw breath.

Sigla flared in the center of the ship. A hole burned through time, broadened, expanded. A figure stepped through the hole: a woman, tall, sinewy. Chestnut hair, tipped with white, flowed around her shoulders and down her back. Long bangs feathered over her forehead, casting her eyes in shadow. She was dressed in the clothes of the Labyrinth—leather pants, boots, leather vest, blouse with loose sleeves. Her feet touched the deck, and time and life surged back into all things.

Surged back into Haplo.

He stared in wonder. "Marit!"

"Haplo?" she asked, her voice low and clear.

"Yes, it's me! Why are you here? How?" Haplo stammered in amazement.

Marit smiled at him. She walked toward him, held out her hand to him. "Xar wants you, Haplo. He has asked me to bring you back to Abarrach."

Haplo reached out his hand to her . . .

# CHAPTER ♦ 18

## WOMBE, DREVLIN

## ARIANUS

♦

"Look out!" Hugh the Hand shouted. Jumping to his feet, he leapt at Marit, caught hold of her wrist.

Blue fire crackled. The sigla on Marit's arms flared. The Hand was flung backward by the shock. He hit the wall, slid down to the floor, clutching his tingling arm.

"What the—" Haplo was staring from one to the other.

The assassin's fingers touched cold iron: his knife, lying on the floor beside him. The numbing shock that had sent his muscles into painful spasms disappeared. Hugh's fingers closed over the hilt.

"Beneath her sleeve!" he shouted. "A throwing dagger."

Haplo stared in disbelief, unable to react.

Marit drew forth the dagger that she wore in a sheath on her arm and flung it all in the same smooth motion.

Had she caught Haplo unaware, her attack would have felled him. His defensive magic would not react to protect him from a fellow Patryn. Particularly not from her.

But even before Hugh's warning, Haplo had experienced a glimmer of distrust, unease.

*Xar wants you,* she had said to him.

And in his mind, Haplo heard the echo of Hugh's words.

*Xar wants you dead.*

Haplo ducked. The dagger fell harmlessly over his head, chest, bounced off, fell to the floor with a clatter.

Marit lunged for her fallen weapon. The dog shot out from underneath the bench, intent on putting its body between its master and danger. Marit tripped over the animal, crashed into Haplo. He lost his balance. Reaching out to save himself from falling, he caught hold of the steering stone.

Hugh the Hand raised the knife, intending to defend Haplo.

The Cursed Blade had other plans. Wrought ages ago, designed specifically by the Sartan to fight their most feared enemies,[1] the knife recognized that it had two Patryns to destroy, not just one. What Hugh the Hand wanted counted for nothing. He had no control over the blade; rather, it used him. That was how the Sartan, with their disdain for mensch, had designed it. The blade needed a warm body, needed that body's energy, nothing more.

The blade became a live thing in Hugh's hand. It squirmed and writhed and began to grow. Appalled, he dropped it, but the blade didn't mind. It no longer had any need of him. Taking the form of a gigantic black-winged bat, the knife flew at Marit.

Haplo felt the runes of the steering stone beneath his hand. Marit had recovered her dagger. She lunged to stab him. His defensive magic, which would have reacted instantly to protect him from an attack by a mensch or a Sartan, was unable to respond to danger from a fellow Patryn. The sigla on his skin remained pale, would not shield him.

Haplo flung up one arm to fend off Marit's attack, attempted to activate the steering stone's magic with the other. Blue and red light flared. The ship soared upward.

"Death's Gate!" Haplo managed to gasp.

The sudden motion of the ship threw Marit off balance, caused her to miss. The knife slashed across Haplo's forearm, leaving a streak of glistening red blood. But he was lying on the deck in an awkward and vulnerable position.

Marit regained her balance swiftly. With the skilled, single-minded purpose of a well-trained fighter, she ignored the ship's erratic motion and went after Haplo again.

He was staring not at her but past her.

"Marit!" he yelled. "Look out!"

She was not about to fall for a trick she had learned to avoid as

---

[1] See Appendix I, *The Accurséd Blade.*

a child. She was more worried about the wretched dog, which was in her way. Marit stabbed at the dog. Something large, with scratching claws, struck her from behind.

Tiny, sharp teeth whose bite was like searing flame sank into the flesh at the base of her skull, above the protective tattoos. Wings flapped against the back of her head. Marit knew her attacker— a bloodsucker. The pain of its bite was excruciating; worse, the creature's teeth were venomous, injecting a paralyzing poison into its victim to bring her down. Within moments she would be unable to move, helpless to stop the bat from draining her life's blood.

Fighting down panic, Marit dropped the knife. Reaching behind her, she grabbed hold of the furry body. The bat had dug its claws deep into her flesh. Its teeth were nipping and slashing, hunting for a large vein. The poison burned through Marit, making her sick and dizzy.

"Break its hold!" Haplo was shouting. "Quick!"

He was trying to help her, but the lurching of the ship made it difficult for him to reach her.

Marit knew what she had to do. Gritting her teeth, she gripped the flapping bat in her hands and yanked on it as hard as she could. The claws tore her flesh out with them; the bat squealed and bit her hands. Every bite shot another dose of poison into her.

She flung the bat away, hurling it with her remaining strength into the wall. She slumped to her knees. Haplo dashed past her; the dog bounded over her. Marit felt her dagger beneath her palm. Her fingers closed on it. She slid it up the sleeve of her blouse. Keeping her head down, she waited for the sickness to pass, waited for her strength to return.

Behind her she heard a snarling and thumping, and then Haplo's voice.

"Hugh, stop that damn knife!"

"I can't!"

The sunlight that had been shining through the porthole was gone. Marit looked up. Arianus had been replaced by a dazzling display of swiftly altering images. A world of green jungle, a world of blue water, a world of red fire, a world of twilight, a world of terrible darkness, and a bright white light.

The thumping ceased. She heard the heavy, labored breathing of the two men, the dog panting.

The images repeated themselves, swirls of color to her dazed mind: green, blue, red, pearl gray, dark, light. Marit knew how Death's Gate worked. She focused on the green.

"Pryan," she whispered. "Take me to Xar!"

The ship altered course immediately.

Haplo was staring blankly at the dog. The dog was staring at the deck. Growling, wondering where its prey had gone, the animal began pawing at the rune-covered wooden hull of the ship, thinking perhaps that the bat had somehow managed to crawl into a crack.

Haplo knew better. He looked around.

Hugh the Hand was holding the weapon—a crude iron knife. Pale and shaken, he dropped it. "I never did trust magic. You got any idea how the damn blade works?"

"Not much," Haplo said. "Don't use it again."

The Hand shook his head. "If we were on solid ground, I'd bury the cursed thing." He looked out the window, his expression dark. "Where are we?"

"Death's Gate," said Haplo, preoccupied. He knelt down beside Marit. "How are you?"

She was shivering hard, almost convulsively.

Haplo took hold of her hands.

Angrily Marit snatched them away, pulled back from him. "Leave me alone!"

"You've got a fever. I can help . . ." he began, and started to brush aside the feathery chestnut bangs that she wore low over her forehead.

She hesitated. Something inside her wanted him to know the truth, knew it would hurt him worse than the knife's blade. But Xar had warned her not to reveal this secret power she possessed, this link to him.

Marit shoved Haplo's hand aside. "Traitor! Don't touch me!"

Haplo lowered his hand. "I'm not a traitor."

Marit eyed him with a grim smile. "Our lord knows about Bane. The dragon-snake told him."

"Dragon-snake!" Haplo's eyes flashed. "What dragon-snake? One who calls himself Sang-drax?"

"What does it matter what the creature calls himself? The dragon-snake told our lord about the Kicksey-winsey and Arianus. How you brought peace when you were ordered to bring war. And all for your own glory."

"No." Haplo's voice grated. "He lies."

Marit made an impatient negating motion with her hand. "I heard what the mensch said for myself. Back there on Arianus. I heard your mensch friends talking." Her lip curled. She cast a scornful glance back at Hugh the Hand. "Mensch friends armed with Sartan weapons—made by our enemy for our destruction! Weapons you undoubtedly intend to use on your own kind!"

The dog whined, started to creep over to Haplo.

Hugh the Hand whistled, spoke gruffly, "Here, boy. Come to me."

The dog gazed woefully at its master. Haplo appeared to have forgotten its existence. Ears drooping, tail hanging limp, the dog wandered over to Hugh and flopped down at his side.

"You betrayed our lord, Haplo," Marit continued. "Your betrayal hurt him deeply. That was why he sent me."

"But I didn't betray him, Marit! I haven't betrayed our people. Everything I've done has been for them, for their own good. The dragon-snakes are the true betrayers—"

"Haplo," the Hand called warningly, casting a significant look out the porthole. "We've changed course, seemingly."

Haplo barely glanced out. "This is Pryan." He eyed Marit. "You brought us here. Why?"

She was rising shakily to her feet. "Xar ordered me to bring you here. He wants to question you."

"He can't very well do that if I'm dead, can he?" Haplo paused, remembering Abarrach. "On second thought, I guess he can. So our lord has learned the forbidden *Sartan* art of necromancy."

Marit chose to ignore the emphasis. "Will you come to him peacefully, Haplo? Surrender yourself to his judgment? Or must I kill you?"

Haplo stared out the window at Pryan—a hollow stone ball, its suns shining in the center. Basking in eternal daylight, the plant life on Pryan grew so thickly that vast mensch cities were built in the limbs of gigantic trees. Mensch ships sailed oceans floating on broad moss plains far above the ground.

Haplo looked at Pryan, but he wasn't seeing it. He was seeing Xar.

How easy it would be. Fall on my knees before Xar, bow my head, accept my fate. Quit the fight. Quit the struggle.

If I don't, I'll have to kill her.

He knew Marit, knew how she thought. Once the two of them had thought alike. She honored Xar. Haplo did, too. How could he not? Xar had saved his life, saved the lives of all their people, led them forth from that heinous prison.

But Xar was wrong. Just as Haplo had been wrong.

"*You* were the one who was right, Marit," he told her. "I couldn't understand then. Now I do."

Not following his thoughts, she eyed him with suspicion.

" 'The evil is in us,' you said. *We* are the ones who give the Labyrinth strength. It feeds off our hatred, our fear. It grows fat on our fear," he said with a bitter smile, recalling Sang-drax's words.

"I don't know what you're talking about," Marit said disdainfully. She was feeling better, stronger. The poison was abating, her own magic acting to dilute it. "I said lots of things I didn't mean then. I was young."

Mentally, silently, she spoke to Xar. *I am on Pryan, Husband. I have Haplo. No, he is not dead. Guide me to the meeting place.*

She rested her hand on the steering stone. Runes flared. The ship had been drifting aimlessly; now it began to fly swiftly through the green-tinged sky. Her lord's voice flowed inside her, drew her to him.

"What is your decision?" Course set, Marit let go the stone. She pulled her dagger from her sleeve, held it firmly, steadily.

Behind her the dog growled low in its throat. Hugh the Hand quieted the animal, petting it gently. He watched intently; his own fate—bound up in Haplo, who would lead him to Alfred—was at stake. Marit kept the human in her line of vision, but she was paying scant attention to him. She discounted him as a threat, as she would discount any mensch.

"Xar's made a terrible mistake, Marit," Haplo told her quietly. "The dragon-snakes are his true enemy. *They're* the ones who will betray him."

"They are his allies!"

"They *pretend* to be his allies. They will give Xar what he seeks. They'll crown him ruler of the four worlds, bow down to him. Then they'll devour him. And our people will be destroyed as surely as were the Sartan.

"Look at us," he continued. "Look what they've done to us. Since when, in the history of our people, have two Patryns fought each other?"

"Since one of them betrayed his people," she returned scornfully. "You are now more Sartan than Patryn. So my lord says."

Haplo sighed. He called the dog to his side. The animal, ears alert, tail wagging happily, trotted over. Haplo scratched its head. "If it were just me, Marit, I'd give up. I'd go with you. I'd die at my lord's hands. But I'm not alone. There's our child. You did bear my child, didn't you?"

"I bore her. Alone. In a Squatter's hut." Her voice was hard, sharp as the blade in her hand.

Haplo was silent, then asked, "A girl-child?"

"Yes. And if you're thinking to soften me, it won't work. I learned well the one lesson *you* taught me, Haplo. Caring about something in the Labyrinth brings only pain. I gave her a name, tattooed the heart-rune on her chest, and then I left her."

"What did you name her?"

"Rue."

Haplo flinched. He was pale; his fingers curled, dug into the dog's flesh.

The animal yelped, gave him a reproachful glance.

"Sorry," he muttered.

The ship had descended, was skimming over the tops of the trees, moving at an incredible speed, far faster than when Haplo had first visited this world.

Xar's magic, drawing them to him.

Below, the jungle was a dizzying green blur. A flash of blue, briefly seen and then gone, was an ocean. The ship was dropping lower and lower. In the distance Haplo could see the sparkling beauty of a white city: one of the Sartan citadels. Probably the one he himself had discovered.

It would be logical for Xar to visit the citadel; he had Haplo's account to guide him.

What does Xar expect my corpse to tell him? Haplo wondered suddenly. Obviously he suspects me of having hidden knowledge. Something I've kept from him. But what? I've told him everything . . . almost . . . And what's left isn't important to anyone but me.

"Well?" Marit demanded impatiently. "Have you made your decision?"

The spires of the citadel loomed above them. The ship was flying over the wall, descending into an open courtyard. Two mensch standing beneath were staring up at them in open-mouthed astonishment. Haplo could not see Xar, but the lord must be somewhere nearby.

If I'm going to make my move, it has to be now.

"I won't go back, Marit," Haplo said. "And I won't fight you. It's what Sang-drax wants us to do." His gaze shifted from the porthole, slid with deliberate slowness around the ship, flicked over Hugh the Hand, returned to Marit.

Haplo wondered how much the human had understood of what had passed. Haplo had spoken in human for the assassin's benefit, but Marit had been using the Patryn language.

Well, if he didn't understand before, he would now.

"I guess you'll have to kill me," said Haplo.

Hugh the Hand dove for the knife—not the Cursed Blade, but Haplo's knife, stained with the human's own blood, which lay on the deck. He intended to distract the woman; he knew he didn't stand a chance of stopping Marit.

She heard him, whirled, stretched out her hand. The sigla on her skin flashed. Runes danced in the air, spun themselves into a flaring rope of fire that wrapped around the human. Hugh screamed in agony and crashed to the deck, the blue and red runes twining around him.

Haplo took advantage of the diversion to grasp the steering stone. He spoke the runes, willed the ship to leave.

Resistance. Xar's magic held them fast.

The dog gave a warning bark. Haplo turned. Marit had dropped the knife. She was going to use her magic to kill him. Sigla on the backs of her hands began to gleam.

The Cursed Blade came to life.

# CHAPTER ♦ 19

# THE CITADEL

# PRYAN

♦

THE CURSED BLADE ALTERED FORM; A TYTAN—ONE OF THE TERRIFYING, MURDER-ous giants of Pryan—stood over them.

The tytan's huge hands were clenched to fists as big around as boulders. Its blind face contorted in rage; it lashed out brutally at creatures it sensed rather than saw.

Marit heard the thing roaring above her, saw on Haplo's face a look of fear and astonishment that was certainly not feigned. Her magic changed swiftly from an offensive attack to a defensive shield.

Haplo plummeted into her, dragged her with him to the deck. The giant's fist swung harmlessly over them. Marit struggled to regain her feet, her mind still concentrating on killing Haplo. She didn't fear the monster until she suddenly realized that her defensive shield-magic was beginning to crumble.

Haplo saw her runes starting to fade, saw her look of astonishment.

"The tytans know Sartan magic!" he shouted to her above the giant's roar.

Haplo himself couldn't believe what was happening, and his confusion hindered his ability to respond. Either the ship had expanded to accommodate the giant, or the giant had shrunk to fit inside the ship.

Hugh the Hand, freed of Marit's spell, lay groaning near one of the bulkheads. The sound attracted the tytan's notice. It turned, raised its enormous foot over the prostrate man, prepared to stamp him to death. Then, unaccountably, the tytan lowered its foot, left him alone. The giant shifted its attention back to the Patryns.

The Sartan blade, Haplo realized. It's not a real tytan at all, but a creation of the blade. It won't hurt its master.

But the Hand was barely conscious; there was no hope now of his controlling the blade, if he ever could—something Haplo was beginning to doubt.

Death's Gate. Perhaps it had been only coincidence, but the bat had disappeared; the blade's magic had failed when they entered Death's Gate.

"Dog, attack!" Haplo cried.

The dog darted around behind the giant, nipped at the tytan's heel. The dog's bite must have seemed less than a beesting to the giant, but apparently hurt it enough to distract it. The tytan swung around, stamping in rage. The dog nimbly sprang to one side, dove in again, sinking its teeth into the other heel.

Haplo cast a defensive spell. Blue sigla flared around him, looking like an eggshell and just as fragile. He turned to Marit, who was crouched on the deck, staring up at the giant. Her sigla were fading. She was muttering the rune-language, apparently about to cast another spell.

"You can't stop it!" Haplo grabbed hold of her. "Not by yourself. We've got to create the circle."

She shoved him aside.

The tytan kicked the dog, sent the animal flying across the deck. Its body crashed into a wall, quivered, and lay still. The tytan's eyeless head turned this way and that, sniffing out its prey.

"Create the circle!" Haplo yelled at her savagely. "It's our only chance. The thing is a Sartan weapon. It means to kill us both!"

The giant's fist hammered down on Haplo's magic shield. The sigla started to crack, began to fade. Marit stared at it. Perhaps she was beginning to understand. Or perhaps the instinct for survival, honed in the Labyrinth, goaded her to action. She reached out, grasped hold of Haplo's hands. He held fast to hers. They spoke the runes swiftly together.

Combined, both their magicks strengthened; they formed a shield stronger than the strongest steel. The tytan's fist slammed down on the glowing rune-structure. The sigla wavered but held fast. Haplo saw a tiny break in it, however. The shield wouldn't last long.

"How do we fight it?" Marit demanded, begrudging his help but aware of the necessity.

"We don't," he said grimly. "We can't. We've got to get out of here. Listen to me: the bat that attacked you vanished when we entered Death's Gate. The gate's magic must somehow disrupt the blade's magic."

The tytan, in a frustrated rage, rained blow after blow down on the glowing shield, kicking at it with its feet, drumming on it with its hands. The cracks widened.

"I'll hold it off!" Haplo yelled above the tytan's roars. "You take us back to Death's Gate!"

"This is a trick," she cried, glaring at him, hating him. "You're only trying to escape your fate. I can fight this thing."

She broke loose of Haplo's grasp. The shield around them burst into flame, engulfing the tytan's hands. It shrieked in pain, snatched it hands back out of the blaze. Sucking in a huge breath, it blew on the fire, and suddenly the flames were engulfing Marit.

She screamed. Her rune-magic acted to protect her, but the sigla on her skin were starting to wither in the heat.

Swiftly Haplo formed his own runes into a huge spear, cast it at the tytan. The spear slammed into the giant's chest. The point penetrated flesh and muscle. The tytan was wounded, though not seriously, and in pain. The flames around Marit died.

Haplo caught hold of her, dragged her to where the steering stone rested. Outside the window, he could see two mensch—an elf and a human—waving their arms and dashing frantically around the ship, as if searching for a way in. He paid them scant attention. He placed his hands on the stone and spoke the runes.

Blinding light flared. The sigla on the ship's walls glowed with dazzling brilliance. The mensch outside the window vanished, as did the citadel and the jungle around it.

They were in Death's Gate. The tytan was gone.

Colors flashed and swirled: blue water, red fire, green jungle, gray storm, darkness, light. Faster and faster the images spun. Haplo was caught in a whirlwind of color. He tried to fix on a single image, but they all swept past him too rapidly. He could see nothing except the colors. He lost sight of Marit, of Hugh, of the dog.

Lost sight of everything except the Sartan blade.

It lay on the deck, a quivering, malevolent force. Once again it was an iron knife. Once again they'd defeated it. But they were nearly finished and the blade's magic was powerful. It had lasted through centuries, perhaps. Survived its makers. How could he destroy it?

The colors—the choices—swirled around him. Blue.

One force existed which might destroy the knife. Unfortunately, it might destroy all of them.

Haplo shut his eyes against the colors and chose blue.

His ship left Death's Gate and slammed into a wall of water.

The blur of colors disappeared. Haplo could see the ship's interior again and, outside the window, the peaceful aqua sea that was the world of Chelestra.

"Where the hell are we now?" Hugh the Hand demanded. He was conscious again, staring in bewilderment out the porthole.

"The fourth world."

Haplo could hear ominous sounds in his ship. A groan from somewhere in the hold, strange whispering sighs, as if the ship were lamenting its fate.

Marit heard them, too. She tensed, looked around in alarm. "What is that?"

"The ship is breaking apart," Haplo answered grimly. His eyes were on the knife. Its runes glowed faintly.

"Breaking apart?" Marit gasped. "That's not possible. Not with the rune-magic to protect it. You're . . . you're lying."

"Fine, I'm lying." Haplo was too tired, too badly hurt, too preoccupied to argue. Keeping a wary gaze on the knife, he cast a glance around at the steering stone. It stood on a wooden pedestal well above the deck. Still, when the ship began to break up that wouldn't matter.

"Give me your vest," Haplo told Marit.

"What?"

"The vest! Your leather vest!" He glared at her. "Damn it, I don't have time to explain! Just give it to me!"

She was suspicious. But the creakings were growing louder; the dismal sighs had given way to sharp cracks. Taking off the leather vest, which was covered with protective runes, Marit flung it at Haplo. He tossed it over the steering stone.

The runes on the Cursed Blade glowed an ugly green. The dog, apparently unhurt and now morbidly curious, crept near, sniffed at the knife. The animal leapt back suddenly, hackles rising.

Haplo looked up at the ceiling. He recalled the last time he'd landed on Chelestra—his ship breaking apart, the rune-magic failing, the water starting to seep through the cracks. Then he'd been amazed, raging, afraid. Now he prayed for a drop.

There it was! A tiny trickle of sea water, running down one of the bulkheads.

"Hugh!" Haplo shouted. "Grab the knife! Put it in the water!"

Hugh the Hand didn't respond. He didn't move. He was crouched against the hull of the ship, holding on to it for dear life, staring with gaping mouth and frantic eyes at the water.

The water. Haplo cursed himself for a fool. The human came from a world where people fought over water; a bucket of the precious liquid was wealth. He had undoubtedly never in his entire life seen this much water. And he certainly hadn't seen it as a terrifying fist closing over the ship, slowly crushing its wooden shell.

Perhaps there was no word in the mensch language on Arianus for drowning, but Hugh the Hand didn't need a word. He could picture such a death vividly. Haplo understood; he'd gone through this himself.

The choking, the smothering, the bursting lungs. Useless to try to explain to Hugh the Hand that he could breathe the water as easily as he could breathe air. Useless to explain to him that if they acted quickly they could leave before the ship broke apart. Useless to remind him he couldn't die. At this juncture, that might not appear to be much of a blessing.

A drop of water, falling from one of the slowly widening cracks in the wooden hull, fell on Hugh's face. He shuddered all over, gave a hollow cry.

Haplo lurched across the deck. Grabbing hold of the assassin, the Patryn dug his nails into Hugh's arm. "The blade! Grab it!"

The knife flew from the deck, sprang into Hugh's hand. It had not altered form, but its greenish glow intensified. Hugh the Hand stared at it as if he'd never seen it before.

Haplo backed swiftly away.

"Hugh!" The Patryn tried desperately to break through the man's terror. "Put the knife in the water!"

A yell from Marit stopped him.

She was pointing out the porthole, her face pale and horrified. "What . . . what is it?"

Foul ooze, like blood, stained the water. The beautiful aqua was dark now, and hideous. Two red-green glowing eyes peered in at them, eyes that were bigger than the ship. A toothless mouth gaped in silent, mocking laughter.

"The dragon-snakes . . . in their true form," Haplo answered.

The knife. That's why the Cursed Blade hadn't changed form. It didn't need to change. It was drawing on the greatest source of evil in the four worlds.

Marit couldn't look away. Slowly she shook her head. "No," she said thickly. "I don't believe . . . Xar would not permit it . . ." She stopped, whispered almost to herself, "The red eyes . . ."

Haplo didn't answer. He waited tensely for the dragon-snake to attack, to batter the ship to pieces, seize them and devour them.

But the dragon-snake didn't, and then Haplo realized it wouldn't. *I grow fat on your fear,* Sang-drax had said to him. There was enough fear and hatred and mistrust on board this ship to feed a legion of dragon-snakes. And with the ship breaking apart slowly, the dragon-snake had only to wait for its victims' magic to diminish and die, wait for them to feel the full extent of their helplessness. Their terror would only increase.

Another snapping crack, a series of cracks from farther back in the ship. Water dripped on Haplo's hand. The sigla, which had flared blue and red at the appearance of the dragon-snake, began to dim; their light—his magic—was growing faint.

Soon his magic would break apart, as his ship was breaking apart.

Revulsion twisting inside him, Haplo reached out and snatched the Cursed Blade from Hugh's unresisting grasp.

The pain was worse, far worse than if he'd taken hold of a red-hot poker. His instinct was to drop it. He gritted his teeth against the pain, held on. The burning iron seared his skin, melted into it, seemed to flow from his hand into his very veins.

The blade came to life, twisted and wrapped around his hand, burrowed insidiously into his flesh. It devoured his bone. It was beginning to devour him.

Reeling, in a blind and frantic effort to free himself of the pain, he stumbled to his knees, thrust his hand into a pool of water forming on the deck.

The Cursed Blade went instantly dark and cold.

Shivering, clutching his wounded hand, afraid of looking at it, Haplo crouched on his knees, doubled over, sick and retching.

A blow hit the ship. A timber above the human snapped, caved in. Hugh the Hand gave a great bellow. Water poured down on top of him, on both of them. Haplo was drenched. His magic was gone.

The dog barked warningly. A red glow lit the interior of the cabin.

Haplo looked outside the window. The Cursed Blade was dead, apparently, but the dragon-snake had not vanished as had the tytan and the bat. The knife had summoned it, and now it would not be dismissed. But the dragon-snake saw that the ship was now breaking apart; those inside had a chance to escape. The snake couldn't afford to wait. Its tail struck the ship again.

"Marit," Haplo whispered. His throat was raw; he couldn't talk.

She was far from where the water was pouring in, and since the ship was listing in the opposite direction, she was still relatively dry.

"The steering stone!" He knew she couldn't hear him; the words had come out a croak. He tried again. "The stone! Use it . . ."

She either heard or seized on the same idea herself. She could see at a glance the effect the water was having on her own magic, and now she understood why Haplo had covered the steering stone with the leather vest.

The dragon-snake's eyes glowed hideously. It read her thoughts, understood her intent. Its toothless maw opened.

Marit cast one frightened glance at it, then resolutely ignored it. She snatched the leather vest off the stone. Crouching over it, protecting the magic from the dripping water with her body, she wrapped her hands around it.

The dragon-snake struck. The ship seemed to Haplo to explode. Water swept him away; he was sinking beneath it.

Then strong arms caught him, held him. A voice spoke to him, soothed him.

All pain vanished. He rested, drifting on the water's surface, at peace with himself.

The voice called again.

He opened his eyes, looked up and saw . . .

Alfred.

# CHAPTER ✦ 20

# THE CITADEL

# PRYAN

✦

"No! don't leave us! take us with you! take us with you!"

"Oh, stop it, Roland, for Orn's sake," the elf snapped testily. "They're gone."

The human glowered at his companion and, more for the sake of defiance than because he thought he might accomplish anything constructive, he continued to wave his arms and shout at the strange ship, which was no longer even in sight.

At length, feeling a fool and growing tired of waving his arms above his head, Roland left off shouting and turned around to take his frustration out on the elf.

"It's your fault we lost them, Quindiniar!"

"Mine?" Paithan gaped.

"Yes, yours. If you'd let me talk to them when they first landed, I could have made contact. But you thought you saw a tytan inside! Hah! One of those monsters couldn't get its little toe into that ship," Roland scoffed.

"I saw what I saw," returned Paithan sullenly. "And you couldn't have talked to them anyway. The ship was all covered with those weird pictures, like that Haplo's ship, when he was here. You remember him?"

"Our savior? I remember. Brought us here to this blasted citadel. Him and the old man.[1] I'd like to have both of them in front of

---

[1] Haplo was tricked by the wizard Zifnab into transporting the human siblings Roland and Rega and the elven siblings Paithan and Aleatha and the dwarf

me right now." Roland swung a clenched fist, which, quite by accident, smacked Paithan in the shoulder.

"Oh, sorry," Roland muttered.

"You did that on purpose!" Paithan nursed his bruised arm.

"Bosh. You got in my way. You're always getting in my way."

"*Me* getting in *your* way! *You're* the one who keeps following me around! We divided this city into two halves. If you'd stay in your half, as we agreed, I wouldn't get in your way."

"You'd like that!" Roland jeered. "Rega and I stay on our side and starve to death while you and your bitch of a sister grow fat—"

"Fat! Fat!" Paithan had switched to elven, as he often did when exasperated—and he seemed to be speaking a lot more elven these days. "Where do you think *we're* getting food?"

"I don't know, but you spend a lot of time in that fool Star Chamber or whatever you call it." Roland was deliberately and irritably speaking human.

"Yes, I'm growing food there. In the darkness. Aleatha and I are living on mushrooms. And don't call my sister names."

"I wouldn't put it past you. Either of you. And I'll call her exactly what she is—a scheming little bit—"

"Scheming little what?" came a throaty, sleepy voice from the shadows.

Roland choked, coughed, glowered in the voice's general direction.

"Oh, hello, Thea," Paithan greeted his sister without enthusiasm. "I didn't know you were here."

An elven woman stepped into Pryan's eternal sunlight. One might guess, from her languorous appearance, that she had just waked from a nap. By the look in her blue eyes, her sleep had been filled with sweet dreams. Her ashen blond hair was disheveled; her clothes appeared to have been thrown on hastily, were just the tiniest bit disarranged. The fabric and lace seemed to want some strong male hand to shift them into proper place—or to take them off and start over.

She stayed in the sunlight only a few moments, long enough to let it shine on her hair. Then she glided back into the shadows cast

Drugar to the Sartan citadel on Pryan. Their adventures are recorded in *Elven Star*, vol. 2 of *The Death Gate Cycle*.

by the high city wall surrounding the plaza. Bright light was damaging to her fair complexion and made wrinkles. Languidly she leaned against the wall and regarded Roland with an amusement which glittered sapphire blue from beneath long and sleepy eyelashes.

"What were you about to call me?" Aleatha asked again, eventually growing bored at hearing him stammer and sputter.

"You know well enough what you are," Roland managed to get out at last.

"No, I don't." Aleatha's eyes opened wide for just a fraction of a second, long enough to absorb him inside; then—as if the effort were too exhausting—she lowered the lashes again. Cast him out. "But why don't you meet me in the maze garden at winetime and tell me."

Roland muttered something to the effect that he'd meet her in hell first and—his face mottled—stalked off.

"You shouldn't tease him like that, Thea," said Paithan when Roland was out of earshot. "Humans are like savage dogs. Baiting only makes them—"

"More savage?" suggested Aleatha with a smile.

"*You* may find toying with him amusing, but it makes him damn difficult to live with," Paithan told his sister.

He began walking back through the human section of the city toward the main part of the citadel. Aleatha fell into slow step beside him.

"I wish you'd just leave him alone," Paithan added.

"But he's the only source of entertainment I have in this dreary place," Aleatha protested. She glanced at her brother; a slight frown marred the delicate beauty of her face. "What's the matter with you, Pait? You never used to scold me like this. I swear, you're getting more like Callie every day—a stringy old maid—"

"Stop it, Thea!" Paithan caught hold of her wrist, jerked her around to face him. "Don't you talk about her like that. Callie had her faults, but she held our family together. Now she's dead and father's dead and we're all going to die and—"

Aleatha snatched her hand away, used it to slap her brother across his face. "Don't say that!"

Paithan rubbed his stinging cheek, regarded his sister grimly. "Hit me as much as you like, Thea, it won't change things. We're going to run out of food eventually. When that happens—" He shrugged.

"We'll go out and find more," Aleatha said. Two spots of fevered color burned in her cheeks. "There's loads of food out there: plants, fruit—"

"Tytans," Paithan said dryly.

Gathering up her full skirts, which were admittedly growing a bit frayed at the hem, Aleatha flounced off, moving at a much more rapid pace than previously.

"They're gone," she said over her shoulder.

Paithan had difficulty keeping up with her. "That's what the last group said when they left. You know what happened to them."

"No, I don't," Aleatha retorted, walking quickly through the empty streets.

Paithan caught up. "Yes, you do. You heard the screams. We all heard them."

"A trick!" Aleatha tossed her head. "A trick to deceive us, trick us into staying in here. The others are probably out there feasting on . . . on all sorts of wonderful things and laughing at us . . ." Despite herself, her voice quavered. "Cook said there was a ship out there. She and her children found it and they flew away from this dreadful place . . ."

Paithan opened his mouth to argue, shut it again. Aleatha knew the truth. She knew well enough what had really happened that terrible night. She and Roland, Paithan and Rega and Drugar, the dwarf, had stood on the steps, watching anxiously as Cook and the others left the safety of the citadel and entered the distant jungle. It was the emptiness and the loneliness that drove them to risk leaving the safety of the citadel's walls. That and the constant quarreling, the arguing over dwindling food supplies. Dislike and distrust had strengthened into fear and abhorrence.

None of them had seen or heard signs of the tytans—the terrifying giants who roamed Pryan—for a long, long time. They all assumed—everyone except Paithan—that the creatures had left, roamed off. Paithan knew that the tytans were still there, knew because he'd been reading a book he'd found in a dusty old library in the citadel.

The book was handwritten in elven—a rather old-fashioned and outdated elven—and was illustrated with lots of pictures, one reason Paithan had chosen it. Other books in the library were written in elven, but they had more writing than pictures. He snored just looking at them.

Some type of godlike beings who called themselves "Sartan" were the ones who had—so they claimed—brought the elves and humans and dwarves to this world.

"Heretical nonsense," his sister Callie would have termed it.

The world of Pryan—world of fire—was one of four worlds, purportedly.

Paithan didn't believe that part, having found a diagram of the supposed "universe"—four balls hanging suspended in midair, as if some juggler had tossed them up and then walked off and left them.

"What kind of fools do they take us for?" he wondered.

A green and lush tropical world whose suns, located in the heart of the hollow planet, shone constantly, Pryan was—according to the book—intended to provide light and food to the other three worlds.

As for the light, Paithan readily conceded that he had more light than he knew what to do with. Food was a different matter. Admittedly the jungle was full of food, *if* he wanted to fight the tytans for it. And how was he supposed to send it to these other worlds anyway?

"Throw it at them, I guess," said Paithan, considerably tickled at the thought of flinging *pua* fruit into the universe. Really, these Sartan must think they were all idiots to believe a tale like this!

These Sartan had built this citadel. And, according to them, they had built a whole lot more citadels. Paithan found this idea intriguing. He could almost believe it. He'd seen their lights shining in the sky. According to the book, the Sartan had brought the elves, humans, and dwarves to live with them in the citadels.

Paithan believed that, too, mainly because he could see evidence with his own eyes of the fact that others like himself had once inhabited this city. There were buildings built the way elves liked them, with lots of gewgaws and curlicues and useless columns and arched windows. And there were buildings meant to house humans —solid and dull and square. And there were even tunnels down below, made for dwarves. Paithan knew because Drugar had taken him down there once, right after they had first entered the city, when the five of them had still been speaking to each other.

The citadel was very beautiful and practical, and the person who had written this book appeared to be baffled by the fact that it hadn't worked. Wars had started. The elves, humans, and dwarves (the writer called them "mensch") had refused to live in peace, had begun to fight each other.

Paithan, however, understood perfectly. There were only two elves, two humans, and one dwarf living in the city now, and these five couldn't get along. He could imagine what it must have been like back then—whenever "then" was.

The mensch (Paithan came to hate that word) populations had grown at an alarming rate. Unable to control the ever expanding numbers, the Sartan (may Orn shrivel their ears and any other part that seemed suitable) had created fearsome beings they called tytans, which were apparently supposed to act as nursemaids to the mensch and also work in the citadels.

The light beaming from the citadel's Star Chambers was so bright that any ordinary mortal who looked on it would be blinded, and so the tytans were created without eyes. To compensate for the handicap (and to control them better), the Sartan had provided the tytans with strong telepathic skills; the tytans could communicate by thought alone. The Sartan had also given the tytans very limited intelligence (such strong and powerful beings would be a threat if they were too smart) and had also endowed them with their rune-magic or something like that.

Paithan wasn't much on reading; he had tended to skim over the boring parts.

The plan had worked, apparently. The tytans roamed the streets, and the elves, humans, and dwarves were too intimidated by the monsters' presence to fight.

All well and good. But what had happened after that? Why did the mensch leave the cities and venture into the jungle? How did the tytans get loose? And where were these Sartan now and what did they intend to do about this mess?

Paithan didn't have the answers, because at that point the book ended.

The elf was miffed. He'd gotten interested in the story in spite of himself and wanted to know how it turned out. But the book didn't tell him. It looked as if it had intended to, since there were more pages bound into it, but these pages were blank.

He'd read enough, however, to know that the tytans had been created in the citadels, and so it seemed more than likely that they should be drawn to the citadels. Especially since the tytans kept asking everyone they met (before they bashed their brains out) questions such as "Where is the citadel?" Once the tytans found the citadel, they wouldn't be likely to leave it.

That's what he'd told the others.

"I'm staying right here, inside these walls. The tytans are still out there, hiding in the jungle, waiting for us. Mark my words," he'd said.

And he'd been right. Horribly right. He would sometimes wake up in a cold sweat, thinking he heard the screams of the dying out in the jungle, beyond the walls.

Paithan had refused to go with Cook and the others. And because he refused to go, Rega—Roland's sister and Paithan's lover—had refused to go. And because Rega had refused to go, Roland had decided to stay. Or perhaps it was because Aleatha—Paithan's sister—had refused to go that Roland had decided to stay. He *said* it was because of Rega, but his eyes kept darting to Aleatha as he spoke. No one was certain quite why Aleatha stayed, except that she was fond of her brother and it would have taken a great deal of effort to leave.

As for Drugar, the dwarf, he stayed because he was given to know that he wasn't welcome to join the party that was leaving. Not that he was particularly welcome among those who stayed behind, but they would never say as much to him aloud, since he was the one who had saved them all from being devoured by the dragon.[2] The dwarf did what he wanted anyway and kept his own counsel about it, rarely talking to any of them.

But apparently Drugar agreed with Paithan, because the dour dwarf had shown no desire to leave the citadel, and when the screaming began he had simply stroked his beard and nodded his head, as if he'd been expecting it.

Paithan thought about all this and sighed and put his arm around his sister's shoulders.

---

[2] Zifnab's dragon. See *Elven Star*, vol. 2 of *The Death Gate Cycle*.

"What were you and Roland doing together in the plaza anyway?" Aleatha asked, indicating by her change of subject that she was sorry she'd hit him. "You looked a couple of idiots when I saw you from the walls—jumping around and shouting at the sky."

"A ship came down," Paithan answered, "out of nowhere."

"A ship?" Her eyes opened wide; she forgot, in her astonishment, that she was wasting their beauty on a mere brother. "What kind of ship? Why didn't it stay? Oh, Paithan, maybe it will come back and fly us out of this horrible place!"

"Maybe," he said, not wanting to dampen her hopes and get his face slapped again. Privately he had his doubts. "As for why it didn't stay, well, Roland doesn't agree with me but I could swear that the people on board were fighting a tytan. I know it sounds crazy, the ship was small, but I saw what I saw. And I saw something else, too. I saw a man who looked like that Haplo."

"Oh, well, then, I'm glad he left," Aleatha said coldly. "I wouldn't have gone anywhere with him! He led us into this dreadful prison, pretending to be our savior. Then he left us. He was the cause of everything rotten that's happened to us. I wouldn't be surprised if he wasn't the one who brought the tytans down on us in the first place."

Paithan let his sister rant on. She had to have someone to blame and, thank Orn, this time it wasn't him.

But he couldn't help thinking that Haplo had been right. If the three races had allied to fight the tytans, maybe their people would be alive right now. As it was . . .

"Say, Thea." Paithan came out of his gloomy reverie as a thought struck him. "What were *you* doing down in the market plaza,[3] anyway? You never walk that far."

"I was bored. No one to talk to except that human slut. Speaking of Rega, she said to tell you that something funny was going on in that beloved Star Chamber of yours."

"Why didn't you say so?" Paithan glared at her. "And don't call Rega a slut!"

Breaking into a run, he dashed through the streets of the shin-

---

[3] Haplo's description of the citadel of Pryan, made on his first journey, places the market plaza right inside the city gates.

ing marble city, a city of spires and domes and wondrous beauty. A city that was likely to become their tomb.

Aleatha watched him go, wondering how he could expend all that energy on something as senseless as going into a gigantic room and fiddling with machines that never did anything and weren't ever likely to do anything. Nothing constructive—such as grow food.

Well, they weren't starving yet. Paithan had attempted to impose some sort of rationing system on them, but Roland had refused to accept it, stating that humans—being bigger—needed more food than elves and so it was unfair of Paithan to allot to Roland and Rega the same amount of food that he allotted to himself and Aleatha.

At which Drugar had spoken up—a rarity for him—and claimed that dwarves, because of their heavier body mass, needed twice as much food as either elves or humans.

At which Paithan had thrown up his hands and said he didn't care. They could gorge themselves. They'd only die that much sooner and he, for one, would be glad to be rid of them.

At which Rega had flown into a rage and said that no doubt he'd be thankful if she was the first one to die and she hoped she was because she couldn't go on living with a man who hated her brother.

At which they'd all stormed off and no one had ended up rationing anything.

Aleatha looked down the empty street and shivered in the bright sunlight. The marble walls were always cold. The sun did nothing to warm them, probably because of the strange darkness that flowed over the city every night. Having been raised in a world of perpetual light, Aleatha had come to enjoy the artificial night that fell on the citadel and nowhere else on Pryan. She liked to walk in the darkness, reveling in the mystery and velvet softness of the night air.

It was especially nice to walk in the darkness *with* someone. She glanced around. The shadows were deepening. The strange night would fall soon. She could either go back to the Star Chamber and be bored to tears watching Paithan dither over his stupid machine or she could go and see if Roland would really meet her at the garden maze.

Aleatha glanced at her reflection in a crystal window of a vacant house. She was somewhat thinner than she had been, but that didn't detract from her beauty. If anything, her narrow waistline only made her full breasts more voluptuous. Artfully she re-arranged her dress to best advantage, brushed her fingers through her thick hair.

Roland would be waiting for her. She knew it.

# CHAPTER ✦ 21

# THE CITADEL

# PRYAN

✦

THE GARDEN MAZE WAS AT THE BACK OF THE CITY, ON A GENTLE SLOPE THAT dipped down from the city proper to the protective wall that surrounded it. None of her companions particularly liked the maze; it had a strange feel to it, Paithan complained. But Aleatha felt drawn to the maze and often walked near it during winetime. If she had to be by herself (and it was getting more and more difficult to find company these days), this was where she liked to be.

"The garden maze was built by the Sartan," Paithan told her, having acquired the knowledge from one of the books he bragged about reading. "They made it for themselves because they were fond of being outdoors and it reminded them of wherever it was they came from. It was off-limits to us *mensch.*" His lip curled when he said the word. "I don't know why they bothered. I can't imagine any elf in his right mind who'd want to go in there. No offense, Thea, but what do you find so fascinating about that creepy place?"

"Oh, I don't know," she'd answered with a shrug. "Perhaps because it *is* kind of frightening. Everything—and everyone— around here is so boring."

According to Paithan, the maze—a series of hedges, trees, and bushes—had once been carefully clipped and maintained. The paths led, by various circuitous routes, to an amphitheater in the center. Here (away from the eyes and ears of the mensch) the Sartan had held secret meetings.

"I wouldn't go into it if I were you, Thea," Paithan had warned her. "According to the book, these Sartan laid some type of magic on the maze, meant to trap anyone who wasn't supposed to be there."

Aleatha found the warning thrilling, just as she found the maze fascinating.

Over the years, abandoned and left to itself, the garden maze had gone wild. Hedges that had once been neatly trimmed now soared high into the air, grew over the paths, forming green and tangled ceilings that shut out the light and kept the maze cool and dark even during the hot daylight hours. It was like venturing into a green tunnel of plant life, for something kept the paths themselves clear, perhaps the strange markings carved into the stone, marks that could be seen on the buildings in the city and on its walls. Marks that Paithan said were some type of magic.

A gate made of iron (a rarity on Pryan, where few people had ever seen the ground) led to an arch formed by a hedge over a stone pathway. Each stone on the path was marked with one of the magical symbols. Paithan had told her that the marks might hurt her, but Aleatha knew better. She'd paid no attention to them before finding out what they were. She'd walked on them many times. They hadn't hurt her feet a bit.

From the gate, the path led straight into the maze. High walls of vegetation soared overhead; flowers filled the air with sweet fragrance.

The path ran straight for a short distance, then forked, slanting off in two different directions, each leading deeper into the maze. The fork was the farthest Aleatha had ever ventured. Both paths took her out of sight of the gate, and Aleatha, though wild and reckless, was not without common sense.

At the fork were a marble bench and a pool. Here Aleatha sat in the cool shadows and listened to hidden birds singing, admiring her reflection and wondering idly what it would be like to wander deeper into the maze. Probably boring and not worth the effort, she'd decided after having seen a drawing of the maze in Paithan's book. She'd been dreadfully disappointed to learn that the paths led to nothing but a circle of stone surrounded by tiers of seats.

Walking down the empty street (so very empty!) that led to the maze, Aleatha smiled. Roland was there, pacing moodily back and forth, casting dark and dubious glances into the bushes.

Aleatha permitted her skirts to rustle loudly, and at the sound Roland straightened, shoved his hands into his pockets, and began to saunter about quite casually, regarding the hedge with interest, as if he had just arrived.

Aleatha smothered a laugh. She'd been thinking about him all day. Thinking how much she *didn't* like him. Thinking that she detested him, in fact. Thinking that he was boorish, and arrogant and . . . well . . . human. Recalling how much she hated him, it was only natural for her to think about the night they'd once made love. There had been extenuating circumstances, of course. Neither had been responsible. Both had been recovering from the terrible fright of being nearly eaten by a dragon. Roland had been hurt and she'd only been trying to comfort him . . .

And why did she have to keep remembering that night and his strong arms and soft lips and the way he'd loved her, a way in which no other man had ever dared to love her . . .

It wasn't until the next day she'd remembered he was human and had peremptorily ordered him never to touch her again. He apparently had been only too glad to obey—judging by what he'd said to her in response.

But she took a grim delight in teasing him—it was the only pleasure she had. And he seemed to take equal delight in irritating her.

Aleatha stepped out into the pathway. Roland, lounging against the hedge, glanced at her and smiled what she considered a nasty smile.

"Ah, I see you came," he said, implying that she had come because of him, robbing her of the line that had been on her lips—implying that he'd come because of her—and thereby making her instantly furious.

And when Aleatha was furious, she was simply sweeter and more charming than ever.

"Why, Roland," she said, with a very natural start of surprise. "Is that you?"

"And who the hell would it be? Lord Dumdum, perhaps?"

Aleatha flushed. Lord *Durndrun* had been her elven fiancé, and while she hadn't loved him and she'd been going to marry him only for his money, he was dead and this human had no right to make fun of him and . . . oh, never mind!

"I wasn't certain," she said, tossing her hair back over a bare shoulder (the sleeve of her dress didn't quite fit properly anymore because she'd lost weight, and it kept slipping down her arm, re-vealing a white shoulder of surpassing loveliness). "Who knows what slimy thing might have crawled up from Below?"

Roland's eyes were drawn to her shoulder. She permitted him to look and yearn (she trusted he was yearning), and then she slowly and caressingly covered her shoulder with a lacy shawl she'd found in an abandoned house.

"Well, if something slimy did crawl up out of nowhere, I'm certain you'd frighten it off." He took a step nearer her, glanced again pointedly at her shoulder. "You're turning all bony."

Bony! Aleatha glared at him, so angry she forgot to be charming. She bounded at him, her hand raised to strike.

He caught her wrist, twisted it, bent down and kissed her. Aleatha struggled exactly the right length of time—not too long (which might discourage him), but long enough to force him to tighten his hold on her. Then she relaxed in his arms.

His lips brushed over her neck. "I know this is going to disappoint you," he whispered, "but I only came to tell you I wasn't coming. Sorry." And with that, he let go of her.

Aleatha had been leaning her full weight on him. When he removed his hold, she tumbled onto her hands and knees. He grinned at her.

"Begging for me to stay? Won't do any good, I'm afraid." Turning, he sauntered off.

Enraged, Aleatha struggled to her feet, but her heavy skirts hampered her, and by the time she was upright and ready to claw his eyes out, Roland had rounded a corner of a building and was gone.

Aleatha paused, breathing heavily. To run after him now would look like just that—running after him. (If she *had* gone after him, she would have discovered him slumped against a wall, shivering and wiping sweat from his face.) Digging her nails into her palms, she stormed through the gate that led into the maze, flounced down the stones marked with Sartan runes, and threw herself on the marble bench.

Certain she was alone, hidden, where no one could see her if her eyes turned red and her nose swelled, she began to cry.

"Did he hurt you?" a gruff voice demanded.

Startled, Aleatha jerked her head up. "What—oh, Drugar." She sighed, at first relieved, then not so. The dwarf was strange, dour. Who knew what he was thinking? And he *had* tried to kill them all once . . .[1]

"No, of course not," she replied scornfully, drying her eyes and sniffing. "I'm not crying." She gave a light little laugh. "I had something in my eye. How . . . long have you been standing here?" she asked, airy, nonchalant.

The dwarf grunted. "Long enough." And what he meant by that, Aleatha hadn't a clue.

His name among the humans was Blackbeard, and he suited it. His beard was long and so thick and full that it was difficult to see his mouth. One rarely knew whether he was smiling or frowning. The glittering black eyes, shining out from beneath heavy, beetling brows, gave no hint of his thoughts or feelings.

Then Aleatha noticed that he had come from the inner part of the maze, the part into which she'd never dared venture. She was intrigued. Obviously no wicked magic had stopped him. She was about to ask him eagerly what he'd seen, how far he'd gone, when he disconcerted her by asking her a question first.

"You love him. He loves you. Why do you play these hurtful games?"

"I? Love him?" Aleatha gave a lilting laugh. "Don't be ridiculous, Drugar. Such a thing is impossible. He's a human, isn't he? And I'm an elf. You might as well ask a cat to love a dog."

"It is not impossible. I know," he answered.

His dark eyes met hers and then their gaze shifted away. He stared into the hedge, gloomy, silent.

Blessed Mother! Aleatha thought, her breath taken away. Though Roland might not love her (and she was quite convinced, at this moment, that he did not and never would), here was someone who did.

Except it was not love which had stared at her hungrily from those eyes. It was more. Almost adoration.

Had it been any other man—elf or human—Aleatha would have been amused, accepting his infatuation as her due, taking his

---

[1] Tytans wiped out Drugar's people. Blaming the humans and elves for abandoning the dwarves, Drugar swore vengeance on Roland, Rega, and Paithan. *Elven Star*, vol. 2 of *The Death Gate Cycle*.

love and hanging it up for show with the rest of her trophies. But her feeling at the moment was not triumph over another conquest. Her feeling was pity—deep and profound.

If Aleatha appeared heartless, it was only because her heart had been hurt so much that she had locked it up in a box and hidden the key. Everyone she had ever cared about had abandoned her—first her mother, then Callie, then her father. Even that fop Durndrun— who had been a sap, but rather a dear sap—had managed to get himself killed by the tytans.

And if she ever *had* been attracted to Roland (Aleatha was careful to put that in the past tense), it was only because he'd never seemed the least bit interested in finding the key to the box containing her heart. Which made the game safe, fun. Most of the time.

But this wasn't a game. Not with Drugar. He was lonely, as lonely as she was herself. Lonelier, for his people, everyone whom he had loved and cared for, were gone, destroyed by the tytans. He had nothing, nobody.

Pity was swallowed by shame. For the first time in her life, Aleatha was at a loss for words. She didn't have to tell him his love was hopeless—he knew that for himself. She didn't worry that he would become a nuisance. He would never mention it again. This time had been an accident—he'd spoken out of sympathy for her. From this moment forward, he'd be on his guard. She couldn't prevent him from being hurt.

The silence was becoming extremely uncomfortable. Aleatha lowered her head, her hair hanging around her face, hiding him from her sight, hiding her from his. She began to pick little holes in the lace shawl.

*Drugar,* she wanted to say. *I'm a horrible person. I'm not worthy. You haven't seen me. Not the real me. I'm ugly inside. Truly, truly ugly!*

"Drugar," she began, swallowing, "I'm a—"

"What's that?" he growled suddenly, turning his head.

"What's what?" she asked, leaping up from the bench. The blood rushed to her face. Her first thought was that Roland had sneaked back and had been spying on them. He would know . . . This would be intolerable . . .

"That sound," said Drugar, brow wrinkling. "Like someone humming. Don't you hear it?"

Aleatha did hear it. A humming noise, as the dwarf said. The humming wasn't unpleasant. In fact, it was sweet, soothing. It reminded her of her mother, singing a lullaby. Aleatha breathed a sigh. Whoever was humming, it certainly wasn't Roland. He had a voice like a cheese-grater.

"How curious," Aleatha said, smoothing her dress, dabbing at her eyes to make certain all traces of tears were gone. "I suppose we had better go see what's causing it."

"Ya," said Drugar, hooking his thumbs into his belt. He waited deferentially for her to precede him down the path, not presuming to walk beside her.

She was touched by his delicacy and, reaching the gate, she paused, turned to face him.

"Drugar," she said with a smile that was not the least flirtatious, but was a smile from one lonely person to another, "have you gone far inside the maze?"

"I have," he answered, lowering his eyes before hers.

"I'd love to go in there sometime myself. Would you take me? Just me. None of the others," she added hurriedly, seeing the frown lines appear.

He glanced up at her warily, perhaps thinking she was teasing. His face softened. "Ya, I'll take you," he said. An odd glint came into his eyes. "There's strange things to be seen in there."

"Truly?" She forgot the eerie humming. "What?"

But the dwarf only shook his head. "It will be the darktime," he said. "And you have no light. You will not be able to find your way back to the citadel. We must go now."

He held the gate open for her. Aleatha swept past him. Drugar shut the gate. Turning to her, he made a clumsy bow, rumbled something deep in his chest, something that was probably in dwarven, for she couldn't understand the words. But they sounded rather like a blessing. Then, turning on his heel, he stalked off.

Aleatha felt a tiny pulse of unaccustomed warmth in her heart, shut in its box.

# CHAPTER 22

# THE CITADEL

# PRYAN

◆

Taking the steps two at a time in his excitement, Paithan dashed up the spiral staircase that led to the very topmost tower of the citadel, into a large room he had named the Star Chamber.[1] He could now see—and hear—for himself that some type of change had befallen his star machine (he took a proprietary interest in it, having discovered it), and he cursed Roland heartily for having kept him from viewing the change as it occurred.

He was also considerably surprised, and considerably alarmed, to receive the message from Rega about the machine. Humans were not comfortable around machinery. They generally tend to distrust it, and when confronted with it, usually break it. Rega had turned out to be worse than most.

Although at first she had evinced interest in the machine and had looked on admiringly as Paithan displayed its more prominent features, she had gradually developed a most unreasonable dislike for the marvelous contraption. She complained about the amount of time he spent with it, accused him of being more interested in it than he was in her.

"Oh, Pait, you are so thick," Aleatha told him. "She's jealous, of course. If that machine of yours were another woman, she'd tear its hair out."

Paithan scoffed at the notion. Rega had too much sense to be

---

[1] Haplo refers to this room in his account as the sanctuary.

jealous of a bunch of gleaming metal clockwork, even though it was more elaborate than any other clockwork device he'd ever seen in his life, resplendent with sparkling stones called "diamonds" and rainbow-makers known as "prisms" and other wonders and beauties. But now he began to think Aleatha might be right, and that was why he was taking the stairs two at a time.

Perhaps Rega had torn up his machine.

He flung open the door, ran into the Star Chamber, and immediately ran back out. The light inside the room was blinding. He couldn't see a thing. Huddling in a shadow cast by the open door, he massaged his aching eyeballs. Then, squinting, he tried to make out what was going on.

But all he could come up with were the obvious facts—his machine was beaming with dazzling, multicolored light while simultaneously grinding, revolving, ticking and . . . humming.

"Rega?" he yelled from behind the door.

He heard a strangled sob. "Paithan? Oh, Paithan!"

"It's me. Where are you?"

"I'm . . . in here!"

"Well, come out," he said with a certain amount of exasperation.

"I can't!" she wailed. "It's so bright. I can't see! I'm scared to move. I . . . I'm afraid of falling in that hole!"

"You can't fall in the 'hole,' Rega. That diamond—I mean the thing you call a rock—is wedged into it."

"Not anymore! The rock moved, Paithan! I saw it! One of those arms picked it up. Down in the hole it was like a fire burning, and the light got so bright I couldn't see, and then the glass ceiling started to open—"

"It's open!" Paithan gasped. "How did it work? Did the panels slide over each other? Like a giant lotus blossom? Like in the picture—?"

Rega, shrieking almost incoherently, informed him just what he could do with his picture *and* his lotus blossoms. Finishing with a hysterical burst, she demanded that he get her the hell out of there.

At that moment the light shut off. The humming stopped. It was dark and silent in the room, dark and silent throughout the citadel, throughout the world—or so it seemed.

But it wasn't truly dark—not like the strange "night" that spread over the citadel for some unknown reason, not dark the way it was Below. For though night might fall on the citadel itself, the light of Pryan's four suns continued to beam down into the Star Chamber, much like an island in a sea of black fog. Once his eyes had adjusted to normal sunlight, as opposed to blinding rainbow-colored starlight, Paithan was able to enter the chamber.

He found Rega flattened against a wall, her hands over her eyes.

Paithan cast a hurried and anxious glance around the chamber. He knew the moment he entered that the light hadn't shut off for good; it was just resting, perhaps. The clockwork above the hole in the floor (he called it the "well") kept ticking. The ceiling panels were closing. He paused to watch, enraptured. The book had been right! The panels, made of glass covered with strange pictures, were shutting up just like the petals of a lotus blossom. And there was an air of expectation, anticipation. The machine was quivering with life.

Paithan was so excited he wanted to run around and examine everything, but his first duty lay with Rega. Hastening to her, he took her gently in his arms. She grasped hold of him as if she were going under for the third time, keeping her eyes squinched shut.

"Ouch! Don't pinch me. I've got you. You can look now," he added more tenderly. She was shivering uncontrollably. "The light's gone out."

Rega cautiously opened her eyes, took one look, saw the ceiling panels moving, and immediately shut her eyes again.

"Rega, watch," Paithan coaxed her. "It's fascinating."

"No." She shuddered. "I don't want to. Just . . . get me out of here!"

"If you'd only take the time to study the machine, my dear, you wouldn't be frightened of it."

"I was trying to study it, Paithan," she said with a sob. "I've been looking at those damn books you're always reading and I came . . . came in here"—she hiccuped—"this winetime to . . . to look around. You . . . you were so . . . interested in it . . . I thought it would make you happy if I was—"

"And it does, dear, it does," said Paithan, stroking her hair. "You came in here and you looked around. Did you . . . touch anything, my dear?"

Her eyes flared open. She went stiff in his arms. "You think I did this, don't you?"

"No, Rega. Well, maybe not on purpose, but—"

"Well, I didn't! I wouldn't! I hate it! Hate it!"

She stamped her foot. The clock gave a lurch. The arm that held the diamond above the well creaked and started to turn. Rega flung herself into Paithan's arms. He held her, watching, fascinated, as a red light started to beam out of the well, pulsing up from its fathomless depths.

"Paithan!" Rega whimpered.

"Yes, yes, dear," he said. "We'll leave." But he made no move to go.

The books provided a complete diagram of the way the Star Chamber worked and explained exactly what it did.[2] Paithan could understand the part that dealt with the machinery, but he didn't understand the part that dealt with the magic. Now if it had been elven magic, he could have comprehended what was going on, for though not magically inclined himself, he had worked with the elven wizards in his family's weapons business long enough to have learned the fundamentals.

The Sartan magic—dealing as it did with such concepts as "probabilities" and making use of the pictures known as "sigla"— was beyond him. He felt as awed and baffled in its presence as he knew Rega must feel in the presence of elven magic.[3]

Slowly, gracefully, silently, the lotus-blossom ceiling started to reopen.

"This . . . this is how it all began, Paithan," Rega whimpered. "I didn't touch anything! I swear it. It's . . . doing this all by itself."

"I believe you, dear. I truly do," he answered. "It's all . . . so wonderful!"

---

[2] A part of this explanation and accompanying diagram can be found in Appendix II.

[3] Humans do use magic, but their magic deals with the manipulation of nature and all things natural, as opposed to elves, who work with mechanical magicks. Elves tend to discount human magic, therefore, considering it crude and backward. This accounts for Paithan's superior attitude. Unfortunately, most humans on Pryan, accustomed to using elven magical technology, feel the same way about their own magic as do the elves. Human wizards are accorded very little respect.

"No, it isn't! It's horrible. We'd better leave. Quickly, before the light comes back on."

"Yes, I guess you're right." Paithan started for the door, moving slowly, reluctantly.

Rega went with him, clutching him so close that their feet tangled.

"Why are you stopping?"

"Rega, darling, I can't walk like this . . ."

"Don't let go of me! Just hurry, please!"

"It's hard to hurry, dearest, with you standing on my foot . . ."

They edged their way across the polished marble floor, circling the well—capped with its gigantic multifaceted jewel—and the seven enormous chairs that faced outward from the hole.

"The tytans sat here," Paithan explained, placing his hand on the leg of one of the chairs, a leg that extended far over his head. "I can see now why the creatures are blind."

"And why they're insane," Rega muttered, tugging him along.

The red light beaming up from the depths of the well was growing brighter. The clockwork hand that held the diamond turned it this way and that. The light glinted and danced off the jewel's sheer planes. The sunlight, shining in through the ever widening panels, was sliced into colors by the prisms.

Suddenly the diamond seemed to catch fire. Light blazed. The clockwork mechanism ticked more rapidly. The machine came to life. The light in the room grew brighter and brighter and even Paithan admitted that it was time to get out. He and Rega ran the rest of the way, sliding across the polished floor, and dashed out the door just as the strange humming sound started again.

Paithan slammed the door shut. The brilliant multicolored rainbow light shone out from the cracks, illuminated the hallway.

The two stood leaning against a wall, catching their breath. Paithan stared at the closed door longingly.

"I wish I could see what was going on! If I could, perhaps I could figure out how it works!"

"At least you got to see it start," said Rega, feeling much better. Now that her rival had, in essence, spurned the devotion of a smitten follower, Rega could afford to be generous. "The humming is quite nice, isn't it?"

"I hear words in it," said Paithan, frowning. "As if it's call-ing . . ."

"As long as it's not calling you," Rega said softly, her hand twining around his. "Sit down here with me a moment. Let's talk."

Paithan, sighing, slid down the wall. Rega curled up on the floor, nestled beside him. He looked at her fondly, put his arm around her.

They made an unusual couple, as unlike in appearance as they were in almost everything else. He was elven. She was human. He was tall and willowy, white-skinned, with a long, foxish face. She was short and full-figured, brown-skinned, with brown hair that hung straight down her back. He was a hundred years old—in his youth. She was in her twenties—in her youth. He was a wanderer and a philanderer; she was a cheat and a smuggler and casual in her relationships with men. The only thing they had in common was their love for each other—a love that had survived tytans and sav-iors, dragons, dogs, and daft old wizards.

"I've been neglecting you lately, Rega," Paithan said, resting his cheek on her head. "I'm sorry."

"You've been avoiding me," she said crisply.

"Not you in particular. I've been avoiding everyone."

She waited for him to offer some explanation. When he didn't, she moved her head out from beneath his chin, looked at him.

"Any reason? I know you've been involved with the ma-chine—"

"Oh, Orn take the machine," Paithan growled. "I'm interested in it, certainly. I thought maybe I could get it to work, even though I'm not really certain what it's meant to do. I guess I hoped it might help us. But I don't think it will. No matter how much it hums, no one will hear it."

Rega didn't understand. "Look, Paithan, I know Roland can be a bastard sometimes—"

"It's not Roland," he said impatiently. "If it comes to that, what's mostly wrong with Roland is Aleatha. It's just . . . well . . ." He hesitated, then blurted it out. "I found some more stores of food."

"You did!" Rega clapped her hands together. "Oh, Paithan, that's wonderful!"

"Isn't it," he muttered.

"Well, of course it is! Now we won't starve! There . . . there *is* enough, isn't there?"

"Oh, more than enough," he said gloomily. "Enough to last a human lifetime, even an elven lifetime. Maybe even a dwarven lifetime. Especially if there aren't any more mouths to feed. Which there won't be."

"I'm sorry, Paithan, but I think this is wonderful news and I don't see what you're so upset about—"

"Don't you?" He glared at her, spoke almost savagely. "No more mouths to feed. We're it, Rega! The end. What does it matter whether we live two more tomorrows or two million more tomorrows? We can't have children.[4] When we die, maybe the last humans and elves and dwarves on Pryan die. And then there will be no more. Ever."

Rega stared at him, stricken. "Surely . . . surely you can't be right. This world is so big. There must be more of us . . . somewhere."

Paithan only shook his head.

Rega tried again. "You told me that each one of those lights we see shining in the heavens is a city, like this one. There must be people like us in them."

"We would have heard from them by now."

"What?" Rega was amazed. "How?"

"I'm not sure," Paithan was forced to admit. "But it says in the book that in the old days, the people living in the cities could communicate with each other. We haven't been communicated with, have we?"

"But maybe we just don't know how . . . That humming sound." Rega brightened. "Maybe that's what it's doing. "It's calling the other cities."

"It's calling someone, I think," Paithan conceded thoughtfully, listening intently. The next sound, however, he heard all too well. A human voice, booming loudly.

"Paithan! Where are you?"

"It's Roland." Paithan sighed. "Now what?"

"We're up here!" Rega shouted. Standing up, she leaned over the rail of the staircase. "With the machine."

---

[4] Due to genetic differences, elves, humans, and dwarves cannot cross-breed.

They heard booted feet clattering up the stairs. Roland arrived, gasping for breath. He glanced at the closed door, the light welling from underneath.

"Is that where . . . this strange sound's . . . coming from?" he demanded, sucking in air.

"What of it?" Paithan returned defensively. He was on his feet, eyeing the human warily. Roland was no fonder of the machine than was his sister.

"You'd better turn the damn thing off, that's what," Roland said, his face grim.

"We can't—" Rega began, but stopped when Paithan stepped on her foot.

"Why should I?" he asked, sharp chin jutting outward in defiance.

"Take a look out the window, elf."

Paithan bristled. "Talk to me that way and I'll never look out another window as long as I live!"

But Rega knew her half-brother, guessed that his belligerent facade was covering up fear. She ran to the window, stared out a moment, not seeing anything. Then she gave a low cry.

"Oh, Paithan! You'd better come see this."

Reluctantly the elf moved to her side, peered out. "What? I don't see . . ."

And then he did see.

It looked as if the entire jungle were moving; it appeared to be advancing on the citadel. Large masses of green were surging slowly up the mountain. Only it wasn't the jungle, it was an army.

"Blessed Mother!" Paithan breathed.

"You said the machine was calling something!" Rega moaned.

It was. It was calling the tytans.

# CHAPTER ♦ 23

## OUTSIDE THE CITADEL

## PRYAN

♦

"MARIT! WIFE! HEAR ME! ANSWER ME!" XAR SENT OUT HIS COMMAND IN SILENCE and it returned to him in silence.

No response.

Frustrated, he repeated her name several times, then ceased. She must be unconscious . . . or dead—the only two circumstances in which a Patryn would refuse to answer such a summons.

Xar pondered what to do. His ship was already in Pryan; he'd been attempting to guide Marit to the landing site when she had vanished. He considered changing course—Marit's last frantic message to him had been from Chelestra. But at length he decided to continue to the citadel. Chelestra was a world made up of magic-nullifying water, water that would weaken his power. It was not a world Xar had much interest in visiting. He would go to Chelestra after he had discovered the Seventh Gate.

The Seventh Gate.

It had become an obsession with Xar. From the Seventh Gate, the Sartan had cast the Patryns into prison. From the Seventh Gate—Xar determined—he would free them.

In the Seventh Gate, Samah had sundered the world, created new worlds out of the old. In the Seventh Gate, Xar would forge his own new world—and it would be all his.

This was the true reason for his journey to Pryan.

The ostensible reason—the reason he gave his people (and Sang-drax)—was to gain ascendancy over the tytans and incorporate them into his army. The real goal was to discover the location of the Seventh Gate.

Xar was certain it must be in the citadel. He made the deduction based on two facts: (one) Haplo had been to the citadel on Pryan and, according to both Kleitus and Samah, Haplo knew the location of the Seventh Gate; (two) as Sang-drax had said, if the Sartan had something they wanted to protect, what better guards than the tytans?

Following Haplo's coordinates, which would lead to the citadel, the Lord of the Nexus, accompanied by Sang-Drax and a small force of about twenty Patryns, eventually reached Pryan. The citadel itself was easy to find. An intensely bright light, made up of bands of brilliant color, beamed from it, acting as a guiding beacon.

Privately Xar was astonished at the massive size of Pryan. Nothing Haplo had written had prepared his lord for what he found. Xar was forced to revise his plans, forced to think that maybe conquering this enormous world with its four ever shining suns was going to be impossible—even with the help of the tytans.

But not impossible if he were master of the Seventh Gate.

"The citadel, My Lord," announced one of his people.

"Bring the ship down inside the walls," Xar commanded.

He could see a perfect landing site—a large, open area just inside the walls, probably a marketplace. He waited impatiently for the ship to set down.

But the ship couldn't land. It couldn't even get close to the site. When it came level with the walls of the citadel, the ship seemed to hit an invisible barrier, bumping into it gently, not damaged, but unable to fly through. The Patryns tried again and again, to no avail.

"It must be Sartan magic, Lord," said Sang-drax.

"Of course it's Sartan magic!" Xar repeated, irritated. "What did you expect to be guarding a Sartan city?"

He hadn't expected it, though, and that was what made him angry. Haplo had entered the citadel. How? The Sartan magic was strong. Xar couldn't unravel it; he couldn't find the beginning of the rune-structure. Such a feat was possible, but it might take him years.

Xar reread Haplo's report, hoping for a clue.

*The city is built up off the jungle floor, rising from behind an enormous wall, rising taller than the tallest trees. A towering, pillared crystal spire balances on a dome formed of marble arches that stand in the city's center. The top of the spire must be one of the highest points in this world. It is from this center spire that the light beams most brightly.*

But in Haplo's case, the light had been white—or so Xar recalled. Not this dazzling array of colors. What had caused the light to alter its aspect? And most important, how was he going to get inside to find out? Xar read on.

*The center spire is framed by four other spires, duplicates of the first; they stand on the platform holding the dome. On a level beneath that stand eight more identical spires. Gigantic marble steppes rise from behind these spires. And finally, at each end of the guard walls stands another pillar. There are four such pillars, placed at the cardinal direction points.*

*A path leads up the mountain straight to a large metal door formed in a hexagon and inscribed with Sartan runes—the city's gate. The gate is sealed shut.*

*Sartan rune-magic would open the gate, but I refused to use the magic of our enemies. I entered by going through the marble wall, using an ordinary solvent rune-structure.*

*That* is the difference, then, Xar reasoned. Haplo had entered by going through the walls. The Sartan magic must extend above the walls, like an invisible dome, to keep out flying enemies such as dragons. The magic of the wall itself was either weaker to begin with or had been weakened over time.

"Land the ship in the jungle," Xar ordered. "As near the citadel as possible."

His crew brought the ship down in a clearing they found some distance outside the walls of the citadel. The huge warship was one of the steam-powered dragon ships used by the Sartan on Abarrach to sail the molten seas. It was completely refitted to suit the Patryns, and it drifted down easily among the treetops, sank into a vast bed of moss.

Shafts of the striated, multicolored light filtered through the thick foliage that surrounded them, slid over the ship, shifting around it in an ever changing pattern.

"My Lord!" One of the Patryns pointed out the porthole.

A gigantic being stood near the ship, so near that had they been standing on the prow, they could have reached out and touched it. The being was shaped like a man, but its skin was the color and the texture of the jungle, so that it blended perfectly with the trees—one reason they had nearly landed on top of it and had not seen it until now. Its huge head had no eyes, but it appeared to be staring fixedly at something. It stood motionless, almost as if it were in a trance.

"A tytan!" Xar was vastly interested. He could see more of them, now that he looked for them. Six or so were around his ship.

He recalled Haplo's report:

*Creatures thirty feet tall. Skin that blends in with its background, making them difficult to see. No eyes; they're blind, but they have other senses that more than make up for their lack of sight. They are obsessed with one thing: the citadels. They ask questions about the citadels of everyone they meet, and when these questions aren't answered satisfactorily (and no one has yet discovered what a satisfactory answer is) the creatures fly into a murderous rage, killing any living being near them. Created by the Sartan to oversee the mensch (and possibly for some other purpose having to do with the light) they use a crude form of Sartan magic. . . .*

*These creatures very nearly destroyed me. They came close to destroying my ship. They are powerful, and I see no way of controlling them.*

"*You* saw no way of controlling them," Xar remarked. "But then, Haplo, my son, *you* are not me.

"Nothing could withstand a fighting force of these creatures!" he added with satisfaction to Sang-drax. "They don't look all that dangerous. They're certainly not bothering us."

The dragon-snake appeared nervous, however. "True, Lord Xar. I think it likely that they are under some type of spell. If you are going to the citadel, you should go now. Before whatever spell they are under wears off."

"Nonsense, I can deal with them," Xar replied with scorn. "What is the matter with you?"

"I sense a presence of great evil," Sang-drax said in a low voice. "A malevolent force—"

"Not these mindless entities, surely," Xar interrupted with a glance at the tytans.

"No. It is intelligent, cunning." Sang-drax was silent a moment, then said softly, "I think we may have fallen into a trap, Lord of the Nexus."

"You were the one who advised me to come," Xar reminded the dragon-snake.

"But it was not I who put the idea into your head, Lord," Sang-drax returned, his single red eye hooded.

Xar was displeased. "First you badger me to come here, now

you're warning me to leave. If you continue talking out of both sides of your mouth, my friend, you'll choke!"

"I am only concerned about my lord's safety—"

"And not your own precious skin, eh? Well, come on, if you're going with me. Or will you stay here, hiding from the 'evil' force?"

Sang-drax made no response, but he also made no move to leave the ship.

Xar opened the hatch, descended the ship's gangplank to the floor of the jungle. He cast a swift glance around, eyed the tytans warily.

The monsters paid him no attention. He might have been a bug at their feet. Their heads were turned in the direction of the citadel. The rainbow light bathed the creatures in radiance.

And it was then he heard the humming sound.

"Who is making that irritating noise?" the lord demanded.

He motioned to a Patryn who stood on the ship's upper deck, ready to run and do whatever his lord might require of him. "Find out where that strange humming sound is coming from and put a stop to it."

The Patryn left swiftly. "My Lord," he reported on his return, "everyone in the ship can hear it, but no one has any idea what is causing it. The sound does not appear to be coming from the ship itself. If you notice, Lord, it seems to be louder out here than inside."

True, Xar admitted. The sound *was* louder out here. He cocked his head. It appeared to be coming from the direction of the citadel.

"There are words in that sound," said Xar, listening intently.

"It's as if it were speaking to someone, Lord," the Patryn offered.

"Speaking!" Xar repeated to himself. "Yes, but what is it saying? And to whom?"

He listened closely and carefully; he could distinguish alterations of pitch and tone that might indicate words being formed. He could almost make out what they were, but never quite. And that, he concluded, was what was so irritating about the sound. All the more reason, then, to reach the citadel.

He stepped onto the moss, started walking in the direction of the citadel. He was not worried about finding a clear path. His magic would cut a swath through the thickest tangle of undergrowth. He kept his eyes on the tytans, however, moving cautiously, prepared to defend himself.

The tytans paid no attention to him. Their sightless heads faced in one direction—the citadel.

Xar had ventured only a short distance away from his ship when Sang-drax suddenly appeared at his side.

"If the citadel is now working, it could mean that Sartan are inside, operating it," Sang-drax warned.

"Haplo reported the citadel uninhabited—"

"Haplo is a traitor and liar!" the dragon-snake hissed.

Xar saw no reason to respond to that. Keeping his attention fixed on the tytans, he ventured farther and farther away from his ship. None of the monsters appeared to take the slightest interest in him.

"More likely, the light has something to do with the starting up of the Kicksey-winsey," Xar returned coldly.

"Or both," Sang-drax rejoined. "Or worse," he added beneath his breath.

Xar flicked him a glance. "Then *I* will find out. Thank you for your concern. You may now return to the ship."

"I have decided to go with you, Lord."

"Indeed? And what of this 'evil force' that so terrified you before?"

"I wasn't terrified," Sang-drax replied sullenly. "I respect it, as you would be wise to do, Lord of the Nexus, for it is your enemy as much as mine. I have been asked to investigate it."

"By whom? I did not give any such command."

"My brethren, Lord. If that meets with your approval?"

Xar detected a note of sarcasm in the snaky voice, disliked the implication. "There is no greater enemy than the Sartan, no more powerful force than theirs—and ours—in the universe. You will do well to remember that. You and your brethren."

"Yes, Lord," Sang-drax said humbly enough, apparently chastened. "I meant no insult. I have found out that the Kicksey-winsey has been started on Arianus. My brethren have asked me to see if there might be some connection."

Xar didn't see how there could be—or why there should be. He gave the matter no more thought, left the clearing, and entered the jungle. His magic caused the tree branches to lift to allow him passage. The tangled vines slithered apart to give him clearance. He looked back at his people, lined up on the deck, ready to come to his defense if necessary. He indicated with a wave of his hand that he was going on. They were to remain with the ship, guard it, keep it safe.

Xar rounded the bole of a tree and suddenly came face to shinbone with one of the tytans. The creature gave a grunt, began to move. The Lord of the Nexus instantly prepared to defend himself. But the tytan had not sensed him, apparently. It was taking a slow and halting step forward.

Xar, staring up at the creature, saw on its sightless face an expression of happiness.

And then he could distinguish the words of the humming.

*Return . . . return to . . .*

And just when he thought he was going to be able to sort out the rest, the humming stopped. The rainbow light went out. And although Pryan's four suns continued to shine in the sky, the jungle seemed vastly darker by contrast.

The tytan shifted its head. The eyeless face turned toward Xar. The tytan no longer looked happy.

# CHAPTER 24

# THE CITADEL

# PRYAN

♦

"Shut the machine off!" Roland yelled.

"I can't!" Paithan shouted.

"It's calling the tytans!"

"Maybe it is and maybe it isn't. Who knows? Besides, look at the tytans. They act like they're drunk . . ."

"Drunk, my ass! You just don't want to turn off your precious machine. You think more of that damn thing than you do of us!"

"Oh, Roland, that's not true—" Rega began.

"Don't you 'Oh, Roland' me!" he snapped at his sister. "It was you who said that very thing last night!"

"But I didn't mean it," she said hastily, with an apologetic smile for Paithan.

"*You* try to shut it down. Go ahead!" Paithan yelled, waving a hand at the door.

"Maybe I will!" Roland said loftily, somewhat daunted but unable to refuse the challenge.

He took a step toward the door. The light went out; the humming stopped.

Roland stopped, too.

"What did you do?" Paithan demanded, pouncing on him angrily.

"Nothing! I swear! I didn't go near the damn thing!"

"You broke it!" Paithan clenched his fists.

Roland clenched his own fists, fell into a fighting stance.

"There's someone out there!" Rega cried.

"Don't try to trick me, Rega." Roland and Paithan were circling each other. "It won't work. I'm going to tie those pointed ears around his neck—"

"Stop it, both of you!" Rega grabbed hold of Paithan, nearly dragging him off his feet, and hauled him over to the window. "Look, damn it! There are two people—two humans, by the look of them—out beyond the gate."

"Orn's ears, there *are* people out there!" Paithan said in astonishment. "They're running from the tytans."

"Oh, Paithan, you were wrong!" Rega said excitedly. "There *are* more people on this world."

"They won't be on it for long," Paithan said grimly. "There must be fifty of those monsters out there and only two of them. They'll never make it."

"The tytans! They've got them! We have to help!" Rega started to run off.

Paithan caught her around the waist.

"Are you mad? There's nothing we can do!"

"He's right, sis." Roland had lowered his fists, was peering out the window. "If we went out there, we'd only die, too—"

"Besides," Paithan added in awed tones, "it doesn't look as if they need our help. Blessed Mother! Did you see that?"

Loosening his hold on Rega in his amazement, Paithan leaned out the window. Roland crowded in beside him. Rega pulled herself up on her tiptoes to look out over their shoulders.

The citadel was built on one of the few mountains tall enough to rise above the mass of Pryan's vegetation. The jungle encircled it, but had not encroached upon it. A path, cut into jagged rock, led from the jungle to the citadel, to the large metal door formed in the shape of a hexagon and inscribed with the same picture-writing the books termed "runes."

Once, many cycles ago, the five trapped in the citadel had run up that path themselves, pursued by a flesh-devouring dragon. It was the dwarf, Drugar, who had figured out how to open that magical door. Escaping inside, they had shut the dragon out.

Now two more people were running along that same treacherous path, attempting to reach the safe haven of the citadel. The tytans, carrying branches clutched in massive fists, were bearing down on their foes, who looked smaller and more fragile than insects.

But then one of the strangers, clad in black robes,[1] turned to face the advancing tytans. The figure raised his hands. Blue light flared around him, danced and twined, and then spread out to form an enormous blue wall, a blue wall that burst into flame.

The tytans fell back before the magical fire. The strangers took advantage of the monsters' confusion to continue running up the path.

"Haplo," Paithan muttered.

"What?" Rega asked.

"Ouch! Do you have to dig your nails into my shoulder? The blue fire reminds me of that Haplo, that's all."

"Maybe. But look, Paithan! The fire isn't stopping the tytans!"

The magical fire was flickering, dying out. The tytans continued their advance.

"But the two have almost reached the gate. They'll be safe enough."

The three fell silent, watching this life-or-death race.

The strangers—the one in black robes and the other dressed in ordinary human-type clothing—had reached the metal gate. They came to a sudden halt.

"What's stopping them?" Roland wondered.

"They can't get in!" Rega cried.

"Sure they can," Roland scoffed. "Any wizard who can work magic like that ought to be able to open a gate."

"That Haplo got in," Paithan said. "Or at least he claimed he did."

"Would you quit yammering about Haplo!" Rega shouted at him. "I tell you they can't get in! We've got to go down there and open the gate for them."

Paithan and Roland exchanged glances. Neither moved.

Rega cast them each a furious look; then, turning, she headed toward the stairs.

"No! Wait! If you open the gate for them, you'll let the tytans in, too!"

---

[1] Probably what led Paithan to deduce that Xar was human. No elf ever wears black, considering the color ill-omened.

Paithan made a grab for her, but this time Rega was prepared. She darted out of his reach and was off and running down the hall before he could stop her.

Paithan swore something in elven and started after her. Noticing he was alone, he stopped, turned. "Roland! Come on! It'll take both of us to fight the tytans off—"

"Not necessary," Roland said. He waved Paithan back to the window. "Drugar's down there. *He's* opening the gate."

The dwarf took the pendant that hung from around his neck and placed it in the center of the runes as he had done once before, only this time he was inside the gate instead of outside. The sigil on the dwarf's pendant burned with blue fire, expanded. Wherever its fire touched one of the sigla on the gate, that sigil burst into blue flame. Soon a circle of magic burned brightly.

The gates swung open. The two strangers darted inside, the tytans roaring on their heels. The magical fire daunted the monsters, however. They fell back. The gates shut; the flames died.

The tytans began to beat on the gates with their fists.

"They're attacking the citadel!" Paithan exclaimed in horror. "They never did that before. Do you think they can get in?"

"How the hell should I know?" Roland retorted. "You're the expert. You're the one whose read all those damn books! Maybe you should turn that machine of yours back on again. That seems to calm them down."

Paithan would gladly have turned the machine on again, but he didn't have any idea how. He couldn't tell Roland that, however, and for the moment, Roland was actually regarding Paithan with a certain amount of grudging respect.

What the human doesn't know won't hurt him, was Paithan's theory. Let him think I'm a mechanical genius. If I'm lucky, the machine will cycle itself back up again. If not, and the tytans manage to break down the wall, well, the truth won't matter much then anyway.

"The machine . . . uh . . . has to rest. It'll come back on soon." Paithan prayed to Orn he was right.

"It had better. Or we're all going to be resting—resting in peace, if you know what I mean."

They could hear clearly, through the open window, the tytans roaring and bashing at the walls in a frantic effort to get inside. Rega was down there now, talking with the human in the black robes.

"One of us ought to go down there," Paithan suggested, prodding Roland.

"Yeah, you should," Roland agreed, prodding Paithan.

Suddenly an enormous shape filled the window, blotting out the sunlight. A dank, dark smell choked them.

Frightened half out of their wits, the two grabbed hold of each other, dragged each other down. A massive green-scaled body slid past the window, scraping along the outside wall of the citadel at tremendous speed.

"A dragon!" Paithan quavered.

Roland said something not repeatable.

A gigantic talon thrust through the window.

"Oh, god!" Paithan quit hugging Roland and hugged the floor.

Roland flung his arms over his head.

But the talon disappeared after breaking out a section of the marble wall. The dragon had apparently used the window to give itself leverage. The green-scaled body slithered off. Sunlight shone through.

Trembling, the two clutched at the windowsill, pulled themselves cautiously back up, peered out over the ledge.

The dragon was sliding down the tower, wrapping its wingless body around tall spires, then dropping onto the courtyard below. Those in the courtyard—Rega, Drugar, and the two strangers—appeared to be frozen with terror. None of them made a move. The dragon lurched toward them.

Paithan moaned and covered his eyes with his hand.

"Rega! Run for it!" Roland screamed out the window.

But the dragon thundered past them without a glance, heading straight for the gates. The Sartan runes flashed blue and red, but the dragon soared right through the magic and through the metal gates as well.

Outside the walls, the dragon reared up to an astonishing height, its head nearly at a level with the citadel's tall spires. The tytans turned and fled, their enormous bodies moving with incongruous fluid grace.

"It saved us!" Paithan cried.

"Yeah, for lunch," Roland said grimly.

"Nonsense!" said a voice behind them.

Paithan jumped, cracked his head on the casement. Roland whirled around, lost his balance, and nearly fell backward out the window. Fortunately Paithan, feeling the need to grab hold of something substantial, grabbed hold of Roland. Both stood staring.

An old man with a stringy white beard, mouse-colored robes, and a disreputable hat was stalking down the hall, waving his arms and looking extremely pleased with himself.

"Dragon's under my complete control. Hadn't been for me, you'd be guava jelly right about now. Showed up in the nick of time —whoever Nick is. *Dukes ate mackinaw,* you might say."

The old man planted himself triumphantly in front of the elf and the human, folded his arms across his chest, and rocked back on his heels.

"What dukes?" Paithan asked feebly.

"*Dukes ate mackinaw,*" repeated the old man, scowling. "With ears as big as yours, you'd think you could hear. I flew down to save your lives, arrived right in the nick of time. *Dukes ate mackinaw.* That's Latin," the old man added importantly. "Means . . . well, it means . . . well, that I showed up . . . in the . . . er . . . nick of time."

"I don't understand." Paithan gulped.

Roland was rendered speechless.

" 'Course you don't understand," said the old man. "You have to be a great and powerful wizard to understand. You're not, by chance, a great and powerful wizard?" He appeared somewhat nervous.

"N-no." Paithan shook his head.

"Ah, there, you see?" The old man was smug.

Roland drew a quivering breath. "Aren't . . . aren't you Zifnab?"

"Am I? Wait!" The old man closed his eyes, held out his hands. "Don't tell me. Let me guess. Zifnab. No. No. Don't believe that's it."

"Then . . . who the devil are you?" Roland demanded.

The old man straightened, threw out his chest, stroked his bearded chin. "Name's Bond. James Bond."

"No, sir," came a sepulchral voice from down the hall. "Not today, I'm afraid, sir."

The old man flinched, drew nearer Paithan and Roland. "Don't pay any attention. That's probably only Moneypenny. Got the hots for me."

"We saw you die!" Paithan gasped.

"The dragon killed you!" Roland gargled.

"Oh, they're always trying to kill me off. But I come back in the last reel. *Dukes ate mackinaw* and all that. You wouldn't have a dry martini about you, would you?"

Measured footfalls echoed in the hallway. The closer the footfalls came, the more nervous the old man appeared, although he was obviously doing his best to ignore the ominous sound.

A very tall, imposing gentleman walked up to the old man. The gentleman was dressed all in somber black—black waistcoat, black vest, black knee-breeches with black ribbons, black stockings and shoes with silver buckles. His long hair was white and tied in the back with a black ribbon, but his face was young, and rather stern about the mouth. The gentleman bowed.

"Master Quindiniar. Master Redleaf. I am pleased to see you again. I trust I find you in good health?"

"Zifnab died!" Paithan insisted. "We saw him!"

"We can't have everything, can we?" The imposing gentleman gave a long-suffering sigh. "Excuse me, please." He turned to the old man, who was staring hard at the ceiling. "I am sorry, sir, but you cannot be Mr. Bond today."

The old man began to hum a tune. "Dum deedle-um dum—dum, dum, dum. Dum deedle-um dum—dum, dum, dum. Bomp—de-um."

"Sir." The imposing gentleman's voice took on an edge. "I really must insist."

The old man appeared to deflate. Taking off his hat, he twirled it around and around by the brim, darting swift glances from beneath his brows at the imposing gentleman.

"Please?" the old man whined.

"No, sir."

"Just for the day?"

"It simply wouldn't do, sir."

The old man heaved a sigh. "Who am I, then?"

"You are Zifnab, sir," said the imposing gentleman with a sigh.

"That doddering idiot!" The old man was quite indignant.

"If you say so, sir."

The old man stewed and fumed and made a complete shambles of his hat. Suddenly he cried, "Ah, ha! I can't be Zifnab! He's dead!" He stabbed a bony finger at Paithan and Roland. *"They'll* tell you! By cracky, I've got witnesses!"

"*Deus ex machina,* sir. You were saved in the final reel."

"Damn the dukes!" Zifnab cried in a towering rage.

"Yes, sir," said the imposing gentleman serenely. "And now, sir, if you will permit me to remind you. The Lord of the Nexus is in the courtyard—"

"The courtyard . . . Blessed Mother! The dragon!" Paithan whirled, almost fell out the window. He caught himself, blinked. "It's gone."

Roland turned. "What? Where?"

"The dragon. It's gone!"

"Not precisely, sir," said the imposing gentleman with another bow. "I believe that would be me to whom you are referring. I am the dragon." The gentleman turned back to Zifnab. "I, too, have business in the courtyard, sir."

The old man looked alarmed. "Will this end up in a fight?"

"I trust not, sir," said the dragon. Then its voice softened. "But I'm afraid I may be gone for some considerable length of time, sir. I know that I leave you in good company, however."

Zifnab reached out a trembling hand. "You will take care of yourself, won't you, old chap?"

"Yes, sir. And you will remember to take your warming drink at night, won't you, sir? It would never do to have you irregular—"

"Uh, yes, yes. Warming drink. Certainly." Zifnab flushed and glanced askance at Paithan and Roland.

"And you will keep an eye on the Lord of the Nexus? Not let him find out about—you know."

"Do I know?" Zifnab asked, puzzled.

"Yes, sir, you do."

"Well, if you say so," Zifnab said with an air of resignation.

The dragon did not seem overly pleased with this, but the old man had placed his hat back on his head and was racing off down the hall.

"Gentlemen." The dragon bowed a last time to Paithan and Roland. Then it disappeared.

"I've got to lay off the hard stuff." Roland wiped sweat from his brow.

"Hey, you two!" Zifnab came to a halt, peered back over his shoulder. "Are you coming?" He pointed majestically down the staircase. "You have a guest! The Lord of the Nexus has arrived."

"Whoever he is," Paithan muttered.

Not knowing what else to do, having no idea what was going on but hoping desperately to find out, Paithan and Roland trailed along reluctantly behind the old man.

As they passed the door of the Star Chamber, the machine started up again.

# CHAPTER ♦ 25

# THE CITADEL

# PRYAN

♦

Xᴀʀ ᴡᴀꜱ ɪɴ ᴀɴ ɪʟʟ ʜᴜᴍᴏʀ. ʜᴇ ʜᴀᴅ ʙᴇᴇɴ ꜰᴏʀᴄᴇᴅ ᴛᴏ ꜰʟᴇᴇ ꜰʀᴏᴍ ᴀ ʙᴜɴᴄʜ ᴏꜰ blind behemoths; then he'd been blocked from entering a gate by magic that even a mensch could unravel. Finally, he owed, if not his life, then at least his dignity and well-being to a dragon. This galled him. This and the knowledge that Haplo had been able to enter this citadel and he, the Lord of the Nexus, could not.

"*If* Haplo was telling the truth," said Sang-drax beneath his breath.

The two stood just inside the gate. Three mensch—two females and a male—were staring at them stupidly, much as Xar might have expected from mensch.

"Haplo told the truth," Xar returned grimly. "I saw into his heart. He was here. He was inside this citadel. And these—these weak-minded mensch managed to get inside." He was speaking in Patryn and so could express his thoughts freely. "And what is the matter with you?"

Sang-drax had been glancing around nervously, his one eye swiveling to take in every part of the citadel—walls, spires, windows, the shadows on the ground below, the blue-green sky above.

"I was wondering where the dragon went, Lord."

"What does it matter? The wyrm's gone. Leave it at that. We have other, more important things to consider."

Sang-drax continued to look about. The mensch were now staring at him, obviously wondering what was wrong with him.

"Stop that!" Xar commanded Sang-drax, further irritated. "You look a fool! One would almost think you were frightened."

"Only for you and your safety, Lord," Sang-drax returned with an oily smile that had a strained quality. The single red eye ceased its roving, fixed itself on the mensch.

One of them, a human female, stepped forward. "Welcome, sirs," she said, speaking human. "Thank you for driving off the tytans. That was wonderful magic!" She was gazing at Xar with reverence and awe.

Xar was pleased, felt better. "Thank you, madam, for permitting me entrance into your city. And you, sir"—he bowed to the dwarf—"for your assistance with the gate."

Xar stared hard at the pendant the dwarf wore around his neck. The Patryn recognized a Sartan sigil when he saw one.

The dwarf, glowering, put his hand over the pendant, thrust it back beneath heavy leather armor.

"I beg your pardon, sir," said Xar humbly. "I didn't mean to be rude. I was admiring your amulet. Might I ask where you acquired it?"

"You can ask," the dwarf said gruffly.

Xar waited.

The dwarf remained silent.

The human female, casting the dwarf an angry glance, slid in front of him, came nearer Xar.

"Don't mind Drugar, sir. He's a dwarf," she added, as if that explained everything. "My name is Rega Redleaf. And this is Aleatha Quindiniar." She gestured toward another female—this one an elf.

The female was quite lovely, for a mensch. Xar bowed to her. "I am charmed, madam."

She gave him a cool, languid nod. "Did that Haplo send you here?"

Sang-drax hastily intervened. "This is Xar. Lord Xar. The man Haplo is my lord's subject. My lord sent Haplo. Haplo did not send my lord."

Rega looked impressed. Drugar's frown deepened. Aleatha stifled a yawn, as if this was all too boring for words. Rega continued introductions. Two males—a human and an elf—had just dashed up.

"This is my brother, Roland, and my . . . er . . . friend, Paithan Quindiniar."

"Hullo, sir." Paithan gave Xar a quick glance, then turned immediately back to Rega. "Have you seen him? Did he come down here?"

"Where've you been during all the excitement, Roland?" Aleatha asked in dulcet tones. "Hiding under your bed?"

"I was not!" Roland said hotly, rounding on her. "I was—"

"Roland." Rega tugged at him. "You're being rude. This is Lord Xar."

"Good to meet you, sir." Roland gave the lord a nod, then turned back to Aleatha. "If you must know, Paithan and I were trapped up in the tower with a—"

"He was right in front of us!" Paithan struck in. "He *must* be here!"

"Who are you talking about?"

"The dragon!" said Roland.

"Zifnab!" said Paithan at the same time.

"Who did you say?" Rega demanded.

"Zifnab."

Rega stared at Paithan in shock.

Xar and Sang-drax exchanged swift glances. Xar's lips tightened.

"Zifnab," Rega repeated in perplexity. "Paithan, that's impossible. He's dead."

"Oh, no, he's not," said Roland.

Aleatha began to laugh.

"It's not funny, Thea," Paithan snapped. "He was here. That was *his* dragon. Didn't you recognize the beast?"

Sang-drax sucked in a breath. The single red eye glistened, narrowed. He made a hissing sound.

"What is it?" Xar asked in Patryn.

"The old man. I know now what he is."

"He's a Sartan—"

"No. Or rather, he was. But not anymore. He has become one of *them*!"

"Where are you going?"

Sang-drax had begun to sidle toward the gate. "Beware the old man, My Lord. Beware—"

An imposing gentleman dressed all in black materialized out of the shadows.

At the sight of him, Sang-drax pointed. *"He's* the dragon, Lord! Trap him! Kill him! Quickly, while he's in this weak body!"

Xar didn't need to be told. The sigla on his skin flared red and blue, burned with the fire that warned him of an enemy.

"Ever the coward, aren't you?" The dragon faced Sang-drax. "This is *our* battle."

"Kill him, Lord!" the dragon-snake urged. He turned to the others, who, not understanding the language, were staring in perplexity. "My brethren." He spoke in human. "Don't be deceived. This man is not what he seems. He is a dragon! And he plans to slaughter us all. Kill him! Swiftly!"

"Go find shelter, friends. I will deal with this," Xar said to the mensch.

But they didn't move. Afraid, confused, too stupid—who knew? Stupid or not, they were in his way.

"Run, fools!" Xar yelled, exasperated.

The imposing gentleman ignored both Xar and the mensch, continued to advance on Sang-drax. Snarling curses, Sang-drax was slowly giving ground, sidling back toward the gate.

"Slay him, My Lord!" he hissed.

Xar gnashed his teeth. He couldn't cast a spell that would kill the dragon without killing the mensch. And he needed them, needed to question them.

Perhaps if they saw the dragon in its true form, they would be frightened into fleeing.

The lord drew a single sigil in the air. The spell was a simple one, not being battle magic. The sigil flared red, expanded, blazed through the air toward the gentleman dressed all in black.

At that moment the gentleman caught hold of the whining Sang-drax by the throat. The sigil struck both of them, flared around them, entwining them in magical flame.

An enormous wingless dragon with bright, shining green scales, the color of the jungle in which it dwelt, reared up over the walls of the city. Confronting it was a huge serpent, its foul body covered in slime, reeking of the dead of centuries. Its head had only one red eye.

Xar was nearly as startled by the sight of this apparition as the mensch were. He had never seen a dragon-snake in its true form. He had read Haplo's description of them on Chelestra, but now Xar understood fully Haplo's loathing, revulsion, even fear. Xar, Lord of the Nexus, who had battled innumerable terrible foes in the Labyrinth, was shaken and unnerved.

The dragon opened massive jaws, closed them on the serpent's neck, just below the toothless head. The serpent's tail lashed out, coiled around the dragon with crushing force, seeking to squeeze the life out of its foe. Twisting and screaming in fury, the two thrashed and flailed, threatening to destroy the citadel. The walls shivered; the gate trembled as the massive bodies crashed into them. If the walls fell, the tytans would be able to enter the city.

The mensch did not flee, but remained rooted to the spot with terror. Xar could not work his magic—either out of fear of hitting Sang-drax or fear *of* Sang-drax. The lord wasn't certain, and his confusion angered him, caused him to hesitate.

And suddenly the two were gone. The dragon and serpent, bound in a deadly embrace, vanished.

The mensch stood staring stupidly at nothing. Xar sought to gather his rattled thoughts. An old man clad in mouse-colored robes wandered out of the shadows.

"Take care of yourself, you sorry excuse for a reptile," Zifnab called, waving good-bye sadly.

# CHAPTER ✦ 26

# THE CITADEL

# PRYAN

✦

XAR STOOD IN AMAZEMENT. THE TWO WERE GONE, DEFINITELY GONE. HE REACHED out mentally, searching for them. He sought them in Death's Gate. He sought them on the other worlds. No trace. They were, quite simply, gone. And he had no idea where.

If one believed Haplo . . .

But Xar didn't. He put that notion out of his mind.

He was baffled, enraged . . . intrigued. If the dragon and its foe were gone from this world, this universe, then they must have found a way out. Which meant that there *was* a way out.

"Well, of course there is!" A hand clapped Xar soundly on the back. "A way out. A way to the Immortal."

Xar turned swiftly. "You!" He scowled.

"Who?" The old man brightened.

"Zifnab!" Xar spat the name.

"Oh." The old man sagged despondently. "Not someone else? You weren't expecting someone else? A Mr. Bond, perhaps?"

Xar recalled Sang-drax's warning. *Beware the old man.* It seemed almost laughable. Still, the old man had escaped from the prisons of Abarrach.

"What are you talking about?" Xar demanded, eyeing the old man with more interest.

"Beats the hell out of me," said Zifnab, quite cheerful. "What was I talking about? I rarely remember. I try not to remember, in fact."

His face went gray. His eyes lost their vague expression, were suddenly focused, suddenly pained. "It hurts—remembering. I don't do it. Not my memories. Other people's memories . . . easier, much easier . . ."

Xar was grim. "'A way out,' you said. 'A way to the Immortal' . . ."

Zifnab's eyes narrowed. "The final *Jeopardy* answer, eh? I have thirty seconds to write down the question. Dum-de-dum, dum, dadoo-de-doo. There! I think I've got it." He looked triumphantly at Xar. "What is the Seventh Gate?"

"What *is* the Seventh Gate?" Xar asked casually.

"That's the question!" Zifnab said.

"But what's the answer?" Xar was rapidly losing patience.

"That's the answer! To the question. Do I win?" Zifnab asked hopefully. "Chance to come back tomorrow?"

"I may give you a chance to stay alive today!" Xar snarled. Reaching out, he took hold of the wizard's arm, gripped it tightly. "Enough foolery, old man. Where is the Seventh Gate? Your companion obviously knew—"

"Why, so did yours," Zifnab countered. "Didn't he tell you? Mind you don't crumple the fabric . . ."

"Companion? Sang-drax? Nonsense. He knows only that I am searching for it. If he had known, he would have taken me to it."

Zifnab looked extremely wise and intelligent—or at least he made the attempt. He drew near Xar, whispered, "On the contrary, he's leading you away from it."

Xar gave the old man's arm a painful twist. "You know where the Seventh Gate is!"

"I know where it isn't," Zifnab said meekly. "If that's any help."

"Leave him alone!"

Preoccupied with the old Sartan, Xar had forgotten the mensch. He turned to find one of them daring to interfere.

"You're hurting him!" The elven female (Xar couldn't recall her name) was attempting to pry his hand off Zifnab's arm. "He's only a daft old man. Leave him alone. Paithan! Come help!"

Xar reminded himself again that he needed these mensch—at least until they had shown him the secrets of the citadel. Xar removed his hand from Zifnab's arm, was about to make some explanatory remark when another mensch dashed up. This one looked scandalized.

"Aleatha! What are you doing? This really isn't any of our business. I apologize, sir, for my sister. She's somewhat . . . well, somewhat . . ." The elf hesitated.

"Pigheaded?" offered a human male, coming up behind the elven female.

Her name was apparently Aleatha. She whirled around, slapped the human male across the face.

At this point, a human female entered the fray. "What did you hit Roland for? He didn't do anything!"

"Rega's right," said the man called Roland. He was nursing a red cheek. "I didn't do anything."

"You said I had the face of a pig!" Aleatha stated haughtily.

"He said you were pigheaded, Aleatha." Paithan attempted to explain. "It doesn't mean the same thing in human that it means in elven . . ."

"Oh, don't pander to her, Paithan!" Rega snapped. "She knows perfectly well what he meant. She speaks human better than she lets on."

"Excuse me, Rega, but this is between me and my sister—"

"Yes, Rega," interjected Aleatha, arching her eyebrows. "We don't need any *outsiders* interfering in our family business."

"Outsiders!" Rega flushed, glared at Paithan. "So that's what you think of me! An outsider! Come on, Roland. We *outsiders* are going back to *our* side of the city!"

Grabbing hold of her brother's arm, Rega hauled him down the street.

"Rega, I never said that . . ." Paithan started to run off after them. Pausing, he glanced back at Xar. "Uh, excuse me, won't you?"

"Oh, Paithan, for Orn's sake, find a backbone!" Aleatha cried.

Paithan didn't answer, continued following after Rega. Aleatha flounced off in another direction.

This left the dwarf, who had not said a word. He glowered darkly at both Xar and Zifnab; then, with a parting grunt, he turned on his heel and trudged off.

Long ago the Sartan and Patryns fought over who would control these creatures. Why did we bother? Xar wondered. We should have tied them all up in a sack and drowned them!

"Haplo knows," Zifnab announced.

"So I've been told," Xar said irritably.

"He doesn't know he knows, but he knows." Zifnab took off his disreputable hat, rubbed his hair until it stood straight up on his head.

"If this is some trick on your part to try to keep Haplo alive, it won't work," Xar snapped testily. "He will die. He may already be dead. And his corpse will lead me to the Seventh Gate."

"Trick." Zifnab sighed. "The trick is on you, I'm afraid, old chap. Die. Yes, Haplo may well die. In a place where *you'll* never find him."

"Ah, then you know where he is?" Xar didn't believe it, but he was playing along, still hoping for something useful.

"Well, of course I know!" Zifnab said, insulted. "He's in—ulp!" The old man clapped his hand over his mouth.

"Yes?" Xar prodded.

"Can't say. Top secret. For your eyes only. My eyes, that is."

Xar had an idea.

"Perhaps I was too precipitous in my decision to execute Haplo," the lord said, musing. "He is a traitor, but I can be generous. I *will* be generous. I pardon Haplo. There, you see. I forgive him —as a father should forgive his erring child. And now you say he is in some type of danger. We will go and find him. You and I. You will lead me to him."

Xar began steering the old man toward the city gate. "We'll go back to my ship. Rescue Haplo . . ."

"I'm touched. Truly touched," said Zifnab, moist-eyed. "My dragon often says that about me, you know. But it's really quite impossible."

Xar began forming a spell. "You *will* come with me, old man . . ."

"Oh, I'd be tickled to death to come with you," Zifnab said cheerfully. "If you were going anywhere. But you're not. Your ship, you see . . ." His gaze shifted to the sky.

Xar's ship was lifting above the treetops, sailing away. The lord was momentarily astounded; then he swiftly cast a spell, a spell that should have taken him instantly on board. The runes flared on his body. He started to leap forward through time and space, but fell back as if he'd struck a wall. Sartan magic. He tried again, only to run into the invisible barrier.

Furious, Xar rounded on the old man, set to cast a spell that would wither the flesh from the fragile bones.

The imposing gentleman dressed all in black stepped out of the shadows. He was bloody and disheveled, his clothes torn, and he looked exhausted. But he took hold of Xar's wrist in his, gripped it with a strength that the Lord of the Nexus with all his magic could not break.

"Leave him alone," said the gentleman. "He's not responsible. Your friend the serpent, the one you know as Sang-drax. He escaped me. He's the one who is blocking your magic. He's the one stealing your ship."

"I don't believe you!"

The lord's ship was now nothing more than a speck in the sky.

"He's taken your form, Lord of the Nexus," said the gentleman. "Your people think Sang-drax is you. They'll obey all his commands —and he'll probably repay them with death."

"If what you say is true, then he must have some urgent need for the ship," Xar said confidently, trying to calm himself, though he cast a swift and frowning glance at his disappearing vessel.

The gentleman was speaking to Zifnab. "You don't look well, sir."

"Not my fault," the old man said, pouting. He pointed an accusing finger at Xar. "I told him I was Bond. James Bond. He didn't believe me."

"What else did you tell him, sir?" the gentleman asked, looking severe. "Nothing you weren't supposed to, I take it?"

"Well, now, that depends," said Zifnab, rubbing his hands together nervously, not meeting the gentleman's eye. "We did have such a nice chat."

The imposing gentleman nodded gloomily. "That's what I feared. You've done damage enough for one day, sir. Time to go inside and have your warming drink. The human female will be happy to make it for you, sir."

"Of course she'd be happy to! Make her day! But she won't!" Zifnab whined querulously. "She doesn't know how. No one makes it the way you do."

"Yes, sir. Thank you, sir. I'm very sorry, sir, but I won't be able to . . . fix your drink tonight." The gentleman had gone extremely pale. He managed a wan smile. "I'm not feeling very well. I'll just take you to your bedchamber, sir . . ."

Once they were gone, Xar could give vent to his anger. He glared around the city's walls, walls that were suddenly prison walls, for though he could walk out of that gate with ease (not counting the tytans, which were suddenly the least of his worries), he had no ship, no way to travel back through Death's Gate. No way to reach Haplo—either dead or alive.

That is, if he believed what the old man had told him.

Feeling weak and old and tired—unusual feelings for the Lord of the Nexus—Xar sat down on a bench in the strange gathering darkness that appeared to be falling on the citadel and nowhere else. Xar tried again to reach Marit, but there was no answer to his urgent summons.

Had she betrayed him? Had Sang-drax betrayed him? . . .

"Would you believe my enemy?" The whisper came from the night, startling Xar. He stared into the shadows, saw glowing there a single red eye.

Xar rose. "Are you here? Come out where I can see you!"

"I am not here in actual physical presence, Lord. My thoughts are with you."

"I had much rather my ship was with me," Xar said angrily. "Bring my ship back to me."

"If you command, Lord, I will." Sang-drax was humble. "But may I present an alternate plan? I overheard the conversation between you and that old fool, who may not be as foolish as he would have us believe. Allow *me* to search for Haplo, while you go on with your business here."

Xar pondered. Not a bad idea at that. He had too much to do, too much at stake to leave now. His people were on Abarrach, poised for war. He had to continue looking for the Seventh Gate; and he still needed to determine whether he had learned the art of bringing life to the dead. Several of those goals might be accomplished here. In addition, he would find out whether Sang-drax was loyal.

He was beginning to see the outline of a plan.

"If I agree to let you search for Haplo, how do *I* return to Abarrach?" Xar demanded, not wanting Sang-drax to think he had the upper hand.

"Another ship is available to you, Lord. The mensch know its location."

Probably inside the city somewhere, Xar reasoned.

"Very well." The lord gave his permission magnanimously. "I

will let you know the moment I hear from Marit. Meanwhile, do what you can to find him on your own. Remember, I want Haplo's corpse—and in good condition!"

"I live only to serve you, Lord Xar," Sang-drax said humbly. The single eye closed in reverence, and then the presence was gone.

"Excuse me, sir," came a voice, speaking elven.

Xar had been aware of the young elf's presence for some time, but, absorbed in his mental conversation with Sang-drax, he hadn't paid any attention. Now was the moment, however, to start putting his plan into action.

The Lord of the Nexus gave an affected start of surprise, peered through the shadows.

"I beg your pardon, young man. I didn't hear you come up. What was your name again? Forgive me for asking, but I'm old and my mind wanders."

"Paithan," said the elf kindly. "Paithan Quindiniar. I came back to apologize for the way we behaved. We've all been under a lot of strain lately. And then, what with the dragon and that horrible serpent and Zifnab . . . That reminds me, have you seen the old man lately?"

"No, I'm afraid not," Xar answered. "I must have dozed off. When I woke up, he was gone."

Paithan looked alarmed. He glanced around anxiously. "Orn take him, the crazy old bugger. I wonder where he's got to? No good searching for him tonight, though. You must be tired and hungry. Please, come, share dinner with my sister and me. We . . . uh . . . usually eat with the others, but I don't suppose they'll be joining us tonight."

"Why, thank you, my boy." Xar reached out a hand. "Would you mind assisting me? I'm somewhat feeble . . ."

"Oh, certainly, sir." Paithan offered Xar his arm.

The Lord of the Nexus clasped the elf close to him, and together —the elf supporting the lord's faltering steps—they proceeded slowly along the streets toward the citadel.

And while they were walking, Xar received a response to his summons.

"Marit," he said silently. "I have been waiting to hear from you . . ."

# CHAPTER ♦ 27

## LOST

♦

Marit sat with her back against a chill stone wall, watching the human assassin keep watch over her. He was leaning back against the wall opposite, a pipe in his mouth and a most foul-smelling smoke issuing from it. His eyelids were closed, but she knew that if she so much as brushed a strand of hair out of her face, she'd see the black glitter of his deep-sunken eyes.

Lying on a pallet on the floor between the two, Haplo slept fitfully, uneasily, not the healing sleep of her kind. Beside him another set of eyes kept careful watch, dividing their attention between her and the master. Hugh the Hand sometimes slept. The dog never did.

Growing irritated at the unrelenting scrutiny, Marit turned her back on both the watchers and, hunkering down, began to hone her dagger. It didn't need honing, nor did it need the sigla redrawn. But fussing with the dagger gave her something to do besides pacing the chill floor—around and around, around and around until her legs ached. Perhaps, though she didn't really expect it, if she quit watching them, the watchers might relax and grow careless.

She could have told them they were worrying over nothing. She wasn't going to harm him. Not now. Her orders had been changed. Haplo was to live.

Knife sharpened, Marit thrust it into a minute crack between two of the large blocks of white polished stone that formed the floors, walls, and domed ceiling of the strange room in which they'd been imprisoned. She slid the dagger along the crack, probing, testing for a weakness she knew wouldn't be there. Sartan runes were engraved on each block. Sartan runes surrounded her, were on the floor, everywhere she looked. The runes didn't harm her, but she avoided touching them. They made her nervous, uncomfortable, just as this room made her nervous and uncomfortable.

And it was impossible to leave.

She knew. She'd tried.

The room was large, well lit, with a diffused white light that shone from everywhere at once and nowhere in particular. A maddening sort of light—it was beginning to annoy her. There was a door, but it was covered with Sartan sigla. And though again the runes didn't react when Marit came near, she was loath to touch the door they guarded.

She couldn't read the Sartan writing; she'd never learned. Haplo could, though. She'd wait until he woke up to tell her what it said. Since he was to live.

Haplo was to live. Marit made a vicious stab into the crack, levered the dagger against the block in a completely futile attempt to wiggle the stone loose. It didn't budge. She was likely to break her dagger first. Angry, frustrated, and—though she refused to admit it—frightened, she snatched the dagger from the crack and hurled it away. The blade skidded across the polished floor, caromed off the wall, and slid back to the center of the room.

The assassin's eyes opened, two glittering slits. The dog lifted its head, regarded her warily. Marit ignored them both, turned her back on them.

"Is Haplo dead?"

"No, Lord. I am afraid I failed in my—"

"He is *not* dead. Has he escaped you?"

"No, Lord. I am with him—"

"Then *why* is he not dead?"

A knife, she could have said. A cursed Sartan knife. He saved my life, she could have said. Saved it even though I'd tried to kill him. All these things she could have said.

"I have no excuse, Lord," was what she did say. "I failed."

"Perhaps this task is too difficult for you, Marit. I have sent Sang-drax to deal with Haplo. Where are you?"

Marit blushed again, hotly, at the memory of her shame-filled reply. "In a Sartan prison, Lord."

"A Sartan prison! Are you certain?"

"All I know, Lord, is that I am in a white room covered with Sartan runes and there is no way out. A Sartan is here, keeping guard on us. He is the one you described, Lord, the one known as Alfred. A friend of Haplo's. This Alfred was the one who brought us here. Our ship was destroyed on Chelestra."

"The two are in this together, undoubtedly. Tell me what happened."

She told him: the strange weapon with the Sartan runes, the tytan, the waters of Chelestra, the steering stone in her hands, the dragon-snakes.

"We were brought here, Lord—by the Sartan."

"He *brought* you? How?"

"He . . . he put his foot in the gate. That's the only way I can describe it.

"I remember the water rising; the ship was breaking apart, our magic failing. I took hold of the steering stone. It was still dry, its magic still working. Images of the worlds flashed before my mind. I grasped the first I saw and clung to it and Death's Gate opened for me. Then the water was washing over me, drowning me, drowning the magic. The gate began to close. The ship began sliding beneath the water; the dragon-snakes were coiled around it.

"A serpent head smashed through the wood, dove straight for Haplo. I reached out, caught hold of him, and dragged him out of the creature's jaws. The horrible red eyes swiveled until they found me. The gate was closing fast, too fast for me to stop it. And then the gate stuck about halfway, as if something had jammed it open.

"A bright light shone on me. Silhouetted against the light was the figure of a stooped and gangling man, who was peering at us worriedly. He reached out his hands to Haplo. I hung on to him and I was pulled through the gate. Just as it began to shut again, I fell and kept on falling."

There had been something else, but it was a vague shadow, on the fringes of her consciousness, and so she did not think it proper to mention it to Xar. It was unimportant anyway. Nothing more than a voice—a kindly voice—saying to her, "There now, I've got him. He's safe. You can let go." She remembered being relieved of a dragging weight and of sinking thankfully into sleep.

"What is the Sartan doing to you?"

"Nothing, Lord. He comes and goes like a thief, creeping in and out of the room. He refuses to look at me or talk to me. The Sartan's only concern is for Haplo. And no, Lord, I have not spoken to the Sartan. Nor will I give him the satisfaction!"

"True. It would make you look weak, vulnerable. What is this Alfred like?"

"A mouse. A scared rabbit. But I assume this is only his disguise, Lord, intended to lull me into a false sense of security."

"Undoubtedly you are right. I wonder one thing, though, Wife. You *saved* Haplo's life on Chelestra. You could have left him to die, it seems."

"Yes, I saved him, Lord. You wanted his corpse."

No mention of the fact that the dragon-snakes terrified her. That it had seemed likely *she* would die on Chelestra, along with Haplo. Xar trusted the dragon-snakes. He knew them better than she did. It was not her place to question . . .

"The dragon-snakes would have brought him to me," Xar returned. "But then I suppose you could not have known that. Describe this prison."

She did so. An empty room, made of polished white stone, covered with Sartan runes. "And thus my magic will not work here," she said ruefully. "I am surprised we are still able to communicate, Husband."

"That is because such magic is internal. It does not attempt to reach into the possibilities, and thus the Sartan magic does not affect it. As you say, Haplo will be able to read the Sartan runes. He will know where you are. Or perhaps his 'friend' will tell him. Haplo won't kill you, will he? Since you tried to kill him?"

"No, Lord. He will not kill me."

It was well Xar could hear only words through the magic. He could not hear her sigh.

"Excellent. On second thought, I think it would be best if you stayed with him."

"Are you certain, Lord? Once I escape this place, I can find a ship. I know I can. I—"

"No. Stay with Haplo. Report to me what he and his Sartan friend say to each other about this room, about Pryan, about any of the other worlds. From now on, Marit, report to me everything Haplo says."

"Yes, Lord." She was now a spy. Her final humiliation. "But what am I to say to him? He'll wonder why I don't try to kill him—"

"You slept with him. You bore his child. He loves you still. Do you need me to elaborate, my dear?"

No, she didn't. And that was how their conversation ended.

Marit's stomach clenched. She was almost physically ill. How could Xar ask such a thing of her? To pretend to make love to Haplo! To ingratiate herself to him, cling to him and, while she was clinging, suck his blood like a leech. No! Such an insidious scheme was dishonorable! No Patryn would agree to it. She was disappointed, bitterly disappointed in Xar, that he could even suggest such a repulsive—

Her anger, her disappointment seeped away.

"I understand. You don't think I would be pretending," she said softly to the absent Xar. "I failed you. I saved Haplo's life. *You* think I am still in love with him, don't you, Lord! Otherwise you would never have asked me to do this."

There had to be a way—another way—to convince Haplo that she was, if not exactly for him, at least no longer against him.

Patryn law! Marit lifted her head, almost smiled, but checked herself, with a stealthy glance at the mensch assassin. It wouldn't do to look suddenly pleased with herself.

She continued to sit quietly in the prison; she had no idea how long. Alfred came and went. She watched him distrustfully. Hugh the Hand watched her distrustfully. The dog watched them all (with the exception of Alfred) distrustfully, and Alfred appeared extremely upset and unhappy about the whole thing.

At length, bone-tired, Marit lay down to sleep. She had nearly drifted off when a voice jerked her to wakefulness.

"Haplo, how are you feeling?"

Hugh the Hand was asking the question. Marit shifted her position slightly so that she could see. Haplo was sitting up on his pallet, staring around in amazement. The dog, with a pleased bark, was on its feet, nosing its master eagerly. Haplo petted it, rubbed its muzzle and jowls. The animal's tail wagged furiously.

"How long have I been out?" Haplo asked.

"Who knows?" the Hand answered with disgust. "How can you tell in this place? I don't suppose you have any idea where we are now?"

Haplo glanced around again, frowned. "I've seen some place like this before . . . but I can't remember . . ."

His gaze flicked over to Marit, held. He'd caught her staring at him. Too late to try to pretend she was asleep. She stiffened, looked away. She was aware suddenly of her dagger, lying in the middle of the floor, lying between them.

"Don't worry," Hugh the Hand grunted, following Haplo's gaze. "Between the dog and me and Alfred, we haven't let her get close to you."

Haplo propped himself up on one elbow. He was weak, far too weak for a Patryn who had been through the healing sleep. The wound on the heart-rune. Such a wound would have doomed him in the Labyrinth.

"She saved my life," he said.

Marit could feel his eyes on her. She wished there was someplace to hide in this damn room, some way to escape. She might even try the door, but she'd look a fool if she couldn't break out. Gritting her teeth, keeping a tight hold on herself, she sat up and pretended to be absorbed in lacing her boot. After all, what Haplo had just said was going to work to her advantage.

The assassin grunted. Removing the pipe from his mouth, he knocked the bowl against the wall, dumped ashes on the floor.

Haplo's attention shifted back to the human.

"Did you say Alfred?"

"Yeah. I said Alfred. He's here. Off somewhere, getting food." He jerked a thumb at the door.

Haplo took in his surroundings. "Alfred. Now I remember what this place reminds me of—the mausoleum, on Arianus."

Marit, recalling Xar's command, listened carefully. The words meant nothing to her, but she felt a chill go over her. Mausoleum. It reminded her of Abarrach—a *world* that was a mausoleum.

"Did Alfred say where we are?"

Hugh smiled—a terrible smile that tightened his lips, darkened his eyes. "Alfred hasn't had much to say to me. In fact, he's been avoiding me."

"I'm not surprised."

Haplo sat up straight, looked down at his hand—the hand that had picked up the cursed Sartan knife. It had been black, the flesh burned off. Now the arm was whole, uninjured. He looked over at her.

Marit knew what he was thinking as well as if he'd said it aloud. She was still close to him, and that irritated her.

"You track my thoughts like a wolfen tracks a wounded man," he'd said once, teasing her.

What she had never told him was how closely he'd been able to track hers. At first she'd hungered for such closeness, one reason that she'd stayed with him so long, longer than any other man she'd ever been with before. But then she'd found herself liking him too much, counting on him, becoming dependent on him. And it was then she'd realized she was going to have his child. It was then she'd left.

Bad enough knowing she'd lose him to the Labyrinth; to have to face losing the child, too . . .

*Be the one who leaves. Don't be the one left.* It had become her credo.

She looked at him and knew exactly what he was thinking. *Someone has healed me. Someone has closed the circle of my being.* He looked at her, wanting it to be her. Why? Why couldn't he realize it was over?

"The Sartan healed you," she said to him. "Not me." Slowly and deliberately, she turned away again.

Which was all very well and all very dignified, but sometime soon she was going to have to explain that she wasn't out to kill him anymore.

Marit wove the runes, hoping to snare her dagger, which was still lying in the center of the floor. Her magic fizzled, petered out; the damn Sartan magic in this dreadful room was unraveling her spells.

"Tell me what happened." Haplo had turned his attention back to Hugh the Hand. "How did we get here?"

The human sucked on his pipe, which had gone out. The dog lay at Haplo's side, crowding as close as it could get, its eyes gazing anxiously into its master's face. Haplo gave it a reassuring pat, and it sighed and nestled even closer.

"I don't remember much," the Hand was saying. "Red eyes and giant serpents and you with your hand on fire. And terror. Being more afraid than I've ever been in my life. Or death."

The assassin smiled wryly. "The ship burst apart. Water filled my mouth and my lungs and then the next thing I knew I was in this room, on my hands and knees, heaving up my guts. And you were lying next to me, with your hand and arm like charred wood. And that woman was standing over you with her dagger and the dog was about to go for her throat, and then Alfred came bumbling through the door.

"He said something to her in that strange language you people talk and she seemed about to answer him when she toppled over. She was out cold.

"Alfred looked at you and shook his head; then he looked at her and shook his head again. The dog had shut up by this time, and I'd managed to get onto my feet.

"I said, 'Alfred!' and walked toward him, only I couldn't walk very well. It was more of a lurch."

The Hand's smile was grim. "He turned around and saw me and gave a kind of croak and then *he* toppled over and *he* was out cold. And then I must have passed out, because that's the last thing I remember."

"And when you came to?" Haplo asked.

Hugh shrugged. "I found myself here. Alfred was fussing over you and that woman was sitting over there, watching, and she wasn't saying anything and neither was Alfred. And I stood up and went over to Alfred. This time I made sure I didn't scare him.

"But before I could open my mouth, he was up like a startled gazelle and took off through that door, muttering something about food and I was to keep watch until you came around. And that was a while ago and I haven't seen him since. She's been here the whole time."

"Her name is Marit," said Haplo quietly. He was staring at the floor, running his finger around—but not touching—a Sartan sigil.

"Her name's Death, my friend, and you're the mark."

Marit drew a deep, shivering breath. Might as well get it over.

"Not any longer," she said.

Rising to her feet, she walked over, picked up her dagger from the stone floor.

The dog leapt up, stood over its master protectively, growling. Hugh the Hand rose, too, his body supple, his movement swift. He said nothing, just stood there, watching her through narrowed eyes.

Ignoring them both, Marit carried the dagger to Haplo. Kneeling down, she offered the dagger to him—hilt first.

"You saved my life," she said, cold, grudging. "By Patryn law, that must settle any quarrel between us in your favor."

"But *you* saved my life," Haplo countered, looking at her with a strange intensity that made her extremely uncomfortable. "That makes us even."

"I didn't." Marit spoke with scorn. "It was your Sartan friend who saved you."

"What's she saying?" Hugh the Hand demanded. She had spoken in the Patryn language.

Haplo translated, adding, "According to the law of our people, because I saved her life, any dispute between us is settled in my favor."

"I hardly call trying to murder you a 'dispute,' " Hugh said dryly, sucking on the pipe and eyeing Marit distrustfully. "This is a ruse. Don't believe her."

"Stay out of this, mensch!" Marit told him. "What do worms such as you know of honor?" She turned back to Haplo. She was still holding the dagger out to him. "Well, will you take it?"

"Won't this put you in disfavor with Lord Xar?" he asked, still looking at her with that penetrating intensity.

She forced herself to keep her eyes on his. "That's my concern. I cannot in honor kill you. Just take the damn dagger!"

Haplo took it slowly. He looked at it, turning it around and around in his hand as if he'd never seen anything like it before in his life. It wasn't the dagger he was examining. It was her. Her motives.

Yes, whatever had once been between them was over.

Turning around, she started to walk away.

"Marit."

She glanced back.

He held the dagger out to her. "Here, you shouldn't go unarmed."

Swallowing, jaw clenched, Marit stalked back, grabbed the dagger, slid it into the top of her boot.

Haplo was about to add something. Marit was turning away so that she wouldn't have either to hear him or to respond, when they were all startled by a flash of rune-light and the sound of a stone door creaking open.

Alfred walked into the room, but when he saw them all staring at him, he started backing hastily out.

"Dog!" Haplo ordered.

Giving a joyful bark, the animal dashed forward. It caught hold of the Sartan's coattails and tugged the reluctant Alfred, tripping and stumbling, into the room.

The door shut behind him.

Caught, Alfred cast a meek and unhappy glance at each of them and then, with an apologetic smile and a slight shrug of his thin shoulders, he fainted.

# CHAPTER 28

## LOST

♦

IT TOOK SOME TIME TO RESTORE ALFRED, WHO APPEARED VASTLY RELUCTANT TO rediscover his consciousness. At length his eyes fluttered open. Unfortunately, the first thing he saw was Hugh the Hand, looming over him.

"Hullo, Alfred," the Hand said grimly.

Alfred turned pale. His eyes rolled back in his head.

The assassin reached down, caught hold of Alfred by his frayed lace collar. "Faint again and I'll choke you!"

"No, no. I'm . . . all right. Air. I need . . . air."

"Let him up," Haplo said.

Hugh the Hand released his grip, backed off. Alfred, gasping, staggered to his feet. His gaze fixed firmly on Haplo. "I'm very happy to see you . . ."

"Happy to see me, too, Alfred?" Hugh the Hand demanded.

Alfred slid a swift glance in Hugh's direction and was apparently sorry he'd done so, because his gaze slid away again quite rapidly.

"Uh, certainly, Sir Hugh. Surprised . . ."

"Surprised?" Hugh growled. "Why are you surprised? Because I was *dead* that last time you saw me."

"Well, yes, as a matter of fact, now that I think of it, you were. Quite dead." Alfred flushed, stammered. "You obviously made a . . . a miraculous re—recovery . . ."

"I don't suppose you'd know anything about that, do you?"

"Me?" Alfred raised his eyes to the level of Hugh's knees. "I'm afraid not. I was rather busy at the time. There was the Lady Iridal's safety to worry about, you see . . ."

"Then how do you explain this?" Hugh the Hand ripped his shirt open. The Sartan rune was visible on his breast, now glowing faintly, as if with pleasure. "Look at it, Alfred! Look what you've done to me!"

Alfred raised his eyes slowly, reluctantly. He cast one stricken glance at the rune, then groaned and covered his face with his hands. The dog, whimpering in sympathy, trotted over and placed its paw gently on Alfred's overlarge foot.

Hugh the Hand glared in fury, then suddenly grabbed Alfred and shook him. "Look at me, damn it! Look at what you've done! Wherever I was, I was content, at peace. Then you wrenched me back. Now I can't live, I can't die! End it! Send me back!"

Alfred crumpled, hung like a broken doll in Hugh's hands. The dog, squashed between the two, looked confusedly from one to the other, uncertain which to attack, which to protect.

"I didn't know I did it!" Alfred was babbling, practically incoherent. "I didn't know. You must believe me. I don't remember . . ."

"You—don't—remember!" Hugh the Hand punctuated each word with a shake that eventually drove poor Alfred to his knees.

Haplo rescued the dog, which was in danger of being trampled, and then rescued Alfred.

"Let him alone," Haplo advised. "He's telling the truth—as weird as that might sound. Half the time he doesn't know what he's doing. Like changing himself into a dragon to save my life. Come on, Hugh. Let him go. He's our way out. At least I hope he is. If we're trapped here, none of this is going to matter anyway."

"Let *him* go!" Scarcely able to breathe around his rage, Hugh the Hand glowered, then finally threw the Sartan to the floor. "Who's going to let *me* go?"

Turning on his heel, he walked to the door, flung it open, and left. Marit, watching closely, noted with interest that the Sartan magic made no apparent attempt to stop the mensch. She considered following him, just to escape this room herself, but instantly abandoned the idea. She couldn't leave Haplo. Her lord had commanded her to stay.

"Dog, go with him," Haplo ordered.

The animal dashed off after Hugh the Hand. Haplo knelt down

beside Alfred. Marit took advantage of the confusion to fade quietly into the background, as much as she possibly could in this wide-open room.

Alfred lay huddled on the floor in a heap, pitiful and pathetic. Marit regarded him with scorn. This Sartan didn't look as if he could raise bread dough, let alone raise the dead. Hugh the Hand must be mistaken.

The Sartan was a middle-aged man, with a bald crown and wispy hair straggling down on the sides of his head; he had a gangly, ungraceful body and large feet and hands—all of which appeared to think they belonged to someone else. He was clad in faded velvet breeches, a velvet coat that didn't fit, shabby hose, and a ruffled shirt decorated with tattered lace.

Taking a frayed handkerchief from a torn pocket, Alfred began to mop his face.

"Are you all right?" Haplo asked gruffly, with a kind of grudging concern.

Alfred glanced up at him, flushed. "Yes, thank you. He . . . he had every right to do that, you know. What I did—*if* I did it, and I truly *don't* remember doing it—was wrong. Very wrong. You recall what I said on Abarrach about necromancy?" He whispered the last word.

" 'When a life is brought back untimely, another dies untimely.' I remember. But look, is there any way you can help him?"

Alfred hesitated a moment. He was about to answer *no*, it seemed; then he sighed. His bony shoulders sagged. "Yes, I think it would be possible." He shook his head. "But not here."

"Then where?"

"Do you remember the chamber . . . on Abarrach? The one they call the Chamber of the Damned?"

"Yes," said Haplo, looking uncomfortable. "I remember. I wanted to go back there. I was going to take Xar, to prove to him what I meant about a higher power—"

"Oh, dear, no!" Alfred protested, alarmed. "I don't believe that would be at all wise. You see, I've discovered what that chamber is. Orla told me."

"Told you what?" Haplo demanded.

"She was convinced that we had discovered the Seventh Gate," Alfred said softly, in awed tones.

Haplo shrugged. "Yeah? So what?"

Alfred looked startled at this reaction; then he sighed. "I guess you wouldn't know, at that. You see, when the Sartan sundered the world—"

"Yes, yes," Haplo interrupted impatiently. "Death's Gate. The Final Gate. I've been through enough gates to last me a lifetime. What about this one? What makes it so special?"

"That was where they were when they sundered it," Alfred said in a low voice. "They were in the Seventh Gate."

"So Samah and Orla and the Council got together in this chamber—"

"More than that, Haplo," Alfred said gravely. "They not only came together in the chamber, they imbued the chamber with magic. They tore apart a world and built four new ones from that chamber—"

Haplo gave a whistle. "And it still exists, with all its magic . . . all its power . . ." He shook his head. "No wonder they put warding runes to prevent anyone's getting inside."

"According to Orla, Samah wasn't responsible for that," Alfred said. "You see, when the magic was complete and the worlds were formed, he realized how dangerous this chamber could become—"

"Worlds that could be created could also be destroyed."

"Precisely. And so he sent the chamber into oblivion."

"Why didn't he just destroy the chamber?"

"He tried," Alfred said quietly. "And he discovered he couldn't."

"The higher power stopped him?"

Alfred nodded. "Afraid of what he'd tapped into, unable or unwilling to understand it, Samah sent the chamber away, hoping it would never be discovered. That was the last Orla knew of it. But the chamber *was* discovered, by a group of Sartan on Abarrach—a group desperately unhappy with what was happening to their own people. Fortunately, I don't believe they had any idea what they'd found."

"Yeah, all right, so we were in the Seventh Gate. What has any of this got to do with Hugh the Hand?"

"I think that if he went into the Seventh Gate, he would be free."

"How?"

"I can't be sure," Alfred answered evasively. "Not that it matters anyway. We're not going anywhere."

Haplo glanced around. "Where the devil are we? And did you escape Samah? This place looks familiar, like that tomb on Arianus. I don't suppose we're back on Arianus?"

"No, no, we're not on Arianus."

Haplo waited patiently for the Sartan to continue.

Alfred kept quiet.

"You do know where we are?" Haplo asked dubiously.

Alfred conceded the point with a reluctant nod.

"Then where are we?"

Alfred wrung his hands together. "Let me think how best to explain. First, I must tell you that I didn't escape Samah."

"I'm not interested—"

"Please, let me finish. Have you traveled through Death's Gate since it's been open?"

"Yes. I went back to Arianus. Why?"

"Images of each of the worlds flashed before your eyes, giving you a choice of where you want to go. Do you recall a world that was very beautiful, a world you've never visited, never seen? A world of blue skies, sunlight, green trees, vast oceans—an ancient, ancient world."

Haplo nodded. "I saw that. I wondered at the time—"

"That's where we are," said Alfred. "The Vortex."

Haplo looked around at the bare white marble. "Blue sky. Sunshine. Wonderful." His gaze returned to Alfred. "You're making even less sense than usual."

"The Vortex. The center of the universe. Once it led to the ancient world—"

"A world no longer in existence."

"True. But the images of it must have been accidentally retained—"

"Or put there deliberately, a Sartan trap for someone traveling Death's Gate who shouldn't have been," Haplo said grimly. "I damn near came here myself. Is this where I would have ended up?"

"Yes, I'm afraid so. Although you'll find it's not bad, once you get used to it. All our wants and needs are provided. The magic sees to that. And it's safe. Perfectly safe."

Haplo was looking around again. "And to think I've been worrying about you in the Labyrinth, picturing you dead or worse. And all the time you've been here." He waved his hand. "Safe. Perfectly safe."

"You were concerned about me?" Alfred asked, his wan face brightening.

Haplo made an impatient gesture. "Of course I was concerned. You can't walk across an empty room without causing some sort of catastrophe. And speaking of empty rooms, how do we get out of this one?"

Alfred didn't reply. Lowering his head, he stared at his shoes.

Haplo eyed him thoughtfully. "Samah said he was sending you and Orla to the Labyrinth. Either he made a mistake or he wasn't quite the bastard he made out to be. He sent you both here." A thought seemed to occur to him. "Where is Orla, anyway?"

"Samah wasn't a bad man," Alfred said softly. "Just a very frightened one. But he's not afraid anymore. As for Orla, she left. She went to be with him."

"And you just stayed here? You didn't go with her? You could have at least gone back to warn the other Sartan on Chelestra—"

"You don't understand, Haplo," Alfred said. "I stay here because I have to. There is no way out."

Haplo stared at him in exasperation. "But you said Orla left—"

Alfred began to sing the runes. His ungainly body was suddenly graceful, swaying and whirling to the rhythm of the song. His hands formed the sigla in the air.

The melody was sad, yet sweet, and Marit was suddenly reminded of the last time she'd held her baby in her arms. The memory hurt her, the song hurt her, and the pain made her angry. She was about to lash out, to disrupt the magic spell he was casting—a spell that was undoubtedly meant to weaken her—when a portion of the stone wall disappeared.

Inside the wall, lying in a crystal coffin, was a Sartan woman. Her face was quiet, her eyes closed. She seemed to smile faintly.

Haplo understood. "I'm sorry . . ."

Alfred smiled sadly. "She is at peace. She left to join her husband." He shifted his gaze to Marit; his expression grew stern. "Orla saw what happened to him, saw how he died."

"He was executed for his crimes." Marit was defensive, defiant.

"He suffered as he made us suffer. He deserved what he got. More, even. Far more."

Alfred said nothing. He cast a fond glance at the woman in the crystal coffin, rested his hand on the window with a gentle touch. Then, slowly, his hand moved to another crystal coffin beside hers. This coffin was empty.

"What's that?" Haplo demanded.

"Mine," Alfred said, "when the time comes. You are right. This place is very much like Arianus."

"Too damn much," said Haplo. "You've found another tomb. 'Perfectly safe!'" He snorted. "Well, you're not crawling into it. You're coming with me."

"I'm afraid not. You're not going anywhere. I've told you, there's no way out." Alfred looked back at Orla. "Except her way."

"He's lying!" Marit cried, fending off panic, fighting a sudden terrifying desire to tear at the solid stone with her bare hands.

"No, he's not lying. He's a Sartan. He can't lie. But he's very good at *not* telling the truth." Haplo eyed Alfred. "Death's Gate is around here somewhere. We'll go out through Death's Gate."

"We don't have a ship," Marit reminded him.

"We'll build one." Haplo kept his gaze on Alfred, who was once more staring at his shoes. "What about it, Sartan? Death's Gate? Is that the way out?"

"The gate swings only one way," Alfred said in a low voice.

Frustrated, not certain what to do, Haplo stared at the Sartan.

Marit knew what to do. Leaning down, she slid the dagger from her boot.

"I'll make him talk."

"Leave him alone, Marit. You won't get anything out of him that way."

"I'll try not to damage your 'friend' too much. You don't have to watch."

Haplo stepped in front of her. He said nothing. He simply put his body between her and Alfred.

"Traitor!" Marit tried to dodge around him.

Haplo caught her, his movement quick and deft. He held on to her tightly. She was strong, perhaps stronger than he was at this moment, and she fought to escape. Their arms and hands locked, and as they held each other fast, a blue glow began to shimmer from each hand, each arm.

The rune-magic, coming to life.

Except that this magic wasn't acting either to attack or to defend. It was acting as it would when any two Patryns touched. It was the magic of joining, of closing the circle. It was a magic of healing, of shared strength, shared commitment.

It began to seep inside Marit.

She didn't want it. She was empty inside, empty and hollow, dark and silent. She couldn't even hear her own voice anymore, just the echo of words spoken long ago coming back to her. The emptiness was cold, but at least it wasn't painful. She'd pushed out all the pain, given birth to it, cut the cord.

But the blue glow, soft and warm, spread from Haplo's hand to hers. It began creeping into her. A tiny drop, like a single tear, fell into the emptiness . . .

"Haplo, you'd better come and see this."

It was Hugh the Hand, standing in the door. His voice was harsh, urgent.

Distracted, Haplo turned. Marit broke free of his grasp. He turned back to her, looking at her, and in his eyes was the same warmth she'd felt in the rune-magic. His hand reached out toward her. She had only to take it . . .

The dog came trotting up. Tail wagging, tongue lolling, it started toward her, as if it had found a friend.

Marit threw her dagger at it.

Her aim was rotten. She was upset, could barely see. The dagger grazed the animal along the left flank.

The dog yelped in pain, flinched away from her. The dagger thudded against the wall somewhere near the assassin's right calf. Hugh put his foot on it. Alfred was staring in horror, so pale it seemed he might faint again.

Marit turned her back on them all. "Keep that beast away from me, Haplo. By law, I can't kill you. But I can kill that damn dog."

"Come here, boy," Haplo called. He examined the animal's wound. "It's all right, dog. Just a scratch. You were lucky."

"In case anybody's interested," Hugh the Hand said, "I found the way out. At least I think it's a way out. You'd better come and look. I've never seen anything like it."

Haplo glanced at Alfred, who had flushed bright red. "What's wrong with it? Is it guarded? Magic?"

"Nothing like that," the Hand answered. "More like a joke."

"I doubt it's a joke. The Sartan don't have much of a sense of humor."

"Someone did. The way out is through a maze."

"A maze . . ." Haplo repeated softly.

He knew the truth then. And Marit knew at the same moment Haplo knew. The emptiness inside her filled, filled with fear, fear that twisted and kicked inside her like a living thing. She was almost sick with it.

"So Samah *did* keep his word," Haplo said to Alfred.

The Sartan nodded. His face was deathly white, his expression bleak. "Yes, he kept it."

"He knows where we are?" Hugh the Hand demanded.

"He knows," Haplo said quietly. "He's known all along. The Labyrinth."

# CHAPTER ♦ 29

# THE LABYRINTH

♦

T HEY LEFT THE ROOM OF WHITE MARBLE AND ITS CRYSTAL COFFINS. FOLLOWING Hugh's lead, they traversed a narrow hallway carved out of gray rough-cut rock. The corridor sloped, straight and even, steadily downward. At its end an arched doorway, also carved out of rock, opened into a gigantic cavern.

The vault of the cavern's roof was high overhead, lost in shadows. A dull gray light, shining from a point far opposite the entrance, glistened off the wet surfaces of huge stalactites. Stalagmites thrust up out of the cavern floor to meet them, like teeth in a gaping mouth. Through gaps in the wet teeth a river of black water swirled, flowing in the direction of the cheerless light.

An ordinary enough cavern. Haplo looked at the arched doorway. Touching Marit's arm, he silently called her attention to a mark scratched above it—a single Sartan rune. Marit looked at it, shuddered, leaned against the chill wall.

She was shivering, her bare arms clasped tightly. Her face was averted; her hair hung over it, hiding it. Haplo knew that if he smoothed back that tangled mass of hair, touched her cheek, he'd feel tears. He didn't blame her. Once he would have wept himself. But now he felt strangely elated. This was, after all, where he'd intended to come all along.

Marit couldn't read the Sartan rune-language, but she could read that one sigil. All Patryns could. They could read them and they had come to hate and detest them.

"The First Gate," said Haplo. "We stand at the very beginnings of the Labyrinth."

"Labyrinth," Hugh the Hand repeated. "Then I was right. That is a maze out there." He gestured beyond the gate.

Rows of stalagmites spread out into the darkness. A path, wet and sleek, led from the arch into the stalagmites. Haplo could see from where he stood the first fork in the path, two diverse courses, slanting left and right, each wandering off amid rock formations that had not been naturally created, but had been formed by magic and fear and hate.

There was one right way. All others led to disaster. And they were standing at the very first gate.

"I've been in a few caves in my life," the Hand continued. He gestured into the darkness with the stem of his pipe. "But nothing like this. I walked out onto the path until I came to that first fork; then I caught a glimpse of where it led." He rubbed his chin. The hair was beginning to grow back on his face and his head, a blue-black stubble that must have itched. "I figured I'd better come back before I got myself lost."

"Getting lost would have been the least of your worries," said Haplo. "The wrong turn in that maze leads to death. It was built that way on purpose. The Labyrinth is more than a maze. It's a prison. And my child is trapped in there."

Hugh the Hand removed his pipe from his mouth, stared at Haplo. "I'll be damned."

Alfred huddled in the back, as far from the arched doorway as he could get and still remain near the group.

"You want to tell him about the Labyrinth, Sartan, or shall I?"

Alfred looked up briefly, an expression of hurt in his eyes. Haplo saw the pain, knew the reason for it, chose to ignore it. Alfred wasn't Alfred anymore. He was the enemy. No matter that they were all in this together now. Haplo needed someone to hate, needed his hate as a strong wall to lean against for support, or he'd fall and maybe never get up.

The dog had been standing beside Haplo, near the open archway, sniffing the air and not liking what it smelled. It shook itself all over, padded to Alfred. The dog rubbed against the Sartan's leg, its plumy tail brushing back and forth slowly, gently.

"I understand how you feel," Alfred said. Reaching out, he gave the dog a timid pat on the head. "I'm sorry."

Haplo's wall of hate began to crumble; fear started climbing up over the pieces. He gritted his teeth. "Damn it, Alfred, stop apologizing! I've told you before, it's not your fault!" The echo came bounding back at him.

*Your* fault . . . *your* fault . . . *your* fault . . .

"I know. I will. I'm s-s-s—" Alfred made a hissing sound like a spent teakettle, caught Haplo's eye, and fell silent.

The Hand looked from one to the other. "I don't give a damn whose fault it is. Somebody explain what's going on."

Haplo shrugged. "A long time ago there was a war between his people and mine. We lost and they won—"

"No," Alfred corrected gently, sadly, "nobody won."

"At any rate, they shut us up in this prison, then went off to find prisons of their own. Is that how you'd put it, Alfred?"

The Sartan did not answer.

"This prison is known as the Labyrinth. It's where I was born. It's where she was born." He gestured at Marit. "It's where our child was born. And where our child lives."

"*If* she lives," Marit muttered beneath her breath.

She had regained a certain amount of control; she was no longer shaking. But she did not look at them. Leaning against the wall, she kept her arms clasped about her tightly, holding herself together.

"It's a cruel place, filled with cruel magic that delights not only in killing, but in killing slowly, torturing, tormenting you until death comes as a friend.[1] The two of us managed to escape, with the help of our lord, Xar. But many don't. Many haven't. Generations of our people have been born, have lived and died in the Labyrinth.

"And there are none of our people now living," Haplo finished quietly, "who started at the First Gate and made it all the way through to the end."

The assassin's expression darkened. "What are you saying?"

Marit turned to him, anger burning her tears dry. "It took our people hundreds of years to reach the Final Gate. And they did it by standing on the bodies of those who fell before them! A dying father points out the way ahead to his son. A dying mother hands her

---

[1] One of the Patryn words for "death" is, in fact, the same as the word for "friend."

daughter to those who will carry the child on. I escaped and now I'm back."

She gulped, a dry, wrenching sob. "To face it all over again. The pain, the fear . . . And no hope of escape. We're too far away."

Haplo wanted to comfort her, but he guessed his sympathy wouldn't be appreciated. Besides, what comfort could he offer? She spoke the truth.

"Well, no use standing around here. The sooner we start the sooner we're finished," he said, and didn't realize the dark import of his words until he heard Marit's bitter laughter.

"I was coming on this journey with the intent of going back inside the Labyrinth," he went on, deliberately brisk, businesslike. "I just hadn't planned on entering from this direction. But I guess one way is as good as another. Maybe the best. Now I won't miss anything."

"You were going back?" Marit stared at him in wonder. "Why?" Her eyes narrowed. "To escape Xar?"

"No," Haplo answered. He didn't look at her. His gaze shifted to the cavern, to the gray light gleaming off the eddies in the dark water. "I was going back to find you. And our daughter."

She seemed about to say something; her lips parted. Then they closed over the words. Her eyes lowered.

"I am going in there now to search for our daughter," Haplo said. "Will you go with me?"

Marit raised her head, her face pale. "I . . . I don't know. I have to think . . ."

"Marit, you don't have much choice. There's no other way out."

"According to the Sartan!" She sneered. "Maybe you trust him. But I don't. I have to think about it."

She saw the pity on Haplo's face. Very well. Let him think she was afraid. Let him think she needed time to bolster her courage. What did it matter to her what he thought?

Her body rigid, she stalked up the path toward the mausoleum. Coming level with Alfred, she glared at him until he cringingly fell back out of her way, stumbling over the dog as he did so. Marit swept past him, disappeared up the corridor.

"Where's she off to?" Hugh the Hand demanded, suspicious. "Maybe one of us should go with her."

"Leave her alone. You don't understand. We both nearly died in there. Going back isn't easy. Are you coming?"

The Hand shrugged. "Either that or spend eternity here. I don't suppose I could die of boredom?" He cocked an eye at Alfred.

"No, I'm afraid . . . not," said Alfred, thinking the question was serious.

Hugh laughed, bitter and sharp. "I'll go with you. What can happen to me?"

"Good." Haplo's spirits lightened. He almost began to think they had a chance. "We can use your skills. You know, when I first contemplated going back inside, I thought of you for a companion. Strange the way it's all worked out. What weapons do you carry?"

Hugh the Hand started to answer, but Alfred interrupted.

"Uh . . . that won't matter," he said in a small voice.

"What do you mean, it won't matter? Of course it matters—"

"He can't kill," said Alfred.

Haplo stared, struck dumb with astonishment. He didn't want to believe it, but the more he thought about it, the more sense it made—at least from a Sartan point of view.

"You understand?" Alfred asked hopefully.

Haplo intimated that he did with a few brief and unrepeatable words.

"Well, I sure as hell don't!" Hugh the Hand snarled.

"You can't be killed. You can't kill. It's as simple as that," said Haplo.

"Think about it," Alfred continued in a low voice. "Have you killed anything—even a bug—since your . . . uh . . . return?"

Hugh stared, his face going sallow beneath the black sprouts of beard.

"That's why no one would hire me," he said harshly. Sweat glistened on his skin. "Trian wanted me to kill Bane. I couldn't. I was supposed to kill Stephen. I couldn't. I was hired to kill you"—he gave Haplo a haunted look—"and I couldn't. Damn it, I couldn't even kill myself! I tried"—he stared at his hands—"and I couldn't do it!"

He looked at Alfred, eyes narrowed. "Would the Kenkari have known that?"

"The Kenkari?" Alfred was puzzled. "Ah, yes. The elves who keep the souls of the dead. No, I don't believe they would have known. But the dead would," he added after a moment's thought. "Yes, they would have known. Why?"

"The Kenkari were the ones who sent me to kill Haplo," the Hand said grimly.

"The Kenkari?" Alfred was amazed. "No, no they would never kill anyone or hire it done. You may be certain, you were sent for some other reason . . ."

"Yes," said the Hand, eyes glittering, "I'm beginning to understand. They sent me to find you."

"Isn't that interesting, Alfred," Haplo added, regarding the Sartan intently. "They sent Hugh the Hand to find you. I wonder why?"

Alfred's eyes slid out from beneath both of their gazes. "I can't imagine—"

"Wait a minute," Haplo interrupted. "What you said can't be right. Hugh the Hand *did* damn near kill me. And Marit as well. He has some sort of magical weapon—"

"*Had*," Hugh the Hand corrected with grim satisfaction. "It's gone. Lost in the sea water."

"A magical weapon?" Alfred shook his head. "From the Kenkari? They are quite gifted in magic, but they would never use their magic to make weapons—"

"Naw," Hugh the Hand growled. "I got it from . . . well, let's just say it came from another source. The blade was supposedly of ancient Sartan make and design. Your people used it during some long-ago war . . ."

"Perhaps." Alfred looked extremely unhappy. "Many magical weapons were made, I'm afraid. By both sides. I don't know anything about this particular one, but my guess is that the weapon itself was intelligent, could act on its own. It used you, Sir Hugh, simply as a bearer, a means of transport. That and your fear and will to guide it."

"Well, it's lost now, so it doesn't matter," Haplo said. "Lost in the waters of Chelestra."

"A pity we cannot flood the universe with such water," said Alfred quietly to himself.

Haplo looked into the cavern, into the dark water that flowed through it. He could hear the water now that he listened, hear it churn and gurgle and lap against the bordering rocks. He could imagine what horrid things swam in its foul currents, what dread creatures might crawl out of its dark depths.

"You're not coming with us, are you," Haplo said.

"No," said Alfred, staring at his shoes. "I'm not."

Almost sick with fear, Marit took her time returning to the white room, knowing she must compose herself before she spoke to Xar. He would understand; he always understood. She had seen him—countless times—comfort those unable to go back into the Labyrinth. He was the only one who'd ever done so. He would understand, but he would be disappointed. Marit entered the round room.

The crystal coffins were no longer visible, covered over by Sartan magic, but she sensed their presence. And being around dead Sartan didn't give her as much pleasure as she might have imagined.

Standing at the opposite end of the room from the coffins, as far away as she could get, she placed her hand on the sigil tattooed on her forehead and bowed her head.

"Xar, My Lord," she murmured.

He was with her immediately.

"I know where we are, Lord," she said softly, unable to check a sigh. "We are in the center of the Labyrinth. We stand at the very first gate."

Silence. Then Xar said, "And will Haplo enter?"

"He claims he will. But I doubt he has the courage." She doubted she had the courage, but she didn't mention that. "No one has ever gone back before, Lord, except you." Still, what do we have if we stay here? Our own tombs.

Marit recalled the face of the woman in the crystal coffin. She rested peacefully, wherever she was. Her death had been an easy one.

"What reason does Haplo give for entering the Labyrinth?" Xar asked.

Marit found it difficult to answer. She hesitated, felt him press her—an uncomfortable sensation.

"The—the child, Lord," she said at last, stammering. She'd almost said, *our* child.

"Bah! What a paltry excuse! He must take me for a fool! I know his *true* reason. He has become ambitious, has Haplo. He has succeeded in seizing control of Arianus. Now he and that Sartan friend of his plan to try to subvert my own people, turn them against me. He will enter the Labyrinth and raise his own army! He must be stopped . . . You doubt me, Marit?"

She sensed his displeasure, almost anger. Yet she couldn't help what she felt. "I think he is serious . . . He has certainly never mentioned . . ."

"Of course he wouldn't." Xar dismissed her admittedly weak arguments. "Haplo is cunning and clever. But he will not succeed. Go with him, Daughter. Stay with him. Fight to stay alive. And do not fear. Your time there will not be long. Sang-drax is on his way to the Labyrinth. Through me, he will find you and Haplo. Sang-drax will bring Haplo to me." *Since you have failed.*

Marit heard the rebuke. She accepted it in silence, knowing she deserved it. But the image of the horrid dragon-snakes she'd glimpsed on Chelestra rose hideously in her mind. Firmly she banished the vision. Xar was asking other questions.

"Haplo and the Sartan. What did they talk about? Tell me everything they have said."

"They spoke of Hugh the Hand, how the Sartan might be able to lift the curse of immortal life from the human. They talked of Abarrach and a chamber there. It is called the Chamber of the Damned—"

"Again that wretched chamber." Xar was angry. "Haplo talks of nothing else! He is obsessed with it! He once wanted to take me to it. I—"

A pause.

A long, long pause.

"I . . . have been a fool. He would have taken me," Xar murmured. His words were soft, brushing across her forehead like the wings of a butterfly. "What did he say about this chamber? Did he or the Sartan mention something called the Seventh Gate?"

"Yes, Lord." Marit was astounded, awed. "How did you know?"

"A fool, a blind fool!" he repeated bitterly, and then he was urgent, compelling. "What did they say about it?"

Marit related all she could remember.

"Yes, that is it! A room imbued with magic! Power! What can be created can be destroyed!"

Marit could feel Xar's excitement; it quivered through her like an electric jolt.

"Did they say where it was on Abarrach? How to reach it?"

"No, Lord." She was forced to disappoint him.

"Speak to him about this chamber further! Find out all you can! Where it is! How to enter!" He grew calmer. "But don't rouse his suspicions, Daughter. Be circumspect, cautious. Of course, that is how they plan to defeat me. Haplo must never come to suspect—"

"Suspect what, Lord?"

"Suspect that I know about this chamber. Keep in contact with me, Daughter . . . Or perhaps I should say *Wife.*"

He was pleased with her again. Marit had no idea why, but he was her lord and his commands were to be obeyed without question. And she would be glad to have his counsel when they were in the Labyrinth. But his next statement proved troubling.

"I will let Sang-drax know where you are."

That brought no comfort to her, though she knew it should. Only unease.

"Yes, Lord."

"Of course, I do not need to tell you—mention none of what we have discussed to Haplo."

"No, Lord."

He was gone. Marit was alone. Very much alone. That was what she wanted, what she'd chosen. He travels fastest who travels alone. And she'd traveled fast, very fast indeed.

All the way back to where she'd started.

The four (and the dog) stood at the entrance to the cavern, the entrance to the Labyrinth. The gray light had grown not brighter, but stronger. Haplo judged it must be midday. If they were going, they should go now. No time was a good time to travel in the Labyrinth, but any time during the daylight was better than at night.

Marit had rejoined them. Her face was pale but set, her jaw clenched. "I will go with you," was all she'd said, and she'd said that much sullenly, with reluctance.

Haplo wondered why she'd decided to come. But he knew asking would do no good. Marit would never tell him, and his asking would only alienate him from her further. She had been like this when they'd first met. Walled up inside herself. He had managed, with patience and care, to find a door—only a small one, but it had permitted him inside. And then it had slammed shut. The child —he knew now that was why she'd left him and he thought he understood.

Rue, she'd named the baby.

And now the door was closed and shuttered, walled up. There was no way in. And from what he could tell, she'd sealed the only way out.

Haplo glanced up at the Sartan sigil shining above the archway. He was entering the Labyrinth, the deadliest place in existence, without any weapons—except for his magic. But that, at least, wasn't a problem. In the Labyrinth, there were always plenty of ways to kill.

"We should go," Haplo said.

Hugh the Hand was ready, eager to get on with it. Of course, he had no idea what he was walking into. Even if he couldn't die . . . and who knew? Against the Labyrinth's cruel magic, the Sartan heart-rune might not protect him. Marit was frightened, but resolved. She was going forward, probably because she couldn't go back.

Either that or she was still hoping to murder him.

And the one person—the last person Haplo would have said he needed or wanted . . .

"I wish you'd come, Alfred."

The Sartan shook his head. "No, you don't. I'd only be in your way. I would faint . . ."

Haplo regarded the man grimly. "You've found your tomb again, haven't you? Just like in Arianus."

"And this time I'm not going to leave." Alfred gazed fixedly downward. He must know his shoes very well by now. "I've caused too much trouble already." He lifted his eyes, cast a quick glance at Hugh the Hand, lowered his eyes again. "Too much," he repeated. "Good-bye, Sir Hugh. I'm really . . . very sorry."

"Good-bye? That's it?" the Hand demanded angrily.

"You don't need me to end the . . . curse," Alfred said softly. "Haplo knows where to go, what to do."

No, Haplo didn't, but then he figured it wouldn't matter anyway. They'd likely never get that far.

He was suddenly angry. Let the damn Sartan bury himself. Who cared? Who needed him? Alfred was right. He'd only be in the way, be more trouble than he was worth.

Haplo entered the Labyrinth. The dog cast one mournful look back at Alfred, then trotted along at its master's heels. Hugh the Hand followed. He looked grim but relieved, always grateful for action. Marit brought up the rear. She was very pale, but she didn't hesitate.

Alfred stood at the entryway, staring at his shoes.

Haplo walked the path carefully. Coming to the first fork, he halted, examined both branches. One way looked much the same as the other, both probably equally bad. The tooth-like rock formations thrust out from all sides, blocking his view. He could see only upward, see what looked like dripping fangs. He could hear the dark water swirling onward, into the heart of the Labyrinth.

Haplo grinned to himself in the darkness. He touched the dog on the head, turned the dog's head toward the entrance.

Toward Alfred.

"Go on, boy," Haplo commanded. "Fetch!"

# CHAPTER ✦ 30

# THE CITADEL

# PRYAN

✦

"I DON'T LIKE THAT HORRID WIZARD, PAITHAN, AND I THINK YOU SHOULD TELL him to leave."

"Orn's ears, Aleatha, I can't tell Lord Xar to leave. He has as much right to be here as we do. We don't own this place—"

"We were here first."

"Besides, we can't send the old gentleman out into the arms of the tytans. It would be murder."

The elf's voice dropped, but not low enough that Xar couldn't hear what was being said.

"And he could prove useful, help protect us if the tytans manage to break inside. You saw how he got rid of those monsters when he first came. Whoosh! Blue lights, magic fire."

"As to that magic fire"—this was the human male, adding his small modicum of wisdom—"the wizard might do the same to us if we make him mad."

"Not likely," Xar murmured, smiling unpleasantly. "I wouldn't waste the effort."

The mensch were having a meeting—a private, secret meeting, or so they supposed. Xar knew all about it, of course. He was seated at his ease in the Sartan library in the citadel. The mensch were gathered down by the garden maze—a good distance away, but Xar clearly heard every word they were saying.

"What is it you don't like about him, Aleatha?" the human female was asking.

What was her name? Xar couldn't recall. Again, he didn't waste the effort.

"He gave me this lovely necklace," the human was continuing. "See. I think it must be a ruby. And look at the cunning little squiggly mark cut into it."

"I got one, too," said the elf Paithan. "Mine's a sapphire. And it has the same squiggle. Lord Xar said that when I wore it, someone would be watching over me. Isn't it pretty, Aleatha?"

"I think it's ugly." The elf female spoke with scorn. "And I think *he's* ugly—"

"He can't help how he looks."

"Something I'm certain *you* can understand, Roland," Aleatha interjected coolly. "As to those 'gifts,' he tried to give me one. I refused. I didn't like the look in his eye."

"Come on, Thea. Since when have you turned down jewels? As for that look, you've seen it a thousand times before. Every man looks at you that way," Paithan said.

"*Then* they get to know her," Roland muttered.

Either Aleatha didn't hear him or she chose to ignore him. "The old man only offered me an emerald. I've been offered better than that a hundred times over."

"And taken them up on their offers a hundred times over, I'll wager," Roland said, more loudly this time.

"Come on, you two, stop it." Paithan intervened. "What about you, Roland? Did Lord Xar give you one of these jewels?"

"Me?" Roland sounded amazed. "Look, Paithan, I don't know about you elves, but among us humans, guys don't give necklaces to other guys. As to guys who *accept* jewelry from other guys, well . . ."

"What are you saying?"

"Nothing, Paithan," Rega intervened. "Roland's not saying anything. He took the necklace; don't let him fool you. I saw him asking Drugar about the jewel, trying to get it appraised."

"What about it, Drugar? How much are they worth?"

"The gem is not of dwarf-make. I cannot tell. But I wouldn't wear one. I get a bad feeling from them." The dwarf's voice was low and gruff.

"Sure you do," Roland scoffed. "Such a bad feeling you'd gladly take every one of them for yourself. Look, Drugar, old buddy, never try to swindle a swindler. I know all the tricks. It *has* to be dwarf-made. Your people are the only ones who dig deep enough below the leaf-level to find jewels like this. Come on. Tell me what it's worth."

"What does it matter what it's worth?" Rega flared. "You'll never get a chance to cash in on it. We're trapped in here for the rest of our lives and you know it."

The mensch all fell silent. Xar yawned. He was growing bored, and this mindless chatter was starting to irritate him. He was beginning to regret giving them the magical gems, which brought every word of what they said to him. Then suddenly he heard what he'd been wanting to hear all along.

"I guess that brings up the real reason for our meeting," Paithan said quietly. "Do we tell him about the ship? Or keep it to ourselves?"

A ship! Sang-drax had been right. The mensch *did* have a ship hidden around here. Xar shut the Sartan book he'd been attempting to read, concentrated on listening.

"What difference does it make?" Aleatha asked languidly. "If a ship really does exist—which I doubt—we can't reach it. We have only Cook's word on it, and who knows what she and her brats thought they saw out there? The tytans have probably smashed it to toothpicks anyway."

"No," Paithan said after another moment's silence. "No, they haven't. And it does exist."

"How do you know?" Roland demanded, suspicious.

"Because I've seen it. You can—from the top of the citadel. From the Star Chamber."

"You mean all this time you knew that the others were telling the truth about what they saw? That a ship was out there and still in good shape and you didn't tell us?"

"Don't shout at me! Yes, damn it, I knew! And I didn't tell you for the simple reason that you would have acted stupid the way you're acting now and rushed out like the others and gotten your fool head bashed in—"

"Well, and so what if I did? It's my head! Just because you're sleeping with my sister doesn't make you my big brother."

"You could use a big brother."

"Oh, yeah?"

"Yeah!"

"Stop it, both of you, please—"

"Rega, get out of my way. It's time he learned . . ."

"You're all behaving like children."

"Aleatha! Where are you going? You shouldn't go into that maze. It's . . ."

"I'll go where I please, Rega. Just because *you're* sleeping with my brother—"

Imbeciles! Xar clenched his fists. For an instant he considered transporting himself down to them, shaking the truth out of them. Or perhaps choking it out of them. He grew calmer, however, and soon forgot about them. But not about what they'd said.

"You can see the ship from the top of the citadel," he muttered. "I'll go up there and look for myself. The elf might well be lying. And they're not likely to come back soon."

Xar had been meaning to take a look inside what the mensch referred to as the Star Chamber, but the elf—Paithan—had the annoying habit of hovering around the room, treating it as if it were his own personal and private creation. He'd very proudly offered to give Xar a tour. Xar had been careful not to evince too much interest, much to Paithan's disappointment. The Lord of the Nexus would examine the Star Chamber in his own good time—by himself.

Whatever Sartan magic happened in the Star Chamber was the key to controlling the tytans. That much was evident.

"It's the humming sound," Paithan had said. "I think that's what's drawing them."

Obvious enough that even a mensch had seen it. The humming sound undoubtedly did have a startling effect on the tytans. From what Xar had observed, the humming sent them into some sort of trance. And when it stopped, they flew into a frenzy, like a fretful child who will only be quiet when it hears its mother's voice.

"An interesting analogy," Xar remarked, transporting himself to the Star Chamber with a spoken word of magic. He disliked climbing the stairs. "A mother's soothing voice. A lullaby. The Sartan used this to control them, and while they were under this influence, they were slaves to the Sartan's will. If *I* could just learn the secret . . ."

Reaching the door that led into the Star Chamber, Xar peered cautiously inside. The machine was shut down. The blinding light was off. The machine had been running erratically ever since the lord's arrival. The elf thought it was supposed to work this way, but

Xar guessed not. The Lord of the Nexus knew little about machinery; he truly missed the child Bane at this moment. The boy had figured out how to work the Kicksey-winsey; he could undoubtedly have solved the mystery of this far simpler machine.

Xar was confident that he himself would solve it in time. The Sartan, as was their custom, had left behind innumerable volumes, some of which must contain something other than their constant whining—complaints about how tough things were, how awful their lives had become. He grew irritated every time he tried to read one.

What with wading through books of useless twaddle, listening to the mensch bicker and quarrel, and keeping an eye on the tytans, who had once again massed outside the citadel's walls, Xar had found very little information to help him.

Until now. Now he was beginning to get somewhere.

He entered the Star Chamber, stalked over to the window, and stared outside. It took him several moments of intense searching to find the ship, partly hidden in the thick jungle foliage. When he located it, he wondered how he could have missed it. His eye was instantly drawn to it—the only ordered thing in a world of wild disorder.

He examined it intently, excited, tempted. The ship was in plain view. He could whisk himself there at this moment. Leave this world, leave the mensch. Return to the Labyrinth, return to find Haplo.

Haplo—who knew the location of the Seventh Gate on Abarrach. Who wanted nothing more than to take his lord with him . . .

Sartan runes.

Xar narrowed his eyes, brought the ship into tighter focus. He could not be mistaken. The hull of the vessel—it was built to resemble some type of giant bird—was covered with Sartan runes.

Xar cursed. The Sartan magic would keep him out as effectively as it had kept him out of the citadel.

"The mensch . . ." he whispered.

They had managed to enter the citadel; they could certainly enter the ship. That dwarf with his amulet and his puny little bit of Sartan rune-magic. The mensch could get inside the ship, take Xar with them. The mensch would be thrilled to leave this place.

But between the mensch and the ship, between Xar and the ship, was an army of tytans.

Xar cursed again.

The creatures—hundreds of them—were camped outside the walls. Whenever the machine flared to life, they swarmed out of the jungle, surrounded the citadel, blind heads turned in the direction of the gate, waiting for it to open. This transfixion lasted as long as the humming and the brilliant starlight. When the machine shut off, the tytans came out of the trance and attempted to break into the citadel.

Their rage was truly frightening. The tytans beat on the walls with their fists and tree-branch clubs. Their silent shouts reverberated in Xar's head until it almost drove him mad. But the walls held; Xar gave grudging thanks to the Sartan for that much at least. Eventually, worn out, the tytans would shuffle back into the cover of the jungle and wait.

They were waiting now. He could see them. Waiting to question the first living being who came out of the citadel, waiting to club him to death when they didn't get the right answer.

This was maddening, truly maddening. *I know now the location of the Seventh Gate—back on Abarrach. Haplo could lead me to it. He will lead me to it. Once Sang-drax finds him . . .*

*But what about Sang-drax? Does Sang-drax know? Has the dragon-snake deliberately lied—*

Movement outside the door. A shuffling sound. *Drat those snooping mensch! Couldn't they leave him alone an instant?*

A rune flared from his hand; the door dissolved. A startled-looking old man, clad in mouse-colored robes, with his hand raised to the now nonexistent door handle, was staring into the room in amazement.

"I say," he said. "What'd you do with the door?"

"What do you want?" Xar demanded.

"This isn't the men's room?" The old man glanced about in wistful expectation.

"Where did you come from?"

The old man shuffled into the room, still looking about hopefully. "Oh, down the hall. Take a right at the potted palm. Third door on the left. I asked for a room with a bath, but—"

"What are you doing here? Were you following me?"

"I don't believe so." The old man considered the matter. "Can't think why I would. No offense, old chap, but you're not exactly my type. Still, I suppose we should make the best of it. Two girls left at the altar, aren't we, my dear? Abandoned at the church door . . ."

The old man had wandered over near the well. A magical shove and Xar would be rid of this irritating fool for good. But Xar found what the old man was saying intriguing.

"What do you mean . . . abandoned?"

"Dumped is more like it," said the old man with increasing gloom. "So I won't get hurt. 'You'll be safe here, sir,' " he mimicked, scowling. "Thinks I'm too old and frail to mix it up in a good brawl anymore. I'll show you, you hyperthyroid toad . . ."

He shook a scrawny fist in the general direction of nothing, then sighed and turned to Xar. "What was the excuse yours gave you?"

"Who gave me?" Xar was playing along. "I'm afraid I don't understand."

"Why, your dragon. Geriatric? Feeble? Slow him down? I—Ah, of course." The old man's vague expression grew disconcertingly sharp. "I understand. Quite clever. Lured you here. Got you here. Left you here. And now he's gone. And you can't follow."

Xar shrugged. The old man knew something. Now to keep him talking. "Are you referring to Sang-drax?"

"On Abarrach, you're too close. Kleitus has already talked too much. He might say more. Sang-drax is worried. Suggests Pryan. Wasn't expecting my dragon, though. Opposing team. Flip side. Change in plans. Haplo trapped in Labyrinth. You here. Not perfect, but better than nothing. Takes ship. *And* people. Leaves you—lurch. Goes to Labyrinth. Kills Haplo."

Xar shrugged. "Dead or alive, it doesn't matter to me."

"That's true." The old man pondered. "So long as Sang-drax brings you the body. But that . . . that's the one thing he *won't* do."

Xar stared out the window. He stared long and hard out the window. Stared long and hard at the ship guarded by the Sartan runes, an army of tytans between him and escape.

"He'll bring him," said Xar at last.

"No, he won't," the old man replied. "Care to wager?"

"Why wouldn't he? What would be his reason?"

"To keep you and Haplo from reaching the Seventh Gate," the old man said triumphantly.

"So," Xar said, turning to face the old man. "You *do* know about the Seventh Gate."

The old man tugged nervously at his beard. "The fourth race at Aqueduct. A horse. Seventh Gate. Six to one. Prefers a muddy track."

Xar frowned. He advanced on the old man, stood so close that his breath disturbed the wispy gray hair. "You *will* tell me. If you don't, I can make the next few minutes very unpleasant for you . . ."

"Yes, I've no doubt you could."

The vague look left the old man's eyes, leaving them filled with an inexpressible pain, a pain Xar could never hope to replicate.

"It wouldn't matter what you did to me." The old man sighed. "I truly don't know where the Seventh Gate is. I never went there. I disapproved, you see. I was going to stop Samah, if I could. I told him so. The Council members sent their guards to bring me by force. They needed my magic. I am powerful, a powerful wizard . . ."

The old man smiled briefly, sadly.

"But when they came, I wasn't there. I couldn't leave the people. I hoped I might be able to save them. And so I was left behind. On Earth. I saw it. The end. The Sundering."

The old man drew in a trembling breath. "There was nothing I could do. No help. Not for them. Not for any of them—the 'deplorable but unavoidable civilian casualties.' . . . 'It's a question of priorities,' Samah said. 'We can't save everyone. And those who survive will be better off.'

"And so Samah left them to die. I saw . . . I saw . . ."

A tremor shook the old man's thin body. Tears filled his eyes and a look of horror began to contort his face—a look so dreadful, so awful, that despite himself, Xar recoiled before it.

The old man's thin lips parted as if he would scream, but no scream came out. The eyes grew wider and wider, reliving horrors only he could see, only he could remember.

"The fires that devoured cities, plains, and forests. The rivers that ran blood-red. The oceans boiling, steam blotting out the sun. The charred bodies of the countless dead. The living running and running, with nowhere to run to."

"Who are you?" Xar asked, awed. "*What* are you?"

The old man's breath rattled in his throat; spittle flecked his lips. "When it was over, Samah caught me, sent me to the Laby-

rinth. I escaped. The Nexus, the books *you* read—mine. My handi-
work." The old man looked faintly proud. "That was before the
sickness. I don't remember the sickness, but my dragon tells me
about it. That was when he found me, took care of me . . ."

"Who are you?" Xar repeated.

He looked into the old man's eyes . . . and then Xar saw the
madness.

It dropped like a final curtain, dousing the memories, putting
out the fires, clouding over the red-hot skies, blotting out the horror.

The madness. A gift? Or a punishment.

"Who are you?" Xar demanded a third time.

"My name?" The old man smiled vacantly, happily. "Bond.
James Bond."

# CHAPTER ♦ 31

# THE CITADEL

# PRYAN

♦

ALEATHA FLOUNCED THROUGH THE GATE LEADING INTO THE MAZE. HER SKIRT caught on a bramble. Swearing, she tore it loose, taking a certain grim satisfaction in hearing the fabric rip. So what if her clothes were in shreds? What did it matter? She would never get to go anywhere, never get to do anything with anybody of interest ever again. . . .

Angry and miserable, she curled up on the marble bench, giving herself up to the luxury of self-pity. Outside the maze, through the hedgerows, she could hear the other three continuing to bicker. Roland asked if they shouldn't go in after Aleatha. Paithan said no, leave her alone, she wouldn't go far and what could happen to her anyway?

"Nothing," said Aleatha drearily. "Nothing will happen. Ever again."

Eventually their voices faded away; their footsteps trailed off. She was alone.

"I might as well be in prison," she said, looking at her surroundings, the green walls of the hedges with their unnaturally sharp angles and lines, strict and confining. "Except prison would be better than this. Every prisoner has *some* chance of escape, and I have none. Nowhere to go but this same place. No one to see except these same people. On and on and on . . . through the years. Wearing away at each other until we're all stark, raving mad."

She flung herself down on the bench and began to cry bitterly. What did it matter if her eyes turned red, her nose dripped? What did it matter who saw her like that? No one cared for her. No one loved her. They all hated her. She hated them. And she hated that horrid Lord Xar. There was something frightening about him . . .

"Don't do that, now," came a gruff voice. "You will make yourself sick."

Aleatha sat up swiftly, blinking back her tears and fumbling for what remained of her handkerchief, which—from being put to various uses—was now little more than a ragged scrap of lace. Not finding it, she wiped her eyes with the hem of her shawl.

"Oh, it's you," she said.

Drugar stood over her, gazing down at her with his black-browed frown. But his voice was kind and almost shyly tender. Aleatha recognized admiration when she saw it, and though it came from the dwarf, she felt comforted.

"I didn't mean that the way it sounded," she said hurriedly, realizing her previous words hadn't been exactly gracious. "In fact, I'm glad it's you. And not any of the others. You're the only one with any sense. The rest are fools! Here, sit down."

She made room for the dwarf on the bench.

Drugar hesitated. He rarely sat in the presence of the taller humans and the elves. When he sat on furniture made for them, his legs were too short to permit his feet to touch the ground; he was left with his limbs dangling in what was to him an undignified and childlike manner. He could see in their eyes—or at least he presumed he could see—that they tended to think less of him as a result.

But he never felt that way around Aleatha. She smiled at him —when she was in a good humor, of course—and listened to him with respectful attention, appeared to admire what he did and said.

Truth to tell, Aleatha reacted to Drugar as she reacted to any man—she flirted with him. The flirtation was innocent, even unconscious. Making men love her was the only way she knew to relate to them. And she had no way at all to relate to other women. She knew Rega wanted to be friends, and deep inside, Aleatha thought it might be nice to have another woman to talk to, laugh with, share hopes and fears with. But early on in her life, Aleatha had understood that her older sister, Callie, unlovely and undesirable, had hated Aleatha for her beauty, at the same time loving her all the more fiercely.

Aleatha had come to assume that other women felt the same as Callie—and admittedly most did. Aleatha flaunted her beauty, threw it into Rega's face like a glove, made of it a challenge. Secretly believing herself inferior to Rega, knowing she wasn't as intelligent, as winning, as likable as Rega, Aleatha used her beauty as a foil to force the other woman to keep her distance.

As for men, Aleatha knew that once they discovered she was ugly inside, they'd leave her. And so she made a practice of leaving them first, except that now there was nowhere to go. Which meant that sooner or later, Roland would find out, and instead of loving her, he'd hate her. If he didn't hate her already. Not that she cared what he thought of her.

Her eyes filled with tears again. She was alone, so desperately alone . . .

Drugar cleared his throat. He had perched on the edge of the bench, his toes just touching the ground. His heart ached for her sorrow; he understood her unhappiness and her fear. In a strange way, the two of them were alike—physical differences keeping them apart from the others. In their eyes, he was short and ugly. In their eyes, she was beautiful. He reached out, awkwardly patted her on the shoulder. To his amazement, she nestled against him, resting her head on his broad chest, sobbing into his thick black beard.

Drugar's aching heart almost burst with love. He understood, though, that she was a child inside, a lost and frightened child, turning to him for comfort—nothing more. He gazed down at the blond, silken tresses, mingling with his own coarse black hair, and he had to close his own eyes to fight back the burn of tears. He held her gently until her sobs quieted; then, to spare them both embarrassment, he spoke swiftly.

"Would you like to see what I have discovered? In the center of the maze."

Aleatha raised her head, her face flushed. "Yes. I'd like that. Anything is better than doing nothing at all." She stood up, smoothing her dress and wiping her tears from her cheeks.

"You won't tell the others?" Drugar asked.

"No, of course not. Why should I?" Aleatha said haughtily.

"They have secrets from me—Paithan and Rega. I know they do. This will be our secret—yours and mine." She extended her hand.

By the One Dwarf, he loved her! Drugar took her hand. Small as his was, hers fit well inside it. He led her by the hand down the maze path until it grew too narrow for them to walk together. Releasing her, he admonished her to stay close behind him, lest she get lost in the myriad turns and twists of the maze.

His injunction was needless. The hedges were tall and overgrown, often forming a green roof that blotted out all sight of the sky or anything around them. Inside it was greenly dark and cool and very, very quiet.

At the beginning of their journey into the maze, Aleatha tried to keep track of where she was going—two right turns, a left, another right, another left, then two more lefts, a complete circle around a statue of a fish. But after that she was confused and hopelessly lost. She kept so near the dwarf she nearly tripped him up, her long skirts constantly getting under his heels, her hand plucking at his sleeve.

"How do you know where you're going?" she asked nervously.

He shrugged. "My people have lived all their lives in tunnels. Unlike you, we are not easily confused once we cannot see the sun or the sky. Besides, there is a pattern. It is based on mathematics. I can explain it," he offered.

"Don't bother. If I didn't have ten fingers I couldn't count that high. Is the center much farther?" Aleatha had never been strongly attracted to physical exertion.

"Not far," Drugar growled. "And there is a place to rest when we get there."

Aleatha sighed. This had all started out to be exciting. It was eerie inside the hedges and fun to pretend that she might be lost, all the time enjoying the comforting knowledge that she wasn't. But now she was growing bored. Her feet were beginning to hurt.

And they still had to go all the way back.

Tired and ill-tempered, she now eyed Drugar suspiciously. He had, after all, tried to kill them all once. What if he was bringing her down here for some nefarious purpose? Far away from the others. No one would hear her scream. She paused, glanced behind, half-toying with the idea of turning around and going back.

Her heart sank. She had no idea which way to turn. Had it been to the right? Or maybe they hadn't turned at all, but taken the path in the middle . . .

Drugar came to a halt so suddenly that Aleatha, still looking behind, stumbled into him.

"I'm . . . I'm sorry," she said, steadying herself with her hands on his shoulders and then snatching her hands away hurriedly.

He looked up at her, his face darkening. "Don't be afraid," he said, hearing the strain in her voice. "We are here." He waved his hand. "This is what I wanted to show you."

Aleatha looked around. The maze had ended. Rows of marble benches, set in a circle, surrounded a mosaic of variously colored stones arranged in a starburst. In the center were more of those strange symbols like those on the pendant the dwarf wore around his neck. Above them was open sky, and from where she stood Aleatha could see the top of the citadel's center spire. She breathed a sigh of relief. At least now she had some idea of where she was—the amphitheater. Though her knowledge wasn't likely to help her much in getting out of this place.

"Very pretty," she said, looking back at the starburst in the multicolored tile, thinking she should say something to keep the dwarf happy.

She would have liked to rest; there was a calm, pleasant feeling to this place that urged her to linger. But the silence made her nervous—that and the dwarf staring at her with his shadowed, dark eyes.

"Well, this has been fun. Thank you for—"

"Sit down," said Drugar, gesturing to a bench. "Wait. You have not yet seen what I wanted you to see."

"I'd love to, really, but I think we should be getting back. Paithan will be worried—"

"Sit down, please," Drugar repeated and his brows came together in a frown. He glanced up at the citadel's spire. "You will not have to wait long."

Aleatha tapped her foot. As usual when her will was thwarted, she was starting to get angry. She fixed the dwarf with a stern and imperious gaze that never failed to cut any man down to size, only this time it lost some of its effectiveness as it slanted down her nose instead of flashing upward from chilling eyes. And it was completely lost on Drugar anyway. The dwarf had turned his back on her and walked over to a bench.

Aleatha gave a final hopeless glance down the path and, sighing again, followed Drugar. Plopping herself down near him, she fidgeted, looked back at the spire, sighed loudly, shuffled her feet, and gave every indication that she was *not* amused, hoping he'd take the hint.

He didn't. He sat, stolid and silent, staring into the center of the empty starburst.

Aleatha was about ready to try her luck in the maze. Getting lost in there wouldn't be nearly as bad as being bored to death out here. Suddenly the light from the Star Chamber, on the top of the citadel, began to glow. The strange humming sound began.

A shaft of strong white light slanted down from the citadel's tower, struck the starburst mosaic.

Aleatha gasped, rose from the bench, would have backed up except that the bench was behind her. As it was, she nearly fell. The dwarf reached out a hand, caught hold of her.

"Don't be afraid."

"People!" Aleatha cried, staring. "There are . . . people there!"

The stage of the amphitheater, which had been empty, was now suddenly crowded with people. Or rather, with wisps of people. They weren't whole, flesh and blood as she and Drugar were. They were transparent shadows. She could see through them—to the other seats in the theater, to the hedgerow of the maze beyond.

Her knees weakening, she sat back down on the bench and watched the people. They stood in groups, talking earnestly, walking slowly, moving from group to group, coming into her view and then passing out of it as they stepped into and then out of the shaft of light.

People. Other people. Humans, elves, dwarves—standing together, talking together, apparently companionably, with the exception of one or two groups who seemed—by their gestures and posture—to be disagreeing about something.

Groups of people gathered for only one purpose, so far as Aleatha was concerned.

"It's a party!" she cried joyfully and leapt up from her seat to join them.

"No! Wait! Stop! Don't go near the light!" Drugar had been viewing the scene with reverent awe. Shocked, he attempted to catch Aleatha as she darted past.

He missed his hold, and she was suddenly in the center of the crowd.

She might as well have been standing in a thick fog.

The people flowed around her, flowed through her. She could see them talking, but couldn't hear them. She was standing near them, but couldn't touch them. Their eyes bright, they looked at each other, never at her.

"Please! I'm here!" she pleaded in frustration, reaching out eager hands.

"What are you doing? Come out of there!" Drugar commanded. "It is a holy place!"

"Yes!" she cried, ignoring the dwarf, talking to the shadows. "I hear you! Can't you hear me? I'm right in front of you!"

No one answered.

"Why can't they see me? Why won't they talk to me?" Aleatha demanded, facing the dwarf.

"They are not real, that is why," Drugar said dourly.

Aleatha looked back. The fog-people slid past her, over her, around her.

And suddenly the light went out, and they were gone.

"Oh!" Aleatha gasped, disappointed. "Where are they? Where did they go?"

"When the light goes, they go."

"Will they come back when the light comes back?"

Drugar shrugged. "Sometimes yes. Sometimes no. But generally, this time in the afternoon, I find them here."

Aleatha sighed. She felt more alone than ever now.

"You said they aren't real. What do you think they are?"

"Shadows of the past, maybe. Of those who used to live here." Drugar stared into the starburst. He stroked his beard, his expression sad. "A trick of the magic of this place."

"You saw your people there," said Aleatha, guessing what he was thinking.

"Shadows," he said again, his voice gruff. "My people are gone. Destroyed by the tytans. I am all that is left. And when I die, the dwarves will be no more."

Aleatha looked back around the floor of the amphitheater, now empty, so very empty.

"No, Drugar," she said suddenly. "You're wrong."

"What do you mean, I am wrong?" Drugar glowered. "What do you know about it?"

"Nothing," Aleatha admitted. "But I think one of them heard me when I spoke."

Drugar snorted. "You imagined it. Don't you think I have tried?" he demanded grimly. His face was haggard and ravaged by sorrow. "To see my people! To see them talking and laughing. I can almost understand what they say. I can almost hear the language of my homeland once again."

His eyes squeezed shut. He turned away from her abruptly, stalked back among the seats of the amphitheater.

Aleatha watched him go. "What a selfish beast I've been," she said to herself. "At least I have Paithan. And Roland, though he doesn't count for much. And Rega's not a bad sort. The dwarf has no one. Not even us. We've done our best to freeze him out. He's come here—to shadows—for comfort.

"Drugar," she said aloud. "Listen to me. When I was standing in the starburst, I said, 'I'm right in front of you!' And then, I saw one of the elves turn and look in my direction. His mouth moved and I swear he was saying, 'What?' I spoke again and he looked confused and glanced all around, as if he could hear me but couldn't see me. I know it, Drugar!"

He cocked his head, looking back at her dubiously but obviously wanting to believe. "Are you certain?"

"Yes," she lied. She laughed gaily, excited. "How could I stand in a group of men and not be noticed?"

"I don't believe it." The dwarf was glum again. He eyed her suspiciously, mistrusting her laughter.

"Don't be mad, Drugar. I was only teasing. You looked . . . so sad." Aleatha walked over to him. Reaching out, she touched the dwarf's hand with her own. "Thank you for bringing me. I think it's wonderful. I . . . I want to come back with you again. Tomorrow. When the light shines."

"You do?" He was pleased. "Very well. We will come. But you will say nothing to the others."

"No, not a word," Aleatha promised.

"Now we should be getting back," Drugar said. "The others will be worried about *you*."

Aleatha heard the bitter emphasis on the last word. "Drugar, what would it mean if those people *are* real? Would it mean that we aren't alone, as we think?"

The dwarf stared back at the empty starburst. "I don't know," he said, shaking his head. "I do not know."

# CHAPTER ♦ 32

## THE CITADEL

## PRYAN

♦

The sudden flaring of the light in the star chamber drove Xar from the room. He managed to rid himself of the old Sartan, foisting him off onto the elf, who had come upstairs to talk nonsense. Figuring that the mensch and the madman would get along well together, Xar left them standing in front of the door to the Star Chamber, both of them staring inanely at the bright light seeping out from underneath.

The old man was expounding on some theory concerning the workings of the chamber, a theory Xar might once have found interesting. Now the Lord of the Nexus could not have cared less. He sought sanctuary in the library, the one place where he was certain the mensch would not bother him. Let the Sartan light shine from this Star Chamber and any others like it. Let it bring light and energy into Death's Gate. Let it light Abarrach's terrible darkness, thaw Chelestra's frozen sea moons. What did Xar care?

What if the old man was right? What if Sang-drax was a traitor?

Xar unrolled a scroll, flattened it out on the desk. The scroll was a Sartan work, portraying the universe as they had remade it—four worlds, air, fire, stone, water, connected by four conduits. Conquering these worlds had seemed so simple in the beginning. Four worlds, populated by mensch, who would fall before Xar's might like rotten fruit dropping from the tree.

But one thing after another had gone wrong.

"The fruit on Arianus isn't all that rotten," he was forced to admit to himself. "The mensch are ripe and strong and intent on clinging to the tree with tenacity. And who could have foreseen the tytans on Pryan? Not even I could have supposed the Sartan would be stupid enough to create giants, endow them with magic, and then lose control over them.

"And the magic-destroying sea on Chelestra? How the devil am I to conquer a world where all some mensch has to do is throw a bucket of water on me to render me harmless!

"I need the Seventh Gate! I need it. Or I might fail."

Failure. In all his long life, the Lord of the Nexus had never permitted that word to enter his brain, had certainly never spoken it aloud. Yet now he was forced to concede it was a possibility. Unless he could find the Seventh Gate—the place where it all began.

The place where—with his help—it would all end.

"Haplo would have shown me, if I had let him. He came to the Nexus, that last time, for that purpose. I was blind, blind!" Xar's fingers, like talons, clenched over the scroll, crushed the ancient parchment, which crumbled to dust in his hands. "I cared. That was my failing. His betrayal hurt me, and I should not have permitted such a weakness. Of all the lessons the Labyrinth teaches, this is the most important: to care is to lose. If only I had been able to listen to him dispassionately, to cut to the core of his being with the cold knife of logic.

"He accomplished what I sent him to accomplish. He did what he was commanded to do. He tried to tell me. I wouldn't listen. And now, perhaps, it is too late."

Xar went over every word of Haplo's—the spoken and the unspoken.

*The sigla had been running consistently along the base of the wall ever since we left the dungeon. At this point, however, they left the base of the wall, traveled upward to form an arch of glowing blue light. I squinted my eyes against the brilliance, peered ahead. I could see nothing beyond but darkness.*

*I walked straight for the arch. At my approach, the runes changed color; blue turned to flaring red. The sigla smoldered, burst into flame. I put my hand in front of my face, tried to advance. Fire roared and crackled; smoke blinded me. The superheated air seared my lungs. The runes on my arms glowed blue in response, but their power did not protect me from the burning flames that scorched my flesh. I fell back, gasping for air . . .*

*Runes of warding . . . I couldn't enter.*

*These runes are the strongest that could possibly be laid down. Something terrible lies beyond that door . . .*

*Standing before the archway, a preposterous, ungainly figure, Alfred began to perform a solemn dance. The red light of the warding runes glimmered, faded, glimmered, and died.*

*We could go in now . . .*

*The tunnel was wide and airy, the ceiling and walls dry. A thick coating of dust lay undisturbed on the rock floor. No sign of footprints or claw marks or the sinuous trails left by serpents and dragons. No attempt had been made to obliterate the (Sartan) sigla; the guide-runes shone brilliantly, lighting our way ahead . . .*

*If it hadn't been too preposterous, Lord, I could have sworn I actually felt a sense of peace, of well-being that relaxed taut muscles, soothed frayed nerves . . . The feeling was inexplicable . . .*

*The tunnel led us straight forward, no twists or turns, no other tunnels branching off this one. We passed beneath several archways, but none were marked with the warding runes as had been the first. Then, without warning, the blue guide-runes came to an abrupt halt, as if we'd run into a blank wall.*

*Which we had.*

*A wall of black rock, solid and unyielding, loomed before us. It bore faint markings on its smooth surface. Sartan runes. But there was something wrong with them.*

*Runes of sanctity.*

*And inside . . . a skull.*

*Bodies. Countless bodies. Mass murder. Mass suicide.*

*Runes appeared, running in a circle around the upper portion of the chamber.*

*"Any who bring violence in here will find it visited upon themselves."*

*Why is this chamber sacred, Lord? What is it sacred to?*

*"I almost had the answer . . . I was so close . . .*

And then Haplo and his party were attacked by . . . Kleitus.

Kleitus knew the location of the Chamber of the Damned! Or, as Xar now supposed he should start considering it, the Seventh Gate. Kleitus had died in that chamber!

Xar went over Haplo's report again and again in his mind. Something about a force opposing them, ancient and powerful . . . a table, an altar, a vision . . .

*The Council set the Sartan the task of contacting the other worlds, to explain to them their desperate peril and beg them to send the aid promised before the Sundering. And what was the result? For months they did nothing. Then suddenly they came forward, prattling nonsense that only a child would believe—*

Of course, Xar realized. How utterly logical. These wretched Sartan on Abarrach, cut off from their people for innumerable generations, had forgotten much of the rune-magic, lost much of their power. A group of them, stumbling across the Seventh Gate, had suddenly rediscovered what had been lost. No wonder they had been intent on hiding it, keeping it for themselves. Making up stories about opposing forces, ancient and powerful. Even Haplo had fallen for their lies.

The Sartan hadn't known what to do with such power.

But Xar did.

If only he could find the chamber. Could he do so, perhaps, *without* Haplo? The Lord of the Nexus walked through Haplo's mind, as he had done on Haplo's return from Abarrach. Xar recognized the dungeons where Haplo had almost died. He had escaped from the dungeons, run down a corridor, guided by blue Sartan rune-lights.

Which corridor? What direction? There must be hundreds down there. The Lord of the Nexus had explored the catacombs beneath the castle in Necropolis. It was a maze worthy of the Labyrinth, a rat's warren of tunnels and corridors—some naturally formed, others burrowed into the rock by magic. It might take a man a lifetime to find the right one.

But Haplo knew the right one. If he escaped from the Labyrinth.

Xar brushed the ashes of the scroll from his hands. "And I am trapped here! Unable to help. A ship within sight. A ship covered with Sartan runes. The mensch can break the runes, they broke them to enter here. But they'd never reach the ship alive because of the tytans. I must . . .

"Alive!"

Xar drew in a deep breath, let it out slowly, thoughtfully. "But who said the mensch need to be alive?"

# CHAPTER ♦ 33

# THE LABYRINTH

♦

THE PATH THROUGH THE CAVERN LEADING INTO THE LABYRINTH WAS LONG AND torturous. It took them hours to traverse, inching their way slowly forward, each of them forced to test every step, for the ground would shift and slide beneath the feet of one person after another had passed over it safely.

"Is the damn rock alive?" Hugh the Hand asked. "I swear I saw it deliberately throw her off."

Breathing heavily, Marit stared down into the black and turbid water swirling beneath her. She had been negotiating a narrow section of rock ledge that ran along the sheer wall of the cavern when suddenly the ledge beneath her feet gave way. Hugh the Hand, following close behind her, caught her as she started to slide down the wet walls. Flattening himself out on the ledge, the assassin held fast to Marit's wrist and arm until Haplo could reach them from the opposite side of the broken ledge.

"It's alive. And it hates us," Haplo answered grimly, pulling Marit up to the relative safety of the section of path on which he stood.

Hugh the Hand jumped across the gap, landed beside them. This part of the trail was narrow and cracked, winding through a jumble of boulders, beneath a curtain of stalactites.

"Maybe that was its last jab at us. We're near the exit . . ."

Only a few feet away was the cavern opening—gray light, straggly trees, fog-damp grass. A heart-bursting dash would take them there. But they were all of them bone-weary, hurting, afraid. And this was only the beginning.

Haplo took a step forward.

The ground shivered beneath his feet. The boulders around him began to wobble. Dust and bits of rock fell in cascades from the ceiling.

"Hold still! Don't anyone move!" Haplo ordered.

They held still, and the rumbling ceased.

"The Labyrinth," Haplo muttered to himself. "It always gives you a chance."

He looked at Marit, who was standing on the path beside him. Her face was scratched, hands cut and bleeding from her fall. Her face was rigid, her eyes on the exit. She knew as well as Haplo.

"What is it? What's the matter?" It was Alfred, quavering.

Haplo turned his head slowly. Alfred was behind, standing on the narrow ledge that had already tried to throw Marit into the roiling black water. Part of that ledge was missing. He'd have to jump for it, and Haplo remembered clearly what a wonder Alfred was at leaping across chasms. His feet were wider than the ledge he would have to traverse. Hugh the Hand had already saved the clumsy and accident-prone Sartan from falling into two pits and a crack.

The dog remained near Alfred, occasionally nipping at his heels to urge him along. Cocking its head, the dog whined unhappily.

"What's wrong?" Alfred repeated fearfully when no one answered.

"The cavern's going to try to stop us from leaving," Marit said coldly.

"Dear me," said Alfred, amazed. "Can it . . . can it do such a thing?"

"What do you think it's been doing?" Haplo demanded irritably.

"Oh, but come now." Alfred took a step forward to argue the point. "You make it sound as if—"

The ground heaved. A ripple passed through it, almost—Haplo could have sworn—as if it laughed. Alfred gave a cry, wavered, twisted. His feet slid out from under him. The dog sank its teeth into his breeches and hung on. Arms flailing wildly, Alfred managed, with the dog's help, to regain his balance. Eyes closed in terror, he flattened himself against the rock wall, sweat trickling down his bald head.

All inside the cavern was suddenly still.

"Don't do that again!" Marit ordered, grinding the words through clenched teeth.

"Blessed Sartan!" Alfred murmured, his fingers trying to dig into the rock.

Haplo swore. "It was you blessed Sartan who created this. How the devil are we going to get out?"

"You shouldn't have brought me," Alfred said in a trembling voice. "I warned you I would only slow you down, put you in danger. Don't worry about me. You go on ahead. I'll just go back . . ."

"Don't move—" Haplo began, then fell silent.

Ignoring him, Alfred had started to walk back, and nothing was happening. The ground remained still.

"Alfred, wait!" Haplo called.

"Let him go!" Marit said scornfully. "He's slowed us up enough already."

"That's what the Labyrinth wants. It *wants* him to go, and I'll be damned if I'll obey. Dog, stop him."

The dog obediently caught hold of Alfred's flapping coattails, hung on. Alfred looked back at Haplo piteously. "What can I do to help you? Nothing!"

"You may not think so, but the Labyrinth does. Strange as it may seem, Sartan, I've got the feeling that the Labyrinth is afraid of you. Maybe because it sees its creator."

"No!" Alfred shrank back. "No, not me."

"Yes, you. By hiding in your tomb, by refusing to act, by keeping 'perfectly safe,' you feed the evil, perpetuate it."

Alfred shook his head. Catching hold of his coattails, he began to tug at them.

The dog, thinking it was a game, growled playfully and tugged back.

"At my signal," Haplo said beneath his breath to Marit. "You and Hugh the Hand make a run for the opening. Be careful. There may be something waiting for us out there. Don't stop for anything. Don't look back."

"Haplo . . ." Marit began. "I don't want to—" She faltered, flushing.

Startled, hearing a different tone in her voice, he looked at her. "To what? Leave me? I'll be all right."

Touched, pleased by the look of concern in her eyes—the first softness he'd seen in her—he reached out his hand to brush the sweat-damp hair back from her forehead. "You're hurt. Let me take a look—"

Eyes flaring, she pulled away from him. "You're a fool." She flicked a disparaging glance at Alfred. "Let him die. Let them all die."

She turned her back on him, fixed her eyes on the cave's opening.

The ground trembled beneath Haplo's feet. They didn't have much time. He held out his hand across the broken ledge. "Alfred," he said quietly, "I need you."

Alfred lifted a haggard, drawn face, stared at Haplo in amazement. The dog, at a silent signal from its master, released its hold.

"I can't do this alone," Haplo continued. He held out his hand, held it steady. "I need your help to find my child. Come with me."

Alfred's eyes filled with tears. He smiled tremulously. "How? I can't . . ."

"Give me your hand. I'll pull you across."

Alfred leaned precariously over the broken ledge, reached out his hand—bony, ungainly, the wrist protruding from the frayed lace of his too-short cuffs. And, of course, he was blubbering. "Haplo, I don't know what to say . . ."

The Patryn caught hold of the Sartan's wrist, clasped it tightly. The ground heaved and buckled. Alfred lost his footing.

"Run, Marit!" Haplo shouted, and began to work his magic.

At his command, blue and red sigla burned in the air. He spun the runes into a blue-glowing rope that snaked from his arm to wrap around Alfred's body.

The cavern was collapsing. Risking a quick glance, Haplo saw Marit and Hugh running madly for the exit. A rock plummeted down from the ceiling, struck Marit a glancing blow. The runes on her body protected her from harm, but the weight of the rock knocked her down. Hugh the Hand picked her up. The two dashed on. The assassin looked behind him once, to see if Haplo was coming. Marit did not look.

Hauling on the rope, Haplo swung the Sartan—arms and legs dangling like a dead spider—across the gap to his side of the ledge.

Just at that moment, the part of the ledge on which Alfred had been standing gave way.

"Dog! Jump!" Haplo yelled.

The dog gathered itself and, as the rock slid out from beneath its feet, hurled its body into the dust-laden air. It slammed into Alfred, sent them both sprawling.

Boulders fell across the path, blocking it, blocking their way out. Haplo picked the Sartan up, shook him. Alfred's eyes were starting to roll back in his head; his body was going limp.

"If you faint, you'll die here. And so will I!" Haplo shouted at him. "Use your own magic, damn it!"

Alfred blinked, stared. Then he drew in a sucking breath. Singing the runes in a quavering voice, he spread his arms and began to fly toward the exit, which was rapidly growing smaller.

"Come on, boy," Haplo commanded the dog and plunged ahead. His rune-magic struck the boulders that blocked his path, burst them apart, sent them bounding out of his way.

Alfred swooped up and out of the cavern opening. His arms flapping, feet stretched out behind him, he looked like a coattailed crane.

A huge rock thundered down on top of Haplo, bowled him over, pinned his leg beneath it. The opening was closing; the mountain itself was sliding down on top of him. A tiny glimmer of gray light was all that remained. Haplo used his magic as a wedge, pried the boulder off his leg, lunged forward, thrusting his hand through the narrowing gap.

The tunnel of light grew wider. Sartan runes flared around his hand, strengthening the glow of the Patryn runes.

"Pull him out!" Alfred was shouting. "I'll hold it open!"

Hugh the Hand grabbed hold of Haplo, pulled him through the magic-wrought tunnel. Haplo scrambled to his feet, began to run. The assassin and Alfred were at his side, the dog barking and racing in front of them. Alfred naturally stumbled over his own feet. Haplo didn't even pause, but swept the Sartan up and kept going. Marit stood on a ridge, waiting for them.

"Take cover!" Haplo shouted at her.

An avalanche of rock and splintered trees roared down the mountainside.

Haplo flung himself face forward on the ground, dragged Alfred down with him. The Patryn's rune-magic sheltered him, and he hoped Alfred had sense enough to use his own magic for protection. Rock and debris bounced off the magical shields, crashed around them. The ground shook, and then suddenly all was quiet.

Slowly, Haplo sat up.

"I guess you won't be going back now, Alfred," he said.

Half the mountain had collapsed in on itself. Gigantic slabs of stone lay across what had been the cavern's entrance, sealing it shut, perhaps forever.

Haplo stared at the ruin with a strange foreboding. What was wrong? He hadn't really planned to come back this way. Perhaps it was nothing more than the instinctive fear of having a door slammed shut at his back. But why had the Labyrinth suddenly decided to seal off their exit?

Marit unknowingly spoke his thoughts.

"That leaves us just one way out now—the Final Gate."

Her words came back, a dismal echo, bouncing off the ruined mountain.

*The Final Gate.*

# CHAPTER ✦ 34

## THE LABYRINTH

✦

"I CAN'T GO ON," ALFRED GULPED, SINKING ONTO A FLAT ROCK. "I HAVE TO rest."

The last panicked dash and the fall of the mountain on top of him had been too much for the Sartan. He sat hunched over, wheezing and gasping. Marit cast a disdainful glance at him, then one at Haplo. Then she looked away.

*I told you,* said her scornful gaze. *You are a fool.*

Haplo said quietly, "There's no time, Alfred. Not now. We're exposed, out in the open. We find cover, then we rest."

"Just a few moments," Alfred pleaded meekly. "It seems quiet . . ."

"Too quiet," Marit said.

They were in a small grove of scrub trees that appeared, from their stunted growth and twisted limbs, to have waged a desperate struggle for life in the shadow of the mountain. A sparse smattering of leaves clung dejectedly to the branches. Now that the mountain had collapsed, the Labyrinth's sun touched the trees for perhaps the first time. But the gray light brought no cheer, no comfort. The leaves rustled mournfully, and that, Marit noticed uneasily, was the only sound in the land.

She drew her knife out of her boot. The dog jumped up, growled. Hugh the Hand eyed her suspiciously. Ignoring the animal, ignoring the mensch, Marit said a few words to the tree in her own language, apologizing for harming it, explaining her dire need. Then she began to hack at a branch.

Haplo, too, had apparently noted the silence. "Yes, it's quiet.

Too quiet. That avalanche must have been heard for miles. You can bet someone is on their way to investigate. And I don't intend to be here when they arrive."

Alfred was perplexed. "But . . . it was only an avalanche. A rock slide. Why would anyone care?"

"Of course the Labyrinth cares. It dropped a mountain on us, didn't it?" Haplo wiped sweat and rock dust from his face.

Marit cut off the branch, began to strip away small twigs and half-dead leaves.

Haplo squatted down on his haunches, faced Alfred.

"Don't you understand yet, damn it? The Labyrinth is an intelligent entity. I don't know what rules it or how, but it knows—it knows everything." He was silent, thoughtful. "But there's a difference about the Labyrinth. I can sense it, feel it. Fear."

"Yes," agreed Alfred. "I'm terrified."

"No, not our fear. Its fear. It's afraid."

"Afraid? Afraid of what?"

Haplo grinned, though his grin was strained. "Strange as it sounds, us; you, Sartan."

Alfred shook his head.

"How many heretical Sartan were sent through the Vortex? Hundreds . . . a thousand?" Haplo asked.

"I don't know." Alfred spoke into the lace of his draggled shirt collar.

"And how many had mountains dropped on them? None, I'll wager. That mountain has been standing there a long, long time. But you—you enter the Vortex and *bam!* And you can be damn sure that the Labyrinth's not going to give up."

Alfred looked at Haplo in dismay. "Why? Why would it be afraid of me?"

"You're the only one who knows the answer to that," Haplo returned.

Marit, sharpening the point of the branch with her knife, agreed with Alfred. Why would the Labyrinth fear a mensch, two returning victims, and a weak and sniveling Sartan? Yet she knew the Labyrinth, knew it as Haplo knew it. It was intelligent, malevolent. The avalanche had been a deliberate attempt to murder them, and when the attempt had failed, the Labyrinth had sealed off their only route of escape. Not that it had been much of an escape route, with no ship to take them back through Death's Gate.

Fear. Haplo's right, Marit realized, with a sudden heady elation. The Labyrinth's afraid. All my life *I've* been the one who was afraid. Now it is. It is as scared as I ever was. Never before has the Labyrinth tried to keep someone from entering. Time and again, it permitted Xar to enter the Final Gate. The Labyrinth even seemed to welcome the encounter, the chance to destroy him. It never shut the gate on Xar, as it tried to shut it on us. Yet not one of us, nor all of us combined, is nearly so powerful as the Lord of the Nexus.

Then why? What does the Labyrinth fear from us? Her elation faded, left her chilled. She needed to talk to Xar, report to him what had occurred. She wanted his counsel. Chopping off another branch, she wondered how she could find an opportunity to slip off by herself.

"I don't understand any of this," said Hugh the Hand, glancing around nervously, his face darkening. "And I wouldn't have believed it if I hadn't seen how that damn Cursed Blade took on a life of its own. But I know fear. I know how it works in a man and I suppose it's no different in a bunch of intelligent rocks. Fear makes a man desperate, reckless." The assassin looked down at his hands, smiled grimly. "I grew rich off other men's fear."

"And it will make the Labyrinth the same," Haplo said. "Desperate, reckless. That's why we can't afford to stop. We've already spent too much time here as it is." The sigla on his hands and arms were glowing a pale blue, tinged with red.

Marit glanced at the tattoos on her body, saw the same warning. Danger was not near, but it wasn't far away either.

Alfred, pale and shaken, rose to his feet. "I'll try," he said gamely.

Marit traced a sigil of healing on the tree, then cut off another branch. Silently she handed the first crude spear she had made to Haplo. He hesitated, astonished that she should think of him, pleased that she was concerned. He accepted the spear, and as he took it, their hands touched.

He smiled that quiet smile of his. The light in his eyes, in that smile, which was so achingly familiar, seeped into Marit's heart.

But the only effect the light had was to illuminate the emptiness. She could see inside every part of her, see the bleak walls, barred windows, shuttered doors.

Better the darkness.

She turned away. "Which direction?"

Haplo didn't answer immediately. When he did, his voice was cool, perhaps with disappointment. Or perhaps she was accomplishing her goal—perhaps he was learning to hate her.

"The top of that ridge up ahead." He pointed. "We should be able to get a view of the countryside, maybe find a path."

"There's a path?" Hugh the Hand stared around in disbelief. "What made it? This place looks deserted."

"It has been deserted, probably for hundreds of years. But yes, there's a path. This is the Labyrinth, remember? A deliberately crafted maze, made by our enemies. The path runs all the way through it. The path leads the way out—in more ways than one. There's an old saying, 'You abandon the path at your peril. You keep to the path at your peril.'"

"Wonderful." Hugh the Hand grunted. Reaching into the folds of his clothing, he drew out his pipe, regarded it with longing. "I don't suppose there's such a thing as stregno in this god-awful place?"

"No, but when we reach one of the Squatter villages, there's a dried leaf mixture that they smoke on ceremonial occasions. They'll give you some." Haplo grinned, turned to Marit. "Do you remember that village ceremony where we—"

"You'd better see to your Sartan friend," she interrupted. She had been thinking of exactly the same time. His hand was on the door of her being, trying to force it open. She put her shoulder to it, barred his entry. "He's limping."

They had only traveled a short distance and already the Sartan was lagging behind.

"I seem to have twisted my ankle," Alfred said apologetically.

"It would have been more useful if he'd twisted his neck," Marit muttered scornfully.

"I'm dreadfully sorry—" Alfred began. He caught Haplo's baleful glance and swallowed the rest.

"Why don't you use your magic, Alfred?" Haplo suggested with elaborate patience.

"I didn't think there was time. The healing procedure—"

Haplo checked an exasperated exclamation. "Not to heal yourself! You can float, fly. As you did just now when you flew out of the cavern. Or have you forgotten already?"

"No, I didn't forget. It's just that—"

"You might even prove useful," Haplo went on quickly. He

didn't want to give Alfred time to think. "You can see what's ahead."

"Well, if you really believe it would help—" Alfred still sounded dubious.

"Just do it!" Haplo said through clenched teeth.

Marit knew what he was thinking. The Labyrinth had left them in peace too long.

Alfred went into his little dance—a hopping sort of dance, on his sore foot. He waved his hands and hummed a tune through his nose. Slowly, effortlessly, he rose into the air, drifted gently forward. The dog, in a high state of excitement, gave a joyful bark and leapt playfully for Alfred's dangling feet as the Sartan sailed overhead.

Haplo, breathing a sigh, turned and started up the ridge. He was almost at the top when the wind hit, slamming into him like a doubled-up fist.

The wind came out of nowhere, as if the Labyrinth had sucked in an enormous breath and was blowing it back out. The blast sent Marit staggering. Hugh the Hand, at her side, was cursing and rubbing his eyes, half-blinded by wind-blown dust. Haplo stumbled, unable to keep his balance.

Above them, Alfred let out a strangled cry. The wind caught hold of the floating Sartan. Arms and legs flapping wildly, he was being flung at incredible speed right into the mountain.

Only the dog was able to move. It raced after Alfred, snapped at the man's flying coattails.

"Catch him!" Haplo shouted. "Drag him—" But before he could finish, the wind smote him a blast from behind, knocked him flat.

Hearing the urgency in its master's voice, the dog bounded high into the air. Teeth closed over fabric. Alfred sagged down; then the fabric tore. The dog tumbled to the ground in a flurry of legs. The wind rolled the animal over and over. Alfred was blown away, and then suddenly he stopped. His body, his clothes, had become entangled in the limbs of one of the stunted trees. The wind fretted and whipped at him in frustration, but the tree refused to let loose.

"I'll be damned," said Hugh the Hand, wiping grit from his eyes. "The branches reached up and grabbed him!"

Alfred hung from the tree limbs, dangling helplessly, gazing about in bewilderment. The strange wind had ceased blowing as suddenly as it had started, but there remained an ominous feeling in the air, a sullen anger.

The dog dashed over to stand protectively beneath Alfred. The Sartan was starting to sing and wave his hands.

"Don't!" Haplo shouted urgently, scrambling to his feet. "Don't move or say or do anything! Especially not magic!"

Alfred froze.

"His magic," Haplo muttered; then he began to swear beneath his breath. "Every goddamn time he uses his magic. And what will happen to him if he doesn't? How can he get through the Labyrinth alive without it? Not that he's going to get through alive *with* it. This is hopeless. Hopeless. You're right," he said bitterly to Marit. "I am a fool."

She could have answered him. *The tree saved him. You didn't see it, but I did. I saw it catch hold of him. Some force is working for us, trying to help us. There is hope. If we've brought nothing else, we've brought hope.*

But she didn't say that. She wasn't certain hope was what she wanted.

"I suppose we'll have to get him down," growled Hugh the Hand.

"What's the use?" Haplo demanded dispiritedly. "I've brought him here to die. I've brought us all here to die. Except you. And maybe that's worse. You'll be forced to just keep on living . . ."

Marit edged close to him. Instinctively, she reached out a hand to comfort him, then realized what she was doing. She stopped, confused. It seemed she was two different people—one hating Haplo, the other . . . *not* hating him. And she didn't much trust either.

Where am *I* in all this? she wondered angrily. What is it I want?

That doesn't matter, Wife. She could hear Xar's voice. What *you* want is not important. Your job is to bring Haplo to me.

And I'll do it, she decided. Me! Not Sang-drax!

Hesitantly Marit brushed her fingers against Haplo's arm.

Startled at her touch, he turned.

"What the human said is true," Marit told him, swallowing. "Don't you understand? The Labyrinth's acting out of fear. And that makes us its equal." She moved closer to him. "I've been think-ing about my child, my daughter. I do sometimes, at night. When I'm all alone, I wonder if *she* is all alone. I wonder if she ever thinks of me, as I think of her. If she wonders why I left her . . . I want to find her, Haplo. I want to explain . . ."

Tears filled her eyes. She hadn't meant that to happen. She lowered the lids swiftly so that he wouldn't see.

But it was too late. And then, because she wasn't looking at him, she couldn't move away from him fast enough to prevent his putting his arms around her.

"We'll find her," he was saying softly. "I promise."

Marit looked up at him. He was going to kiss her.

Xar's voice was in Marit's head. *You slept with him. You bore his child. He loves you still.* This was perfect. What Xar wanted. She would lull Haplo into feeling secure around her; then she would disable him, capture him.

She closed her eyes. Haplo's lips touched hers.

Marit shivered all over and suddenly shrank back, pulled away.

"You'd better go get your Sartan friend out of the tree." Her voice was sharp as the knife clutched tightly in her hand. "I'll keep watch. Here, you'll need this."

Marit handed him the knife, left him, not looking back. She was shaking all over, tremors tightening her arms and the muscles of her thighs, and she walked blindly, hating him, hating herself.

Reaching the top of the ridge, she leaned against a huge boulder, waited for the shaking to cease. She permitted herself one swift glance behind to ascertain what Haplo was doing. He had not followed her. He had gone off, the dog trotting along at his heels, to try to extricate Alfred from the treetop.

Good, Marit told herself. The trembling was under control. She quelled her inner turmoil, forced herself to scan the area carefully, closely, searching for telltale signs of an enemy.

She felt calm enough to talk to Xar.

But she didn't get the chance.

# CHAPTER 35

## THE LABYRINTH

♦

Aᴌғʀᴇᴅ ᴅᴀɴɢʟᴇᴅ ʜᴇʟᴘʟᴇssʟʏ ғʀᴏᴍ ᴛʜᴇ ᴛᴏᴘ ᴏғ ᴛʜᴇ ᴛʀᴇᴇ; ᴀ sᴛᴜʀᴅʏ ʟɪᴍʙ ʀᴜɴ-
ning up the back of his frock coat supported him like a second—and
in Alfred's case firmer—backbone. The Sartan's legs and arms
waved feebly; there was no way he could get himself down.

The dog paced beneath, mouth open in a tongue-lolling grin, as
if it had treed a cat. Haplo, arriving on the scene, stared upward.

"How the devil did you manage that?"

Alfred spread his hands. "I . . . I really haven't any idea."
Twisting his head, he struggled to peer over his shoulder. "If . . . if
it didn't sound too strange, I'd say the tree caught me as I went
flying past. Unfortunately, it now appears reluctant to let me go."

"I don't suppose there's any chance of that back seam on your
coat ripping?" Haplo called.

Alfred shifted his weight experimentally, began to sway back
and forth. The dog, cocking its head, was fascinated.

"It's a very well-made coat," Alfred returned with an apologetic smile. "The dressmaker to Her Majesty, Queen Anne, fashioned the first one for me. I became quite fond of it and so I've . . .
well . . . I've made them myself from the same pattern ever since."

"*You* made it."

"I'm afraid so."

"Using your rune-magic?"

"I've become rather good at tailoring," Alfred answered defensively.

"Raising people from the dead and tailoring," Haplo muttered. "Just what I need."

The sigla on his body continued to glow faintly, but now they had begun to itch and burn. The danger, whatever it was, was drawing nearer. He peered up at the ridge. He couldn't see Marit, but then he shouldn't be able to see her. He guessed she had hidden herself in the shadow of a large rock.

"I don't remember the damn tree being this tall," Hugh the Hand remarked, craning his neck to see. "You could stand on my shoulders and we still wouldn't be able to reach him. If he'd unbutton his coat and free his arms from the sleeves, he'd drop down."

Alfred was considerably alarmed at the suggestion. "I don't think that would work, Sir Hugh. I'm not very adept at things of that sort."

"He's right there," Haplo agreed grimly. "Knowing Alfred, he'd end up hanging himself."

"Can't you"—Hugh the Hand glanced at Haplo's blue-glowing skin—"magic him down?"

"Using the magic drains my strength, just as running or jumping drains yours. I'd rather conserve it for important things like surviving, not little things like getting Sartan out of trees." Haplo tucked the dagger into his belt, walked over to the base of the tree. "I'll climb up there and cut him loose. You stay down here and be ready to catch him."

Hugh the Hand shook his head, but couldn't suggest any other option. Removing the pipe from his mouth, he slid it safely into his pocket and took up a position directly underneath the dangling Alfred. Haplo climbed the tree, tested the limb holding the Sartan before crawling out on it. He had been afraid, by the look of it, that the branch wouldn't hold his weight. But it was stronger than he'd supposed. It bore his weight—and Alfred's—easily.

"Caught him as he went flying past," Haplo repeated in disgust. Still, he'd seen stranger things. Most of them involving Alfred.

"It's . . . it's an awfully long fall," Alfred protested in a trembling voice. "I could use my magic . . ."

"Using your magic's what got you here in the first place," Haplo interrupted, crawling gingerly out onto the limb, flattening himself in order to distribute his weight evenly.

The branch sagged. Alfred gasped in terror, waved his arms, and kicked his feet. The limb creaked ominously.

"Hold still!" Haplo ordered in irritation. "You'll bring us both down!" He slid his dagger between the coat and the branch, began to cut through the seam.

"What . . . what do you mean—my magic got me into this?" Alfred asked, closing his eyes tightly.

"That wind didn't pick up any of the rest of us and try to impale us on a mountain. Just you. And the mountain didn't start to collapse until *you* began to sing those damn runes of yours."

"But why?"

"Like I said, you tell me," Haplo grunted.

He was about halfway through, cutting slowly, hoping to let Alfred down as easily as possible, when he heard a low whistle. The sound went through him like a bolt of hot iron, burning him, piercing him.

"What an odd-sounding bird," said Alfred.

"It's not a bird. It's Marit. Our signal for danger."

Haplo gave the knife a jerk, slit the coat seam in one long, jagged tear. Alfred had time for one wild yell; then he was plummeting through the air. Hugh the Hand stood stolidly, feet planted firmly, body braced. He caught Alfred, broke the Sartan's fall, but the two went over together in a heap.

Haplo, from his vantage point in the tree, looked to the ridge. Marit detached herself from the boulder long enough to point to her left. She gave another low whistle and added a series of three catlike howls.

Tiger-men.

Marit raised her hands, spread all ten fingers wide, then repeated this gesture twice.

Haplo swore softly. A hunting pack, at least twenty of the fierce beasts, who were not really men at all, but were known as such because they walked upright on two strong hind legs and used their front paws, complete with prehensile thumbs, like hands.[1]

---

[1] Tiger-men are taller than most humans, with thick fur pelts and long tails. They can run on back legs or drop down on all fours, are capable of leaping incredible distances, and are as much at home in trees as on the ground. They are adept at using weapons, but prefer killing with fang and claw, dragging down their prey and sinking their teeth into the neck, ripping out the throat. They know rune-magic, using it primarily to enhance their weapons. They kill for sport as well as food.

They could, therefore, use weapons, and were skilled with one known as a cat's paw, intended to cripple rather than kill. A disk-shaped piece of wood with five sharp stone "claws" attached, the cat's paw was either thrown or flung from a sling. Its magic was weak against Patryn magic, but effective. No matter what part of a sigla-covered body it struck, the cat's paw inserted its claws through the small breaks in the tattoos, bit deep into muscle, and clung there tenaciously. Often hurled at the legs of a victim, the cat's paw tearing into a calf muscle or thigh felled the prey with deadly efficiency.

Tiger-men prefer their meat fresh.

Haplo cast a fleeting glance behind him at the ruined mountain, knew before he looked that it was useless. No hope of crawling back into that cave. He scanned the horizon, then noticed that Marit was waving to him, urging him to hurry.

Haplo slid down the tree. Hugh the Hand was picking Alfred up, attempting to help him stand. The Sartan crumpled like a rag doll.

"Looks like in the fall he did something to his other ankle," Hugh the Hand said.

Haplo swore again, louder and more graphically.

"What's all that hand-waving and shrieking about?" the assassin asked, looking in Marit's direction.

She was no longer visible, having retreated behind the boulder again to keep the tiger-men from seeing her. Although, if what Haplo suspected was true, they didn't need to see her. They knew what they were looking for and probably where to find it.

"Tiger-men are coming," Haplo said shortly.

"What're they?"

"You have house cats on Arianus?"

Hugh the Hand nodded.

"Imagine one taller, stronger, faster than I am, with teeth and claws to match."

"Damn." Hugh looked impressed.

"There's a hunting pack, maybe twenty of the beasts. We can't fight them. Our only hope is to outrun them. Though where we're going to run to is beyond me."

"Why don't we just lie low? They couldn't have spotted us yet."

"My guess is they know we're here. They've been sent to kill us."

Hugh the Hand frowned skeptically but didn't argue. Reaching into his pocket, he fished out his pipe, stuck it between his teeth, and stared down at Alfred, who was rubbing his injured ankles and trying to look as if the massage was helping.

"I'm really very sorry—" he began.

Haplo turned away.

"What do we do about him?" the Hand asked in a low voice. "He can't walk, much less run. I could carry him . . ."

"No, that would weigh you down. Our only chance is to run and keep running until we drop. Tiger-men are fast, but only in short bursts. They're not good at long distances."

A low and urgent whistle from Marit emphasized the need for haste. Haplo glanced over at the dog, then back at Alfred.

"You've ridden dragon-back, haven't you?"

"Oh, yes." Alfred perked up. "In Arianus. Sir Hugh would remember. It was when I was tracking Bane—"

But Haplo wasn't listening. He pointed at the dog, began speaking the runes softly. The animal, aware something involving it was about to happen, was on its feet, its tail, its entire body seeming to wag with excitement. Blue sigla flared from Haplo's hand, flashed through the air, and twined about the dog.

The runes sparkled over its body like the 'lectric zingers of the Kicksey-winsey gone mad. The dog began to grow in size, expanding, enlarging. It came to Haplo's waist; then its muzzle was level with his head, and then it was looking down at its master, tongue lolling, bathing them all in a rain of slobber.

Hugh the Hand gasped and staggered backward. Shaking his head, he rubbed his eyes. When he looked again, the dog was even bigger. "I've had drunken hallucinations that weren't this bad."

Alfred sat on the ground, stared up at the magically transformed animal with a doleful expression. Halting the magic, Haplo started toward the injured Sartan. Alfred made a pathetic attempt to stand, scrabbling backward up a convenient boulder.

"I'm much better. Truly I am. You go on ahead. I—"

His protestations were cut short by an exclamation of pain. He would have fallen, but Haplo planted his shoulder in the Sartan's middle, lifted him, and tossed him onto the back of the dog before

Alfred knew precisely what had happened, where he was, or which end of him was up.

Once he figured all these out, he realized he was sitting on the back of the dog—now the size of a young dragon—and he was well above the ground. Giving a low moan, shutting his eyes, Alfred flung his arms around the dog's neck and hung on for dear life, nearly choking the animal.

Haplo managed to pry loose the Sartan's death-like grip, at least enough to let the dog breathe.

"Come on, boy," he said to the animal. He looked over at the assassin. "You all right?"

Hugh the Hand gave Haplo a quizzical glance. "You people could take over the world."

"Yeah," said Haplo. "Let's go."

He and the assassin set off at a run. The dog—with Alfred clinging and groaning and keeping his eyes shut—trotted easily along behind.

Haplo—keeping low—crept up the side of the ridge to join Marit. He left the others at the bottom, awaiting his signal before proceeding.

"What have we got?" he asked softly, though by now he could see for himself.

Off to his left, a large group of tiger-men was crossing the plain below. They loped along at a leisurely pace on two legs. They didn't pause to look around, but kept coming. And there were at least forty.

"This is no ordinary hunting pack," Haplo said.

"No," Marit agreed. "They're too many of them. They're not fanning out, not stopping to sniff the air. And they're all armed."

"All heading straight in this direction. And us with our backs against the mountain." Haplo scanned the vast plain in discouragement. "And no help down there."

"I'm not so sure," Marit said, sweeping her hand to her right. "Look over there, on the horizon. What do you see?"

Haplo looked, squinted. Gray clouds hung low; fingers of mist dragged over the tops of a distant stand of fir trees. The jagged peaks of snow-capped mountains could be seen when the mist lifted. And there, above the dull green of the firs, about halfway up the side of one of the mountains . . .

"I'll be damned!" Haplo breathed. "A fire."

Now that his attention was drawn to the brilliant spot of orange, he wondered that he hadn't noticed it immediately, for it was the only splotch of color in the dismal world. He let hope, kindled by the flame, warm him an instant, then quickly stamped it out.

"A dragon attack," he said. "It has to be. Look how far it is above the treetops."

Marit shook her head. "I've been watching the fire while you were down there fooling with the Sartan. It burns steadily. Dragonflame comes and goes. It may be a village. I think we should try for it."

Haplo looked at the tiger-men, steadily decreasing the distance between themselves and their prey. He looked back at the flame, which continued to burn steadily, brightly, almost defiantly lighting the gloom. Whatever decision they made would have to be made soon. Heading for the fire would carry them down the ridge, into the plains, clearly into view of the tiger-men. It would be a desperate race.

Hugh the Hand crawled up on his belly beside Haplo.

"What is it?" he grunted. His eyes widened at the sight of the cats moving purposefully toward them. But he said nothing beyond another grunt.

Haplo pointed. "What do you make of that?"

"A beacon fire," Hugh the Hand said promptly. "There must be a fortress near here."

Haplo shook his head. "You don't understand. Our people don't build fortresses. Mud and grass huts, easily put up, easily abandoned. Our people are nomads—for reasons like that." He glanced at the tiger-men.

Hugh the Hand chewed thoughtfully on the pipe stem. "It sure as hell looks like a beacon fire to me. 'Course," he added dryly, removing the pipe, "in a place where house cats are as big as men and dogs are as big as trees, I could be mistaken."

"Beacon fire or not, we have to try for it. There's no other choice," Marit insisted.

She was right. No other choice. And no more time to stand here arguing about it. Besides, if they could just make the forest safely, that might discourage their pursuers. The tiger-men didn't like the forests, the territory of their longtime foes, wolfen and snogs.

Wolfen and snogs—other threats they'd have to face. But—one way of dying at a time.

"They'll spot us the moment we break cover. Run down the ridge and across the plains. Make straight for the trees. If we're lucky, they won't follow us into the forest. Not much use in setting an order of march. Try to keep together." Haplo looked around, brought the dog forward with a gesture.

Alfred opened his eyes, took one look at the band of tiger-men moving toward them, gave a groan, and shut his eyes again.

"Don't faint," Haplo told him. "You'll fall off and I'll be damned if I'm going to stop and put you back on."

Alfred nodded, clutched the dog's fur even more tightly.

Haplo pointed toward the woods. "Take him there, boy," he ordered.

The dog, realizing this was serious work now, cast a baleful glance at the tiger-men and then stared at the forest with fixed determination.

Haplo drew in a deep breath. "Let's go."

They plunged down the side of the ridge. Almost instantly, wild cat screams rose on the air—horrible sounds that raised the hair on the back of the neck, sent shivers through the body. Fortunately, the ridge was made of granite, solid and hard, and they were able to scramble down it swiftly. Moving at an angle away from the tiger-men, the small band reached the level plains ahead of their pursuers.

The ground was now smooth and flat; whatever type of vegetation had once covered it appeared to have been deliberately cut down, allowing them to run unobstructed. The thought occurred to Haplo, bounding swiftly over the dark black dirt, that he might have been dashing across lush farmland perched high in the moss-beds of Pryan. The idea was ludicrous, of course. His people were hunters and gatherers, fighters and roamers, not farmers. He put the thought out of his mind, put his head down, and concentrated on pumping his legs.

The level ground was an advantage to Haplo and his group, but it was also a distinct advantage to the tiger-men. Haplo, glancing behind, saw that the creatures had dropped to all fours, their powerful limbs galloping with ease over the dirt and plant stubble.

Their slant-eyes glittered green; the glistening fangs in their panting mouths were spread wide in grins of bloodlust and the thrill of the chase. The dog had raced on ahead, Alfred bumping and jouncing, his legs flung up and back and sideways. The dog easily outdistanced those on foot. Casting a worried backward glance at its master, it started to slow, waited for him to catch up.

"Go on!" Haplo shouted.

The dog, though seemingly unhappy about leaving him behind, did as it was told. It sped for the woods.

A clunk at Haplo's left side caused him to look down. The wicked sharp edges of a cat's paw shone white against the soil. The weapon had fallen short of its mark, but not by much. He increased his speed, using his magic to enhance his body's strength and stamina. Marit was doing the same.

Hugh the Hand was keeping up gamely when suddenly he pitched forward and lay face down in the dirt. Blood dribbled from a wound on his head. A cat's paw lay at his side. Haplo veered off course to help. Another cat's paw whined through the air.

Haplo ignored it. The assassin was out cold.

"Marit!" Haplo called.

She glanced back, first at him, then at their pursuers gaining on them. She made a swift motion with her hand that said, *Leave him! He's finished!*

Haplo had his hand under Hugh's left shoulder, was dragging the unconscious man to his feet. Marit appeared at the human's right side. Something struck Haplo in the back, but he paid little attention to it. A cat's paw, but it had landed the wrong way, claws outward.

"Join the circle!" he told Marit.

"You're crazy!" she retorted. "You'll get us all killed! And for what? A mensch!" Her tone was bitter, but when she looked at Haplo, he was startled and warmed to see grudging admiration in her eyes.

Catching hold of Hugh the Hand, she whispered the runes beneath her breath. The blue and red glow from her body flowed over the human as Haplo's magic flowed over him from the other side. Hugh the Hand began to stumble forward, legs acting at the magic's command, not his own. He ran in a sleepwalking stupor, reminding Haplo of the automaton back on Arianus.

Their combined magic kept the human going, but only at a cost to both the Patryns. The forest appeared to be farther off than it had at the beginning of their mad dash. Haplo could hear the tiger-men close behind them now, hear the thud of their paws in the dirt, the low growls and whines of pleasurable anticipation of the kill.

No more cat's paws were thrown. Haplo wondered why at first, then realized grimly that the beasts had decided their crippling weapons were no longer necessary. The prey was obviously wearing out.

Haplo heard a snarl. Marit screamed a warning; she let Hugh fall. A heavy weight hit Haplo from behind, dragged him down. Fetid breath on his face sickened him; claws tore at his flesh. His defensive magic reacted—blue rune-fire crackled. The tiger-man howled in pain; the weight on top of Haplo lifted.

But if one tiger-man had caught him, others wouldn't be far behind. Haplo levered himself up with his hands, struggled to regain his feet. He could hear Marit's shrill battle cries, caught a glimpse of her jabbing at one of the tiger-men with a wooden spear. Haplo drew his dagger as another tiger-man struck him, this time from the side. He and the tiger-man went down, rolling over and over, Haplo stabbing with the knife, the tiger-man tearing at the Patryn's unprotected face with ripping claws.

A loud booming bark, roaring like thunder, erupted from overhead. The dog had dropped off Alfred, returned to join the fray. Grabbing hold of the tiger-man on top of Haplo, the dog yanked the beast off and began to shake it back and forth, hoping to break its spine.

And suddenly, astonishingly, Haplo heard calls and yells coming from the forest. Arrows whistled above him; several of the tiger-men shrieked and slumped to the ground.

A group of Patryns emerged from the trees. Hurling spears and javelins, they drove the tiger-men away. Another flight of arrows sent the beasts fleeing back across the plains in thwarted rage.

Haplo was dazed and bleeding; the cuts on his face burned like fire. "Marit," he said, trying to find her in the confusion.

She stood over the body of a tiger-man, her bloodied spear in her hand. Seeing her unhurt, Haplo relaxed. Several Patryns had hold of Hugh the Hand, and, although obviously perplexed at the sight of a man bereft of tattoos, they were carrying him gently but hastily into the shelter of the woods.

Haplo wondered wearily what they must think of Alfred.

A woman knelt down beside Haplo. "Can you walk? We

caught the tiger-men by surprise, but a pack that large will soon get its courage back. Here, I will lend you my help—"

The woman reached for Haplo's hand to assist him to his feet, perhaps to share her magic with him. But someone moved in front of the woman. Marit's hand clasped his.

"Thank you, Sister," said Marit. "He has help already."

"Very well, Sister," said the woman with a smile and a shrug. She turned to keep an eye on the tiger-men, who had retreated but were prowling about at a safe distance.

Haplo, with Marit's assistance, rose stiffly to his feet. He'd fallen with one knee bent at an angle, and when he tried to put his weight on it, pain shot through his leg. Reaching up his hand, he gingerly touched his face, drew his fingers back red with blood.

"You were lucky, the claws just missed your eye," Marit told him. "Here, lean on me."

Haplo's injury wasn't serious; he could have managed to walk on his own. But he didn't particularly want to. He draped his arm over Marit's shoulder. Her strong arms encircled him, supported him.

"Thanks," he said softly. "For this and—"

She cut him off. "We're even now," she returned. "Your life for mine."

And though her voice was chill, her touch was gentle. He tried to see into her eyes, but she kept her face averted from his. The dog had transformed back to its normal size, was gamboling happily at his side.

Looking ahead, into the forest, Haplo saw Alfred standing on one foot like an ungainly bird, peering out at them, wringing his hands in anxiety. The Patryns had carried Hugh the Hand into the woods. He had regained consciousness, was already attempting to sit up, waving off both their aid and their baffled and curious inspection.

"We would have made it safely," Marit said abruptly, "if you hadn't stopped to help the mensch. It was foolish. You should have left him."

"The tiger-men would have killed him."

"But according to you, he can't die!"

"He can die," said Haplo, accidentally putting his injured leg to the ground. He winced. "He comes back to life and the memory comes back as well. The memory's worse than the dying." Pausing a moment, he added, "We're a lot alike—he and I."

She was silent, thoughtful. He wondered if she understood. They had almost reached the edge of the woods. Stopping, she looked sideways at him.

"The Haplo I knew would have left him."

What was she saying? He couldn't tell by her tone. Was it oblique praise?

Or denunciation?

# CHAPTER ◆ 36

## THE LABYRINTH

◆

THE TIGER-MEN SET UP A HOWL OF DISAPPOINTMENT WHEN THE PATRYNS ENTERED the woods.

"If you and your friends can manage to go on a little farther without healing," the woman told Haplo, "we should push ahead. The tiger-men have been known to follow prey into the forest before now. And in such large numbers, they won't give up easily."

Haplo looked around. Hugh the Hand was pale; blood covered his head; but he was on his feet. He couldn't understand the woman's words, but he must have guessed their import. Seeing Haplo's questioning glance, the assassin nodded grimly.

"I can make it."

Haplo's gaze shifted to Alfred. He was walking on two feet as well as he ever walked on two feet, which meant that even as Haplo looked at him, Alfred tripped over an exposed tree root. Regaining his balance, he smiled; his hands fluttered. When he spoke, he spoke human. As did Hugh the Hand.

"I took advantage of the confusion . . . When they went out to help you, while no one was looking, I . . . well . . . The idea of riding on the dog again . . . I thought it would be easier . . ."

"You healed yourself," Haplo concluded.

He also spoke human. The Patryns were watching them. They could use their magic to understand the mensch language but they weren't doing it; probably out of politeness. They wouldn't need their magic in order to understand Sartan language, however—a language based on the runes. While they might not like it, they would have no difficulty recognizing it.

"Yes, I healed myself," Alfred replied. "I deemed it best. Save time and trouble . . ."

"And unfortunate questions," Haplo said softly.

Alfred glanced sideways at the other Patryns and flushed. "That too."

Haplo sighed, wondered why he hadn't thought of this sooner. If the Patryns discovered Alfred was a Sartan—their ages-old enemy, an enemy that they'd been taught to hate from the moment they could understand what hatred was—there was no telling what they might do to him. Well, Haplo would try to keep up the pretense that Alfred was a mensch, like Hugh the Hand. That would be difficult enough to explain—most Patryns living in the Labyrinth would have never heard of any of the so-called "lesser" races. They all would have heard of the Sartan.

Alfred was looking sideways at Marit.

"I won't betray you," she replied scornfully. "At least not yet. They might take out their wrath on the rest of us."

With a scathing glance at the Sartan, she left Haplo's side. Several of the other Patryns were moving on, to act as scouts for the trail ahead. Marit joined them.

Haplo dragged his thoughts back to the immediate, dangerous circumstances. "Keep near Hugh," he ordered Alfred. "Warn him not to mention anything about Sartan. We don't want to give them ideas."

"I understand." Alfred's gaze followed Marit, walking with several of the Patryn men. "I'm sorry, Haplo," he added quietly. "Because of me, your people have become your enemies."

"Forget it," Haplo said grimly. "Just do as you're told. Here, boy."

Whistling to the dog, he began to limp on down the trail. Alfred fell back to walk beside Hugh the Hand.

The Patryns left the two strangers alone, though Haplo noticed that several Patryns took up places behind, their eyes on Hugh and Alfred, their hands never far from their weapons.

The woman—the leader of what Haplo assumed was a hunting party—joined him, walked along beside. She was burning with questions; Haplo could see the glittering light in her brown eyes. But she would not ask them. It was for the headman of the tribe to question a stranger—even the strangest of strangers.

"I am called Haplo," he said, touching briefly the heart-rune on his left breast. He wasn't required to tell her his name, but he did so out of courtesy and to indicate his gratitude for her rescue.

"I am Kari," she replied, smiling at him, touching her own heart-rune.

She was tall and lank, with the hard-muscled body of a Runner. Yet she must be a Squatter; otherwise what was she doing leading a hunting party?

"It was lucky for us you came when you did," Haplo remarked, limping along painfully.

Kari did not offer to assist him; to do so would have been an insult to Marit, who had made it clear that she had some sort of interest in Haplo. Kari slowed her own pace to match his. She kept quiet watch as they walked, but she didn't appear particularly concerned that they were being followed. Haplo could see no indication from the sigla on his skin that the tiger-men were trailing them.

"It was not luck," Kari replied calmly. "We were sent to find you. The headman thought you might be in trouble."

Now it was Haplo's turn to burn with questions, but—out of politeness—he dared not ask them. It was the headman's prerogative to explain his reasons for doing something. Certainly the rest of the tribe would never consider offering explanations of their own, putting their words into another's mouth.

The conversation lagged a bit at this point. Haplo glanced about with a nervousness that was not all feigned.

"Don't worry," said Kari. "The tiger-men are not following us."

"It wasn't that," Haplo answered. "Before we met them, we saw flames. I was afraid that perhaps a dragon was attacking a village nearby—"

Kari was amused. "You don't know much about dragons, do you, Haplo?"

Haplo smiled and shrugged. It had been a nice try. "All right, so it isn't dragon-fire—"

"It is our fire," Kari said. "We built it."

Haplo shook his head. "Then apparently you're the ones who don't know much about dragons. The blaze can be seen a long way off—"

"Of course." Kari continued to be amused. "It is meant to be seen. That's why we light it on the tower. It is a welcome fire."

Haplo frowned. "Forgive me for saying this, Kari, but if your headman has made this decision, it seems to me that he must suffer from the sickness.[1] I'm surprised you haven't been attacked before now."

"We have been," Kari said nonchalantly. "Many, many times. Far more in past generations than these days, of course. Very few things in the Labyrinth are strong enough or daring enough to attack us now."

"Past generations?" Haplo's jaw sagged.

Who in the Labyrinth could speak of past generations? Few children knew their own parents. Oh, occasionally some large Squatter tribe might date itself back to a headman's father, but that was rare. Generally the tribes were either wiped out or scattered. Survivors joined up with, were absorbed into other tribes.

The past, in the Labyrinth, went back no further than yesterday. And one never spoke of a future.

Haplo opened his mouth, shut it again. To ask any more would be insulting. He'd already overstepped the bounds as it was. But he was uneasy. He glanced more than once at the telltale sigla on his skin. None of this made sense. Were they being lured into some sort of elaborate trap?

We are, he reminded himself, in the very heart, at the very beginning of the Labyrinth.

"Come, speak freely, Haplo," Kari said, sensing his discomfort, perhaps his suspicion. "What question is in your mind?"

"I've come here for a purpose," he said to her. "I'm looking for someone. A little girl. Her age would be seven, maybe eight gates. She is called Rue."

Kari nodded calmly.

"You know her?" Haplo's pulse quickened with hope. He couldn't believe it. He had found her already . . .

"I know several," Kari answered.

"Several! But how—"

---

[1] Probably a reference to Labyrinth sickness—a form of insanity affecting Patryns, brought on by the terrors and hardship of life in the Labyrinth.

"Rue is not an uncommon name in the Labyrinth," Kari said with a wry smile.

"I . . . I suppose not," Haplo mumbled.

To be honest, he'd never thought about it, never considered the possibility that there might be more than one child in the Labyrinth named Rue. He was not used to thinking of people in terms of names. He couldn't recall his parents' names. Or the name of the headman in the tribe that had raised him. Even Marit. She had been "the woman" to him, when he thought about her. The Lord of the Nexus was just that—his lord.

Haplo looked down at the dog trotting along next to him. The animal had saved his life—and he'd never bothered to give it a name. It wasn't until he had passed through Death's Gate, wasn't until he had entered the worlds of mensch, that he'd really become conscious of names, come to think of people as separate beings—important beings, distinct and individual.

And he wasn't the only one who had a problem with names. Haplo slid a glance back at Alfred—traipsing down the path, stumbling over any obstacle that presented itself, tripping over smooth ground if nothing else was available.

What's your true name, Sartan? Haplo wondered suddenly. And why haven't you ever told anyone?

The Patryns had covered a long distance. Haplo's leg was giving him increasing trouble, causing him increasing pain before Kari finally called a halt. The gray gloom was darkening; night was coming. It was dangerous to travel through the Labyrinth at any time, but far more dangerous after dark.

They had reached a clearing in the forest, near a stream. Kari examined it, consulted with her party, then announced that they would camp here for the night.

"Heal yourselves," she told Haplo. "We have food for you. Then sleep in peace. We will keep watch."

The Patryns brought them hot food, cooking it over a small fire that they built in a clearing. Haplo was astounded at their boldness, but said nothing. To have registered any sort of protest would have been to question Kari's authority, something that—as a stranger and one who'd been rescued by her—he had no right to do. He was relieved to note that they were at least sensible enough not to allow the blaze to smoke.

Once her guests were served, Kari asked courteously if there were other comforts she could provide for them.

"Your two friends do not speak our language," she said, with a glance at Hugh and Alfred. "Are their needs different from ours? Is there anything special we can bring them?"

"No," Haplo replied. "Thank you."

He had to give her credit. That, too, had been a nice try.

Kari nodded and left. She set the watch, posting lookouts on the ground and in the trees. Then she and the rest of her people sat down to eat. She did not ask Haplo and the others to join her circle. This could be taken for a bad sign—one didn't share food with one's enemy. Or again, it might be courtesy, an assumption that since the two strangers did not speak the language they would be more comfortable alone with their companions.

Marit returned, silently joined them. She kept her eyes on her meal—a mixture of dried meat and fruit wrapped and cooked in grape leaves. The dog shared Haplo's meal, then flopped over on its side and, with a tired sigh, fell sound asleep.

"What's going on, Haplo?" Hugh the Hand questioned, keeping his voice low. "These people may have saved our lives, but they don't seem overfriendly. Are we their prisoners now? Why are we hanging around with them?"

Haplo smiled. "It's nothing like that. They're uncertain of us. They've never seen people like you two and they don't understand. No, we're not their prisoners. We could leave anytime we wanted and they'd never say a word. But it's dangerous traveling in the Labyrinth—as you've seen. We need to rest, heal our wounds, build up our strength. They'll escort us to their village—"

"How do you know you can trust them?" the Hand demanded.

"Because they're my people," Haplo returned quietly.

Hugh the Hand grunted. "That little murderer Bane was one of *my* people. So was that accursed father of his."

"It's different with us," said Haplo. "It's this place, this prison. For generations, ever since we were sent here, we've had to work together to simply survive. From the moment we're born, our lives are in someone else's keeping—either father or mother, or maybe complete strangers. It doesn't matter. And it continues like that throughout our lives. No Patryn would ever hurt or kill or . . . or . . ."

"Betray his lord?" Marit asked.

She flung her food to the ground. Jumping to her feet—startling the sleeping dog to wakefulness—she stalked off.

Haplo started to call her back, faltered, and fell silent. What could he say?

The other Patryns had stopped talking to stare at her, wondering what was wrong, where she was going. Marit grabbed a water skin and walked down to the small stream, where she made a pretense of filling it. There were no stars or moon in the Labyrinth, but the firelight reflected off the leaves of the trees, glanced off the surface of the stream, providing enough light to see by. She took care to keep within the light—to do otherwise was to invite trouble.

The other Patryns went back to the meal and their talk. Kari followed Marit with her eyes, then turned a cool, thoughtful gaze on Haplo.

He was cursing himself for a fool. What had he been thinking about? My people—so superior. He was beginning to sound like a Sartan. Well, the late Samah, at least. Certainly not Alfred—a Sartan who had difficulty feeling superior to dirt worms.

"So what's your point?" Hugh the Hand asked, filling in the awkward silence.

"Nothing," Haplo muttered. "Never mind." Maybe they did in fact have to worry about these Patryns. *We were sent to find you.* The tiger-men had been sent to find them, too. And Haplo was lying to his people, deceiving them, bringing the ancient enemy into their midst.

A Patryn male, who had accompanied Marit during the day, went to the stream, started to sit down beside her. She turned her shoulder to him, averted her face. Shrugging, the Patryn walked off.

Haplo stood up painfully, limped down to the stream. Marit was sitting alone, shoulders hunched, knees drawn up, her chin resting on her knees. *Rolling herself into a ball,* Haplo had once teasingly described this position.

Hearing his footsteps, she glanced up, frowning, ready to repel any intrusion. Seeing that it was him, she relaxed somewhat, did not drive him away, as he had more than half-expected.

"I came for some water," he said stupidly.

She made no comment. The inane remark certainly didn't deserve one. He bent down, cupped his hand, drank, though he wasn't really thirsty. He sat down beside her. She did not look at him, but stared into the water, which was clear and cold and fast-running.

"I asked about our daughter," he said. "There are several girls in the village about her age named Rue. I don't know why, but I didn't expect that."

She said nothing, stared at the water. Picking up a stick, she thrust it into the stream. The water altered course, swirled around it in whorls and ripples, kept going.

"I hate this place," she said abruptly. "I loathe it, fear it. I left it. But I never really left it. I dream of it, always. And when I came back, I was frightened, but a part of me . . . a part of me . . ." She swallowed, frowned, shook her head angrily.

"—felt as if you'd come home," he finished for her.

Her eyes blinked rapidly. "But I haven't," she said in a low voice. "I can't." She glanced over her hunched shoulder at the Patryns, gathered together. "I'm different." Another moment's silence, then she said, "That's what you meant, wasn't it?"

"About Hugh and me being alike?" Haplo knew exactly what she was thinking, feeling. "Now I'm beginning to understand how the Sartan came to name Death's Gate. When we passed through Death's Gate, you and I both died, in a way. When we try to come back here, come back to our old life, it isn't possible. We've both changed. We've both *been* changed."

Haplo knew what had changed him. He wondered very much what had happened to change Marit.

"But I didn't feel like this when I was in the Nexus," Marit protested.

"That's because being in the Nexus isn't truly leaving the Labyrinth. You can see the Final Gate. Everyone's thoughts are centered in the Labyrinth. You dream about it, as you said. You feel the fear. But now, you dream about other things, other places . . ."

Did Hugh the Hand dream? Did he dream about that haven of peace and light he'd described? Was that what made it so hard, so very hard to come back?

And what did Marit dream?

Whatever it was, she obviously wasn't going to tell him.

"In the Labyrinth, the circle of my being encompassed only myself," Haplo went on. "It never really included anyone else, not even you."

She looked over at him.

"Just as yours never really included me," he added quietly.

She looked away again.

"No names," Haplo continued. "Only faces. Circles touched, but never joined—"

She shivered, made a sound, and he stopped talking, waited for her to say something.

She kept silent.

Haplo had hit some vital part of her, but he couldn't tell what. He went on talking, hoping to draw her out. "In the Labyrinth, my circle was a shell protecting me from feeling anything. I planned to keep it that way, but first the dog broke the circle, and after that, when I went beyond Death's Gate, other people just sort of seeped inside. My circle grew, expanded.

"I didn't intend it. I didn't want it. But what choice did I have? It was either that or die. I've known fear out there, worse than any fear in the Labyrinth. I healed a young man—an elf. I was healed by Alfred—my enemy. I've seen wonders and horrors. I've known happiness, hurt, sorrow. I've come to know myself.

"What changed me? I'd like to blame it on that chamber. That Chamber of the Damned. Alfred's Seventh Gate. A brush with the 'higher power' or whatever it was. But I don't think that was the cause. It was Limbeck and his speeches and Jarre calling him a druz. It was the dwarf maid Grundle and the human girl, Alake, who died in my arms."

Haplo smiled, shook his head. "It was even those four irritating, quarreling mensch on Pryan: Paithan, Rega, Roland, and Aleatha. I think about them, wonder if they've managed to survive."

Haplo touched the skin of his forearm; the tattoos were glowing faintly, indicating danger, but a danger that was far away. "You should have seen how the mensch stared when they first saw my skin start to glow. I thought Grundle's eyes were going to roll out of her head. Now, among my own people, I feel the way I did among the mensch—I'm different. My journeys have left their mark on me and I know that they must be able to see it. I can never be one of them again."

He waited for Marit to say something, but she didn't. She jabbed the stick into the water and huddled away from him. Obviously she wanted to be alone.

Standing up, he limped back to his bed, to heal himself—as far as possible—and try to sleep.

$\blacklozenge$

"Xar," Marit pleaded silently after Haplo had gone. "Husband, Lord, please help me, guide me. I'm so afraid, so desperately afraid. And alone. I don't know my own people anymore. I'm not one of them."

"Do you blame me for that?" Xar questioned mildly.

"No," Marit answered, poking the stick into the stream. "I blame Haplo. He brought the mensch here, and the Sartan. Their presence puts us all in danger."

"Yes, but it may work for us in the end. You say you are at the very beginning of the Labyrinth. This village, from what you describe, must be an incredibly large one, larger by far than any I ever knew existed. This suits me well. I have formed a plan."

"Yes, Lord." Marit was relieved, vastly relieved. The burden was to be lifted from her shoulders.

"When you reach the village, Wife, this is what you will do. . . ."

It was now extremely dark; Haplo could barely find his way back to the group. Hugh the Hand looked up at him hopefully, a hope that died when he saw that Haplo's hands were empty. "I thought you'd gone to get us something more to eat."

Haplo shook his head. "There is nothing more. We have a saying: 'The hungrier you are, the faster you'll run.' "

The Hand growled, and—scowling darkly—he went to the stream to fill his stomach with water. He moved silently, stealthily, as he always moved, as he had trained himself to move. Marit didn't hear him coming, apparently, and when he drew near, she gave a violent start.

"A guilty start," the Hand told Haplo later, describing the incident. "And I could have sworn I heard her talking to someone."

Haplo brushed it off; what else could he do? She was hiding something from him, of that he was certain. He longed to be able to trust her, but he couldn't. Did she feel the same about him? Did she want to trust him? Or was she only too happy to hate him?

Marit walked over to join the circle of Patryns, tossing down her water skin among them as an offering. Perhaps she was out to prove that she, at least, was still one with her people.

Kari looked over at Haplo, extending an invitation. He could have joined them if he had wanted, but he was too tired, too sore to move. His leg ached and the scratches on his face burned like fire. He needed to heal himself, to close the circle of his being—as best he could, considering the circle was torn and would be forever.

He scraped together a bed of dried fir needles and lay down.

Hugh the Hand sat down beside him.

"I'll take the first watch," the assassin offered quietly.

"No, you won't," Haplo told him. "To do so would be an insult, would look as if we didn't trust them. Lie down. Get some rest. You, too, Alfred."

The Hand thought he was going to argue; then he shrugged and stretched himself out on the ground, propped up against the curved bole of a tree. "Anything says I've got to fall asleep?" he asked, crossing his legs and taking out his pipe.

Haplo smiled tiredly. "Just don't make it look too obvious." He petted the dog, which had curled up beside him. It raised its head lazily, blinked at him, went back to its dreams.

Hugh the Hand stuck the pipe between his teeth. "I won't. If anyone asks, I'll say I'm troubled with insomnia. Eternal insomnia." He cast a dark glance at Alfred.

The Sartan flushed, his face reddening in the glow cast by the fire. He had been attempting to find himself a place to sleep, but first he'd struck his head on a buried rock; then he'd apparently sat down on an anthill, because he suddenly leapt to his feet and began slapping at his legs.

"Stop it!" Haplo commanded irritably. "You're drawing attention to yourself."

Alfred collapsed hastily to the ground. A faint expression of pain crossed his face. He reached underneath him, removed a pine cone, and tossed it away. Catching Haplo's disapproving glance, the Sartan hunkered down in the dirt and attempted to look comfortable. Surreptitiously, his hand slid underneath his bony posterior, removed another pine cone.

Haplo closed his eyes, began the healing process. Slowly the pain in his knee receded, the burning cuts on his face closed. But he couldn't sleep. Eternal insomnia, as Hugh the Hand had put it.

The other Patryns set the watch, doused the fire. Darkness closed over them, lit only by the softly glowing sigla on the skin of his people. Danger was around them, always around them. Marit did not return to her group, nor did she stay with the other Patryns, but chose a place to sleep about halfway between both.

Hugh the Hand sucked on the empty pipe. Alfred began to snore. The dog chased something in a dream.

And just when Haplo had decided that he couldn't sleep, he slept.

# CHAPTER ◆ 37

## THE CITADEL

## PRYAN

◆

Xᴀʀ ʜᴀᴅ ʀᴇᴀᴄʜᴇᴅ ᴀ ᴅᴇᴄɪsɪᴏɴ. ʜɪs ᴘʟᴀɴs ᴡᴇʀᴇ ꜰᴏʀᴍᴇᴅ; ɴᴏᴡ ʜᴇ sᴇᴛ ᴀʙᴏᴜᴛ putting them into action. He had arranged with Marit for the Patryns of the Labyrinth to deal with Haplo, keep him safe until Sang-drax reached him.

As for Sang-drax, Xar had concluded that the question of the dragon-snake's loyalty was not a factor. After much thought on the matter, Xar was confident that Sang-drax's primary motivation was hatred—the dragon-snake hated Haplo, wanted revenge. Sang-drax would not rest until he had sought out Haplo and destroyed him. That would take some time, Xar reasoned. Even for someone as powerful as Sang-drax, the Labyrinth was not easily traversed. By the time the dragon-snake had his coils wrapped around Haplo, Xar would be there to see to it that his prize was not damaged beyond usefulness.

Xar's immediate problem was the killing of the mensch. Given the lord's power and skill in magic, the murder of two elves, two humans, and a dwarf (none of them overly intelligent) should not be a concern. The Lord of the Nexus could have destroyed them all simultaneously with a few gestures in the air and a spoken word or two. But it was not the manner of their dying that worried him, it was the condition of the corpses after death.

He studied the mensch under various circumstances for a day or two, and concluded that, even dead, they would never be able to stand up to the tytans. The elven male was tall, but thin, with fragile bone structure. The human male was tall with good bones and muscle. Unfortunately, this male appeared to be suffering from pangs of thwarted love and consequently had let his body go to ruin. The human female was stocky, but muscular. The dwarf, though short in stature, had the strength of his race and was the best of a bad lot. The elven female was hopeless.

It was essential, therefore, that the mensch in death should be better than they were in life. Their corpses had to be fit and strong. And, most important, they had to be endowed with a strength and stamina the wretches did not currently possess. Poison was the best way to murder them, but it needed to be a special concoction—one that would kill the body and at the same time make it healthier. A most intriguing dichotomy.

Xar began with a flask of ordinary water. Working the rune-magic, considering the possibilities, he altered the water's chemical structure. At last he felt confident that he had succeeded; he had developed an elixir that would kill—not immediately, but after a short period, say an hour or so, during which the body would begin a rapid acceleration of muscle and bone tissue, a process that would later be further enhanced by the necromancy.

The poison had one drawback: the bodies would wear out far faster than ordinary corpses. But Xar did not need these mensch long; they had only to buy him enough time to reach the ship.

The elixir finished, including the final additive of a pleasing flavor of spiced wine, Xar prepared a feast. He concocted food, then placed the poisoned wine in a large silver pitcher in the center of the table, and went to invite the mensch to a party.

The first one he came across was the human female—he could never recall her name. In his most charming manner, Xar asked her to join him that evening for a dinner of the most wonderful delicacies, all compliments of the lord's magical talent. He urged her to bring the others, and Rega, excited by this break in their dull routine, hastened to do just that.

She went hunting for Paithan. She knew, of course, where to look for him. Opening the door to the Star Chamber, she peered inside.

"Paithan?" she called, hesitant about entering. She hadn't gone into the chamber since the time the cursed machine had nearly blinded her. "Could you come out here? I have something to tell you."

"Uh, I can't leave right at the moment, sweetheart. I mean, well, it might be a while . . ."

"But, Paithan, it's important."

Rega took a tentative step inside the doorway. Paithan's voice was coming from an odd direction.

"It will have to wait . . . I'm not really able . . . I've gotten myself in a bit of a . . . Can't quite figure out how to get down, you see . . ."

Rega couldn't see, at least not at the moment. Irritation overcoming her fear of the light, she walked into the Star Chamber. Hands on her hips, she glared around the room.

"Paithan, quit playing games this instant. Where are you?"

"Up . . . up here." Paithan's voice drifted down from above.

Astonished, Rega tilted her head, stared in the direction indicated. "Name of the ancestors, Pait, what are you doing up there?"

The elf, perched on the seat of one of the enormous chairs, peered back down at her. He looked and sounded extremely uncomfortable. "I came up here to . . . um . . . well . . . see what it was like from up here. The view, you know."

"Well, how is it?" Rega demanded.

Paithan winced at the sarcasm. "Not bad," he said, glancing around and feigning interest. "Really quite nice . . ."

"View—my ass!" Rega said loudly.

"I can't, dear. Not from this angle. If you could bend over—"

"You climbed up there to try to figure out how the damn chair works!" Rega informed him. "And now you can't get back down. What did you have in mind? Pretending you're a tytan? Or maybe you thought the machine would mistake you for a tytan! Not but what it might. You've got all the brains of one."

"I had to try something, Rega," Paithan excused himself plaintively. "It seemed like a good idea at the time. The tytans are the key to this machine. I just know it. That's why it's not working properly. If they were here—"

"—we'd all be dead," Rega inserted grimly, "and there'd be nothing to worry about, least of all this stupid machine! How did you get up there?"

"Going up was easy—the chair legs are sort of rough with lots of footholds, and elves were always pretty fair climbers and—"

"Well, just come down the same way."

"I can't. I'll fall. I tried once. My foot slipped. I was barely able to hang on. I could just picture myself pitching head first into that well." Paithan clutched the edge of the chair seat. "You can't believe how deep and dark that well looks from up here. I'll bet it goes clear into the center of Pryan. I could imagine myself falling and falling and falling . . ."

"Don't think about it!" Rega told him irritably. "You're only making it worse!"

"It can't get much worse," Paithan said miserably. "Just looking down, I feel like I might throw up." His face did have a greenish tinge.

"This whole business makes me feel like *I* might throw up," Rega muttered, taking a step or two backward, just to be out of range. She eyed him thoughtfully. "The first thing I'm going to do— if and when I ever get him out of here—is lock the door to this damn room and throw away the key."

"What did you say, dear?"

"I said what if Roland tosses up a length of rope? You could secure it to the arm of the chair, then shinny down it."

"Do you have to tell your brother?" Paithan groaned. "Why can't *you* do it?"

"Because it's going to take a strong arm to throw the rope that far," Rega returned.

"Roland will never let me live this down," Paithan said bitterly. "Look, I've got an idea. Go ask the wizard—"

"Eh?" came a quavering voice. "Someone call for a wizard?"

The old man wandered into the room. Seeing Rega, he smiled, doffed his decrepit hat. "Here I am. Glad to be of service. Bond's the name. James Bond."

"The *other* wizard!" Paithan hissed. "The useful one!"

"Great Scott!" The old man froze. "It's Dr. No! He's found me! Don't be afraid, my dear." He reached out trembling hands. "I'll save you—"

"I can't get Lord Xar." Rega was explaining to Paithan. "That's what I came to tell you. He's busy planning a party. We're all invited—"

"A party. How wonderful!" The old man beamed. "I'm quite fond of parties. Have to get my tux out of mothballs—"

"A party!" Paithan repeated. "Yes, that would be great fun!

Aleatha loves parties. We'll get her away from that strange maze where she spends all her time now—"

"*And* get her away from the dwarf," Rega added. "I haven't said anything because, well, she *is* your sister, but I think there's something sort of odd going on there."

"What are you implying?" Paithan glared down at Rega.

"Nothing, but it's obvious that Drugar adores her and, let's face it, she's not really choosy about men—"

"Oh, yes. After all, she *did* fall for your brother!" Paithan said viciously.

Rega flushed in anger. "I didn't mean—"

The old man, following Rega's gaze upward, gave a violent start. "I say! It *is* Dr. No!"

"No—" Paithan began.

"You see!" Zifnab yelled, triumphant. "He admits it!"

"I'm Paithan!" Paithan shouted, leaning farther over the edge of the chair seat than he'd intended. Shuddering, he slid hurriedly backward.

"The fool is stuck up there," Rega explained in icy tones. "He's scared to come down."

"I'm not either," Paithan retorted sullenly. "I have the wrong shoes on, that's all. I'll slip."

"You're sure he's not No?" the old man asked nervously.

"Yes, he's not No. I mean no, he isn't . . . Never mind." Rega was starting to feel dizzy herself. "We've got to get him down. Do you have any spells?"

"Dandy spell!" the old man said immediately. "Fire . . . Fire . . . Fireball! That's it! We set the chair legs on fire and when they burn up—"

"I don't think that will work!" Paithan protested loudly.

The old man snorted. " 'Course it will. The chair goes up in flames, and pretty soon the seat doesn't have a leg to stand on and whoosh! Down she comes!"

"Go get Roland," Paithan said in resigned tones. "And take *him* with you," he added, with a dark glance at the old man.

"Come on, sir," said Rega. Trying not to laugh, she guided the old man, protesting, out of the Star Chamber. "Yes, I *do* think it would be fun to set the chair on fire. I wouldn't even mind setting Paithan on fire. But maybe some other time. Perhaps you could go help Lord Xar with the party arrangements . . ."

"Party," the old man said, brightening. "I do *love* a good party!"

"And hurry!" Paithan's voice cracked in panic. "The machine's starting up! I think the starlight's about to come on!"

As Paithan had said, Aleatha had been spending most of her time with Drugar in the maze. And, as she had promised, she had told no one about her discovery. She might have, if they'd been nice to her; Aleatha rarely troubled herself with the bother of keeping secrets. But the others, including Roland (especially Roland), were all just as idiotic and juvenile as always.

"Paithan's involved with that stupid machine of his," Aleatha told Drugar as they traversed the maze. "Rega's involved with trying to uninvolve Paithan with the stupid machine, and, as for Roland, who knows—or cares—what he's doing." She sniffed. "Let them hang around with that horrid, ugly Xar. You and I have found *interesting* people. Haven't we, Drugar?"

Drugar agreed. He always agreed with everything she said and was more than willing to take her into the maze anytime she wanted to go.

They had gone the very next morning, when the star machine was on, but, as Drugar had warned her, the fog-people weren't around. Aleatha and the dwarf waited for a long time, but no one came. The starburst mosaic in the amphitheater remained deserted.

Aleatha, bored, wandered around the mosaic, staring down at it.

"Why, look, Drugar," she said, kneeling. "Isn't this pattern the same one that's on the city gate?"

Drugar bent over to examine it. Yes, it was the same pattern. And in the center of the runes was an empty place, the same as the empty place on the city gate.

Drugar fingered the amulet he wore around his neck. When he placed that amulet in the empty place, the gate opened. His fingers grew cold; his hand shivered. He backed away from the starburst hurriedly and glanced at Aleatha, fearing she had noticed, would have the same idea.

But Aleatha had already lost interest. The people weren't here. The place was—for her—boring. She wanted to leave, and Drugar was quite ready to leave with her.

That afternoon, however, the two came back. The light from the star machine was on and shining brightly. The people were walking around the same as before.

Aleatha sat and watched them in mingled frustration and joy, tried to listen to them.

"They're talking," she said. "I can see their mouths move. Their hands move when they talk, help shape their words. They're real people. I know they are! But where are they? What are they talking about? It's so irritating not to know!"

Drugar fingered his amulet, said nothing.

But her words stuck in the dwarf's mind. The two returned to the maze the next afternoon, and the afternoon after that. The dwarf now began to view the fog-people the way Aleatha viewed them—as real people. He began to notice things about them; he thought he recognized some of the dwarves from the day previous. Elves and humans looked alike to him; he couldn't tell whether they were the same or not. But the dwarves—one in particular—he was certain had been there before.

This dwarf was an ale merchant. Drugar could tell by the plaiting of his beard—it was knotted in the guild braids—and by the silver mug. Hanging from a velvet ribbon around the dwarf's neck, the mug was used to offer customers a taste of his brew. And apparently his ale was good. The dwarf was well-to-do, to judge by his clothes. Elves and humans greeted him with respect, bowing and nodding. Some of the humans even dropped down on one knee to talk with the dwarf, putting themselves at his eye level—a courtesy Drugar had never in his life imagined a human offering a dwarf.

But then, he'd never in his life had much to do with humans or elves, for which he'd always been grateful.

"I've named that elf right there Lord Gorgo," Aleatha said. Since the fog-people wouldn't talk to her, she'd started talking about them. She'd begun to give them names and imagine what their relationships were to each other. It amused her, in fact, to stand right next to one of the shadowy men and discuss him with the dwarf.

"I knew a Lord Gorgo once. His eyes stuck out just like that poor man's eyes stick out. He *does* dress well, though. Much better than Gorgo, who had no taste in clothes. That woman he's with— frightful. She must not be his wife—look how she's clutching him. Low-cut dresses appear to be the fashion there, but if *I* had *her* bosoms, I'd button my collar up to my chin. What very handsome human males they have there. And walking about as freely as if they owned the place. These elves treat their human slaves very carelessly. Why, look, Drugar, there's that dwarf with the silver mug. We saw him yesterday. And he's talking to Lord Gorgo! And here's a human coming up to join them. I believe I shall call him Rolf. We had a slave once named Rolf, who . . ."

But Drugar had stopped listening. Taking hold of the amulet, the dwarf left the bench where he'd been sitting and for the first time ventured out into the midst of the people who seemed so real and were so false, who talked so much and were so silent.

"Drugar! You're here with us!" Aleatha laughed and whirled in a dance, her skirts billowing around her. "Isn't it fun?" Her dance ceased; she pouted. "But it would be more fun if they were real. Oh, Drugar, sometimes I wish you'd never brought me here! I like it, but it makes me so homesick . . . Drugar, what are you doing?"

The dwarf ignored her. Removing the amulet from around his neck, he knelt down in the center of the starburst and placed the amulet in the empty spot, just as he had placed it in the same empty spot in the center of the city gate.

He heard Aleatha scream, but the sound was distant, far distant, and he wasn't certain he was even hearing it at all . . .

A hand clapped him on the back.

"You, sir!" A voice boomed, speaking dwarven. A silver mug waved in front of Drugar's nose. "You'll be a stranger to our fair city, I'm wagering. Now, sir, how would you like a taste of the finest ale in all of Pryan?"

# CHAPTER ♦ 38

# THE LABYRINTH

♦

Haplo woke the next morning, healed and rested, and lay quietly for long moments, listening to the sounds of the Labyrinth. He had hated this place while he was trapped here. It had taken from him everything he had ever loved. But it had given him everything he had ever loved as well. Only now did he realize it; only now did he come to admit it.

The tribe of Squatters that had taken him in when he was a boy, after his parents had been killed. He couldn't remember any of their names, but he could see their faces in the pale gray light that was little more than a brightening of the darkness, but was morning to the Labyrinth. He hadn't thought about them in a long time, since the day he'd left. He'd put them out of his mind then, as he'd assumed they must have put him out of their minds. Now he knew better.

The men who'd rescued that frightened little boy might still think about him. The old woman who'd housed and fed him must wonder about him, wonder where he was, what had happened to him. The young man who'd taught him the art of inscribing the sigla on weapons might be interested to know that his teaching had proved valuable. Haplo would have given a great deal now to find them, to tell them, to thank them.

"I was taught to hate," he mused, listening to the rustle of small animals, the bird calls he'd never truly heard until now, never truly forgotten. He rubbed the jowls of the dog, which was snoozing with its head on its master's chest. "I was never taught to love."

He sat up suddenly, disturbing the dog, which yawned, stretched, and dashed off to annoy foraging squirrels. Marit lay by herself, apart from Haplo and his group, apart from the other Patryns. She slept as he remembered seeing her sleep, curled up in the same tight ball. He remembered sleeping beside her, his body wrapped around hers, his stomach pressed against her back, his arms cradling her protectively. He wondered what it might have been like, sleeping with her and the baby, the child between them, sheltered, protected, loved.

To his astonishment, his eyes burned with tears. Hastily, embarrassed and half-angry at himself, he rubbed the moisture dry.

A stick snapped behind him.

Haplo started to turn, but before he could hoist himself up, Hugh the Hand had leapt to his feet, was confronting Kari.

"It's all right, Hugh," Haplo said, standing up. He spoke human. "She let us know she was coming."

True enough. Kari had stepped on the stick on purpose, courteously calling attention to her nearness.

"These you term mensch, don't they require sleep?" she asked Haplo. "My people noticed your friend was awake all night."

"They have no rune-magic to protect them," Haplo explained, hoping she hadn't taken offense. "We have been through many dangers. He . . . that is, *they*"—Haplo had to remember to include Alfred—"are naturally nervous, being in such a strange and terrifying place."

*And why have they come to this strange and terrifying place?* was the question on Kari's lips. Haplo could hear the words as surely as if she'd spoken them. But to ask such a question was not her duty. She gave Hugh the Hand a pitying look, spoke a few words in Patryn to Haplo, then handed over a chunk of hard bread.

"What was that all about?" the Hand wondered, glowering darkly after Kari.

Haplo grinned. "She says that you must be able to run like a rabbit, otherwise you'd never have lived this long."

Hugh the Hand wasn't amused. He glanced around grimly. "I'm amazed anything lives long around here. There's a bad feeling to these woods. I'll be glad to get out of them." He stared morosely at the lumps of colorless dough Haplo held in his hands. "That breakfast?"

Haplo nodded.

"I'll pass." Pipe in his mouth, the assassin wandered over to the stream.

Haplo glanced to where Marit had been sleeping. She was awake now, doing what a Patryn always did first thing in the morning—checking old weapons, making new ones. She was eyeing a spear, a full-sized one with a sigla-engraved rock head. It was a fine weapon, most likely a gift from one of the Patryns. Haplo recalled the man who had met her by the stream. Yes, he'd been carrying a spear like that.

"Very fine," Haplo said, coming up to her. "Well made."

Marit jumped up, her hand tightening reflexively around the haft of the spear.

"I'm sorry," he said, startled at her reaction. "I didn't mean to scare you."

Marit shrugged, cold, nonchalant. "I didn't hear you coming, that's all. This horrible place," she said abruptly, glancing around. "I'd forgotten how much I hate it!" Taking out a knife—another present, probably—she began improving a sigil carved on the spear's head. She had not once looked directly at him. "I hate it," she repeated in a low voice.

"This may sound strange," said Haplo, "but I was thinking this morning that it was sort of good to be back. My memories aren't all bad—" Impulsively he reached out to her.

Her head snapped back. She whipped around. Her hair, flying, struck him, stung his face. She held the spear between them. "We are even now. I saved your life. I owe you nothing. Remember that."

Spear in hand, she walked off. Several of Kari's group were heading out, going to scout the path ahead. Marit joined them, took her place beside the man who had given her the spear.

Confused, Haplo stared after her. Yesterday she had claimed him as hers, warned Kari away from him. Last night she'd talked to him. She had been glad—or so he had thought—to have him near her.

All was ended. All was suddenly different. What had happened between then and now?

Haplo couldn't guess. Kari and her people were breaking down their crude camp, preparing to travel. The birds had fallen silent. The only sounds were the angry chattering of three squirrels, up a tree, throwing nutshells at the dog, barking beneath. Haplo looked at his skin; the sigla glowed softly. Danger, not near, but not far. Never far.

He gnawed at a piece of bread. It filled the stomach; that was about all he could say for it.

"Could . . . could I have some of that?" Alfred was standing beside him, eyeing the bread.

Haplo practically threw it at him.

Alfred fumbled, caught it, nibbled at a corner. He started to say something, but Haplo interrupted.

"Here, stupid dog!" He whistled. "Stop that noise!"

The animal, hearing the sharp and unaccustomed note of rebuff, fell immediately silent. Head down, it trotted back meekly, wondering what it had done wrong.

"Aren't you hungry?" Alfred ventured.

Haplo shook his head.

"You really should eat—"

"You're in danger here," Haplo said grimly.

Alfred looked alarmed, nearly dropped the bread. He glanced fearfully around him, probably expecting to see packs of tiger-men swarming through the trees. Instead he saw only Hugh the Hand, stripped to the waist, plunging his head and shoulders into the rushing stream. Nearby, Kari and her group were ready to move out.

Kari waved to Haplo, motioned for him and his friends to join them. He waved back, indicating that she was to go on ahead. Kari looked at him dubiously, frowning. It wasn't wise to split up. He knew that as well as she. But then, he thought bitterly, he wasn't really part of her group anyway. He smiled reassuringly, held his hand up, palm out, to indicate that he would be all right, that they'd catch up in a moment. Kari shrugged and left.

"What you said about danger . . . I don't understand—" Alfred began.

"You should go back."

"Back where?" Alfred stared, helpless, confused.

"To the Vortex. Hugh the Hand'll go. Hell, you couldn't pry him loose from you. You'd stand a pretty fair chance of making it, I think. The tiger-men—if they're still around—will be tailing us."

"But the Vortex is destroyed."

"Not for you, Sartan. I've seen your magic! You killed the king dragon-snake. You raised the dead. You could probably lift up the pieces of that damn mountain and put it back together again."

Alfred protested. "You said I wasn't to use my magic. You saw what happened—"

"I think the Labyrinth will let you—especially if it knows you're leaving."

Alfred flushed. His head down, he glanced at Haplo sideways. "You . . . you said you needed me . . ."

"I lied. I don't need you. I don't need anyone. What I came to do is hopeless anyway. My child is dead. Murdered in your damn prison. Go on, Sartan. Get out."

"*Not* 'Sartan.' My name is—"

"Don't say Alfred!" Haplo was suddenly furious. "That isn't your name! Alfred's a mensch name you took when you decided to hide out by becoming a mensch. No one knows what your real name is, because it's a Sartan name and you've never trusted anybody enough to tell them. So just—"

"It is Coren."

"What?" Haplo blinked, pulled up short.

"My name is Coren," Alfred repeated quietly.

"I'll be damned." Haplo mulled over what he knew of Sartan rune-language. "That means 'to choose' or something like that."

Alfred smiled faintly. " 'Chosen.' Me—chosen. Ludicrous, isn't it? The name doesn't mean anything, of course. It's quite common among Sartan. Almost every family has—er—*had* a boy they named Coren. Hoping for a self-fulfilling prophecy. You see why I never told you. It wasn't that I didn't trust you. I didn't want you to laugh."

"I'm not laughing," Haplo said.

Alfred looked very uncomfortable. "You should be. It's really quite amusing."

Hugh the Hand, shaking the water off his head and shoulders, walked back up from the stream. He stopped to stare around the empty clearing, probably wondering what had happened to the others.

"You didn't think that name of yours was so amusing when you woke up and found yourself alone in that mausoleum, did you, Coren?" Haplo asked quietly.

Alfred was red again, then pale. His hands trembled. He

dropped the bread—to the extreme gratification of the dog. Sinking onto a tree stump, Alfred sighed, his breath rattling in his throat.

"You're right. Chosen. Chosen to live when everyone I had ever loved had died. Why? For what? They were all so much better. So much more worthy." Alfred looked up, his pale face hard. His trembling hand clenched. "I hated my name then. I *hated* it. I was happy to take the name I bear now. I planned to forget the other one. And I succeeded. I had forgotten it—until I met you."

Alfred sighed again. He smiled sadly.

Haplo looked back at the assassin, made him a sign.

Hugh swung himself easily up into the branches of a tree, gazed ahead, in the direction the other Patryns had taken. He motioned back, raised one finger.

So Kari was keeping an eye on them. She'd left one of the group to wait for them. Courtesy again. She was concerned, didn't want them to get lost.

Haplo snorted.

Alfred was prattling on, obviously deeply relieved to talk.

"Whenever you spoke to me, Haplo, even though you called me Alfred, I kept hearing Coren. It was frightening. And yet it felt good to me, all at the same time. Frightening because I didn't understand. Yet good—you reminded me of my past, my distant past, when my family and friends were still alive.

"How could you do this? I wondered. Who are you? At first I thought you might be one of my people, but I knew immediately that wasn't right. Yet you obviously weren't a mensch. And then I remembered. I remembered the ancient history. I remembered the stories about the—forgive me—the old enemy.

"That night on Arianus, when we were imprisoned in the vat, I cast a spell on you, put you to sleep."

Haplo stared, astonished. "A spell on *me!* You?"

Alfred flushed. "I'm afraid so. It was only a sleep spell. You wore the bandages around your hands, to hide the tattoos. I crept over, lifted one of the bandages, and I saw . . ."

"So that's how you knew." Haplo motioned for the assassin to join them. "I wondered. And as fascinating as this trip down memory lane has been, Coren, it doesn't change the fact that you're in danger and you should leave—"

"But it does," Alfred said, standing up so swiftly that he startled the dog. It bounded to its feet with a whuff, ears up, hackles raised, wondering what was wrong. "Now I know what my name means."

"It's just a name, damn it! It doesn't mean anything. You said so yourself."

"But it does mean something—to me. You have taught me, Haplo. You even said it. Not 'chosen,' past tense. But 'to choose.' Present tense. Everyone else has always made my choices for me. I faint." Alfred spread his hands helplessly. "Or fall down. Or"—he cast a guilty glance at Hugh the Hand—"when I *do* take action, I 'forget.' "

Alfred stood up very straight, very tall. "But now that's different. I choose to be here, Haplo. You said you needed me. You made me ashamed. You had the courage to come into this dreadful place —for what? For ambition? For power? No. You came for love. The Labyrinth is afraid. Yes, but not of me. It's afraid of you, Haplo. You have brought into it the one weapon it doesn't know how to fight."

Reaching down, Alfred timidly petted the dog, stroked its silky ears. "I know it's dangerous and I'm not certain how much help I can be, but I choose to be here," he said softly, not looking at Haplo. "I choose to be here with you."

"They're watching us," said Hugh the Hand, coming up from behind. "In fact, four of them have started back in this direction. They're all armed. Of course, it *could* be that they like us so much they can't bear to let us out of their sight. But I doubt it."

The Hand took the pipe out of his pocket, studied it thoughtfully. Putting it into his mouth, he spoke through his teeth. "She betrayed us, didn't she?"

"Yes," said Haplo, looking far back the way they'd come, far back to the ruined mountain.

# CHAPTER 39

# THE CITADEL

# PRYAN

♦

ROLAND, REGA, AND PAITHAN STOOD OUTSIDE THE STAR CHAMBER. BRIGHT LIGHT welled out from under the door. Both Paithan and Roland were rubbing their eyes.

"Can you see yet?" Rega asked anxiously.

"Yeah," said Roland bitterly. "Spots. If you've blinded me, elf—"

"It'll go away." Paithan was surly. "Just give it time."

"I *told* you not to look down!" Roland snarled. "But no. You have to go stare into that damn well and pass out—"

"I did not! My hands slipped! As for the well"—Paithan shivered—"it's fascinating, in a creepy kind of way."

"Sort of like your sister," Roland sneered.

Paithan aimed a blow in the human's general direction. Missing, slamming his fist into a wall, he groaned and began to suck on his bleeding knuckles.

"Roland's just teasing, Pait," said Rega. "He doesn't mean anything. He's so in love with her himself he can't see straight."

"I may never be able to see anything!" Roland retorted. "As for my being in love with that slut—"

"Slut!" Paithan hurled himself bodily at Roland. "Apologize!"

The two went down in a heap, rolling around, pummeling each other.

"Stop it!" Rega stood over them, screaming and occasionally kicking the one who happened to roll nearer her. "Stop it, both of you! We're supposed to be going to the party . . ." Her voice died away.

Xar had appeared at the bottom of the stairs leading to the Star Chamber. Arms crossed over his chest, he was staring up at them, the expression on his face dark and grim.

"Party," Rega repeated nervously. "Paithan! Xar's here! Get up. Roland, come on! You look like idiots! Both of you!"

Still not able to see too well, but hearing the note of tension in Rega's voice, Paithan left off hitting, staggered to his feet. His face burned with shame. He could imagine what the old man must be thinking.

"You knocked a tooth loose," Roland mumbled. His mouth was bloody.

"Shut up!" Rega hissed.

The aftereffects of the bright light were wearing off; Paithan could see the wizard now. Xar was trying to look as if he found them amusing, but though the lines around his eyes were crinkled in a tolerant smile, the eyes themselves were colder and darker than the well in the Star Chamber. Staring into them, Paithan had the same sort of queasy feeling in his stomach. He even found himself taking an involuntary step backward, away from the edge of the staircase.

"Where are the other ones?" Xar asked, voice pleasant, benign. "I want all of you to come to my party."

"What other ones?" Rega asked, hedging.

"The other female. And the dwarf," Xar said, smiling.

"You ever notice how he never seems to remember our names?" Roland said out of the corner of his mouth to Paithan.

"You know"—Rega gulped—"Aleatha was right. He *is* ugly." She reached out, clasped hold of Paithan's hand. "I really don't want to go this party."

"I don't think we have much choice," Paithan said quietly. "What excuse could we offer?"

"Tell him we just don't want to go," Roland said, edging behind Paithan.

"*Me* tell him? What's wrong with *you* telling him?" Paithan snapped.

"I don't think he likes me."

"Where is your sister, elf?" Xar's brows came together over his nose. "And the dwarf?"

"I don't know. I haven't seen them. We'll . . . go look for them!" Paithan offered hurriedly. "Won't we?"

"Yeah. Right now."

"I'll help."

Roland and Rega and the elf clattered down the stairs. At the bottom, they stopped. Xar stood before them, blocking their way. The two humans shoved Paithan to the front.

"Uh, we're just going to find Aleatha . . . my sister," Paithan said faintly. "And the dwarf. Drugar. The dwarf."

Xar smiled. "Hurry. The food will grow cold."

"Right!" Paithan wormed his way around the wizard and bolted for the door.

Rega and Roland were right behind him. None of them stopped running until they were out of the main building, standing on the wide marble steppes that overlooked the empty and deserted city below. The citadel had never appeared quite so empty or so deserted as it did now.

"I don't like this," Rega said, her voice shaking. "I don't like him. What does he want with us?"

"Hush, be careful," Paithan warned. "He's watching us! No, don't look. He's up there, on a balcony."

"What are we going to do?"

"What *can* we do?" Roland demanded. "We go to his party. Do you want to make him mad? Maybe you don't remember what he did to those tytans, but I do. Besides, how bad can it be? I say we're all jumping at our own shadows."

"Roland's right. It's only a party. If the wizard wanted to do anything bad to us—and there's no reason why he should—then he could do it from where he's standing."

"I don't like the way he looked at us," Rega said stubbornly. "And he seems too eager. Excited."

"At his age and with his looks, he probably doesn't get invited to a lot of parties," Roland suggested.

Paithan glanced at the dark-robed figure, standing still and silent on the balcony. "I think we should humor him. We'd better find Drugar and Aleatha right away."

"If they've gone into that maze, you won't find them at all, much less right away," Rega predicted.

Paithan sighed, frustrated. "Maybe you two should go back and I'll try to find Aleatha—"

"Oh, no!" Roland said, latching on to Paithan firmly. "We're all going."

"Well," Paithan began, "I suppose then that we should split—"

"Look! There's Aleatha now!" Rega cried, pointing.

The broad steppe they stood on overlooked the back of the city. Aleatha had just appeared around the corner of a building, her tattered dress a bright spot of color against the white marble.

"Good. That only leaves Drugar. And surely the old man won't mind if we're missing the dwarf—"

"Something's wrong with her," Roland said suddenly. "Aleatha!"

He went dashing down the stairs, racing toward Aleatha. She had been moving toward them—running toward them, in fact. Paithan tried to remember the last time he'd ever seen his sister run. But now she had stopped and was leaning against the wall of a building, her hand pressed over her breast as if in pain.

"Aleatha!" Roland said, coming up to her.

Her eyes were closed. Opening them, she looked at him thankfully, and with a sob reached out to him, nearly fell into his arms.

He clasped her, held her fast. "What's wrong? What's the matter?"

"Drugar!" Aleatha managed to gasp.

"What did he do to you?" Roland cried, clutching her fiercely. "Did he hurt you? By the ancestors, I'll—"

"No, no!" Aleatha was shaking her head. Her hair floated around her face in an ashen-blond, shimmering cloud. She gasped for breath. "He's . . . disappeared!"

"Disappeared?" Paithan came up, Rega alongside. "What do you mean, Thea? How could he disappear?"

"I don't know!" Aleatha lifted her head, her blue eyes wide and frightened. "One minute he was there, next to me. And the next . . ."

She put her head against Roland's chest, began to cry. He patted her on the back, looked questioningly at Paithan. "What's she talking about?"

"Beats me," said Paithan.

"Don't forget Xar," Rega inserted quietly. "He's still watching us."

"Was it the tytans? Thea, don't go getting hysterical . . ."

"Too late," Rega said, eyeing her.

Aleatha was sobbing uncontrollably. She would have fallen but for Roland.

"Look, something terrible must have happened to her." He lifted her tenderly in his arms. "She doesn't normally come apart like this. Not even when the dragon attacked us."

Paithan had to agreed. He was now growing anxious and upset himself. "But what should we do?"

Rega took charge. "We've got to get her calmed down long enough for her to tell us what happened. Take her back into the main building. We'll go to the stupid party, get her a glass of wine to drink. If something dreadful *did* happen—like the tytans broke in and snatched Drugar—then Lord Xar should know about it. He may be able to protect us."

"Why would the tytans come in and snatch Drugar?" Paithan asked—a perfectly logical question, but one which went unanswered.

Roland couldn't hear him over Aleatha's gulping sobs, and Rega gave the elf a disgusted look and shook her head at him.

"Get her a glass of wine," she repeated, and the three returned in a procession back to the main building.

Xar met them at the door, frowned at the sight of the hysterical elven woman.

"What is wrong with her?"

"She's had some sort of shock," Paithan said. Rega had elected him spokesperson with a jab in his back. "We don't know what's wrong because she's too upset to tell us."

"Where is the dwarf?" Xar asked, frowning.

At this, Aleatha gave a strangled scream. "Where is the dwarf? That's a good one!" Covering her face with her hands, she began to laugh wildly.

Paithan was growing more and more worried. He had never seen his sister this upset over anything. "He's been going into the maze—"

Rega chimed in nervously. "We thought a glass of wine—"

Both realized they were talking at once and fell silent. Xar gave Rega a sharp look.

"Wine," he said. His gaze went back to the elf woman. "You are right. A glass of wine will improve her spirits immensely. All of you must take one. Where did you say the dwarf was?"

"We didn't," Paithan returned somewhat impatiently, wondering why this emphasis on Drugar. "If we can just get Aleatha calmed down, perhaps we'll find out."

"Yes," Xar said softly, "we will calm her down. And then we will find out all we need to know. This way." He sidled around behind them, extended his arms. "This way."

Paithan had seen human farmers walking their fields at harvest time, sweeping their scythes through the tall grain, cutting it down with broad strokes. Xar's arms were like those scythes, sweeping the small group up, cutting them down. Paithan's instinct was to bolt. He forced himself to go along with the others, however.

What's there to be afraid of? he asked, feeling foolish. He wondered if the other two shared his apprehensions and cast them a quick glance. Roland was so worried about Aleatha he would have walked right off a cliff without knowing it. But Rega was obviously nervous. She kept peering over her shoulder at Xar as he urged them forward with those scythe-blade arms.

He shepherded them toward a large circular room that might have formerly served as either a banquet hall or a meeting room. A round table stood in the center. The room was beneath the Star Chamber, and it was one place in the deserted citadel that none of the mensch ever entered.

At the arched doorway, Paithan came to a sudden stop, so sudden that Xar bumped into him, the old man's gathering arm encircling him. Rega halted beside Paithan and, reaching out her hand, plucked her brother's sleeve, alerting Roland to their whereabouts.

"What is it now?" Xar's voice had an edge to it.

"We . . . we don't go in here," Paithan said.

"This room doesn't want us in here," Rega added.

"Nonsense," Xar snapped. "It's only a room."

"No, it's magical," Paithan said in a low, awed voice. "We heard voices. And the globe—" He paused, stared.

"It's gone!" Rega gasped.

"What is?" Xar was mild again. "Tell me."

"Why . . . there used to be a crystal globe, hanging over the table. It had four strange lights inside. And when I went over to look at it, I put my hand on the table and suddenly I heard voices. They spoke in a strange language. I couldn't understand them. But they didn't seem to want me in here. So . . . I left."

"And we've never been back since," Rega said, shivering.

"But now the globe is gone." Paithan looked hard at Xar. "You moved it."

Xar appeared amused. *"I* moved it? And why would I do such a thing? This room is no different from any other in the citadel. I found no globe, heard no voices. But it does make an excellent place for a party, don't you agree? Come, please, come inside. No magic, I assure you. Nothing will harm you—"

"Look at all that wonderful food!" Roland gasped. "Where did all that come from?"

"Well," Xar said modestly, "perhaps a little magic. Now, please, come, sit, eat, *drink . . ."*

"Put me down," Aleatha commanded in a perfectly calm, if somewhat tear-ragged, voice.

Roland jumped, almost dropped her. He'd been staring at the food.

"We have to go back!" Aleatha wriggled in his arms. "Put me down, you dolt! Don't you understand? We have to go to the maze! Drugar went with them. We have to make him come back."

"Drugar went where? With who?" Paithan demanded.

"Put me down!" Aleatha glared at Roland, who—his face grim —dumped her unceremoniously on the floor.

"I hope you don't think I enjoyed that," he said coldly and walked over to the delicacy-laden table. "Where's the wine?"

"In a pitcher." Xar gestured, his gaze on Aleatha. "Where did you say the dwarf was, my dear?"

She cast him a haughty glance, turned her back on him, spoke to Paithan. "We were in the maze. We found . . . the theater. There are people there, lots of people. Elves and humans and dwarves . . ."

"Quit kidding, Thea . . ." Paithan flushed, embarrassed.

"Where's the wine?" Roland mumbled, his mouth full.

"I'm serious," Aleatha cried, stamping her foot. "They're not real people. They're only fog-people. We can see them when the starlight comes on. But . . . but now . . ." Her voice quivered. "Drugar's . . . one of them! He's . . . changed into fog."

She grabbed hold of Paithan's arm. "Just come, will you?" she insisted angrily.

"Maybe after we have some food." Paithan attempted to placate his sister. "You should eat something, too, Thea. You know how you see things on an empty stomach."

"Yes!" Xar hissed the word unpleasantly. "Eat, drink. You will all feel much better."

"I found the wine pitcher," Roland called. "But it's empty. The wine's all gone."

"What?" Xar whipped around.

Roland held out the empty pitcher. "See for yourself."

Xar snatched the pitcher, glared inside. A small amount of reddish liquid sloshed around in the bottom. He sniffed at it. He raised his gaze to the four, who shrank back, alarmed at his fury.

"Who drank this?"

From beneath the table came a thin, strident voice, raised in song.

"Goldfinger . . ."

Xar's face blanched, then went red with outrage. Reaching beneath the table, he caught hold of a protruding foot, tugged on it, dragged the foot out. The rest of the old man came along with it, sliding on his back, singing happily to himself.

"You drank the wine . . . all the wine!" Xar could barely talk.

Zifnab gazed up at him with watery eyes. "Lovely bouquet. Exquisite color. Slightly bitter finish, but I suppose that must be due to the poison . . ." He lay on his back, began singing again. "You only live twice . . ."

"Poison!" Paithan caught hold of Rega, who clutched at him.

Roland choked on the food, spit it out all over the floor.

"He's lying!" said Xar harshly. "Don't believe the old fool. This is a prank . . ."

The Lord of the Nexus bent down swiftly, put his hand on the old man's chest, began to mutter and move his fingers in a strange pattern. But suddenly the old man's face contorted in pain. He let out a horrible cry. His hands clawed at the air, his body twisted and twitched. Reaching out, he grabbed hold of the hem of Aleatha's skirt.

"Poison! He meant . . . for you!" Zifnab gasped.

His body curled in on itself; he writhed in agony. Then he stiffened, shuddered. A final convulsive scream, and the old man lay still. His eyes were open, wide and staring. His hand was locked firmly on to Aleatha's skirt. He was dead.

Horror-stricken, Paithan stared at the corpse. Roland was off in a corner, heaving his guts out.

Xar's eyes swept over them, and Paithan saw the gleam of the scythe blade sweeping past, mowing them down.

"It would have been a painless death," Xar said. "Swift, simple.

But this fool has changed all that. You must die. And you *will* die . . .''

Xar reached out his hand toward Aleatha.

She stood terrified, unable to move, her dress caught in the corpse's grip. Aleatha had a dim impression of Paithan leaping in front of her, knocking aside the wizard's hand . . .

Wanting only to escape this horrible place, this terrible man, the hideous corpse, Aleatha tore her skirt from the dead man's hand and ran, panic-stricken, from the chamber.

# CHAPTER 40

# THE LABYRINTH

♦

"WHAT DO YOU MEAN, 'SHE'S BETRAYED US'?" ALFRED ASKED NERVOUSLY.

"Marit's told them you're a Sartan," Haplo answered. "And that I brought you into the Labyrinth."

Alfred gave the matter careful thought. "Then she's only really betrayed *me. I'm* the one putting you in danger." He thought longer, brightened. "You could tell them that I am your prisoner. That . . ." His words died out at the sight of Haplo's grim expression.

"Marit knows better. She knows the truth. And I've no doubt she's told them. I just wonder," Haplo added somberly, staring into the forest, "what else she's told them."

"Are we just going to stand here?" Hugh the Hand demanded, scowling.

"Yes," said Haplo quietly. "We're just going to stand here."

"We could run—"

Haplo pointed. "A good idea. I've been trying to convince Coren here to—"

"Alfred," the Sartan corrected meekly. "Please. That is my name. I . . . I don't know that other person. And no, I'm not going back."

"I go where he goes," said Hugh the Hand. The Patryns were in sight now and moving closer. "We can fight."

"No," said Haplo, not pausing, not even considering, "I won't fight my own people. Bad enough . . ." He stopped, let it hang.

"They're taking their own sweet time. Maybe you made a mistake about her?"

Haplo shook his head. "They know we're not going anywhere." His mouth twisted in a grim smile. "Besides, they're probably trying to figure out what to do with us."

Hugh the Hand gave him a puzzled look.

"You see," Haplo explained. "They're not used to taking another Patryn prisoner. There's never been any need." He looked around at the gray sky, the dark trees. When he spoke, it was softly, to himself. "This was always a terrible place, dangerous, deadly. But at least we were united—one against it. Now, what have I done? . . ."

The Patryns, led by a stoic Kari, surrounded the three.

"Serious charges have been leveled against you, Brother," she said to Haplo.

Her gaze went to Alfred, who flushed clear up his bald scalp and managed to look extremely guilty. Kari frowned, glanced back at Haplo. Probably she was expecting him to deny everything.

Haplo shrugged his shoulders, said nothing. He began walking. Alfred, Hugh the Hand, and the dog followed. The Patryns closed ranks behind them.

Marit was not among them.

The group moved silently through the forest, the Patryns ill at ease, uncomfortable. When Alfred fell—as he did repeatedly, circumstances and his surroundings combining to make him clumsier than usual—the Patryns waited grimly for him to regain his feet. They did not offer help, nor would they permit Haplo or Hugh to go near the Sartan.

At first they'd regarded him with grim-faced enmity. But now, after he'd tumbled headlong over a tree root, walked into a bog, and nearly brained himself on an overhanging limb, they began exchanging questioning glances among themselves, even as they redoubled their watchfulness. It could, of course, all be an act, designed to lull them into complacency.

Haplo recalled thinking exactly the same thing himself the first time he'd met Alfred.

Boy, did they have a lot to learn.

As for the human assassin, the Patryns treated him with disdain. Most likely they had never heard of mensch; Haplo himself had not learned of the existence of these "lesser races" until Xar informed him.[1] But Marit would have told them that Hugh the Hand lacked the rune-magic, was therefore harmless. Haplo wondered if she had thought to tell them that this man could not be killed.

When his fellow Patryns looked at Haplo at all, which was rarely, they were shadow-eyed and angry. Again he wondered uneasily what Marit had told them. And why.

The trees began to thin out. The hunting party was nearing the edge of the forest, and at this point, Kari called a halt. Before them stretched a vast open field of short-cropped waving grass. Haplo was astonished to see signs that some animal had been grazing in the area. If these were mensch, he would have guessed they were raising sheep or goats. But these weren't mensch. They were his people and they were Runners, fighters—not shepherds.

He would have liked very much to ask Kari, but she wouldn't answer any question of his now; wouldn't so much as tell him whether it was day or night.

Across the grass, about a hundred paces away, a river of dark water churned and hammered through steep banks. And beyond that . . .

Haplo stared.

Beyond the river, with its black and ugly water, was built a city.

A city. In the Labyrinth.

He couldn't believe it. But there it was. Blinking didn't cause it to disappear. In a land of Squatters, nomads who spent their lives trying to escape their prison, was a city. Built by people who weren't trying to escape. People who were settled, content. Not only that, but they'd lit the beacon fire, the call to others: come to us, come to our light, come to our city.

Strong buildings, made of stone, covered with rune-markings, stood stolidly on the side of a gigantic mountain, on the top of which burned the beacon fire. Probably, Haplo guessed, these buildings had started as caves. Now they extended outward, the floors of some resting on the roofs of others. They marched down the mountainside in an orderly manner, gathered together at the bottom. The

---

[1] Xar learned of the existence of the mensch in the Nexus, reading the literature left behind by the Sartan.

mountain itself seemed to stretch out protective arms around the city built on its bosom; a large wall, made of the mountain's stone, encircled the city. Rune-magic, inscribed on the wall, enhanced its defenses.

"My goodness," said Alfred, "is . . . is this usual?"

No, not usual.

Marit was here. She was obviously not pleased at being here, but with the dangerous river crossing to be made, out in the open, a prey to any enemy, she'd been forced to wait for the rest of the party. She stood apart from the others, her arms crossed over her chest. She did not look at Haplo, pointedly avoided looking at him.

He would have liked to talk to her. He took a step toward her, but several Patryns moved to block his way. They appeared uncomfortable; perhaps never in their lives had they feared or distrusted one of their own.

Haplo sighed, wondered how he could make them understand. He raised his hands, palms outward, indicating he meant no harm, that he would obey their rules.

But the dog was under no such constraints. The trip through the forest had been a boring one for the animal. Whenever it had sniffed up something interesting, prepared to set off in pursuit, its master had called it sharply to heel. This would have been bearable if the dog had been made to feel that its presence was appreciated. But Haplo was preoccupied, wrapped in dark and gloomy thoughts, and refused to pat the dog's head or acknowledge its friendly licks.

If it hadn't been for Alfred, the dog would have considered this trip a waste of footpad. The Sartan, as usual, had proved highly diverting. The dog had recognized that it was going to be responsible for steering Alfred safely through the forest. Certain minor disasters couldn't be helped—a dog can only do so much. But the animal successfully averted several major catastrophes—such as pulling Alfred out of the tangles of a loathsome bloodvine and knocking him flat when he would have otherwise walked into a spike-lined pit, a trap set by roving snogs.

At last they had reached level, unobstructed ground, and while the dog knew that this didn't necessarily mean Alfred was safe, the Sartan was, for the moment, standing perfectly still. If anyone could get himself in trouble standing still it was Alfred; but the dog considered that it might relax its vigil.

The Patryns gathered at the edge of the forest, while several of their number fanned out to make certain that they would be safe crossing the river. The animal looked at its master, saw—with regret —that nothing could be done for him beyond a licked reminder that a dog was here and available for comfort. An absentminded pat was the animal's reward. The dog glanced about for new diversion and saw Marit.

A friend. Someone not seen in a few hours. Someone who—by the looks of her—needed a dog.

The dog trotted over.

Marit stood in the shadow of a tree, staring at nothing that the dog could see. But what she was doing might have been important, and so the dog padded up softly, so as not to disturb her. The dog pressed its body against Marit's leg, looked up at her with a joyful grin.

Startled, Marit jumped, which made the dog jump, too, causing both to fall backward, eye each other warily.

"Oh, it's you," Marit said, and while not understanding the words, the dog understood the tone, which, while not exactly welcoming, wasn't unfriendly either.

The woman sounded lonely and unhappy, desperately unhappy. The dog, forgiving her for startling it, once again came forward, tail wagging, to renew old acquaintance.

"Go away," she said, but at the same time her hand caressed the dog's head. The caress changed to a desperate clutch; her fingers dug painfully into the animal's flesh.

This was not very comfortable, but the dog restrained a yelp, sensing that she was in pain herself and that somehow this helped. The animal stood calmly at the woman's side, letting her maul its ears and crush its head against her thigh, wagging its tail slowly and gently, giving its presence, since it could give nothing more.

Haplo lifted his head, looked over at them. "Here, dog! What are you doing? Don't bother her. She doesn't like you. Keep close to me."

Marit's fingers had stopped their painful kneading, were soft and stroking. But suddenly she jabbed sharp nails into the dog's flesh.

Now it yelped.

"Get!" Marit said viciously, pushing the animal away.

The dog understood. It always understood.

If only it could impart such understanding to its master.

"We can cross now. It's safe," Kari reported. "Safe enough, at any rate."

Made of a single narrow span of rock, carved with runes, the bridge across the river was no wider than a man's foot. Slick with the spray of the turbid water rushing far below, the bridge was part of the defenses the Patryns had established around their city. Only one person could cross at a time, and that with the utmost care. One slip and the river would claim its victim, drag him down into its bone-chilling black and foaming rapids.

The Patryns, accustomed to the crossing and bolstered by their natural magic, ran over the bridge with ease. Once on the other side, several headed for the city, probably alerting the headman to their coming. Marit crossed over in one of the first groups, but—Haplo noticed obliquely—she waited on the shore.

Kari came up to Haplo. She and three other Patryns were spread out along the riverbank, keeping watch on the woods behind them. "Have your people cross now," she said. "Tell them to hurry." She looked down at the sigla on her skin, on Haplo's. Both glowed blue, brighter than before.

Hugh the Hand, pipe in his mouth, frowned down at the narrow bridge, examined it closely; then, shrugging, he strolled across with nothing more than a wobble or two, a pause to ascertain his footing. The dog trotted along behind, pausing midway to bark at something it thought it saw in the water.

And that left Haplo. And Alfred.

"I . . . I have to . . . to . . ." The Sartan stared at the bridge and stammered.

"Yes, you have to," Haplo replied.

"What's the matter with him?" Kari asked irritably.

"He's afraid of . . ." Haplo shrugged, left the rest of the sentence unsaid. Kari could fill in the blank.

She was suspicious. "He possesses magic."

"Didn't Marit tell you about that, too?" Haplo knew he sounded bitter, but he didn't particularly care. "He can't use his magic. The last time he did, the Labyrinth caught it, used it on him. The way the chaodyn will catch a thrown spear, use it on the one who threw it. Damn near killed him."

"He is our enemy—" she began.

"That's strange," Haplo said quietly. "I thought the Labyrinth was our enemy."

Kari opened her mouth, shut it again. She shook her head. "I don't understand this. Any of this. I will be glad to turn you over to Headman Vasu. You had better find some way to get your friend across—quickly."

Haplo went over to where Alfred stood, staring with wide, frightened eyes at the narrow bridge. Kari and her three companions kept an uneasy watch on the forest behind them. The other Patryns waited for them on the opposite shore.

"Come on," Haplo urged. "It's just a river."

"No, it isn't," Alfred said, with a shuddering glance at the rushing water. "I get the feeling . . . it hates me."

Haplo paused, startled. Well, yes, as a matter of fact, the river might very well hate him. He considered telling Alfred a comforting lie, but knew Alfred wouldn't believe him. The truth was probably better than whatever Alfred might dredge up out of his imagination.

"This is the River of Anger. It winds through the Labyrinth, runs deep and fast. According to legend, this river is the one thing in the Labyrinth we Patryns created. When the first of our people were cast into this prison, their rage was so terrible that it spewed forth from their mouths, became this river."

Alfred stared at him in horror.

"The water is deathly cold. Even I, protected by my rune-magic, could only survive in it a short time. And if the cold doesn't kill you, the water will batter you to death on the rocks, or the weeds will drag you down and hold you underneath the water until you drown."

Alfred had gone white. "I can't . . ."

"You crossed the Fire Sea," said Haplo. "You can cross this."

Alfred smiled faintly. A tinge of color returned to his pale cheeks. "Yes, I did cross the Fire Sea, didn't I?"

"Crawl on your hands and knees," Haplo advised, prodding Alfred toward the bridge. "And don't look down."

"I crossed the Fire Sea," Alfred was repeating to himself.

Reaching the narrow span, he blanched, gulped, and, drawing in a deep breath, placed his hands on the wet stone. He shivered.

"And you'd better hurry," Haplo advised, leaning over to speak in his ear. "Something nasty's gaining on us."

Alfred stared at him, his mouth open. He might have thought Haplo was just saying this to urge him on, but the Sartan saw the blue glow on the Patryn's skin. Nodding dismally, Alfred squinched his eyes tight shut and, by feel alone, started crawling across.

"What's he doing?" Kari demanded, amazed.

"Crossing the bridge."

"With his eyes closed?"

"He doesn't manage all that well with his eyes open," Haplo said dryly. "I figure this gives him a chance."

"It's going to take him the rest of the day," Kari observed after a tense few moments spent watching Alfred inching his way along.

And they didn't have the rest of the day. Haplo scratched at his hand; the rune-glow, warning of danger, was growing brighter. Kari peered back into the forest. The Patryns on the opposite shore watched with dark expressions.

Several people had arrived, coming from the direction of the city. In their midst was a young man, probably near Haplo's age. Absorbed in mentally urging Alfred along, Haplo would not have noticed one man among the rest except that this particular man was markedly unusual.

Most Patryns—male and female alike—are lean and hard-muscled, from lives spent either in running or in fighting to survive. This man's sigla-covered flesh was soft, his body rounded, shoulders heavy, stomach protruding. But by the deferential way the other Patryns treated him, Haplo guessed that this was the headman—Vasu, a name that meant "bright," "beneficent," "excellent."

Vasu came to stand on the shoreline, watching, listening with slightly inclined head as several Patryns explained what was happening. He gave no commands. Kari was, by rights, in charge here. It was her group. In this situation, the headman was an observer, taking control only if things began to fall apart.

And so far, everything was going well. Alfred was making progress. Better than Haplo had dared hope. The bridge's rock surface, though wet, was rough. The Sartan was able to dig his fingers into cracks and crevices and pull himself along. Once his knee slipped. Catching himself, he managed to hang on. He straddled the bridge with his legs. Eyes tightly shut, he gamely kept going.

He was halfway across when the howl rose from the forest.

"Wolfen," said Kari, with a curse.

The howling sounds made by the wolfen are eerie and un-nerving. The howl is bestial, but there are words in it, singing of torn flesh and warm blood and cracked bones and death. One howl rose from the forest; others answered it.

Alfred, startled and alarmed, opened his eyes. He saw the black water boiling below. Panic-stricken, he flung himself flat, clung to the bridge, and froze.

Haplo swore. "Don't faint! Damn it, just don't faint!"

Wolfen don't howl, don't make their presence known, unless they are ready to attack. And by the sounds, it was a pack of them, far too many for Kari and her small band to fight alone.

Vasu made a swift gesture with his hand. The Patryns ranged along the bank, taking aim with bow and arrow and spear, prepared to cover their crossing. Calling to Alfred to keep moving, Hugh the Hand edged down near the bridge as far as he dared, ready to pull the Sartan to shore.

Haplo jumped on his end of the bridge.

"You'll never make it!" Kari cried. "The bridge's magic only permits one person to cross at a time. I will take care of this."

She raised her spear, aimed it at Alfred.

Haplo grabbed her arm, stopped her throw. She wrestled away from him, glared at him.

"He's not worth the lives of three of my people!"

"Get ready to cross," Haplo told her.

He started forward, but at same time the dog leapt past Hugh the Hand, landed on the bridge, and headed for the Sartan.

Haplo paused, waited. The magic would certainly thwart him, but it might not affect the dog. Behind him, he could hear the wolfen crashing through the underbrush. The howls were growing louder. Alfred lay on his belly, staring down in horrible fascination at the water, unable to move.

The dog ran lightly over the bridge. Reaching Alfred, the ani-mal barked once, tried to rouse him from his stupor.

Alfred didn't even seem to hear it.

Frustrated, the dog looked to its master for help.

Kari lifted her spear. Across the water, Vasu made a sharp, peremptory motion with his broad hand.

"His collar!" Haplo shouted. "Grab the collar!"

Either the dog understood or it had reached the same conclu-sion. Digging its teeth firmly into Alfred's collar, the dog tugged.

Alfred moaned, grasped the bridge even more tightly.

The dog growled, deep in its throat. *Collar or flesh? Which will it be?*

Gulping, Alfred let go of his desperate hold. The dog, edging its way backward across the narrow span, dragged the limp and unresisting Sartan along with it. Hugh the Hand and several Patryns waited at the far end. Catching hold of Alfred, they hauled him up safely onto the shore.

"Go!" Kari ordered, her hand on Haplo's shoulder.

She was in charge; it was her privilege to be the last one to cross. Haplo didn't waste time arguing, but hastened over the bridge. When he was clear, the other Patryns followed behind him.

The wolfen broke from the forest just as Kari set her foot on the span. The wolfen barked in dismay at the sight of their prey escaping and dashed after Kari, hoping to catch one at least. A rain of spears and arrows—enhanced by the rune-magic—flew across the river and halted their pursuit. Kari reached the other side safely. Marit stood waiting for her, pulled the woman up onto the bank.

The wolfen ran onto the bridge. The sigla on the rock flared red; the wet stone burst into magical flame. The wolfen fell back, snarling and snapping. They paced the bank, staring at their prey with yellow, hungry eyes, but they dared not cross the river.

Once Kari was safe, Haplo went to see how Alfred was doing. Vasu also walked over to take a look. The headman moved with grace for such a flabby and ungainly man. Reaching the Sartan's side, the Patryn chieftain stared down at his prisoner.

Alfred lay on the bank. He was the color of something that had been in the river several days. He shook until his teeth rattled. His limbs twitched and jerked with leftover terror.

"*Here* is the ancient enemy," Vasu said and it seemed he sighed. "*Here* is what we have been taught to hate."

# CHAPTER ♦ 41

## THE CITADEL

## PRYAN

♦

"Run, Aleatha!" Roland shouted and jumped in front of Xar.

The Lord of the Nexus caught the human by the throat and flung him to one side as if he'd been one of the elves' magical talking dolls. Xar called on the possibilities, worked the rune-magic. Within the blinking of an eye, every arched doorway that led into and out of the circular chamber was walled up, sealed shut.

This done, Xar glanced around, then began to curse bitterly. He'd trapped three mensch in the chamber. Only three. The elf female had escaped.

But perhaps, Xar reflected, this is all for the best. She will lead me to the dwarf.

Xar turned back to his captives. One of them—the elf male— was staring down at the dead body of the old man, at the empty pitcher lying on the floor beside him.

The elf raised his head, turned a horrified face to Xar. "You poisoned the wine? You meant for us to drink it?"

"Of course I did," Xar returned testily. He had no time for mensch inanities. "And now I will have to take your lives in a manner far less suitable to my needs. However, there are compensations." He nudged the corpse with his toe. "I have an extra body. I hadn't counted on that."

The mensch huddled together, the human female kneeling over the human male, who was lying on the floor, his throat torn and bleeding as if claws had raked it.

"Don't go anywhere," said Xar with fine sarcasm. "I'll be back."

He used the rune-magic to escape the sealed room, went after the elf female and the dwarf. And, most importantly, the dwarf's Sartan amulet.

*Run, Aleatha!*

Roland's warning pounded in her heart, throbbed in her ears. And above the words, she could hear the footsteps of the terrible wizard.

*Run, Aleatha! Run!*

Consumed by fear, she ran.

She could hear the dread footfalls behind her. Lord Xar was pursuing her. And it seemed to her that he, too, was whispering Roland's last words to her.

"Run, Aleatha," he was urging her.

His voice was terrifying, laughing at her, mocking. It impelled her to run faster, kept her from being able to think coherently. She ran to the one place where instinct told her she might be safe—the maze.

Xar discovered Aleatha easily. He watched her dash down the street in a flurry of torn silken skirt and tattered petticoat. He pursued her at his leisure, driving her as he might have driven sheep. He wanted her terror, wanted panic. Half-mad, she would unwittingly lead him to the dwarf.

Too late, Xar realized his mistake. He realized it when he saw the maze, saw Aleatha racing for it, saw the Sartan runes that surrounded the entrance.

Aleatha vanished inside. Xar halted outside, glared balefully at the Sartan runes, and considered this latest difficulty.

The three trapped inside the circular chamber stared at the bricked-up walls, at each other, at the corpse of the old man, lying twisted and cold on the floor.

"This isn't real," Rega said in a small, tight voice. "This isn't happening."

"Maybe you're right," Paithan said eagerly and hurled himself at the brick wall that had once been a door.

He smashed into it, groaned in pain, and slid to the floor. "It's real enough, all right." A bleeding gash in his forehead proved it.

"Why is Xar doing this to us? Why . . . why kill us?" Rega quavered.

"Aleatha." Roland sat up, blinked dazedly. "Where's Aleatha?"

"She escaped," Rega said gently. "Thanks to you."

Roland, gingerly touching his bleeding throat, managed a smile.

"But Xar went after her," Paithan added. He looked at the magic brick walls, shook his head. "I don't think she stands much of a chance."

Roland was on his feet. "There must be a way out!"

"There isn't," Paithan said. "Forget it. We're finished."

Roland ignored him, began hammering on the bricks and shouting. "Help! Help us!"

"You ninny!" Paithan scoffed. "Just who do you think's going to hear you?"

"I don't know!" Roland turned on him savagely. "But it beats the hell out of standing here whining and waiting to die!" He turned to the wall, was about to beat on it again, when the imposing gentleman, dressed all in black, stepped through the bricks as if he were walking through the erstwhile door.

"Excuse me, sir," he said deferentially to the astounded Roland, "but I thought I heard you call. Might I be of assistance?"

Before Roland could answer, the imposing gentleman saw the corpse. His face paled.

"Oh, dear, sir. What *have* you done now?"

The gentleman knelt beside the body, felt for a pulse. Finding none, he looked up. His expression was terrible, stern, fey.

Paithan, alarmed, caught hold of Rega, pulled her close. The two stumbled backward into Roland.

The imposing gentleman stood up . . .

. . . and kept standing.

His body grew taller and taller, rose higher and higher. His frame filled out. An enormous scaled tail thrashed in anger. Reptile eyes flared in fury. The dragon's voice shook the sealed room.

"Who has killed my wizard?"

◆

Aleatha ran through the maze. She was lost, hopelessly lost, but she didn't care. In her terror-frazzled mind, the more lost she was, the better her chances of losing Xar. She was so frightened, she didn't realize he was no longer pursuing her.

The hedges tore at her dress, caught her hair, scratched her hands and arms. The stones on the path bruised her tender feet. A stabbing pain tore at her side every time she drew a breath. Footsore, dazed, she was forced by sheer exhaustion to stop her panic-stricken dash. She sank down onto the path, gulping and sobbing.

A hand touched her.

Aleatha shrieked, fell backward into the hedge. But it wasn't the black robes and cruel face of Xar that loomed over her. It was the black-bearded and concerned face of the dwarf.

"Drugar?" Aleatha couldn't see very well through a blood-tinged haze. Was the dwarf real—or still one of the fog-people?

Yet the touch of his hand had been real.

"Aleatha!" Drugar bent down, his expression anxious. He didn't try to touch her again. "What is the matter? What has happened?"

"Oh, Drugar!" Aleatha timidly reached out her hand, gingerly touched his arm. Finding him solid and substantial, she clutched at him frantically, grabbing on to him with strength born of hysteria, nearly dragging him off his feet. "You're real! Why did you leave me alone? I was so frightened! And then . . . then Lord Xar. He— Did you hear that?"

She turned, stared fearfully behind her. "Is he coming? Do you see him?" She struggled to stand. "We have to run, get away . . ."

Drugar was not accustomed to dealing with hysteria; dwarves are never hysterical. He knew something dire had happened; he needed to find out what. He had to get Aleatha calmed down and he didn't have time to coddle her (as was his instinctive tendency). He was momentarily at a loss, but a memory from his past—recently revived by his mind-shattering experience—came to his aid.

Dwarven children are noted for their stubbornness. A dwarven baby, not getting its way, will sometimes hold its breath until it turns blue and loses consciousness. On such occasions, the parent will throw water into the child's face. This causes it to gasp, involuntarily draw in a breath.

Drugar didn't have any water, but he did have ale, brought

with him to prove that where he had been wasn't an illusion. He uncorked the clay bottle and tossed ale into Aleatha's face.

Never in her life had such a thing happened to Aleatha. Dripping and sputtering, she returned to herself—with a vengeance. All the horrors she had witnessed and experienced were deluged, drowned in a flood of foul-smelling brown liquid.

She was quivering with rage. "How dare—"

"Lord Xar," said Drugar, latching on to the one thing she'd said that made sense. "Where is he? What did he do to you?"

His words brought back everything, and at first Drugar feared he'd gone too far. Aleatha began to shake. The dwarf held up the clay bottle. "Drink," he ordered. "Then tell me what has happened."

Aleatha drew in a deep breath. She detested ale, but, taking the bottle, she swallowed some of the cool liquid. The bitter taste made her gag, but she felt better. With many fits and starts and ramblings, she told Drugar all she had seen, all she had heard.

Drugar listened, his expression grim, his hand continually stroking his beard.

"They're probably all dead by now." Aleatha choked on her tears. "Xar murdered them, then came after me. He may be in here now, looking for me. Us, I mean. He kept asking about you."

"Did he, now?" Drugar fingered the amulet he wore at his throat. "There is one thing we can do, one way to stop him."

Aleatha peered at the dwarf hopefully through her sodden mass of hair. "What?"

"We must open the gate, let the tytans into the city."

"You're mad!" Aleatha stared at the dwarf, began to edge away from him.

"No, I am not mad!" Drugar caught hold of her hand. "Listen to me. I was coming to tell you. Look! Look at this!" He held up the ale. "Where do you think I got this?"

Aleatha shook her head.

"You were right," Drugar continued, "the fog-people are not shadows. They are real. If it hadn't been for you, I would have never . . . never . . ."

The dwarf's eyes shimmered. He cleared his throat, frowned in embarrassment. "They live in another citadel, like this one. I was there, I saw it. My people, your people. Even humans. They live together in a city and they get along. They live!" Drugar repeated, his eyes shining. "They are alive. My people! I am not the last of my kind."

He looked down at the clay bottle with affection. "They gave me this, to bring back. To prove my words."

"Another city." Aleatha was following him slowly. "You went to another city. Elves and humans. Ale. You brought back ale. Pretty dresses . . ." Her shaking hands smoothed her own torn gown. "Can . . . can I go there with you, Drugar? Can we go now! We'll escape Xar—"

Drugar shook his head. "There is still a chance the others are alive. We have to open the gate, let the tytans in. They will help us stop Xar."

"They'll kill him," said Aleatha in a dull and lifeless voice, her spirit crushed. "They'll kill us, too, but I guess that doesn't matter—"

"They will not," Drugar said sternly. "You must trust me in this. I learned something while I was in the citadel. It was all a mistake, all a misunderstanding. 'Where is the citadel?' the tytans kept asking. All we had to say to them was: 'Here. Here is the citadel. Come inside.' "

"Truly?" Aleatha looked hopeful, then wary. "Show me. Take me to that place."

Drugar frowned. "Do you want your brother to die?" The dwarf's voice grew harsh. "Do you want to save Roland?"

"Roland," Aleatha repeated softly, drooping. "I love him. I really do love him. I don't know why. He's so . . . so—" She sighed. "He told me to run. He jumped in front of me. He saved my life . . ."

"We will go now," Drugar urged. "We will go and see what has happened to them."

"But we can't leave the maze," Aleatha said, the hysterical edge tinting her voice. "Xar's out there, waiting for us. I know he is—"

"Perhaps he has left," Drugar said. He began walking back up the path. "We will see."

Aleatha watched him go. She was terrified of following him, but she was even more terrified of being left alone. Gathering her torn skirts, she hastened after the dwarf.

Xar could not go into the maze. The Sartan runes blocked his entry. He cursed and paced, considered the possibilities. He could blast his way through the hedge, but he'd probably have to burn down the entire maze to find the mensch. And charred corpses would not be of much use to him.

Patience was what was required of him now. The elf female would have to emerge sometime, Xar reasoned. She couldn't spend her life in there. Thirst, hunger would drive her out. The other three mensch were safely ensconced in the walled room. He could wait here for as long as necessary.

Xar expanded his range of hearing, listened for her. He heard her, running and sobbing, heard her fall. Then he heard another voice.

Xar smiled. He'd been right. The dwarf. She'd led him to the dwarf. He listened to their conversation, ignored most of it. What an inane story. The dwarf was drunk; that much was obvious. Xar laughed aloud at the suggestion that the citadel's gates be opened to the tytans. Mensch were more stupid than he'd thought.

"I will open the gates, dwarf," Xar said. "When you are dead! And you can make friends with the tytans then!"

The two were emerging from the maze. Xar was pleased. He hadn't expected them to come out so soon.

He strolled over to one of the nearby buildings and hid in the shadows. From here he could see the entrance to the maze, yet remain unobserved. He would allow them to get far enough from the maze so that they could not run back to it for protection.

"I will kill these two now," he said to himself. "Leave their bodies here for the time being. When the others are dead, I will return for the corpses, begin the preparations to raise them."

He could hear the heavy footfalls of the dwarf, moving down the path, nearing the entrance. The elf female was with him, her footfalls much lighter, barely discernible. But he could plainly hear her frantic whispers.

"Drugar! Don't go out there! Please. I know he's there. I know it!"

Perceptive, these elves. Xar forced himself to wait patiently and was rewarded by the sight of the dwarf's black-bearded face popping out around the corner of the hedgerow. The face vanished again immediately, then, after a pause, reappeared.

Xar was careful not to move, was one with the shadow in which he hid.

The dwarf advanced a tentative step, hand on an ax he wore at his belt. He looked up the street and down. At length he gestured.

"Aleatha, come now. It is safe. Lord Xar is nowhere in sight."

The elf female crept out. "He's here somewhere, Drugar. I know he is. Let's run!"

She caught hold of the dwarf's hand. Together they began running up the street—away from the maze, straight toward Xar.

He let them get close; then he stepped out into the street, directly in front of them.

"What a pity you had to miss my party," he said to the dwarf. Raising his hand, Xar wove the runes that would slay them both.

The sigla shimmered in the air, swept down on the stunned mensch in a bright flash and, suddenly, began to unravel.

"What—?" Furious, Xar started to recast his magic; then he saw the problem.

The dwarf stood in front of the elf female. In his hand he held the amulet with the Sartan runes. The amulet was protecting them both.

Not for long. Its magic was limited. The dwarf had no idea how to use it beyond this feeble attempt. Xar strengthened his spell.

His sigla burned, flared. Their light was blinding and burst upon the dwarf, upon his puny amulet, with a roar of fire. A shattering explosion, a cry of pain, a terrible scream.

When the smoke cleared, the dwarf lay on the pavement. The elf female knelt over him, pleading with him to get up.

Xar took a step toward her to finish her off.

A voice thundered through the air, halted him.

"*You* killed my wizard!"

A dark shadow obliterated the sun. Aleatha looked up, saw the dragon, saw that it was attacking Xar. She didn't understand, but understanding didn't matter. She bent over Drugar. Tugging on his beard, she begged him, pleaded with him to wake up, to help her. She was so frantic, she never noticed that her hands—where they touched the dwarf—were covered with blood.

"Drugar, please!"

The dwarf's eyes opened. He looked up at the lovely face, so near his own, and he smiled at her.

"Come on, Drugar!" she urged tearfully. "Stand up! Hurry! The dragon—"

"I'm going . . . to be with . . . my people . . ." Drugar told her gently.

"No, Drugar!" Aleatha choked. She saw the blood now. "Don't leave me . . ."

He frowned to quiet her. With his fast-fading strength, he pressed the amulet into her hands. "Open the gate. The tytans will help. Trust me! You must . . . trust me!" He stared up at her, pleading.

Aleatha hesitated. The magic thundered around her; the dragon roared in fury; Xar's voice chanted strange words.

Aleatha clasped her hands tightly around the dwarf's.

"I trust you, Drugar," she said.

His eyes closed. He gasped in pain, yet he smiled. "My people . . ." He breathed softly, finally.

"Drugar!" Aleatha cried, clutching the amulet in her blood-stained hands.

Xar's magic flashed. A tremendous wind, raised by the violent lashing of the dragon's gigantic tail, blew her hair into her face.

Aleatha was no longer crying. She was calm now, surprised at her calmness. Nothing mattered anymore. Nothing.

Holding fast to the amulet, unnoticed by either the wizard or the dragon, the elf kissed the dwarf tenderly on his forehead. Then she rose to her feet and walked, with purpose and resolve, down the street.

Paithan and Roland and Rega stood knee-deep in a vast pile of bricks, fallen timbers, and tumbled blocks of marble.

"Are . . . are any of us hurt?" Paithan asked, looking around in dazed confusion.

Roland lifted his foot, displacing an enormous mound of bricks that had been covering it. "No," he said hesitantly, as if he couldn't believe it himself. "No, I'm all right. But don't ask me how."

Rega brushed rock dust from her face and out of her eyes. "What happened?"

"I'm not sure," Paithan answered. "I remember the man in black asking about his wizard and then he was a dragon shrieking about his wizard and then . . . then . . ."

"The room sort of exploded," Roland continued. He climbed

up and over the rubble until he reached them. "The dragon's head bashed through the ceiling and the room started collapsing and I remember thinking, 'This is it, pal. You're finished.'"

"But we're not," said Rega, blinking. "We're not finished. I wonder how we survived?" She gazed around at the terrible destruction. Bright sunlight flooded the room; the dust sparkled in it like myriad tiny jewels.

"Who cares how we survived?" Roland said, heading for a large hole that had been blasted through the wall. "We did, and that's enough for me. Let's get the hell out of here! Xar is probably after Aleatha!"

Helping each other, Paithan and Rega clamored over a pile of bricks and rubble.

Before he left, Paithan glanced behind. The circular room, with its round table, was destroyed. Whatever voices had once spoken in that room would speak no more.

The three ran out of the hole in the wall just in time to see a gigantic ball of fire illuminate the sky. Frightened, they fell back, took shelter in a doorway. A boom shook the ground.

"What is it? Can you see?" Roland demanded. "Do you see Aleatha? I'm going out there."

"No, you're not!" Paithan caught hold of him. "I'm just as worried about her as you are. She's my sister. But you won't help her by getting yourself killed. Wait until we know what's going on."

Roland, sweating and ashen-faced, stood trembling; he seemed prepared to race off anyway.

"The dragon's fighting Xar," Rega whispered, awed.

"I think you're right," Paithan agreed, pondering. "And if the dragon kills Xar, we're probably next."

"Our only hope is that they kill each other."

"I'm going to go find Aleatha!" Roland ran down the stairs.

"Roland! Don't! You'll be killed!" Rega went running after him.

"There's Aleatha! Over there! Thea!" Paithan yelled. "Thea! We're up here!"

He dashed down the steps to the street level. Aleatha was at the bottom, walking along the street. She either couldn't hear her brother's shout, or she was ignoring him. She walked swiftly, didn't stop, although now Roland had added his powerful voice to the elf's weaker one.

"Aleatha!" Roland raced past Paithan. Reaching Aleatha, he grabbed hold of her arm.

"You're hurt!" he cried, seeing blood on the front of her dress.

Aleatha stared at him coldly. "Let go of me."

She spoke so calmly and with such authority that Roland, amazed, let go.

Aleatha turned, continued walking down the street.

"What's the matter with her? Where's she going?" Paithan asked breathlessly, coming level with Roland.

"You can see where she's going!" Rega gasped. "The gate."

"And she's carrying Drugar's amulet . . ."

The three caught up with Aleatha. This time Paithan stopped her. "Thea," he said, his voice shaking, "Thea, take it easy. Tell us what happened. Where's Drugar?"

Aleatha looked at him, looked at Roland and Rega, seemed at last to know who these people were. "Drugar's dead," she said faintly. "He . . . died saving me." She held fast to the amulet.

"Thea, I'm sorry. It must have been terrible for you. C'mon, now. Back to the citadel. It's not safe out here."

Aleatha pulled away from her brother. "No," she said with that strange calm. "No, I'm *not* going back. I know what I have to do. Drugar told me to do it. They're real, you see. Their city is real. And their dresses are very beautiful."

Turning, she started off again. The city gate was in plain sight now. The starlight beamed out from the Star Chamber; the odd humming vibrated in the air. Explosions and crashes shook the citadel from inside. Outside the walls, the tytans stood in a hypnotic trance.

"Thea!" Paithan called desperately.

The three leapt to catch her.

Aleatha whipped around, held the amulet up before her, as she had seen Drugar hold it up before Xar.

Startled, the others fell back. Either the magic of the amulet stopped them, or else it was Aleatha's commanding presence.

"You don't understand," she said. "That's what this whole thing has been all along. A misunderstanding. Drugar told me. 'The tytans will save us.' " She looked at the gate. "We just . . . didn't understand."

"Aleatha! Drugar tried to kill us once!" Rega cried.

"You can't trust him! He's a dwarf!" Paithan shouted.

Aleatha gave him a pitying glance. Sweeping her tattered skirts up in her hand, she walked over to the gate, placed the amulet in the center.

"She's gone mad!" Rega whispered, frantic. "She's going to get us all killed!"

"What does it matter?" Roland asked suddenly, with a reckless laugh. "The dragon, the wizard, the tytans . . . One of them's bound to kill us. What the devil does it matter which?"

Paithan tried to move, but his body seemed extremely tired, unwilling to support him. "Thea, what are you doing?" he cried, anguished.

"I'm going to let the tytans in," Aleatha replied.

The amulet flared. The gate swung open.

# CHAPTER ✦ 42

# ABRI

# THE LABYRINTH

✦

Escorted by Vasu, Haplo and his companions walked through the giant iron gates that led into the streets of Abri. No other Patryns guarded them; the headman had taken this responsibility on himself. He told Kari and her people to go to their homes, rest after their labors. But the Patryns gathered—at a respectful distance—to view the strangers. Word spread swiftly and soon the streets were crowded with men, women, and children, more curious than hostile.

Of course, Haplo thought grimly, the lack of guards doesn't mean they trust us. After all, we're trapped inside a walled city, with only one way out—rune-guarded, man-guarded gates. No, Vasu's not taking much of a chance.

Abri was, as its name meant, a shelter of rock. The buildings were all made of stone. The streets were dirt, little more than wide tracks, hard packed by long use. But the roads were smooth and level, well suited to the wagons and handcarts that trundled up and down. The buildings were utilitarian, with square corners and small windows that could be sealed up swiftly when the city was under attack.

And, in case of dire necessity, there were caves in the mountains to which the population could flee for protection. No wonder the Labyrinth had found it difficult to destroy Abri and its people.

Haplo shook his head. "And yet it's still a prison. How can you choose to stay here, Headman? Why don't you try to escape?"

"You were a Runner, I am told, Haplo."

Haplo glanced at Marit, on the other side of Vasu. Marit kept her eyes forward, her chin jutted out. She was cold and impenetrable, solid and forbidding as the stone walls.

"Yes," Haplo replied. "I was a Runner."

"And you succeeded in escaping. You reached the Final Gate."

Haplo nodded, unwilling to talk about it. The memory was not a pleasant one.

"And what is the world like beyond the Final Gate?" Vasu inquired.

"Beautiful," said Haplo, his thoughts going to the Nexus. "A city, immense, enormous. Forests and rolling hills, food in abundance—"

"Peaceful?" Vasu asked. "No threat? No danger?"

Yes, Haplo was about to respond; then, remembering, he kept silent.

"There is a threat, then?" Vasu persisted gently. "Danger?"

"A very great danger," Haplo replied in a low voice. He was thinking of the dragon-snakes.

"Were you happy there, in your Nexus, Haplo? Happier there than you were here?"

Haplo glanced again at Marit. "No," he said quietly.

She still did not look at him. She didn't need to. She understood his meaning. A flush as of a burning fever rose from her neck, suffused her cheeks.

"Many of those walking free are in prison," observed Vasu.

Haplo met the headman's eyes, was startled, impressed. The eyes were brown, soft as the body. But they were lit from behind by an inner light, intelligence, wisdom. Haplo began to revise his opinion of this man. Ordinarily, the headman in the tribe is chosen because he is the strongest, a survivor. Thus the headman or headwoman is often one of the oldest members of the tribe, hard and tough. This Vasu was young, flabby, and could never have withstood a challenge from another tribal member. Haplo had wondered, on first encounter, how a weak, soft man like Vasu had managed to retain his hold over a proud, fierce people.

He was beginning to understand why.

"You are right, Headman!" Alfred spoke up. His face was radiant; he was regarding Vasu with awe. And, Haplo noted, the Sartan was actually managing to walk without falling over himself. "You are right! I've been keeping myself prisoner for so long . . . so long." He sighed, shook his head. "I must find a way to set myself free."

"You are a Sartan," Vasu said, the wonderful eyes turning on Alfred, turning him inside out. "One of those who cast us in here?"

Alfred blushed.

Haplo gritted his teeth, expecting stammering, apologies, the usual.

"No," Alfred said, pausing, drawing himself up to his full height. "No, I am not. I mean, yes, I am a Sartan. But no, *I* am not one who cast you in here. My ancestors were responsible, not me. I take responsibility for myself, for my own actions." The blush increased; he looked over sadly at Hugh the Hand. "Those are burden enough."

"An interesting argument," said Vasu. "We are not responsible for the crimes of our fathers, only for our own. And we have one here who is an immortal, or so I'm told."

Hugh the Hand took the pipe from his mouth. "I can die," he said bitterly. "I just can't be killed."

"Another prisoner." Vasu was sympathetic. "Speaking of prisons, why did you return to the Labyrinth, Haplo?"

"To find my daughter."

"Your daughter?" Vasu raised an eyebrow. The answer had taken him by surprise, though he must have heard as much from Kari. "When was the last time you saw her? What tribe was she with?"

"I never saw my child. I have no idea where she is. Her name is Rue."

"And this is the reason you came back? To find her?"

"Yes, Headman Vasu. That is the reason."

"Look around, Haplo," said Vasu softly.

Haplo looked. The street in which they stood was filled with children: boys and girls at play and at work, stopping to stare with bright eyes at the strangers; babes riding in harness on a parent's back; toddlers getting underfoot, tumbling down, only to stand up again with the stubborn persistence of the very young.

"Many are orphans," Vasu said gently, "who come to us by way of the beacon fire. And many of them are named Rue."

"I know my search seems hopeless," Haplo argued, "but—"

"Stop it!" Marit cried suddenly, angrily. She rounded on him. "Stop lying! Tell him the truth!"

Haplo stared, truly astonished. All of them stopped walking, waited to see what would happen next. Crowds of Patryns moved near, watching, listening. At a gesture from Vasu, the Patryns moved back a discreet distance, but still they waited.

Marit turned to face the headman. "Have you heard of Xar, the Lord of the Nexus?"

"Yes," said Vasu, "we have heard of him. Even here, in the center of the Labyrinth, we have heard of Lord Xar."

"Then you know that he is the greatest one of our people ever to have lived. Xar saved this man's life." Marit pointed at Haplo. "Xar loves this man like a son. And this man has betrayed him."

Marit flung back her head, regarded Haplo with scorn.

"He is a traitor to his own people. He has conspired with the enemy"—her accusatory gaze went to Alfred—"and with the mensch"—her eyes shifted to Hugh the Hand—"to destroy Xar, Lord of the Patryns. Haplo's true reason for coming to the Labyrinth is to raise an army. He plans to lead that army from the Labyrinth in a war against his lord."

"Is this true?" Vasu asked.

"No," Haplo replied, "but why should you believe me?"

"Why indeed, traitor?" came a voice from the crowd. "Especially since your minion carries an ancient knife of foul magic, wrought by the Sartan for our destruction!"

Astonished, Haplo looked to see who had spoken. The voice sounded vaguely familiar, perhaps that of the man who had accompanied Marit on the trail. Oddly, though, Marit herself appeared startled, perhaps even troubled by this latest accusation. She, too, it seemed, was trying to locate the person who had spoken.

"I had such a weapon." Hugh the Hand took the pipe from his mouth, spoke up boldly. "But it was lost, as *she* well knows!" He pointed the pipe stem at Marit.

Only it wasn't a pipe.

"Blessed Sartan!" cried Alfred in horror.

The assassin held the Cursed Blade, the iron knife, inscribed with Sartan runes of death.

Hugh the Hand flung the weapon from him. The knife fell to the ground and lay there squirming, wriggling like a live thing.

The sigla tattooed on Haplo's skin flared to life, as did the runes on Vasu and Marit and every other Patryn in the vicinity.

"Pick it up!" Alfred said through pale and trembling lips.

"No!" The Hand shook his head vehemently. "I won't touch the damn thing!"

"Pick it up!" Alfred commanded, his voice rising. "It feels threatened! Quickly!"

"Do it!" Haplo said grimly, dragging back the dog, which was trotting over to take a sniff.

Reluctantly, gingerly, as if he were preparing to grab a poisonous snake by the back of the head, Hugh the Hand bent down, retrieved the knife. He glared at it.

"I swear . . . I didn't know I had it! My pipe . . ."

"The blade would not let him go," Alfred intervened. The Sartan looked miserable. "I wondered at the time, when you said it was lost. The blade would find a way to stay with him, and it did so, by changing its form to that of his most valued possession . . ."

"Headman Vasu, I would most respectfully suggest that you disperse your people," Haplo said, tense, his gaze on the knife. It was still glowing, although not quite as brightly as before. "The danger is very great."

"And it grows proportionately," Alfred added in a low voice, his face flushed with shame. So much for the crimes of the fathers. "With all these people around it . . ."

"Yes, I sense that," Vasu said grimly. "You, return to your homes. Take the children indoors."

Take the children. One little girl was trying to see, moving near, not understanding the danger. Her face was oval, her chin pointed—not unlike Marit's. The child would be about the right age . . .

A man came to the girl, laid his hand protectively on her shoulder, drew her back. His eyes met Haplo's for a brief instant. Haplo felt his face burn. The man led the child away.

The crowd dispersed swiftly, obeying the headman's orders without question. But Haplo could see faces, eyes, watching him balefully, distrustfully from the shadows. He could guess that many hands were on weapons.

And whose had been the voice that spoke? And what force had caused the knife to reveal its true nature?

"Alfred," said Haplo, thinking back, "why didn't the knife change when the tiger-men attacked us?"

Alfred shook his head. "I'm not sure. But as you recall, Sir Hugh was knocked out by a blow to the head."

Or maybe it was the knife itself that had summoned the tiger-men.

"Never before in the history of Abri, which has been here since the beginning, has one of our own brought such danger to us," Vasu was saying. The brown eyes were hard, stern and unforgiving.

"You must imprison them, Headman," Marit told him. "My lord Xar is coming. He will deal with them."

So, Xar is coming, Haplo thought. How long has she known? A lot was beginning to make sense now . . .

"I do not want to imprison one of our own kind. Will you, Haplo, wait in Abri for Lord Xar?" Vasu asked. "Will you give me your word of honor that you will not attempt to flee?"

Haplo hesitated. He could see his own reflection in the headman's brown eyes, so marvelously clear and soft. And in that moment, he made his decision. He came to know himself.

"No, I will not make such a pledge, for I could not keep it. Lord Xar is my lord no longer. He is being guided by evil. His ambition is not to rule but to enslave. I've seen where such ambition leads. I will no longer follow or obey him." Haplo added quietly, "I will do all within in my power to thwart him."

Marit sucked in a sharp breath. "He gave you life!" She spat at his feet, turned on her heel, and stalked off.

"So be it," said Vasu. "I have no choice but to deem you and your two companions a danger to the people. You will be held in prison to await the arrival of Lord Xar."

"We will go peacefully, Headman," said Haplo. "Hugh, put the knife away."

Scowling, not at Haplo but at the Cursed Blade, the assassin thrust it securely into his belt. "I suppose this means I've lost my pipe," he said glumly.

Vasu made a gesture and several Patryns appeared out of the shadows, ready to escort the prisoners.

"No weapons," Vasu commanded. "You will not need them."

He looked back at Haplo, who saw something in the brown eyes, something perplexing, unfathomable.

"I will accompany you," Vasu offered. "If you don't mind?"

Haplo shrugged. He wasn't in a position to mind.

"This way." Vasu was brisk, efficient. He even offered a hand to Alfred, who had slipped on a pebble and was now lying on his back looking helpless, like an upturned turtle.

With the headman's help, Alfred struggled to his feet. His stooped shoulders were bowed as if, once again, he had taken on some enormous burden.

They walked toward the mountain, their destination probably the caverns, deep underground—caverns far below the beacon fire burning its welcome through the gray mists.

The dog crowded against Haplo's leg, looked up at him questioningly with its liquid eyes. *Do we go along with this indignity?* it asked. *Or do you want me to put a stop to it?*

Haplo gave the animal a reassuring pat. With a sigh that said the dog hoped Haplo knew what he was doing, the animal trotted along meekly at its master's side.

That strange look in the headman's eyes. What did it mean? Thinking of this, wondering, Haplo remembered Kari's saying Vasu had sent her out deliberately to find them, bring them back.

How had Vasu known? *What* did Vasu know?

When Marit had left, she had not gone far, only far enough to take her out of Haplo's sight. Keeping to the shadows of a tall, sheltering oak tree, she waited to see Haplo and the others marched off to prison. She was trembling with what she told herself was outrage. Haplo had admitted his guilt, actually admitted it! And to make such statements, to accuse Xar of being guided by evil! It was monstrous!

Xar was right about Haplo. He was a traitor. And Marit had done the right thing in obeying Xar's commands, in having Haplo arrested and held prisoner until Xar could come for him. And Xar would come soon, perhaps any moment.

She would tell her lord, of course, what Haplo had said. And that would seal Haplo's fate. Which was right and just. Haplo was a traitor . . . a traitor to them all . . .

Then why this gnawing doubt?

Marit knew why. She had told no one about the Sartan knife. No one.

She watched until the three were well out of sight; then she suddenly became aware that several fellow Patryns were approaching her, eyeing her curiously, probably wanting to discuss this unusual occurrence in their lives.

Marit was in no mood to talk. Pretending she didn't see them, she turned and walked away, trying to look as if she knew where she was going. Actually, she didn't. She didn't even see where she was going. She needed to think, to try to figure out what was wrong . . .

Her skin itched. The sigla on her hands and arms were glowing faintly. Odd. She raised her head swiftly. She had come farther than she'd intended, was near the wall surrounding Abri. Danger was everywhere in the Labyrinth; she should not be surprised to feel the warning magic. Yet the city had seemed so safe, so secure.

A hand closed over her arm. Marit had her dagger out of its sheath before she saw who held her.

A fellow Patryn.

She lowered the dagger, but kept it in her hand. She could not see the man's face; his hair was long and unkempt and hung over his eyes. The tingling warning signs had not abated. If anything, they were now stronger.

Marit drew back, away from the strange Patryn. As she did so, she noticed that his magic was not reacting to the danger; the tattoos on his skin were not glowing. And then she saw that the runes could not glow; they were not true rune-structures, only copies.

Marit wasted no time in talk or in wondering who or what this creature might be. Those who waited to ask questions rarely lived long to hear the answer. Certain species in the Labyrinth, such as the boggleboe, had the power of shape-shifting. Gripping her dagger, Marit lunged at the impostor.

Her weapon vanished, changed to smoke that drifted harmlessly through the air.

"Ah, you recognize me," said a familiar voice. "I thought you might."

She hadn't; not really. She had known he wasn't a Patryn, but she had not recognized him—until he brushed the tangled hair back from his face to reveal the single red eye.

"Sang-drax," she said ungraciously. She should have been pleased to see him, but her unease grew. "What do you want?"

"Didn't Lord Xar inform you of my coming?" The single red eye blinked.

"My lord informed me that *he* was coming," Marit said coldly. Her thoughts went to the hideous sight of the dragon-snakes of Chelestra. She didn't like being around Sang-drax, wanted to get away from him. "Perhaps Xar is here? If so, I will go—"

"My lord has been unfortunately detained," Sang-drax interrupted. "He has sent me to retrieve Haplo."

"My lord said *he* was coming," Marit reiterated, not liking this change, wondering what was going on. "He would have told me otherwise if he were not."

"Lord Xar finds it a bit difficult to communicate just at the moment," Sang-drax replied, and though his tone was respectful, it seemed to Marit that the dragon-snake smirked.

"If my lord sent you for Haplo, then you had better go and find him," Marit said coldly. "What do you want with me?"

"Ah, getting to Haplo is proving rather a problem," Sang-drax said. "I managed to have him arrested, but I—"

"You were the one!" Marit said. "You knew about the knife!"

"I mean no disrespect, but Headman Vasu is a weak-minded fool. He was prepared to let Haplo and his Sartan friend roam the city at will. My lord Xar would not have liked that. I saw that *you* were not going to act"—Sang-drax's red eye glinted—"and so I was forced to do what I could.

"As I was about to say, my goal was to have Haplo placed in a dungeon, where he will be rendered helpless—he and his Sartan friend. I will be able to capture him quite easily without endangering your people." The dragon-snake inclined his head; the red eye slid shut for an instant.

"But now you can't get to him," Marit guessed.

"Too true." Sang-drax shrugged, smiled in a deprecating manner. "The guards would recognize me immediately as an impostor. But if *you* were to take me in . . ."

Marit gritted her teeth. It took a physical effort to remain standing this close to the dragon-snake. Every instinct urged her to kill it or run.

"We should hurry," Sang-drax added, noting her hesitation. "Before the guards can get organized."

"I must speak to my lord first," Marit said, her way clear. "This countermands Xar's earlier orders to me. I must make certain this is *his* will."

Sang-drax was obviously displeased. "My lord may be difficult to reach. He is, shall we say, otherwise occupied." His voice had an ominous tone.

"Then you will have to wait," Marit returned. "Haplo isn't going anywhere."

"Do you honestly believe that?" Sang-drax gave her a pitying look. "Do you believe that he will stay meekly in his cell, waiting for Xar to come for him? No, Haplo has some plot in mind, you may count upon it. I repeat, I must capture him now!"

Marit didn't know what to believe, but one thing was certain: she didn't believe Sang-drax. "I will speak to my lord," she said resolutely. "When I receive *his* instructions, I will obey them. Where can I find you?"

"Don't worry, Patryn. *I* will find you." Turning, Sang-drax left, continuing on his way down the deserted street.

Marit waited until the dragon-snake was about twenty paces from her; then, keeping to the shadow of the wall, she followed him.

What was he really after? Marit didn't believe Xar had sent him, nor did she believe Sang-drax's implications that Xar was in some sort of trouble.

She would see where Sang-drax went, discover what he was up to.

The dragon-snake, maintaining his Patryn form, rounded a corner of a building. He was taking care, Marit noticed, to keep to the shadows himself, taking care to avoid any true Patryn. He didn't run into many. This part of the city, near the wall, was mostly deserted. The buildings here were older, probably dating to a time before the wall had been constructed, and had probably been left behind as another line of defense. A perfect place for the dragon-snake to hide.

But how had Sang-drax entered the city? Patryns manned the walls and the gate; their magic would keep out all but the most powerful intruder. Yet Sang-drax was here, and he had obviously remained unobserved; otherwise the city would be in an uproar.

Doubt began to edge its sharp point into Marit's mind. How powerful was the dragon-snake? She had always assumed that he was less powerful than she. The Patryns are the strongest force in the universe—aren't we? Isn't that what Xar said, time and again?

*Guided by evil*, Haplo had said.

Marit put Haplo out of her mind.

Sang-drax turned into an alley with no way out. Marit paused at the entrance, not wanting to find herself trapped. The dragon-snake continued down the alley, moving at a leisurely pace.

Marit crossed to the opposite side of the alley and entered a doorway from which she could watch unobserved.

The dragon-snake glanced behind him occasionally, but never more than a glance and an uninterested one at that. He was about halfway down the alley when he stopped, looked more carefully up and down. Then he stepped into a shadowed doorway and disappeared.

Marit waited tensely, not wanting to move closer until she was certain he wasn't going to reemerge.

Nothing happened; nothing stirred. The alley was empty. But she could hear voices, low and indistinct, coming from the building Sang-drax had entered.

Marit traced a series of sigla in the air. Tendrils of fog began to swirl down the alley. She waited patiently, worked the magic slowly. The sudden appearance of a thick fog-bank would look extremely suspicious.

When she could no longer see the squat, square shape of the building across from her, Marit walked across the alley, using the enveloping cloud as cover. She had already marked her destination —a window in the building's side, on a wall that ran perpendicular to the alley.

Sang-drax would have had to be standing in the alley itself, watching for her, to have seen her. And he was nowhere in sight. As it was, she would be only a vague shape, made visible by the faint warning glow of the runes on her bare hands and arms.

Reaching the window, she flattened herself against the wall, then risked a look inside.

The room was small, bare. Former nomads, Patryns didn't have much use for furniture in their dwellings, no such things as tables and chairs. Mats for sitting and pallets for sleeping were all the furnishings considered necessary.

Sang-drax stood in the middle of the empty room, talking to four other Patryns—who were not Patryns, Marit quickly determined. She couldn't see the rune-markings clearly—the fog outside had caused the interior of the building to grow quite dark. But the very fact that the room was dark was the determining factor. A true Patryn's sigla would have been glowing, even as Marit's were.

More dragon-snakes, disguised as Patryns. They spoke the Patryn language well—all of them. Marit found this disturbing. Sang-drax spoke her language, but then he had spent a great deal of time with Xar. How long had these other snakes had her people under observation?

"—are proceeding. Our people are massed at the Final Gate. We wait only for your signal," one of the dragon-snakes was saying.

"Excellent," Sang-drax replied. "My signal will not be long in coming. The armies of the Labyrinth are gathering. At what passes for dawn in this land, we will attack this city and destroy it. When the city is leveled, I will allow a handful of 'survivors' to flee, to spread their tale of destruction, stir up terror at our coming."

"You will not permit Alfred the Sartan to survive?" asked another in a hissing voice.

"Of course not," Sang-drax replied harshly. "The Serpent Mage will die here, as will Haplo the Patryn. Both are far too dangerous to us, now that Lord Xar knows about the Seventh Gate. It is only a matter of time before either Haplo or the Serpent Mage figures out that he has been there. Curse that fool Kleitus for telling Xar in the first place."

"We must find a way to deal with the lazar," observed one dragon-snake.

"All in good time," Sang-drax returned. "When this is finished, we will return to Abarrach, take care of the lazar, then deal with Xar himself. First, however, we will conquer and control the Labyrinth. When we seal shut the Final Gate, the evil trapped in this place will grow a hundredfold—and our power along with it. Our kind will thrive and multiply here, safe from interference, assured of a continual source of nourishment. Fear, hatred, chaos will be our harvest—"

"What was that?" A dragon-snake turned its head toward the window. "A spy?"

Marit had made no sound, although what she had overheard very nearly caused her to sink, weak-kneed, to the ground.

Sang-drax was walking toward the window.

Silent, soft-footed, Marit glided into the thick fog, ran swiftly down the alley.

"Did she hear?" The dragon-snake asked.

Sang-drax dispelled the fog with a wave of his hand. "She heard," he replied with satisfaction.

# CHAPTER ♦ 43

# THE CITADEL

# PRYAN

♦

THE STARLIGHT SHONE BRIGHTLY FROM THE CITADEL'S TOWER. THE FAINT HUMming sound, whose words could be heard but not distinguished, vibrated through the streets. Outside the walls, the tytans stood in their trance. Inside, Aleatha was holding the amulet on the gate.

"We'd better run for it," advised Paithan, licking dry lips.

"I'm not leaving without Aleatha," said Roland.

"I'm not going without Roland," said Rega, standing next to her brother.

Paithan regarded them both with exasperation and despairing fondness. "I won't go anywhere without you two." Bracing himself, he added, "I guess this means we're all going to die."

"At least we'll be together," Rega said softly, reaching out one hand to hold Paithan's while her other took her brother's.

"We'll be safe as long as the light keeps shining." Roland was considering the matter. "Paithan, you and I'll run to the gate, grab Aleatha, and then head for the citadel. Then—"

At that moment the gates swung open and the starlight suddenly went off. The tytans outside the walls began to stir about. Paithan tensed, waiting for the tytans to surge inside and start bashing them into the ground. He waited . . . and waited.

The tytans remained unmoving, sightless heads turned toward the open gate. Aleatha stood before them, just inside the gate. "Please," she said, with the gracious gesture of an elf queen, "please, come inside."

Paithan groaned. He exchanged glances with Roland. The two made ready to dash forward.

"Stop!" Rega ordered, awed. "Look!"

Quietly, humbly, reverently, the tytans dropped their tree-sized clubs to the ground and began to file peacefully up the hill to the gate.

The first tytan to reach the gate stopped and turned its sightless head toward Aleatha.

*Where is the citadel? What must we do?*

Paithan shut his eyes. He couldn't look. Next to him, Roland moaned in anguish.

"Here is the citadel," Aleatha said simply. "You are home."

Wounded and exhausted, Xar sought refuge inside the library. He managed to make his way that far before he collapsed onto the floor. For long moments he lay there, his body bleeding and broken, too weak to heal himself.

The Lord of the Nexus had fought many powerful opponents in his long lifetime. He'd fought many dragons, but never one as strong in magic as this wingless beast of fury.

But the lord had given as good as he'd got.

Lightheaded, dazed with pain and loss of blood, Xar had no very clear idea what had happened to the dragon. Had he killed it? Wounded it so severely it had been forced to withdraw? He didn't know, and at this moment he didn't particularly care. The beast had disappeared. Xar must heal himself quickly, before those fool mensch found him in this weakened state.

The Lord of the Nexus clasped his hands together, closed the circle of his being. Warmth spread through him, sending him into the restorative sleep that would return him fully to strength and health. He very nearly succumbed to it, but an urgent voice, calling to him, woke him up.

Swiftly he shook off the drowsiness. There was no time for sleep. In all probability the dragon was lurking somewhere, healing itself.

"Marit, you come to me in good time. Have you obeyed my commands? Are Haplo and the Sartan in prison?"

"Yes, Lord. But I fear you've . . . you've made a terrible mistake."

"*I've* made a mistake." Xar was upright, rigid, lethal. "What do you mean, Daughter—I've made a mistake?"

"Sang-drax is a traitor. I overheard him plotting. He and the others of his kind are going to attack this city and destroy it. Then they plan to seal shut the Final Gate. Our people will be trapped. You must come—"

"I will come," Xar said, barely able to contain his anger. "I will come and deal with Haplo and this Sartan, who have obviously subverted you to their foul cause—"

"No, Lord. I beg of you! You must believe me . . ."

Xar silenced her voice as he would silence the woman herself when he next encountered her. She was probably attempting to invade his thoughts, spy on him.

*This is one of Haplo's tricks—trying to lure me back into the Labyrinth with these foolish tales.*

"I will return to the Labyrinth," Xar said grimly, rising to his feet, his strength renewed, far more than if he'd slept a fortnight. "And both of you, my children, will be sorry to see me."

But first he needed to find the mensch, particularly that elf woman who had run off with the dwarf's amulet.

Xar listened, magically extending his hearing, listened for the bickering voices of the mensch, the hideous growl of the dragon. He had a difficult time hearing either at first. The irritating humming from the top of the citadel seemed louder than ever. Then, fortunately, the humming ceased, the light shut off.

And then he heard the mensch, and what he heard amazed and appalled him. They were opening the gates to the tytans! The idiots, the fools, the . . .

Words failed him.

Xar strode over to the solid stone wall, drew a sigil on the marble. A window appeared, as if one had existed in that wall all along. Xar was able to see the gate now, could see the mensch huddled together like the stupid sheep they were. He watched the gate open, saw the tytans marching inside.

Xar waited—with a certain grim anticipation—for the tytans to beat the mensch to a bloody pulp. It would only serve them right, though their deaths in such a manner considerably upset his plans. Still, he might be able to take advantage of the tytans' momentary distraction to make good his escape.

To Xar's astonishment, the tytans walked past the four mensch, not quite oblivious to them—one tytan actually picked up the human male and moved him from its path with a gentle hand—but neither paying them much attention. The giants' eyeless heads tilted upward. The light of the citadel came back on, beamed down on them, illuminated them, made them almost beautiful.

The tytans were heading in Xar's direction. Their destination was the citadel.

The seven chairs. Giants who could not see, who would not be affected by the mind-shattering light. The tytans were coming back to the citadel to fulfill their destiny—whatever that might be.

But most important—the gate stood open. The tytans were distracted. The dragon was nowhere around. This was Xar's chance.

He left the library, moved swiftly through the building, exiting from the back just as the tytans were entering at the front.

Keeping to the side streets, Xar hastily made his way to the gate. Once it was in sight, he stopped to reconnoiter. Only seven tytans had entered the citadel. The rest remained outside, but on their faces was the same beatific expression worn by those within. The three mensch stood just inside the gate, staring in bug-eyed astonishment at the tytans. The fourth mensch, the elf woman, stood directly in Xar's path, blocking the gate. His gaze focused eagerly on the bloodstained amulet she held in her hands.

The amulet would get him past the Sartan runes, onto the Sartan ship. Apparently he no longer had to worry about the tytans.

The seven tytans were walking slowly and steadily, two abreast, toward the citadel. Xar took a chance, stepped out in plain sight. The tytans walked past, never noticing him.

Excellent, he thought, rubbing his hands.

He walked swiftly to the gate.

Of course the sight of him threw the mensch into an uproar. The human woman shrieked; the elven male yammered; the human male dashed forward to do Xar bodily harm. The lord tossed a sigil at them as he might have tossed a bone to a pack of ravening wolves. The sigil struck them and the mensch went very quiet, stood very still.

The elven female had turned to face him. Her eyes were wide and frightened.

Xar approached her, his hand outstretched.

"Give me the amulet, my dear," he said to her softly, "and no harm will come to you."

The elf's mouth opened, but no words came out. Then, drawing

a deep breath, she shook her head. "No!" She hid the amulet behind her back. "This was Drugar's. I . . . I don't care what you do
to me, you can't have it. Without it, I can't travel to the other
city . . ."

Nonsense, all of it. Xar had no idea what she was talking about,
didn't care. He was about to suck her dry, leave her a pile of dust—
with the amulet resting safely on top—when one of the tytans
stepped through the gate and came to stand in front of Aleatha.

*You will not harm her.* The voice resounded in Xar's head. *She is
under our protection.*

Sartan magic, crude but immensely powerful, shone from the
tytan as the starlight shone from the top of the citadel.

Xar could have fought the magic, but he was weak from his
battle with the dragon, and besides, a fight wasn't necessary.

The lord simply chose the possibility that he was standing behind the elf woman instead of in front. She had the amulet clutched
in her hands, safely—so she thought—behind her back. Xar
switched places, reached out, plucked the amulet from her fingers,
and hastened out the gate.

Behind him, he could hear the elf woman crying in dismay.

The tytans paid no heed to Xar as he ran past them, on his way
into the jungle, on his way to the ship and, from there, to the Labyrinth.

"Poor Drugar," said Rega softly. She brushed her hand across
her eyes. "I wish . . . I wish I'd been nicer to him."

"He was so alone." Aleatha knelt beside the body of the dwarf,
holding his cold hand in her own.

"I feel rotten," said Paithan. "But who knew? I thought he
*wanted* to be by himself."

"Which of us bothered to ask?" Roland said quietly. "Too busy
thinking about ourselves."

"Or some machine," Paithan added beneath his breath. He cast
a surreptitious glance in the direction of the Star Chamber.

The tytans were up there now, probably sitting in those huge
chairs. Doing what? The machine was dark; the starlight hadn't
come on for a long time now. Yet the air quivered with tension, a
good tension, a suppressed excitement. Paithan wanted more than
anything to go up there and see for himself. And he would go. He
wasn't afraid of the tytans anymore. But he owed this to Drugar. He

owed a lot to Drugar . . . and it seemed the only way he could repay him was to stand over the dwarf's body and feel wretched.

"He looks happy," Rega ventured.

"Happier than he was here with us," Paithan muttered.

"Come on, Aleatha," Roland said, helping her to stand. "There's no need for you to cry. *You* were kind to him. I . . . I have to say I admire you for that."

Aleatha turned, looked at him in astonishment. "You do?"

"So do I, Aleatha," said Rega timidly. "I used to not like you very much; I thought you were weak and silly. But you're the strongest one of all us. I want . . . I really want to be your friend."

"You're the only one of us with any eyes," Paithan added ruefully. "The rest of us were as blind as the tytans. You saw Xar for what he was. And you saw Drugar for what *he* was."

"Lonely," Aleatha murmured. She stared down at the dwarf. "So very lonely."

"Aleatha, I love you," Roland said. Reaching out, he took hold of her shoulders, drew her near. "And what's more, I like you."

"You *like* me?" Aleatha repeated, amazed.

"Yes, I do." Roland flushed, uncomfortable. "I didn't use to. I loved you, but I didn't like you. You were so . . . beautiful." He said the word with contempt. Then his eyes grew warm; he smiled. "Now you're beautiful."

Aleatha was confused. She touched her hair, which was filthy, unkempt, straggling over her thin shoulders. Her face was streaked with dirt, stained with tears, her nose swollen, her eyes red. He loved her, but he hadn't liked her. Yes, she could understand that. No one had ever liked her. Not even herself.

"No more games, Aleatha," Roland said softly, his grip on her tightening. His gaze went to the body of the dwarf. "We never know when the game's going to come to an end."

"No more games, Roland," she said, and rested her head against his chest.

"What do we do about Drugar?" Paithan asked after a moment's silence. His voice was husky. "I don't know anything about dwarven burial customs."

*Take him to his people,* came a tytan's voice.

"Take him to his people," Aleatha repeated.

Paithan shook his head. "That'd be fine, if we knew where they were. Or even if they were still alive . . ."

"I know," said Aleatha. "Don't I?"

"Who are you talking to, Thea?" Paithan looked a little frightened.

*You know,* came the answer.

"But I don't have the amulet," she said.

*You don't need it. Wait until the starlight shines.*

"This way," said Aleatha confidently. "Come with me."

Taking off her shawl, she laid it reverently over the dwarf's body. Roland and Paithan lifted Drugar. Rega went to walk at Aleatha's side. Together they entered the maze.

"Can I stand up now?" came a peevish voice.

"Yes, sir, but you must hurry. The others might be back at any moment."

The pile of bricks began to move. A few on top slid down, clattered to the floor.

"Please be quiet, sir!" intoned the dragon.

"You *could* give me a hand," muttered the peevish voice. "Or a claw. Whatever you've got available at the moment."

The dragon, with a long-suffering sigh, began to sift through the rubble with a green-scaled forearm. Snagging the old man by the collar of his mouse-gray robes—now brick-reddish robes—the dragon hauled the old man up out of the ruin.

"You dropped that wall on me on purpose!" the old man said, shaking his clenched fist.

"I had to, sir," the dragon answered gloomily. "You were breathing."

"Well, of course I was breathing!" the old man cried in high dudgeon. "A fellow can only hold his breath so long, you know! I suppose *you* expected me to turn blue and pass out!"

A bright and happy gleam lit the dragon's eyes; then it sighed, as over something lost, gone forever.

"I meant, sir, that you were being obvious about your breathing. Your chest was rising and falling. At one point, you even made a sound. Not a very corpse-like thing to do—"

"Beard flew up my nose," the old man muttered. "I thought I was going to sneeze."

"Yes, sir," said the dragon. "*That* was when I dropped the wall on you, sir. And now, sir, if you're *quite* ready . . ."

"Are they all right?" the old man asked, peering out the hole in the wall. "Will they be safe?"

"Yes, sir. The tytans are inside the citadel. The seven chosen will take their places in the seven chairs. They will begin to channel the energy up from the well, use their mental powers to beam it out into Pryan and, eventually, through Death's Gate. The two humans and the two elves will be able to communicate with others of their kind in the other citadels. And now that the tytans are back under control, the humans and the elves will be able to venture forth into the jungle. They will find others of their races—and the dwarven race as well. They will lead them to safety inside these walls."

"And they'll live happily ever after," the old man concluded, beaming.

"I wouldn't go that far, sir," said the dragon. "But they'll live as happily as can reasonably be expected. They will have plenty to keep them busy. Particularly after they've made contact with their people on the other worlds of Arianus and Chelestra. *That* should give them quite a bit to think about."

"I'd like to stay and see that," said the old man wistfully. "I'd like to see people happy, working together, building their lives in peace. I don't know why"—he frowned—"but I think it would help me get over these terrible dreams I have sometimes."

He began to tremble. "You know the dreams I mean. Horrible dreams. Dreadful fires and buildings falling and the dying . . . I can't help the dying . . ."

"Yes, you can, Mr. Bond," said the dragon gently. He passed a clawed hand over the old man's head. "You are Her Majesty's finest secret agent. Or perhaps you would rather be a certain befuddled wizard today? You were always rather fond of that one—"

The old man pursed his lips. "Nope. No wizards. I don't want to get typecast."

"Very good, Mr. Bond. I think Moneypenny is trying to get hold of you."

"She's always trying to get hold of me!" the old man said with a cackle. "Well, off we go. Let's be quick about it. Mustn't keep Q waiting."

"I believe the initial is M, sir—"

"Whatever!" the old man snapped.

The two began to fade into the air, became one with the dust.

The table built by the Sartan lay shattered beneath the bricks and the fallen stone.

Many cycles later, when Paithan, along with his wife, Rega, had become rulers of the city named Drugar, the elf commanded that this chamber be sealed off.

Aleatha claimed she could hear voices inside it, sad voices, talking a strange language. No one else could hear them, but since Aleatha was now High Priestess of the Tytans and her husband was High Priest Roland, no one questioned her wisdom.

The chamber was made into a memorial for a rather daft old wizard who had twice given his life for them, and whose body—so far as any of them knew—lay buried beneath the rubble.

# CHAPTER ♦ 44

# ABRI

# THE LABYRINTH

♦

"Excuse me, Haplo . . ."

Alfred's whisper drew Haplo away from an internal struggle. He looked over at the Sartan, not sorry to put his mental weapons down, turn his dark thoughts to something else, probably equally dark.

"Yes, what is it?"

Alfred cast a fearful glance at their guards, marching at their side, edged his way closer to Haplo.

"I—Oh, dear me! Where did *that* come from?"

Haplo caught hold of Alfred, kept him from walking straight into a solid rock wall.

"The mountain's been here a long time," Haplo said, and steered Alfred into the cavern entrance.

He kept fast hold of the Sartan, whose fumbling feet discovered every loose rock, every crack and fissure. The guards, after a long, frowning scrutiny, apparently decided Alfred was harmless, for they left him alone. Most of their attention was centered on Hugh the Hand.

"Thank you," Alfred murmured. "What . . . what I wanted to ask . . . and this may sound like a stupid question . . ."

"Coming from you?" Haplo was amused.

Alfred smiled, embarrassed. "What I was wondering is about this prison. I didn't think your people did that sort of thing . . . to each other."

"I didn't think we did," Haplo said pointedly.

Vasu, who had been walking alongside, as silent and preoccupied as Haplo himself, looked up.

"Only in cases of dire necessity," the headman replied gravely. "Mainly for the prisoner's own good. Some of our people suffer from what we call Labyrinth sickness. In the lands out beyond the walls, the sickness usually leads to death."

"Out beyond these walls," Haplo added grimly, "a person with Labyrinth sickness puts his or her entire tribe in danger."

"What happens to them? What do they do?" Alfred asked.

Haplo shrugged. "Usually they go crazy and jump off a cliff. Or charge a pack of wolfen alone. Or drown themselves in the river . . ."

Alfred shuddered.

"But we have discovered that, with time and patience, these people can be helped," Vasu said. "We keep them in a place where they are safe, where they can do no harm to themselves or to others."

"And that's where you're going to be putting us," Haplo said.

"Essentially it's where you're putting yourselves," Vasu replied. "Isn't that true? If you wanted to leave, you could do so."

"And bring destruction on my own people? I didn't come here to do that," Haplo replied.

"You could leave this human—and the knife he carries—behind."

Haplo shook his head. "No, it's my responsibility. I brought the knife in here—unknowingly, but I brought it. Between the three of us"—he took in Alfred and Hugh the Hand—"maybe we can figure out how to destroy it."

Vasu nodded in understanding and agreement.

Haplo was silent a moment; then he said quietly, "But I won't let Xar take me."

Vasu's expression hardened. "He will not take you without my consent. That I promise you. I will hear what he has to say and make my judgment accordingly."

Haplo almost laughed out loud. Struggling, he maintained a straight face. "You've never met Xar, Headman Vasu. My lord takes what he wants. He's not accustomed to being denied anything."

Vasu smiled indulgently. "Meaning that I won't have any say in the matter." He patted his round stomach complacently. "I may look soft, Haplo. But don't underestimate me."

Haplo remained unconvinced, but arguing would not have been polite. When the time came, he alone would have to deal with Xar. Haplo went back to his dark inner struggle.

"I can't help but wonder, Headman Vasu"—this was Alfred—"how exactly do you keep people imprisoned? Considering that our magic is based on possibilities and with the vast range of possibilities for escape available . . . Not that I plan to try to escape," he added hastily. "And if you'd prefer not to tell me, I understand—"

"It is really quite simple," Vasu answered gravely. "In the realm of possibility, there is always the possibility, that there are no possibilities."

Alfred's eyes glazed over.

The dog nipped him on the ankle, saved him from falling into a hole.

"No possibilities," Alfred repeated, thinking. He shook his head, baffled.

Vasu smiled. "I will be happy to explain. As you must surmise, the reduction of all possibilities to no possibilities is an extremely difficult and complex spell to cast. We place the person in a small, enclosed area, such as a prison cell or a dungeon. The need for such an enclosure is due to the nature of the spell, which requires that, within this area, time itself must be stopped, for only by stopping time can one stop the possibility of things occurring within time. It would be neither feasible nor advisable to stop time for the entire population of Abri.

"Thus we have constructed what is known as a 'well'—a small chamber deep inside the cavern where time literally comes to a halt. A person exists within a frozen second and, during that second, so long as the magic is operative, there exists no possibility of escape. The person within the cell continues to live, but—if held for a long period—would not physically change, would not age. People suffering from Labyrinth sickness are never kept in here long, just long enough for us to counsel and heal them."

"How ingenious!" Alfred was admiring.

"Isn't it," Haplo remarked dryly.

Worried and alone, Marit roamed the city streets until long after the Labyrinth's grayness had darkened to night. Numerous Patryns offered her hospitality, but Marit refused, regarded them warily, suspiciously.

She didn't trust them, couldn't trust her own people anymore. The knowledge grieved her. She felt more alone than ever.

I should go to Vasu, she thought. Warn him, but of what? My story sounds wild, implausible. Snakes disguised as Patryns. An attack on the city. Sealing shut the Final Gate . . .

"And why should I trust Vasu?" she asked herself. "Perhaps he's in league with them. I must wait for my lord. Those are my orders. And yet . . . And yet . . ."

*Guided by evil . . .*

Haplo would believe her. He was the one person who would, the one person who would know what to do. Yet to take this to him was to betray Xar's trust.

*I came to find my daughter . . .*

And what about that daughter, that baby she'd given up so long ago? What would happen to her, to all the daughters and the sons of the Patryns if the Final Gate was sealed shut? Was it possible Haplo had been telling the truth?

Marit turned her steps toward the mountain dungeon.

The streets were dark and silent. The Patryns holed up in their dwellings to keep themselves and their families safe from the insidious evil of the Labyrinth, evil whose strength increased at night.

She passed the houses, the lighted windows, heard voices from inside. Families together. Safe, for the moment . . .

Her steps quickened, driven by fear.

Abri had started inside the mountain, but no Patryns lived there now. The need to lurk in caves, like hunted animals, was over for them.

Entrances into the mountain had been sealed up, a Patryn told her in answer to her question. Closed off, used only in time of emergency. One entrance remained open, the entrance that led to the dungeons.

Marit headed for it, rehearsing what she would say to the guards, figuring how to convince them to let her see Haplo. It was only when she noticed that her arm was itching, burning, that she realized she wasn't the only one intent on entering the cavern.

Marit could see the cavern entrance, a black hole against the grayer, softer darkness of night. Two Patryns stood guarding it. Except that they weren't Patryns. No runes glowed on their skin.

Marit blessed the magic for its warning. Otherwise she would have walked right into their arms. Hiding in the shadows, she watched and listened.

Four shapes converged on the cavern. The voices of the guards, soft and hissing, slid through the night.

"You can approach safely. No one has been around."

"Are the prisoners alone in there?"

Marit recognized Sang-drax's voice.

"Alone and trapped in a time well," was the report.

"A marvelous irony," said Sang-drax. "By imprisoning the only people who could save them, these fool Patryns will be responsible for their own destruction. We four will enter. You two stay here, make certain we are not disturbed. I don't suppose you know where they are being held?"

"No, we could not very well accompany them, could we? We would have been recognized."

Sang-drax shrugged. "No matter. I will find them. I can smell the scent of warm blood even now."

The false Patryns laughed.

"Will you be long at your 'task'?" one asked.

"They deserve to die slowly," said another. "Especially the Serpent Mage, who murdered our king."

"I must make their deaths quick, unfortunately," Sang-drax replied. "The armies are gathering and I need to be on hand to organize them. And you must hasten to the Final Gate. But do not be disappointed. We will feast on blood tomorrow and, once the Final Gate is sealed, for all eternity."

Marit reached for her dagger. The single red eye swiveled, glanced over at her. She cowered into the darkness. The red eye mesmerized her, conjured up images of death—terrible, tortured. She wanted to run and hide. Her hand fell, nerveless, from the dagger's hilt.

The red eye laughed, passed on.

Helpless, Marit watched the four dragon-snakes enter the cave. The other two took up their positions outside.

Once Sang-drax had disappeared, Marit recovered. She had to get inside the cavern, had to get inside that magical room to warn Haplo, to free him, if possible. The thought of Xar came fleetingly to her mind.

"If my lord were here," she reasoned, "if he heard the dragon-snakes as I have heard them, he would do the very same thing."

Marit lifted the sharpened stick she carried with her. The throw would be easy from this distance. As she held the crude spear in her hand, she remembered the terrible dragon-snake she had seen in the waters of Chelestra. What if she only wounded one? Would it change back to its original form? She imagined the gigantic serpents, wounded and thrashing about, wreaking havoc on her people.

And even though I might kill both of them, how can I reach Haplo ahead of Sang-drax? She was wasting time. Leave the dragon-snakes for now. Her magic would take her to Haplo, as it had once before, on Arianus. She drew the sigla in the air, imagined herself with Haplo . . .

Nothing. The magic failed. Of course, she cursed bitterly. He is in a prison. He can't get out. I can't get in!

"Vasu," she said to herself. "I must find him. He holds the key. He can take me there."

And if the headman proved reluctant . . .

Marit fingered her dagger. She'd force him to obey her. But now she had to find out where he lived . . . and quickly.

Marit ran into the street, searching for some wakeful Patryn who could give her information. She hadn't gone far when she stumbled into a man, muffled in a cloak, who stepped out of the shadows.

Startled, nervous, Marit fell back a pace. "I must find Headman Vasu," she said, eyeing the cloaked figure suspiciously. "Don't come near me. Just tell me where he lives."

"You have found him, Marit," said Vasu, throwing back the hood of his cloak.

She could see her glowing skin reflected in his eyes. And she saw, beneath his cloak, the sigla on his skin glowing.

Marit clutched at him gratefully, never stopping to wonder how he came to be here. "Headman, you must take me to Haplo! Right now!"

"Certainly," Vasu said. He took a step toward the cavern.

"No, Headman!" Marit dragged him back. "We must use the magic. Haplo is in dire peril. Don't ask me to explain—"

"You mean from the intruders?" Vasu asked coolly.

Marit gaped at him.

"I have been aware of them ever since they came. We have kept them under surveillance. I am pleased to know," he added with more gravity, the brown eyes intent on her, "that you are not in league with them."

"Of course not! They are hideous, evil." Marit shivered.

"And Haplo and the others?"

"No, Headman, no! Haplo warned me . . . He warned Xar . . ." Marit fell silent.

"And what *of* Lord Xar?" Vasu asked her gently.

*Guided by evil . . .*

Marit shook her head. "Please, Headman, there is no time! The dragon-snakes are in the cave right now! They are going to kill Haplo—"

"They will have to find him first," Vasu said. "And they may discover that task more difficult than they imagine. But you are right. We should make haste."

The headman gestured, and the streets Marit had thought slumbered so peacefully were suddenly alive with Patryns. No wonder she hadn't seen them. They were all cloaked, to hide the glowing, warning runes on their bodies. At a sign from Vasu, the Patryns left their posts and began gliding stealthily toward the cavern.

Vasu took hold of Marit's arm, swiftly traced a series of runes with his hand. The sigla surrounded them, blue and red, and then there was darkness.

Haplo lay on a pallet on the floor, gazing up into the shadows. Like the walls of the small, squarish cavern, the ceiling was covered with sigla, gleaming faintly, red and blue. That and four small burning cresset-stones, placed in the corners of the chamber, gave the only light.

"Relax, boy," he said to the dog.

The animal was restive and unhappy. It had been pacing about the small chamber until it began to make Haplo himself nervous. He ordered it again to settle down. The dog obeyed, relapsing by his side. But though it lay still, it kept its head up, ears pricking to sounds only it could hear. Occasionally it would growl deep in its throat.

Haplo soothed it as best he could, patting it on the head and telling it that all was fine.

He wished someone would pat him on the head, tell him the same thing. Neither of his companions was much comfort.

Alfred was enthralled by the chamber, by the sigla on the walls, by the spell that reduced all possibilities to a single possibility that there were no possibilities. He asked questions, gabbled on about how brilliant it all was until Haplo wished for just one other possibility, and that was a window out of which he could throw Alfred.

Eventually, thankfully, the Sartan fell asleep and was now sprawled on his pallet, snoring softly.

Hugh the Hand had not said a word. He sat bolt upright, as far from the glowing wall as he could get. His left hand clasped and unclasped. Occasionally he would absentmindedly lift his hand to his mouth, as if he held his pipe. Then, remembering, he would scowl and lower his hand back to his leg, where it lay clasping and unclasping.

"You could use the pipe," Haplo advised him. "It would be a real pipe, so long as nothing threatens you."

Hugh the Hand shook his head, glowered. "Never. I know what it is. If I put in my mouth, I could taste the blood on it. Curse the day I ever saw it."

Haplo lay back on his pallet. Stranded in time, he was trapped within this chamber, but his thoughts were free to roam beyond it. Not that they were doing much good. His thoughts kept traveling in the same circle—going nowhere, coming back to the beginning.

Marit had betrayed him. She was going to turn him over to Xar. Haplo should have expected as much—after all, she had been sent to kill him. But if so, why hadn't she tried to kill him when she had the chance? They were even. She had saved his life. The law was satisfied, if she had ever cared about the law. Perhaps that had just been an excuse. Why the change? And Xar was coming for him now. Xar wanted him. Why? Or did it matter? Marit had betrayed him . . .

He looked up to find Marit standing over him.

"Haplo!" She gasped in relief. "You're safe! You're safe!"

Haplo was on his feet, staring at her. And suddenly she was in his arms, and he was in her arms, neither with any clear idea of how it happened. The dog, not to be left out, crowded between them.

He held her tightly. The questions didn't matter. None of it mattered. Not the betrayal, not whatever danger had brought her here. At that moment, Haplo could have blessed it. And he could have wished this moment frozen in time, with no possibility of its ending.

The sigla on the walls flared and went dark. Vasu stood in the center of the room, the spell broken.

"Sang-drax," Marit said, and that was all she needed to say. "He's here. He's coming to kill you."

"What? What? What's going on?" Alfred was sitting up, blinking sleepily at them like an aging owl.

Hugh the Hand was on his feet, poised, ready for trouble.

"Sang-drax!" Suddenly Haplo felt extremely tired. The wound over his heart began to throb painfully. *"He* was the one who knew about the cursed knife."

"Yes," Marit answered, her fingers digging into his arms. "And, oh, Haplo! I heard Sang-drax and the other dragon-snakes talking! They're going to attack the city and—"

"Attack Abri?" Alfred repeated, startled. "Who is Sang-drax?"

"He's one of the dragon-snakes of Chelestra," Haplo said grimly.

Alfred went ashen, staggered backward against the wall. "How . . . how did those monsters get here?"

"They entered Death's Gate—courtesy of Samah. They're in every world now, spreading chaos and evil. And they're here now, too, apparently."

"And preparing to attack Abri?" Vasu couldn't believe it. He shrugged. "Many have tried—"

"Sang-drax spoke of armies," Marit said urgently. "Maybe thousands! Snogs, chaodyn, wolfen—all our enemies. Coming together. Organized. They're going to attack at dawn. But first he's going to kill you, Haplo, and—someone called the Serpent Mage, who killed the king dragon-snake."

Haplo looked at Alfred.

"That wasn't me!" Alfred protested. He had gone so pale he seemed almost translucent. "It wasn't me!"

"No," said Haplo. "It was Coren."

Alfred shuddered, stared down miserably at his feet. His shoes appeared to be doing strange things on their own, shuffling in and out, toes and heels clattering on the stone floor.

"How did you find out all this?" Vasu demanded.

"I recognized Sang-drax," Marit said, uncomfortable. "I knew him from . . . someplace else. He asked me to take him to Haplo.

He claimed Xar sent him to bring Haplo back. I didn't believe him. I refused to do so, and when he left me, I followed him. I overheard him talking to the others. They didn't know I was listening . . ."

"Oh, yes, they did," Haplo interrupted. "He had no need to use you to get to me. They *wanted* you to know their plans. They want our fear—"

"They've got it," Alfred whispered unhappily.

"Haplo, they're on their way here!" Marit said desperately. "They're going to kill you. We've got to get out—"

"Yes," said Vasu. "Time for questions later." He obviously had a great many questions. "I will take you—"

"No, I don't think you will," came a hiss from the darkness.

Sang-drax, still in Patryn form, and three of his fellows appeared in the chamber, walking through a wall.

"This will be simple, like shooting rats in a barrel. A pity I don't have time to make it more fun. I would so like to see you suffer. Especially you, Serpent Mage!" The red eye focused on Alfred, glowing malevolently.

"I think you have the wrong person," Alfred said meekly.

"I think we don't. Your disguise is as easy to penetrate as my own." Sang-drax whipped around to face Vasu. "Try if you like, Headman. You won't find that your magic does you much good."

Vasu stared in astonishment at the sigla he had cast, burning, in the air. The runes were coming unraveled, their magic dying, dwindling to meaningless wisps of smoke.

"Oh, dear," said Alfred, and slid gracefully to the floor.

The dragon-snakes moved in. The dog, snarling and yapping, crouched in front of Haplo and Marit. She held her spears in her hand. Haplo had her dagger. Not that the weapons would do them much good.

Weapon . . . weapon . . .

The Patryns were moving nearer and nearer. Sang-drax had chosen Haplo. The snake's hand was outstretched, reaching for the heart-rune.

"I will finish what I began," he said.

Haplo fell back, pulling Marit and the snarling dog with him. He came up against Hugh the Hand.

"The Sartan knife!" Haplo whispered. "Use it!"

Hugh the Hand drew forth the Cursed Blade, jumped in front

of Haplo. Sang-drax laughed, preparing to slaughter the human, then finish off the Patryns.

Sang-drax found himself confronting a tytan, wielding a tree branch for a club.

Roaring, the giant struck savagely at the dragon-snake. Sang-drax ducked, fell back. The other snakes fought the tytan, hurling spears and magic. But their magic did nothing to stop the Cursed Blade.

"Retreat!" Sang-drax called. He grinned wickedly at Haplo. "A clever ploy. But now what will *you* do? Come, friends. Let their own weapon finish them."

The dragon-snakes vanished.

"Hugh, call it off!" Haplo cried.

But in the presence of its ancient enemy, the Cursed Blade continued to try to kill. The tytan raged around the chamber, bashing its club into walls, its sightless head sniffing them out.

Sigla burned again in the air, but almost immediately dwindled and died.

"I feared as much." Vasu swore in frustration. "The snakes have cast some type of spell in this chamber. My magic won't work."

The tytan rounded on them, its head swiveling in response to Vasu's voice.

"Don't attack!" Haplo halted Marit, who was prepared to hurl her spear. "If it doesn't feel threatened, perhaps it will leave us alone."

"I think so long as any Patryn remains alive, it will feel threatened," Hugh the Hand said grimly.

The tytan approached.

Hugh the Hand ran in front of the tytan, shouting at it, hoping to distract it. Haplo grabbed hold of the comatose Alfred, who was in danger of being trampled by the monster's lumbering feet, and pulled him into a corner.

Vasu and Marit tried circling around the giant, planning to attack it from behind. But the tytan sensed their movement. It whirled, struck. The tree branch whistled horribly, crashed into the wall behind Marit. If she had not thrown herself flat, the blow would have crushed her skull.

Haplo slapped Alfred across the face. "Wake up! Damn it, wake up! I need you!"

The dog added its help, covered Alfred's cheeks with sloppy wet licks. The tytan's huge, stamping feet shook the cavern. Hugh the Hand stood protectively in front of Haplo. Vasu was attempting to cast another spell and not having much success.

"Alfred!" Haplo shook the Sartan until his teeth rattled.

Alfred opened his eyes, took one terrified look at the howling tytan, and, with a gentle groan, shut his eyes.

"No, you don't!" Haplo gripped the Sartan by the neck, forced him to sit upright. "That's not a real tytan. It's the Sartan knife! There must be some sort of magic you can use to stop it! Think, damn it! Or it's going to kill us all!"

"Magic," Alfred repeated, as if this were a new and original concept. "Sartan magic. Why, you're right. I believe there might be a way."

He clambered unsteadily to his feet. The tytan paid no attention to him. Its sightless head was fixed on the Patryns. A massive hand reached down, brushed Hugh the Hand to one side. The tytan headed for Haplo.

Alfred stepped in front of the giant. Solemnly, a comic figure in his shabby finery, his wispy hair trailing down from the bald spot on his head, he raised a trembling hand and, in a shaking voice, said, "Stop."

The tytan vanished.

On the cavern floor, at Hugh's feet, was the Cursed Blade. It quivered an instant, its sigla gleaming. Its light flared, then went out.

"Is it safe now?" Haplo asked, staring hard at the knife.

"Yes," said Alfred. "So long as nothing threatens Sir Hugh again."

Haplo glared at him. "Do you mean to tell me that you could have done that all along? Just say *stop* in Sartan?"

"I suppose so. It didn't occur to me until you mentioned it. And I wasn't really certain it would work. But once I thought about it, it seemed logical to me that the knife's Sartan maker would have provided the user with some means of control. And it would have, in all probability, been something simple that could be taught easily to mensch . . ."

"Yeah, yeah," Haplo said wearily. "Save the explanation. Just teach the damn word to Hugh, will you?"

"What does all this mean?" The assassin was in no great hurry to retrieve his weapon.

"It means that from now on you can control the knife. It won't attack anything you don't want it to. Alfred will teach you the magic you need to know."

"We can leave," said Vasu, staring around the chamber. "Whatever spell those creatures cast has ended. But I've never faced such power. It's far greater than my own. Who are they? What are they? Who created them? The Sartan?"

Alfred blanched. "I'm afraid so. Samah told me that he once asked the creatures that very question. 'Who created you?' 'You did, Sartan,' they said."

"Odd," remarked Haplo quietly. "That's the very same answer they gave me when I asked, 'Who created you?' 'You did,' they said."

"What does it matter who created them?" Marit cried impatiently. "They're here and they're going to attack the city. And then, when it's destroyed . . ." She shook her head, arguing with herself. "I can't believe it. Surely Sang-drax was bluffing."

"What else did they say?" Haplo asked.

"Sang-drax said he was going to seal shut the Final Gate."

# CHAPTER ✦ 45

# ABRI

# THE LABYRINTH

✦

Vasu made ready to leave the caverns, to prepare his people to face a dawn attack. He offered to take Hugh the Hand and Alfred with him; not that they could be of much help, but the headman wanted to keep watch on both of them—and the cursed knife. Marit should have gone with him—she could be of help—but when the headman looked in her direction, she was intently looking somewhere else and refused to catch his eye.

Vasu glanced at Haplo, who was playing with the dog, also keeping his gaze averted. The headman smiled and, taking Hugh and Alfred with him, departed.

Haplo and Marit were alone, not counting the dog. It flopped on its belly on the floor, hiding what might have been a grin with its nose in its paws.

Marit, suddenly uneasy, seemed astonished to find that they were the only two people in the room.

"I guess we should go. There's a lot of work—"

Haplo took her in his arms. "Thank you," he said, "for saving my life."

"I did it for our people," Marit said, stiff in his grasp, still not looking at him. "You know the truth about Sang-drax. You're the only one. Xar—" She paused, horrified. What had she been about to say?

"Yes," said Haplo, his grip on her tightening. "I know the truth about Sang-drax. And Xar does not. Is that what you were going to say, Marit?"

"It's not his fault!" she protested. Against her will and inclination, she found herself relaxing in Haplo's strong arms. "They flatter him, beguile him. They don't let him see their true shape—"

"I used to tell myself that," Haplo said softly. "But I stopped believing it. Xar knows the truth. He knows they are evil. He listens to their flattery because he enjoys it. He thinks he controls them. But the more he thinks that, the more they control him."

Xar's sigil burned into Marit's skin. Her hand started to touch it, rub it as one rubs a bruise, to rub out the pain. She caught herself. The thought of Haplo seeing that mark turned her stomach to water.

And yet, she asked herself angrily, why shouldn't he see it? Why should I be ashamed? It is an honor, a great honor. He is wrong about Xar. Once my lord knows the truth about the dragon-snakes . . .

"Xar is coming," she said stubbornly. "Perhaps he will arrive during the battle. He will save us, his people, fight for us, as he has always fought for us. And then he will understand. He will see Sang-drax for what he is . . ."

Marit pushed Haplo away, turned her back on him. She put her hand to her forehead, scratched the mark hidden beneath her thick hair. "I think we should help with the defenses. Vasu will be needing us—"

"Marit," said Haplo, "I love you."

The sigil on her forehead was like an iron band around her skull, tightening, constricting. Her temples throbbed.

"Patryns don't love," Marit said thickly, not turning around.

"No, we only hate," Haplo replied. "Maybe if I had loved more and hated less, I wouldn't have lost you. I wouldn't have lost our child."

"You'll never find her, you know."

"Yes, I will. I have, in fact. I found her today."

Marit turned, stared at him. "What? How could you be certain—"

Haplo shrugged. "I'm not. In fact, I don't suppose it was her. But it could have been. And it's because of her we'll fight. And we'll win because of her. And somehow, for her sake, we'll keep Sang-drax from shutting the Final Gate . . ."

Marit was in his arms again, holding him fast. The circles of their beings joined to form one circle, unbroken, never ending.

Seeing that no one was likely to need a dog for a while, the animal sighed contentedly, rolled over, and went to sleep.

Outside the caverns, walking the streets of Abri, Vasu made his preparations for war. Surrounded by a hostile environment, continually under threat, if not attack, the city walls were reinforced with magic; the very roofs of the dwelling places were marked with protective runes. Very few of the Labyrinth's creatures attempted to attack Abri. They lurked beyond the walls, in the forests, waiting to ambush groups of farmers, pick off the herders. Occasionally one of the winged beasts—dragons, griffins, the like—would take it into its head to raid within the city walls. But such an occurrence was rare.

It was this talk of armies that worried Vasu. As Haplo had said, the monsters in the Labyrinth had up until now remained largely unorganized. The chaodyn often attacked wolfen. Wolfen were continually defending their territory against roving tiger-men. Marauding dragons killed whatever looked fit to eat. But Vasu wasn't deluding himself. Such minor rivalries and disputes would be fast forgotten if a chance came to band together and invade the fortress city that had stood against them for so long.

Vasu sounded the alarm, gathered the people together in the large central meeting place, and told them of their danger. The Patryns took the dire news calmly, if grimly. Their silence spoke their support. Dispersed, they went about their tasks efficiently, with a minimum of talk. Weapons had to be gathered, their magic strengthened. Families parted, said good-bye briefly, without tears. Adults took up duty on the walls. Older children led younger ones into the mountain caverns, which were unsealed to receive them. Scouting parties, shrouded in black to hide the runes that now glowed ominously, slipped out of the iron gate, ranged along the river, reinforcing the magic on the bridges, attempting to gauge the strength and disposition of the enemy.

"What about that damn fire?" Hugh the Hand squinted up at the beacon flame. "You say there are dragons around here. That will draw them like moths."

"It has never been doused," said Vasu. "Not since the beginning." He glanced down at the gleaming sigla on his skin. "I don't think it will make much difference," he added dryly. "The moths are already swarming."

Hugh the Hand shook his head, unconvinced. "Mind if I take a look around at the rest of your defenses? I've had some experience in this sort of thing."

Vasu appeared dubious.

"The Cursed Blade will be safe enough now," Alfred assured him. "And Sir Hugh knows how to control it. Tomorrow, though, if there is fighting—"

Hugh the Hand winked. "I've got an idea about that. Don't worry."

Alfred sighed, gazed bleakly around the city.

"Well, we have done all we can," Vasu said, echoing Alfred's sigh. "I, for one, am hungry. Would you like to come to my house? I am certain you are in need of food and drink."

Alfred was pleased, astonished. "I would be honored."

As they walked through the city, Alfred noticed that no matter how busy or preoccupied, every Patryn they met accorded Vasu some show of respect, even if it was nothing more than a slight inclination of the head or a gesture of a hand, drawing a swift ritual friendship sigil in the air. Vasu unfailingly returned the sign with one of his own.

His home was no different from any of the other Patryn dwellings, except that it appeared older than most and stood apart. Braced against the mountain, it was like a stalwart guard who plants his back against a secure surface to take on his foes.

Vasu entered first. Alfred followed, tripping over the doorstep but managing to catch himself before he fell face first on the floor. The dwelling was clean and neatly kept and, like all Patryn homes, almost devoid of furniture.

"You are not marr—er . . . joined?" Alfred asked, seating himself awkwardly on the floor, his long legs folding beneath him with difficulty.

Vasu was taking bread from a basket suspended from the ceiling. Rows of sausages, also hanging from the ceiling, brought Alfred a fond memory of Haplo's dog.

"No, I live alone for now," Vasu replied, adding some type of unrecognizable fruit to the simple meal. "I haven't been headman very long. I inherited the position from my father, who only recently died."

"I am sorry for your loss," Alfred said politely.

"His life was one well lived," Vasu returned. "We celebrate such lives, not mourn them." He placed the food on the floor between them, sat down himself. "Our family has held this position for generations. Of course, any man or woman has the right to challenge us, but no one ever has. My father worked hard to govern well, govern justly. I strive as best I can to emulate his good example."

"It seems you are succeeding."

"I hope so." Vasu's troubled gaze shifted to the small window, out into the darkness. "My people have never faced so great a challenge, so grave a threat."

"What about the Final Gate?" Alfred asked timidly, aware that such matters were really none of his business, that he knew very little about it. "Shouldn't someone be sent to warn . . . somebody?"

Vasu sighed softly. "The Final Gate is far, far from here. They would never reach it in time . . . or alive."

Alfred looked at the food, but he had very little appetite.

"But enough dismal talk." Vasu returned to the meal with a cheerful smile. "We need the strength food offers us. And who knows when we may have time to eat again? Shall I offer the blessing? Or will you?"

"Oh, you, please!" Alfred said hastily, blushing. He had no idea what a Patryn might consider a proper blessing.

Vasu extended his hands, began to speak. Alfred joined in the words unconsciously, repeating them without thinking—until it occurred to him that Vasu was speaking the blessing in Sartan.

Alfred's breath caught in his throat, making such a strange half-strangled clicking noise that it caught the headman's attention. Vasu ceased the blessing in the middle, looked up.

"Are you all right?" he asked, worried.

Alfred stared wildly and confusedly at Vasu's glowing, tattooed skin. "You're not . . . Are you? . . . You can't be . . . S-s-sartan!"

"About half," Vasu said imperturbably. He held up his arms, gazed at the sigla with pride. "Our family has adapted over the centuries. In the beginning, we wore the tattoos only for disguise. Not to delude the Patryns, mind you; we only wanted to fit in. Since then, through intermarriage, we have come to be able to use the magic—although not as well as a full-blooded Patryn. But what we lack, we compensate for by using Sartan magic."

"Intermarriage! But . . . the hatred?" Alfred thought back to the River of Anger. "Surely you must have been persecuted . . ."

"No," said Vasu quietly. "They knew why we were sent here."

"The Vortex!"

"Yes, we came from beneath the mountain, where we were sent because of our heretical beliefs. My ancestors opposed the Sundering; they opposed the building of this prison. They were a danger, a threat to the established order. Like yourself, or so I must imagine. Although you are the first Sartan to arrive in the Vortex in many long ages. I had hoped that things had changed."

"You are still here, aren't you?" Alfred said quietly, pushing his food around with trembling fingers.

Vasu regarded him for a long moment in silence. "I suppose explanations would be too long, too complex."

"Not really." Alfred sighed. "We Sartan locked ourselves in our own prison, just as surely as we locked you in yours. Our prison walls were pride; our iron bars were fear. Escape was impossible, for that would have meant tearing down the walls, opening up the barred gates. We dare not do that. Our prison not only kept us in, you see—it kept *them* out. We stayed inside, and shut our eyes, and went to sleep. And we've been asleep all these years. When we woke, everything had changed except us. And now our prison is the only place we know."

"But not you," said Vasu.

Alfred blushed. "I can take no credit for it." He smiled faintly. "I met a man with a dog."

Vasu was nodding. "It would have been easy for our people, when we were first sent here, to give up and die. It was the Patryns who kept us alive. They took us in, accepted us, protected us from harm until we grew strong enough to protect ourselves."

Alfred was beginning to understand. "And it must have been a Sartan idea to build this city."

"I think perhaps it was. Somewhere back in long-forgotten times. It would be natural for the Sartan, who came from cities and liked to live in large groups. We could see the advantages gained by banding together, dwelling in one place, working to make it strong.

"Even back in the ancient world, the Patryns were nomads, tended to be loners. The family unit was—and still is—important to them. But in the Labyrinth, many families were wiped out. The

Patryns had to adapt or cease to survive. They did so by expanding the family unit into the tribe. The Patryns learned the importance of banding together for mutual defense from the Sartan. And the Sartan learned the importance of family from the Patryns."

"The worst in both our peoples brought us to this end." Alfred spoke with emotion. "The worst perpetuated it. You have taken the best and used it to build stability, find peace in the midst of chaos and terror."

"Let us hope," said Vasu somberly, "that this is *not* the end."

Alfred sighed, shook his head.

Vasu observed him closely. "The intruders called you the Serpent Mage."

Now Alfred smiled; his hands fluttered. "I know. I have been called that before. I don't know what it means."

"I do," said Vasu unexpectedly.

Alfred looked up, astonished.

"Tell me what happened to earn you this title," Vasu said.

"Why, that's just it. I don't know. You think I'm being evasive. Or that I don't want to help. I do! I would give anything . . . Let me try to explain.

"To make a long story short, I woke from my sleep to find myself alone. My companions had all died. I was on the air world of Arianus, a world populated by mensch."

He paused, looked at Vasu to see if he understood. Apparently he did, though he said nothing. His attentive silence encouraged Alfred to proceed.

"I was terrified. All this magical power"—Alfred stared at his hands—"and I was alone. And afraid. If anyone discovered what I could do, they might . . . try to take advantage. I could imagine— the coercion, the pleadings, the urgings, the threats. Yet I wanted to live among the mensch, to be of service to them. Not that I was much help."

Alfred sighed again. "Anyway, I developed a most unfortunate habit. Whenever danger threatens, I . . . faint."

Vasu looked amazed.

"It was either that or use my magic, you see," Alfred continued, his face red. "But that's not the worst. Apparently I have worked some very remarkable magic—quite remarkable, in fact—and I don't remember doing it. I must have been fully conscious at the time, but when it's all over I haven't the slightest memory of it. Well,

I guess I do. Deep inside." Alfred laid his hand on his heart. "Because I feel uncomfortable whenever the matter comes up. But I swear to you"—he gazed earnestly at Vasu—"I can't consciously remember!"

"What sort of magic?" Vasu asked.

Alfred swallowed, licked dry lips. "Necromancy," he said in a low, anguished voice, barely audible. "The human, Hugh the Hand. He was dead. I brought him back to life."

Vasu drew in a deep breath, let it out slowly. "And what else?"

"I was told that I . . . I changed into a serpent—a dragon, to be exact. Haplo was in danger, on Chelestra. And there were children . . . The dragon-snakes were going to kill them." Alfred shuddered. "They needed my help, but, as usual, I fainted. At least, that's what I thought I did. Haplo tells me that I didn't. I don't know." Alfred shook his head. "I just don't know."

"What happened?"

"A magnificent dragon—green and gold—appeared out of nowhere and fought the snakes. The dragon destroyed the king snake. Haplo and the children were saved. The only thing I remember was waking up on the beach."

"Indeed, a serpent mage," Vasu said.

"What *is* a serpent mage, Headman? Does it have anything to do with these dragon-snakes? If so, how is that possible? They were unknown to the Sartan at the time of the Sundering—at least so far as I can determine."

"It seems odd that you—a pure-bred Sartan—don't know," Vasu responded, regarding Alfred with some misgiving. "And that I —a half-breed—do."

"Not so strange," Alfred said, smiling bleakly. "You have kept the fire of memory and tradition burning brightly. In our obsession with trying to put back together what we destroyed, we let our fire go out. And then I was very young when I went to sleep. And very old when I woke up."

Vasu considered this in silence; then, relaxing, he smiled. "The Serpent Mage has nothing to do with those you call dragon-snakes, although it is my guess that they have been around far longer than you credit them. 'Serpent Mage' is a title denoting ability—nothing more.

"At the time of the Sundering, there was a hierarchy of magi among the Sartan, denoted by animal names. Lynx, Coyote, Deer

. . . It was very involved, complicated." Vasu's remarkable eyes were fixed on Alfred. "Serpent was near the top. Extraordinarily powerful."

"I see." Alfred was uncomfortable. "I suppose there was training involved, years of study—"

"Of course. With that much power comes responsibility."

"The one thing I've never been very good at."

"You could be of immense help to my people, Alfred."

"If I don't pass out," Alfred said bitterly. "But then again, you might be happier if I did. I could bring more danger to you than I'm worth. The Labyrinth seems to be able to turn my magic against me—"

"Because you're not in control of your magic. Or of yourself. Take control, Alfred. Be the hero of your own life. Don't let someone else play that role."

"Be the hero of my own life," Alfred repeated softly. He almost laughed. It was so very ludicrous.

The two men sat together in companionable silence. Outside, the black began to soften to gray. Dawn—and battle—approached.

"You are two people, Alfred," said Vasu at length. "An inner person and an outer. A chasm exists between the two. Somehow you must bridge it. The two of you must meet."

Alfred Montbank—middle-aged, balding, clumsy, a coward.

Coren—life-giver; a creature of power, strength, courage, the chosen.

These two could never come together. They had been apart far too long.

Alfred sat dejected. "I think I would only fall off the bridge," he said miserably.

A horn sounded, a call of warning. Vasu was on his feet. "Will you come with me?"

Alfred attempted to look brave. Squaring his shoulders, he stood up . . . and tripped over the corner of the rug.

"One of us will come," he said, and picked himself up with a sigh.

# CHAPTER ♦ 46

## ABRI

## THE LABYRINTH

♦

BY THE GRAY LIGHT OF DAWN, IT SEEMED TO THE PATRYNS THAT EVERY ENEMY IN the Labyrinth was ranged against them.

Until that moment, when they looked out over the walls and stared in horrified awe, some had doubted, not believed the warnings. They thought the headman's fears exaggerated. There had been intruders in the city, but they had done no harm. A few packs of wolfen might attack. Or perhaps even a legion of the hard-to-kill[1] chaodyn. How could such vast forces as the headman spoke of gather unobserved? The forest and the surrounding lands had been no more dangerous than normal.

Now the land crawled with death.

Wolfen, chaodyn, tiger-men, snogs, and hosts of other monsters, born and bred by the evil magic of the Labyrinth, were massed along the riverbank, their ranks rippling with activity, until it seemed that they formed another River of Anger.

The forest concealed the numbers hidden within, but the Patryns could see the tops of the trees swaying, stirred by the movement of armies below. Dust rose from where giant trees were being

---

[1] Insect-like creatures, the chaodyn have a hard outer shell that is extremely difficult to penetrate even with magical weapons. A chaodyn must be struck directly, die instantly, or else an attacker will find himself facing two where one stood before.

felled to serve as bridges and battering rams, were being made into ladders to scale the walls.

And beyond the forest, the grass plains that lay fallow, ready for the planting, sprouted a hideous crop. Springing up in the night like weeds that thrive on darkness, the ranks of the foe stretched to the horizon.

Leading the armies were creatures never before seen in the Labyrinth: huge serpents, without wings or feet, gray-scaled, their wrinkled bodies dragging over the ground. They oozed slime that poisoned the land, the water, the air—anything they touched. Their foul smell, of rot and decay, was like a film of oil on the wind. The Patryns could taste it on their tongues and in their throats, feel it coating their arms and hands, obscuring their vision.

The red eyes of the serpents burned hot with bloodlust. Their toothless mouths gaped wide, sucking in the terror and the fear the sight of them inspired, gorging on it, growing fat and strong and powerful.

One of the serpents, however, had only one eye. And it scanned the top of the city walls with evil intent, as if searching for someone in particular.

The dawn came, gray light shining from a source never seen, serving only to illuminate, doing little to warm or cheer. But this day the gray was brightened by a halo of blue, an aura of red. The Patryns' rune-magic had never before gleamed so brilliantly, reacting to the powerful forces arrayed against it with power of its own.

The sigla flared on the protecting wall, its light so dazzling that many standing on the riverbank, awaiting the signal to attack, were forced to shade their eyes against it. The bodies of the Patryns themselves gleamed as if each individual burned with his or her own vibrant flame.

Only one person stood in darkness, forlorn, almost suffocating with terror.

"This is hopeless!" Alfred peered over the edge of the battlements. His hands, gripping the wall, shook so that fragments of rock dislodged, came down in a rain of gritty dust that covered his shoes.

"Yes, it is hopeless," answered Haplo beside him. "I'm sorry I got you into this, my friend."

The dog pattered back and forth nervously along the wall, whining because it couldn't see, occasionally alert and growling at

the sound of a wolfen's challenging howl or a dragon-snake's taunting hiss. Marit stood next to Haplo; her hand was twined fast in his.
They looked at each other every so often, smiling, finding comfort
and courage in each other's eyes.

Alfred, watching them, felt that comfort include him. For the
first time since he had met Haplo, Alfred saw the Patryn almost
whole, almost at peace. He was not fully whole, not completely—
the dog was with him still. Whatever had led Haplo to come back to
the Labyrinth had led him home. And he was content to stay here,
to die here.

*My friend,* he had said.

Alfred heard the words dimly above the shrieks of the invading
foe. The words kindled a small fire inside him.

"Am I?" he asked Haplo timidly.

"Are you what?"

The conversation had moved on, at least between Haplo and
Marit and Hugh the Hand. Alfred hadn't been listening to them.
He'd been listening to the voice across the chasm.

"Your . . . what you said. Friend," Alfred said shyly.

"Did I say that?" Haplo shrugged. "I must have been talking to
the dog." But he was smiling.

"You weren't, were you?" Alfred said, red with pleasure.

Haplo was silent. The armies below them hooted and howled,
gibbered and cursed. Haplo's silence wrapped around Alfred like a
comforting blanket. He couldn't hear the screams of death. Only
Haplo, when he spoke.

"Yes, Alfred, you are my friend." Haplo held out his hand—the
hand that was powerful, tattooed on the back with blue runes.

Alfred extended his hand—white, shriveled, with knobby
wrists and thin bones, its flesh cold and clammy with fear.

The two hands met, clasped, gripped each other firmly.

Two people, reaching across a chasm of hate. At that moment,
Alfred looked inward and met himself.

And he was no longer afraid.

Another shrill blast of the trumpet and the battle began.

The Patryns had either destroyed the bridges across the river or
set magical traps on them. These obstructions halted the enemy only
momentarily, were no more than a minor inconvenience. The nar-

row rock bridge that had cost Alfred some painful moments exploded in a flash of magic, taking out a host of the enemy who had foolishly ventured onto it.

But before the last fragments had fallen down into the raging water, six logs were hauled by tusked behemoths to the river's bank. Dragons—true dragons of the Labyrinth[2]—lifted the logs with claw and with magic and dropped them down. Legions of the dread host swarmed across. If any of their number slipped and fell into the torrent—which many did—they were abandoned to their fate.

Higher up among the cliffs stood permanent bridges of stone. These the Patryns left standing, but used the magic of their engraved sigla to confound the enemy, arousing an intense fear in those trying to cross, causing the ones in front to turn and flee in panic, disorganizing and stampeding those in the rear.

The Patryns guarding the walls were heartened by the sight, assuming that the bulk of the enemy would be unable to reach the city. Their cheering died when the enormous serpents reared up and crashed headlong into the under-section of the bridges, a part left unprotected by magic. The sigla on the sides flashed wildly, but cracks spread through it, disrupting the magic, weakening it—in some cases completely destroying it. The enemy commanders rallied their troops with furious shouts. The retreat was halted, the armies of the Labyrinth raced across the damaged bridges, which trembled beneath the weight, but held.

By midmorning, the sky above Abri was dark with the wings of dragons and griffins, gigantic bats, and leather-winged birds of prey that swooped down on the Patryns from above. Hordes of chaodyn, wolfen packs, and tiger-men dashed across the no-man's-land below. Siege towers were raised, ladders thrust up along the sides of the walls. Battering rams thundered against the iron gates.

---

[2] As opposed to the evil serpents (dragon-snakes) or the good dragons of Pryan. The Labyrinth dragons are descendants of those of ancient Earth, pre-Sundering. They are hideous reptiles, large, with vast wingspan, powerful in magic and abominably evil. They do not kill a victim outright, but enjoy taking prisoners and will torment their victims for days, allowing them to die slowly. Haplo mentions elsewhere that the dragons of the Labyrinth are the one creature he never fought. He ran for his life whenever he feared one was near. So far as Haplo records, Xar, Lord of the Nexus, was the only Patryn ever to fight a Labyrinth dragon and survive.

The Patryns rained down magic on their foes—spears kindled into bolts of flame, javelins burst overhead in a shower of flesh-consuming sparks, arrows that could not miss flew directly to the heart of the chosen victim. Smoke and magical fog obscured the sight of the monsters descending from the air; several crashed head-long into the mountain. The magic of the rune-inscribed walls and buildings of Abri repelled invaders. Ladders thrown up against the walls turned from wood to water. Siege towers caught fire and burned. Iron battering rams melted, the molten metal consuming all those who stood near it.

Daunted by the force and power of the Patryn magic, the armies of the enemy faltered and fell back. Alfred, watching from his place on the walls, began to think he'd been wrong.

"We're winning," he said excitedly to Haplo, who had paused to rest.

"No, we're not," Haplo said grimly. "That was only the first wave. Meant to soften us up, force us to expend our weapons."

"But they're retreating," Alfred protested.

"Regrouping. And this"—Haplo held out a spear—"is my last. Marit's gone to find more, but she won't be successful."

Archers were on their hands and knees, searching for any arrow dropped or spent. They pulled shafts out of the bodies of the dead for use against their killers. On the ground below, those too old to fight hunched over the few remaining weapons, hastily inscribing them with sigla, replicating them with magic that was already starting to wane.

And it still wouldn't be enough to hold back the foes, already massing for the next attack. All along the battlements, the Patryns drew knife and sword, prepared to face the assault, which would be fought hand to hand.

Marit returned, carrying two javelins and a broken spear. "All I could find."

"May I?" Alfred asked, his hand hovering over the weapons. "I can replicate them."

Haplo shook his head. "No. Your magic—remember? Who knows what these might turn into."

"I can't be of any help," Alfred said, discouraged.

"At least," Haplo observed, "you didn't faint."

The Sartan looked up, mildly astonished. "No, I didn't, did I?"

"Besides, I don't think it will matter at this point," Haplo said dryly. "You could make spears from every branch of every tree in the forest and it wouldn't matter. The dragon-snakes are leading this attack."

Alfred stared over the top of the wall. His knees weakened; he very nearly lost his balance. The dog edged close, bolstering him with an encouraging lick and a wagging tail.

The River of Anger had frozen, probably from the magic of the serpents. Armies of creatures now marched across its solid black surface. Surrounding the city, the serpents began to fling themselves bodily at the walls. The sigla-inscribed stone shook beneath the blows. Cracks speared through the structure, small at first, then growing larger. Time and again, the serpents attacked the very bones of Abri. The cracks spread and began to widen, dividing the runes, weakening the magic.

The Patryns atop the walls fought the serpents with every weapon, every magical spell they could think to cast. But weapons struck the gray-scaled skin and bounced off harmlessly; magic burst over the serpents, did no damage. It was afternoon. The armies of the enemy stood on the frozen river and cheered the serpents on, waited for the walls to fall.

Headman Vasu climbed up to where Haplo stood atop the wall. A shuddering blow rocked it beneath his feet. "You said you once fought these creatures, Haplo. How can we stop them?"

"Steel," Haplo yelled back. "Inscribed with magic. Drive it into the head. Can you find me a sword?"

"That would mean fighting them outside the wall," Vasu shouted.

"Give me a group of our people skilled with sword and dagger," Haplo urged.

"We would have to open the gates," Vasu said, his expression dark.

"Just long enough to let us out. Then shut them behind us."

Vasu shook his head. "No, I can't permit it. You would be trapped out there . . ."

"If we fail, it won't matter," Haplo returned grimly. "Either we die out there or we die in here. And out there, we've got a chance."

"I'll go with you," Marit offered.

"So will I," said Hugh the Hand, frustrated, eager for action.

The assassin had tried fighting, but every spear he threw went wide of its mark; the arrows he shot might have been flowers for all the damage they did.

"You can't kill," Haplo reminded him.

The Hand grinned. "They don't know that."

"You've got a point," Haplo admitted. "But maybe you should stay here, protect Alfred . . ."

"No," said Alfred resolutely. "Sir Hugh is needed. You will all be needed. I'll be all right."

"You sure?" Haplo regarded him intently.

Alfred flushed. Haplo wasn't asking if Alfred was sure he'd be all right, but if he was sure about something else. Haplo had always been able to see through him. Well, friends could do that sort of thing.

"I'm sure," Alfred said, smiling.

"Good luck, then, Coren," Haplo said.

Accompanied by the dog and Hugh the Hand, the Patryns—Haplo and Marit—left, disappearing into the fog and smoke of battle.

"Good luck to you, my friend," Alfred said softly.

Closing his eyes, he delved into the very depths of his being—a place he had never before visited, consciously at least—and began to search among the clutter and the refuse for the words of a spell.

Kari and her band of hunters volunteered to go with Haplo to fight the serpents. They armed themselves with steel, taking the time to inscribe the magic on the blades as Haplo instructed.

"The head of the serpent is the only vulnerable part that I know of," Haplo told them. "Between the eyes."

No need to add what they could all see, that the serpents were powerful, that the lashing tails could batter them until their own shielding magic gave way, the enormous bodies crush them, the gaping toothless maws devour them.

Four serpents crawled around the walls, including Sang-drax.

"He's ours," said Haplo, exchanging glances with Marit, who nodded grim agreement. The dog barked in excitement, dashed in circles in front of the gate.

The walls continued to hold, but they wouldn't much longer. Cracks spread from base to top now; the flaring light of the runes was starting to dim and in places had gone out. Hosts of the enemy

were taking advantage of the weakness to throw up ladders, begin
scaling the walls. The attacking serpents occasionally knocked
down their own allies, but paid little heed. Another swarm arrived
to take the places of the dead.

Haplo and his group stood by the gates.

"Our blessing on you," Vasu said, and, raising his hand, he
gave the signal.

Patryns who were guardians of the gate's magic placed their
hands on the runes. The sigla flashed and darkened. The gates began to open. Haplo and his people dashed out rapidly, squeezing
through the crack. Seeing the breach in the defenses, a pack of
wolfen let out a howl and flung themselves at it. The Patryns cut
them down swiftly. Those few wolfen who managed to win through
were caught between the iron gates as they boomed shut.

Haplo and those with him were now locked outside their own
city, with no way back in. The gates would not—by Haplo's own
orders—open again until the serpents were dead.

The magic of the Patryns' swords and their own bodies shone
brightly. At Haplo's command, the teams separated, spread out,
breaking off into small groups to challenge the serpents individu-
ally, prevent them from banding together, draw them away from
the walls.

The serpents mocked them, turned from their destruction to
eliminate these petty nuisances and go back to the task at hand.
Only Sang-drax understood the danger. He shouted a warning, but
it wasn't heeded.

One serpent, seeing puny creatures attacking it, dove straight
down upon them, intending to seize them in its jaws and fling the
bodies back over the walls.

Kari, flanked by three of her people, stood fast against the horror descending on her. Gripping her sword, she waited until the
terrible head was right above her; then, with all her strength, she
plunged the sharp blade—its magic flaming blue and red—into the
reptile head.

The blade bit deep. Blood spurted. The serpent reared up in
agony, yanked the sword from Kari's hands. Blinded by the blood
that rained down on her, sickened by the foul, poisonous smell, Kari
fell to the ground. The serpent's gigantic body rolled to crush her,
but her people dragged her out from beneath it. The serpent's tail
lashed out, would have smashed them, but its thrashings grew fee-

ble. The serpent head crashed to the ground, just missing the wall, and lay still.

The Patryns cheered; their enemies cursed. The other serpents, more cautious now that one of their number had been slain, viewed their attackers with respect, making the Patryns' work far more dangerous.

The head of the one-eyed serpent loomed over Haplo.

"This will be our last meeting, Sang-drax!" he called.

"True enough, Patryn. You have outlived your usefulness to me."

"Because I'm no longer afraid of you!" Haplo retorted.

"Ah, but you should be," Sang-drax returned, his snake-head swiveling, trying to see Marit and Hugh, who lurked on his blind side. "As we speak, several of my kind are speeding toward the Final Gate, with orders to seal it shut. You will be trapped here for all eternity!"

"The people of the Nexus will fight them!"

"But they cannot win. *You* cannot win. How many times have you struck me down only to see me rise again!"

Sang-drax's head dove for Haplo, but the move was only a feint. The serpent's tail whipped around, struck Haplo from behind. The Patryn's body magic protected him, or the blow would have broken his spine. The tail knocked him flat, stunned him. His sword flew from his hand.

The dog stood protectively over its fallen master, teeth bared, hackles raised.

The serpent ignored Haplo, however. He was down and no longer a threat. The red eye found Marit. Sang-drax's jaws opened wide, swooped in for the kill. Marit stood waiting—apparently frozen with terror—making no move to defend herself. The jaws were snapping shut when a heavy weight struck the serpent on its blind side.

Hugh the Hand had thrown himself bodily onto the serpent's head. Using a rune-covered Patryn dagger, he tried to stab into the gray scales. But the dagger broke. The Hand hung on tenaciously, fingers clutching the empty eye socket. He had hoped that the Cursed Blade might come to life, attack this foe for him, but perhaps the serpents were controlling the knife now, as they seemed to have done in the past. Hugh could do nothing but hang on, at least hamper the serpent's attack, give Marit and Haplo time to kill it.

Sang-drax flailed about, shaking his head, trying to break the human's grip. Hugh the Hand was strong and hung on with grim determination. Yellow lightning crackled along the serpent's gray skin. The assassin bellowed in pain. An electrical surge jolted through his body, caused him to loosen his hold in agony.

He slid to the ground, but he'd bought Marit time enough to move in close. She drove her sword into Sang-drax's head. The blade bit into the serpent's jaw and up into the snout, causing pain, but not killing.

Marit tried to free her sword, but Sang-drax flung his head up, jerked it from her blood-slick grasp.

Haplo was on his feet, his sword in hand. But he was staggering, hurt and confused. Marit ran to grab his sword. His hand closed over hers.

"Behind me!" he whispered urgently.

Marit understood his plan. She crowded behind him, taking care to keep clear of his sword arm, which now dangled limply at his side. The dog danced in front, jumping into the air, snapping and taunting the serpent with shrill yelps and barks.

In hideous pain, seeing his foe weak and wounded, Sang-drax plunged down for the kill. Too late he saw the shining blade lifted to meet him, saw the magic flare in a radiance that blinded his one good eye. He could not stop his downward momentum, but he could at least destroy the man who was about to destroy him.

Marit stood up. The serpent's plunging head had narrowly missed her. She had been ready to join in the attack, but at the last moment Haplo had shoved her backward. The serpent's head smashed down, impaled itself on Haplo's blade. Gripping his sword with both hands, Haplo plunged the sword deep into Sang-drax, then both he and his dog disappeared without a cry beneath the serpent's flailing head.

Around her other battles were raging. One of the serpents had slain the Patryns who attacked it and was now assisting its fellow. Kari had gone to the aid of her people, fighting for their lives. Marit spared them only a glance. She could see Haplo, covered with blood —his own and the serpent's. He was not moving.

She ran to him, tried to lift the heavy head of the dead serpent off him. Hugh the Hand, sitting up, shaking his head muzzily, called out a warning.

Marit turned. A wolfen was closing in for the kill. It leapt on her, knocked her down, claws mauling her, fangs tearing at her throat.

And then suddenly it was off her. Opening her eyes, Marit had the wild impression that the wolfen was flying away backward, when she realized it was being carried upward in the claws of a creature more beautiful and wonderful than anything she had ever seen in her life.

A dragon, green-scaled and golden-winged, with a burnished crest that shone like a sun, flew down into the gray of the smoke-filled sky. It caught hold of the wolfen, flung the beast to its death against the sharp rocks of a cliff face. Then the dragon swooped low and snagged the dead serpent, dragged it away from Haplo.

The other serpents, alarmed by the sight of this new foe, left off their battle against the Patryns, turned to fight the dragon.

Marit lifted Haplo in her arms. He was alive; the sigla on his skin gleamed a faint blue. But blood soaked his shirt, over the heart-rune. His breathing was labored and shallow. The dog—amazingly on its feet and uninjured after being buried by the serpent—trotted over to give its master an anxious lick on the cheek.

Haplo opened his eyes, saw Marit. Then he saw—above her—the glistening green and flashing gold wings of the wondrous dragon.

"Well, well," he whispered, smiling. "Alfred."

"Alfred!" Marit gasped in astonishment, stared upward.

But a shadow blocked her sight. A figure loomed over her. She couldn't tell what or who it was at first, could see nothing more than a black shape against the bright radiance cast by the dragon. Haplo's breath caught in his throat; he struggled vainly to sit up.

And then a voice spoke and then Marit knew.

"So that is your friend Alfred," said Xar, Lord of the Nexus, peering upward. "Truly—a very powerful Sartan."

The lord's gaze shifted back down to Marit, to Haplo. "A good thing for me he is otherwise occupied."

# CHAPTER ♦ 47

## ABRI

## THE LABYRINTH

♦

Xar FOUND THE CITY OF ABRI BY THE BEACON FIRE. BURNING ON THE TOP OF THE mountain, above the smoke and mists, above the shimmer of the magic protecting the city, the beacon fire shone bright, and Xar made directly for it.

He had taken his ship into the ruins of the Vortex; there are advantages to traveling in a ship with Sartan runes, although it had been an uncomfortable journey for the Patryn. Leaving Pryan, he had not had time to reconstruct the sigla on the outside of the ship. He had been cautious about altering those on the inside. He knew he might very well need all his strength for whatever he faced in the Labyrinth.

Although not easily impressed, Xar had been appalled by the numbers of enemy forces attacking the city. Arriving at the outset of the battle, he had watched from a safe location, high in the mountains, near the beacon fire and its flame. Xar warmed himself by the fire as he watched the armies of chaos attack his people.

He was not surprised to see the dragon-snakes. He had admitted to himself that Sang-drax would betray him.

The Seventh Gate. It all had to do with the Seventh Gate.

"You know that if I find it, I will control you," he told the dragon-snakes whose gray, slime-covered bodies were launching their assault on the city walls. "The day Kleitus told me of the Seventh Gate—*that* was the day when you began to fear me. That was when you became my enemy."

It didn't matter to Xar that Haplo had warned him of the

dragon-snakes' treachery all along. Nothing mattered for Xar now except the Seventh Gate. It loomed large in his vision, blotting out everything else.

His task now was to find Haplo among the thousands of Patryns battling the foe. Xar was not unduly worried. Knowing men and women as he did, he was fairly certain that wherever he found Marit—and that would be easy, since they were joined—he would find Haplo. Xar's only concern was that the meddlesome Sartan, Alfred, might interfere.

The battle was taking a long time. The Patryns defended themselves well; Xar felt a swelling of pride in his heart. His people. And once he found the Seventh Gate, he would raise them to glory. But he was fast losing patience. Time wasted here was time that could be used to find that very gate. He placed his hand on the sigil, was about to summon Marit, about to go down and search for Haplo himself, when he saw the city gate open, saw the small band of heroes come forth to drive away the dragon-snakes.

And of course—Xar knew without bothering to look—Haplo would be among them. His last battle with Sang-drax had ended in a draw; each had given and taken wounds that would not heal. Haplo would not miss this opportunity to finish off his enemy, despite the odds against him.

"Of course you won't," Xar said, observing the duel with interest and approval. "You are my son."

The lord waited until the battle was ended and Sang-drax destroyed; and then Xar called on the rune-magic to lift him up and carry him down to the bloody ground below.

Marit's first reaction, on seeing Xar, was one of vast relief. Here was the strong father who would—once again—defend, protect, and succor his children.

"My Lord, you have come to aid us!"

Haplo tried to sit up, but he was extremely weak and in pain. Blood soaked his shirt front, had even stained the leather vest he wore over it. He felt the jagged edges of broken bones grind together; any movement at all was sheer agony.

Marit helped him, lending him her strength, her support. She looked up to find Xar's eyes dark on her, but she was too battle-dazed, too elated by his presence to notice the shadow he cast over them.

"My Lord." Haplo's voice was weak. Xar had to kneel beside him to hear him. "We can hold our own here. The gravest threat, the greatest danger is at the Final Gate. The dragon-snakes plan to seal it shut. We . . ." He choked, coughed.

"We will be trapped in this prison house, Lord," Marit continued urgently. "Its evil will grow; the dragon-snakes will see to that. The Labyrinth will become a death chamber, without hope, for there will be no way to escape."

"You are the only one of us who can reach the Final Gate in time, Lord," Haplo said, every word costing him obvious pain. "You are the only one who can stop them."

He sank back into Marit's arms. Her face was near his, her anxiety and concern for him obvious. The three paid no heed to the battle raging around them; Xar's magic enclosed them in a cocoon of safety and silence, protected them from death and the turmoil of war.

Xar's gaze turned, his eyes searched far, far into the distance, until he could see the Final Gate from where they stood—which, with his magical power, was within the realm of possibility. His face grew drawn and grave, the brows came together, the eyes narrowed in anger. He was seeing, Marit guessed, the terrible battle being waged, the people of the Nexus leaving their peaceful homes to defend the only means of escape for their brethren caught inside.

Was the battle already taking place? Or was Xar seeing the future?

His gaze came back, and the eyes were hard and cold and calculating. "The Final Gate will fall. But I will open it again. When I have found the Seventh Gate, then I will take my revenge."

"Lord Xar, what do you mean?" Marit stared at him, not understanding. "Lord, do not worry about us. We will manage here. You must save our people."

"I intend to do so, Wife," Xar said curtly.

Marit flinched.

Haplo heard the word, felt the quiver run through the arms whose touch was so comforting, so welcome. He opened his eyes, looked up at her. Her face was streaked with blood—his own, her own, the dragon-snake's. Her hair was disheveled, and now he could see, on her forehead, the mark, the entwined sigla—hers and Xar's.

"Leave him to me, Wife," Xar commanded.

Marit shook her head, crouched over Haplo protectively. Xar reached down, laid his hand on her shoulder. She cried out and slumped to the ground, her body limp, its rune-magic disrupted.

Xar turned to Haplo. "Don't fight me, my son. Let go. Let go of the pain and the despair, the heartache of this life."

The Lord of the Nexus slid his arms beneath Haplo's broken body. Haplo made a feeble attempt to free himself. The dog dashed up, barked at Xar frantically.

"I know I cannot hurt the animal," Xar said coldly. "But I can hurt her."

Marit, curled up, helpless, moaned and shook her head. The sigil on her forehead blazed like fire.

"Dog, stop," Haplo whispered through ashen lips.

The dog, whining, not understanding but trained to obey, fell back. Xar lifted Haplo in his arms as easily and tenderly as if he were a small injured child.

"Rise, Wife," he said to Marit. "When I am gone, you will need to defend yourself."

The magic that held her paralyzed released her. Weak, Marit stood up. She took a step nearer Xar, nearer Haplo.

"Where are you taking him, Lord?" she asked, hope fighting a final struggle in her heart. "To the Nexus? The Final Gate?"

"No, Wife." Xar's voice was cold. "I return to Abarrach." He looked with satisfaction on Haplo. "To the necromancy."

"How can you let this evil happen to your people, Lord?" she cried in anger.

Xar's eyes flared. "They have suffered all their lives. What is one more day or two or three? When I come back in triumph, when the Seventh Gate is open, their suffering will end!"

It will be too late! The words were on her lips, but she looked into Xar's eyes and dared not say them. Catching hold of Haplo's hand, she pressed it against her own heart-rune. "I love you," she said to him.

His eyes opened. "Find Alfred!" He spoke without a voice, his lips moving, stained with his own blood. "Alfred can . . . stop them . . ."

"Yes, find the Sartan," Xar sneered. "I am certain he will be more than happy to defend the prison his kind built."

The lord spoke the runes; a sigil formed in the air. The flaring rune struck Marit, slashed across her forehead.

The pain seared through her as if he'd cut her with a knife. Blood flowed down over her eyes, blinding her. Gasping, dizzy with the agony and the shock, she fell to her knees.

"Xar! My Lord!" she cried wildly, wiping the blood from her eyes.

Xar ignored her. Bearing Haplo in his arms, the lord walked calmly across the field of battle. A shield of magic surrounded them, protected them.

Trotting along behind, unnoticed and forlorn, was the dog.

Marit sprang to her feet with some desperate notion of stopping them, attacking Xar from behind, rescuing Haplo, but at that moment a whirlwind of sigla spun about them—all three of them, including the dog—and all three were gone.

# CHAPTER 48

# ABRI

# THE LABYRINTH

♦

THE BATTLE CAME TO AN END WITH THE EVENING. THE DRAGON-SNAKES WERE vanquished, destroyed; they no longer threatened to breach the walls. The wondrous green dragon—the likes of which no one had ever before seen in the Labyrinth—joined with the Patryns to defeat the serpents. The walls held, their magic swiftly reinforced. The gate stood fast. Hugh the Hand was the last one through before it shut. He bore Kari in his arms. He had found her lying wounded beneath a score of dead chaodyn.

He carried her inside the gate, gave her into the arms of her people.

"Where are Haplo and Marit?" the Hand demanded.

Vasu, directing the renewing of the gate's magic, looked at him in sudden consternation. "I thought they were with you."

"They haven't come in here?"

"No, they haven't. And I've been here the entire time."

"Open the gate again," Hugh ordered. "They must still be out there."

"Open it!" Vasu commanded his people. "I will come with you."

Hugh the Hand, glancing at the pudgy headman, was about to protest, but then remembered that he could not kill.

The gate swung open; the two men ran out into a host of the enemy. But with their leaders dead, the lust for battle seemed to have drained from the foe. Many were beating a retreat across the river, and these were creating confusion among the ranks.

"There!" Hugh the Hand pointed.

Hurt and bewildered, Marit was wandering alone near the base of the wall. A pack of wolfen, drawn by the scent of blood, were tracking her.

Vasu began to sing in a deep baritone.

Hugh the Hand decided the man had gone mad. This was no time for an aria! But suddenly an enormous bush, with long, spearing thorns, thrust up out of the ground, surrounded the wolfen. Thorns caught their thick fur, held them fast. Supple branches wrapped around their paws. The wolfen howled and shrieked, but the more they fought to escape, the more entangled they became.

Marit did not even notice. Vasu continued singing; the thorns grew deeper, denser. Above, Patryns waited until Marit was safe to finish off the wolfen trapped in the bush.

Hugh the Hand ran to her, caught hold of her. "Where is Haplo?"

She stared at him from eyes almost gummed shut by clotted blood. Either she couldn't see him clearly or she didn't recognize him. "Alfred," she said to him in Patryn. "I must find Alfred."

"Where is Haplo?" Hugh repeated in human, frustrated.

"Alfred." Marit spoke the name over and over.

Hugh saw that he would get nothing from her in her dazed condition. He swept her up in his arms and ran back to Vasu. The headman sheltered them in his magic until they had safely reached the gate.

When night fell, the beacon fire still burned bright. The magic of the sigla on the walls glimmered and flickered, but their light continued to shine. The last of the foe slunk off into the wilderness, leaving their dead behind.

The elders who had spent the day inscribing the weapons with death-dealing runes now spent the night restoring life to those injured and dying.

Marit's head wound was not life-threatening, but the healers could not heal it completely. Whatever weapon had torn her flesh must have been poisoned, they told Hugh the Hand when they showed him the raw and inflamed mark on her skin.

But at least Marit was conscious—far too conscious, as far as the healers were concerned. They had difficulty keeping her in her bed. She kept demanding to see Vasu, and at last they sent for him, since nothing else would calm her.

The headman came—exhausted, grieving. The city of Abri stood, but many had given their lives, including Kari. Including someone Vasu dreaded to name, especially to the woman who watched him draw near her sickbed.

"Alfred," Marit said immediately. "Where is he? None of these fools knows or will tell me. I must find him! He can reach the Final Gate in time to fight the dragon-snakes! He can save our people."

Patryns could not lie to each other, and Vasu was Patryn enough to know that she would see through his deceit, no matter how kindly meant.

"He is a serpent mage. He changed into dragon form—"

"I know all that!" Marit snapped impatiently. "Surely he has changed back by now. Take me to him!"

"He . . . did not return," Vasu said.

The life drained from Marit's eyes. "What do you mean?"

"He fell from the skies, perhaps mortally wounded. He'd been fighting a legion of dragons . . ."

" 'Perhaps'!" Marit grabbed the word, clung to it. "You didn't see him die! You don't know if he's dead!"

"Marit, we saw him fall—"

She rose from her bed, shoving aside the restraining hands of the healers. "Show me where."

"You can't go out there," Vasu said sternly. "It's too dangerous. There are roving bands of wolfen and tiger-men, furious at their defeat, waiting to catch one of us alone."

"The human assassin. Where is he?"

"Here, Marit." Hugh the Hand stood up. He had been watching by her bedside, unseen, unnoticed. "I'll go with you. I need to find Alfred myself," he added grimly.

"He is our only hope," Marit said. Her eyes glimmered with tears for a moment. "He is Haplo's only hope." She blinked the tears away and reached for her weapons, which the healers had set aside.

Vasu did not ask what she meant. Xar's magic had not blinded the headman's eyes. He had seen the Lord of the Nexus, had witnessed the meeting of the three. He had seen Xar leave with Haplo . . . and the dog. He had guessed that the Lord of the Nexus was not traveling to the battle of the Final Gate.

"Let her go," he said to the healers.

They stood aside.

Vasu led Marit and Hugh the Hand to the wall. He pointed out to them where he had seen the dragon—flaming green and gold—fall from the skies. He opened the gate of Abri and saw them depart into the darkness.

Then he stood for long, long hours, until the dawn, watching in despair a sullen red glow that lit the horizon in the direction of the Final Gate.

# APPENDIX ✦ I

## THE ACCURSÉD

## BLADE

✦

## SPECULATIONS[1]

✦

OF ALL THE UNFORTUNATE THINGS MY PEOPLE DID JUST BEFORE THE SUNDERING, the development of a weapon such as this cursed knife—now in the possession of Sir Hugh—is one of the most deplorable. Here is evidence that we involved innocent people—humans, elves, dwarves, the very people we were *supposed* to be protecting—in our battle against the Patryns.

That the blade was intended for use by the mensch is beyond doubt. I have examined it, examined the runes inscribed on it, and I am convinced. It was crafted in haste—that much is obvious from its crude design and manufacture—and therefore, most probably, the blades were turned out in large quantities.

Were Samah and the Council members so terrified of the Patryns that they armed entire legions of mensch with these heinous weapons? I can only suppose that the answer is, sadly, yes. Yet nowhere have I read that any wars involving mensch took place in the final days of pre-Sundering Earth. Such battles as did occur between Patryn and Sartan were generally fought on an individual basis, terrible tourneys of magic which invariably proved fatal to one or both combatants.

But from information about those last days obtained from my dear Orla, I think I can speculate on what happened. Consumed by fear, terrified that the Patryns were forming their own armies (this may or may not have been the case), Samah and the Council de-

---

[1] Written by Alfred Montbank sometime during his sojourn in the Labyrinth.

cided to prepare a defense, armed vast numbers of mensch with these magical weapons. I doubt they meant to send the mensch to war. (For one thing, Samah wouldn't trust them!) Most likely, the mensch armies were to be used as cover, to fight a delaying action, allowing the Sartan time to enter the Seventh Gate and proceed with the Sundering.

Such a battle apparently never took place. Perhaps the mensch revolted (I hope so!), or perhaps even Samah felt some twinges of conscience over forcing others to fight his battles for him. Apparently most of the cursed weapons were either destroyed in the Sundering or confiscated by the Sartan before establishing the mensch on the new worlds.

How did this one escape? It undoubtedly fell into the hands of an unscrupulous elf who, impressed by the weapon's power, decided to keep it for himself. The blade itself would be a willing ally, eager to assist in its own survival. The elf was trained in the blade's use, but, due to circumstance—perhaps his untimely death—such information was not passed along to future generations. Only the blade was handed down. The elf could have no idea he was passing on such a deadly legacy.

How does the blade work?

The following are my speculations based on Hugh's and Haplo's accounts of the blade in action, and my own study of the sigla inscribed on the weapon. (An interesting point: in enhancing the weapon with rune-magic, we Sartan did exactly what we had always claimed we despised the Patryns for doing, giving life to that which is not meant to have it!)

1. The first action the blade takes is to block the enemy's ability to sense danger. Thus Haplo had no warning that Hugh the Hand was stalking him in the Factree, never knew that the assassin was waiting in ambush on the ship.

2. The blade's second action reduces an enemy's possibilities of retaliation. The blade cannot eliminate all possibilities; that would take far greater power than the blade possesses. But it can and does limit the choice of options to those it can easily handle.

3. The blade's third action analyzes both the enemy's strength and weakness and reacts accordingly. Sometimes this reaction is a very simple one for the blade to perform, as in the unfortunate "fight" between the two elf brothers. The blade, facing a dueling dagger, had only to turn itself into a sword to kill its foe. When

Hugh the Hand first encountered Haplo, the blade changed itself to an ax against Haplo's knife.

Notice, however, that when the blade encounters additional opponents, its strength increases. The blade became a bat when attacking both Marit and Haplo. When this attack failed, the blade turned into a tytan.

Also of interest is the fact that the blade appears to draw on the memories and thoughts of the victims. Haplo says that he does not recall thinking specifically of tytans during the brief stop their ship made in Pryan (admittedly, he did have a great deal on his mind!), but it seems logical to me that he must have at least had the giants he encountered on that world in his subconscious.

And that is all I have been able to determine about the blade so far. As to any further speculations, I would have to see the blade in action (something I'd rather *not* do!) to be able to provide additional information on it.

I take this moment to add some information that I have acquired on the Cursed Blade.[2] The first bit of information is good: the blade can be controlled by the user. All one has to do is to say the word "stop" in Sartan.

The second piece of information is very bad. Apparently the blade can also be controlled by outside forces! I have evidence that the dragon-snakes are able to wield some sort of influence over it.

The weapon was created out of fear, designed to kill, and so it would naturally be drawn to the dragon-snakes. They, in turn, appear to be able to control the blade's magic. They cannot, it seems, cause the blade to turn against its user. But the snakes can direct the blade's actions and reactions to suit their own purposes. Haplo thinks now that it was the Cursed Blade that brought the tiger-men down on us. And the blade apparently issued some sort of call to the dragon-snakes, alerting them to its presence in Abri.

There *must* be some way to destroy this weapon. Unfortunately, I can't think of any at the moment, but then my mind is rather flurried. Perhaps if I had time to reflect and study the matter further . . .

(Editor's note: Here the text ends.)

---

[2] This last is written in an agitated style, from which we must conclude that Alfred probably recorded this information just before the Siege of Abri.

## Starchamber of the Pryan Citadels

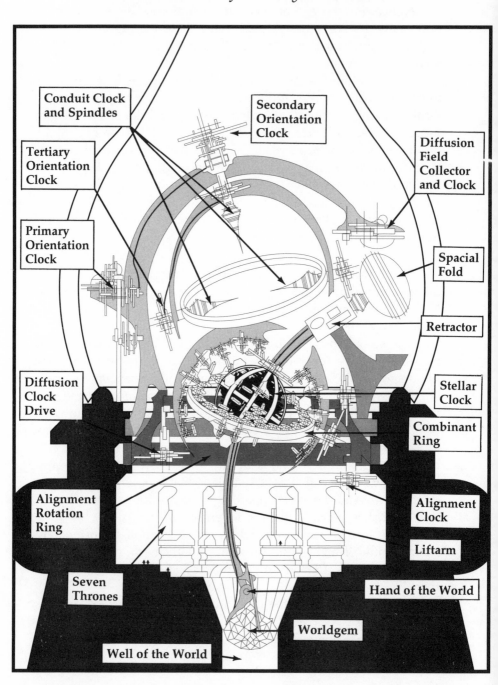

Conduit Clock
and Spindles

Secondary
Orientation
Clock

Diffusion
Field
Collector
and Clock

Tertiary
Orientation
Clock

Primary
Orientation
Clock

Spacial
Fold

Retractor

Diffusion
Clock
Drive

Stellar
Clock

Combinant
Ring

Alignment
Rotation
Ring

Alignment
Clock

Liftarm

Seven
Thrones

Hand of the World

Worldgem

Well of the World

# APPENDIX ◆ II

# THE STAR CHAMBERS

# OF PRYAN

◆

*Being excerpts from* The Book of Stars *as written by Paithan, Lord Master of Drugar Citadel, who has edited and amended the text.*[1] *May the reader enjoy the enlightenment of the stars.*

## EYE OF SUNS[2]

Pryan is a world of power. It keeps the other worlds beyond our own operating. Its heartbeat brings the lifeblood of power, heat, and light to these Sundered Realms. Without the power of the stars that shine above our home and the strength of our light, worlds beyond our understanding only sleep, half dead from lack of nourishment.

Pryan's stationary suns, keep all of their life-giving power within the confines of the world's vast interior. The suns' light brings life to the world's inhabitants. Yet this important function is but a portion of its true purpose of creation.

The light of Pryan's suns—which originates from four separate celestial bodies rather than the single sun perceived by us from our distant ground—is transferred either directly or indirectly into the rock that is the foundation of the world. I myself have seen this very

---

[1] I am indebted to the tytans and to my sister, Aleatha, for the translation of Sartan runes.

[2] A phrase, peculiar to the Sartan, which means "a perspective from on high" or, in this case, an overview.

rock and affirm that it does in fact exist.[3] This rock foundation then collects the energy generated by the suns and forests above it, and stores it in ever increasing amounts deep within its stone. The energy is then collected by the citadel, whose roots sink deep into the foundations of Pryan. These roots radiate energy from the citadel and store it in the well—known as the Well of the World. Only the cap of the Worldgem holds this energy in place.[4]

## GENERAL STRUCTURE AND MOTION

The Star Chamber's lower area houses Seven Thrones, which surround and face the Well of the World. These thrones are immense, so that tytans may sit comfortably in them. The presence of the tytans is essential for the operation of the machine. The throne chamber is separated from the chamber above by a framework and the mechanism for the Star Machine.

This second chamber is enclosed by a huge dome formed of several curved panels to resemble the petals of a lotus blossom. Each panel is made up of colored glass mounted in a lattice work of metal. The glass is inscribed with Sartan runes which, according to the tytans, channel the light into the Star Machine. When the machine is operating, the panels open fully to shine forth its power.

The Star Machine itself has two major parts: the lower clockworks called the Stellar Clock and the upper known as the Conduit Clock. Both sections of the mechanism are suspended by mobile mountings over the Seven Thrones. The Worldgem is held at the end

---

[3] Paithan adds this for those who live on the high surface of Pryan. There the ground consists of the tops of immense trees whose roots remain unknown to those who are born, live, and die in their bows.

[4] "Well of the World" and "Worldgem," in addition to many other fanciful names in the text, are undoubtedly Paithan's constructions. While they do reflect his romantic nature, they are not necessarily instructive in terms of the function of the machine itself. The term "Worldgem," however, may be a mensch rendering of the Sartan *Eort-Batu'h* rune. *Eort* signifies life and power— a cross structure in magic that bridged Fire and Water magics. *Batu'h* would refer to the concept of "foundation" rather than a crystalline stone. If this is the case, then this "Worldgem" is the focal point of a life or power wave—probably the emissions from the "well."

of the Liftarm, suspended from the Stellar Clock down into the Well of the World, which is located in the floor.

The Worldgem seals the Well of the World. A gigantic arching metal arm ending in a metal hand grips the gem and holds it in place while the machine is dormant. This extends downward from a retraction mechanism that pulls the Worldgem out of the well when conditions merit.[5] The arm itself is retracted into a Spatial Fold—a marvelous magic sphere.

The Stellar Clock is cradled inside two opposing mounted rings which are in turn set on a massive swivel mount. The retracted Worldgem and the two rings surrounding it can be positioned in any configuration.

The major mounting for the Stellar Clock is called the Alignment Rotation Ring.[6] This is a rotating mount which can turn the entire lower clockwork around the axis of the well. An Alignment Clock, which is driven by the Primary Orientation Clock and sequenced independently by Babbage Difference Engines,[7] turns the Alignment Rotation Ring and, with it, the Stellar Clock.

Inside the Alignment Rotation Ring is mounted the Diffusion Ring. An amazing number of gears, rods, and cams are positioned along this arc. They swivel and otherwise adjust the orientation of convex mirrors, prisms, and gems which all find their focal point on the Stellar Clock. As with the Alignment Rotation Ring, the Diffusion Ring can be tilted by the Diffusion Clock Drive, which appears to operate on the same principles as the Alignment Clock.

A third ring is mounted inside the Diffusion Ring and is called the Combinant Ring. This ring, too, is fitted with a vast number of gears, screws, and clockworks which support concave mirrors, prisms, and gems. It, too, focuses on the Stellar Clock. Its name implies the combining of force and would seem to act counter to the Diffusion Ring around it. Perhaps these two—the Diffusion Ring

[5] I am still not sure just what these "conditions" might be.

[6] This is a direct translation of the Sartan rune-structure. I'm not sure what it means. I feel like a child examining with wonder the workings of my father's old watch and trying to understand how it operates.

[7] This again is a direct translation from the runes.

and the Combinant Ring—act to cancel each other out and keep forces balanced.[8]

The Upper Alignment Ring is the foundation mount for the Conduit Clock. Like the Alignment Rotation Ring, the Upper Alignment Ring also rotates around the axis of the Well of the World being driven by the Primary Orientation Clock.[9] It is this clockwork which seems to provide the power for the rest of the device as well.

The Primary Orientation Clock is mounted on a great curving frame that can be rotated by the Upper Orientaton Ring. Near the top of this frame is set the Secondary Orientation Clock, which traverses the upper curve of the frame via a screw device.

This Primary Orientation Clock and Secondary Orientation Clock then positions the fork and rings of the Conduit Clock into alignment with spindles mounted below it.[10] These Conduit Spindles apparently interact with the power generated in the lower mechanism in order to be transferred to the other Realms.


THE MACHINE
IN MOTION

I have not been present when the machine is in full motion, for the light in the room is so bright as to blind the viewer. Only the tytans can withstand that light, and they cannot give sufficient description.

Still, I have witnessed the earlier stages of the process. Energy build-up in the Well triggers the mechanism into action. The energy is then carried up the Liftarm and sets the machine in motion. This is the beginning of the cycle.

[8] On the other hand, it could be that the Diffusion Ring separates the power drawn up from the roots of the world into more basic wave forms and narrower spectra of energy, which could then be recombined selectively through the Combinant Ring.

[9] I find no drive or power mechanism for this clockwork which normally would have a weight-and-pendulum arrangement. I surmise that within the mechanism itself is some means of gaining energy from the stream of force coming from the Well of the World. In fact, I suspect that this is the purpose of the Diffusion Field Collector shown in the drawing.

[10] According to the tytans, these conduits link the Sundered Realms to each other.

As the machine begins to move, the Alignment Rotation Drive turns the Alignment Rotation Ring, the Diffusion Ring, and the Combinant Ring. The mirrors of both lower rings and the Stellar Clock begin to rotate into position. Gems and prisms flash as they orient themselves. The Liftarm begins to raise the Worldgem out of the Well and into the Stellar Clock. A powerful, throbbing light issues from the Well of the World as the gem rises higher into the machine. The Conduit Clock also begins to move, shifting the position of its rings and spindles. I have noticed that this orientation differs each time the motion begins and is never exactly repeated.

During this process, the lotus-blossom sections of the dome start to open. It is at this point that the Worldgem is set into the center of the Stellar Clock and the entire chamber is filled with such brilliant light that further observation is impossible. It is this light that we used to believe were the "stars."

## IN CLOSING

The tytans now operate the Star Chamber. Its powerful light radiates from the tallest spire of our city. Darkness, too, still comes to our city regularly in each cycle, yet even through the darkness this light shines. Across the heavens, we view the constant light of a thousand stars. The citadel was built by those who are now gone. We see our purpose here as a sacred trust to add our light to those that shine in the sky. Someday others in far distant worlds may see that light and find their way home.

# Kicksey-winsey

*Textured for Synthesizer and People with Odd*
*(Perhaps Even Electrical) Appliances*

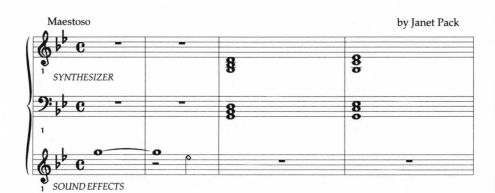

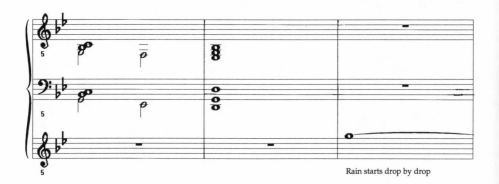

Steady rain

Torrential rain

Hum and factory sounds begin softly—continue to end

Rain and factory sounds fade to end
(five more measures total)

*For the "Roadies" in Minneapolis—*
*We'll have to convene and try this someday!*

PERFORMANCE NOTES

Set your synthesizer for a dark, sonorous sound (French horns an octave below their normal range, a contrabass bassoon, or something akin to Atmospheres on a Kurzweil) until Measure 39. The Geg March begins in the left hand, the Welves Hymn weaves against it in the upper register. Change the voicing to brighter sounds, such as cello and recorder. Return to the deeper voice you used initially at Measure 74 to finish.

The Special Effects are designated by using shaped notes (one to a sound). They appear on specific staff lines and spaces. Wind is always a whole note, often tied to another, on G2 (the second G above Middle C). The following are descriptions of sounds in the score:

**Wind**—Always crescendo to decrescendo, panning from one speaker to the other. Appears as a whole note G2.

**Thunder**—Begins and ends in distance as a rumble. Approaches quickly—by Measure 13 should be a sharp crack. Appears as an oblique diamond on F2 or G2.

**Rain**—Hard drops on metal. Use hard mallets on a metal bar or heavy box. Appears as text below third staff.

**Metallic moan**—Protesting shriek, as if a large machine is reluctantly starting. Appears as X of five dots on C2.

**Whistle**—Shrill, suddenly released. Appears as a small s on A1.

**Whirr**—Similar to a dentist's drill in the middle range. Appears as a comma on F1.

**Scrape**—Use a ratchet or a metal file or grater against something hard. Appears as an oblique 9 on E1 (usually held for two beats).

**Balloon**—Let air escape from partially stretched neck, more "phffft" than a whistle. Or get someone good at making raspberries or Bronx cheers. If you opt for the latter, stay out of the performer's way—this could get damp! Appears as an elongated O on B1.

**Clank**—Use the type of metal kitchen bowl with an attached metal hanger (it produces a secondary sound). Strike with wooden dowel, a drum stick, or gently with the side of a hammer or hard rubber mallet. Appears as a flower.

**Zizz**—Electricity running up a Jacob's ladder. Appears as a point-down triangle on either D2 or E2.

**Whump**—An occasional unexplainable sound. Should be ominous and hollow, therefore used sparingly. Appears as a square on B1.

**Hum**—Starts in Measure 26, continues throughout piece, fading into background at end. Similar to a large electrical generator. Appears as text under third staff.

**Factory sounds**—Some synthesizers come equipped with mechanical background noises (on a Kurzweil it's called Alien Factory). Use these, or come up with your own. Begins in Measure 26 along with the Hum and runs for length of piece. Appears as text beneath third staff.

Now get a group together, follow the cues (approximately), and have fun!